LAXDÆLA SAGA

ADVISORY EDITOR: BETTY RADICE

MAGNUS MAGNUSSON is an Icelander who has been resident in Scotland for most of his life. After a career in newspaper journalism in Scotland, he is now a freelance author and broadcaster, best known as the presenter of the BBC quiz programme *Mastermind*. He studied English and Old Icelandic at Oxford University, and his hobby is translating from Icelandic, both old and new. With Hermann Pálsson he has translated three other Saga volumes for Penguin Classics, *Njal's Saga*, *King Harald's Saga* and *The Vinland Sagas*; in preparation is *Gisli's Saga*, and future plans include *Grettir's Saga*.

HERMANN PÁLSSON studied Icelandic at the University of Iceland and Celtic at University College, Dublin. He was formerly Professor in Icelandic at the University of Edinburgh, where he taught from 1950 to 1988. He is the General Editor of the New Saga Library and the author of many books on the history and literature of medieval Iceland; his more recent publications include *Legendary Fiction in Medieval Iceland* (with Paul Edwards) and *Art and Ethics in Hrafnkel's Saga*. In addition to the three other Saga translations with Magnus Magnusson, Hermann Pálsson has translated *Hrafnkel's Saga* and (with Paul Edwards) *Egil's Saga*, *Orkneyinga Saga*, *Eyrbyggja Saga*, *Seven Viking Romances*, all for the Penguin Classics, and *Vikings in Russia*.

LAXDÆLA SAGA

*

Translated with an Introduction by
**MAGNUS MAGNUSSON AND
HERMANN PÁLSSON**

PENGUIN BOOKS

PENGUIN BOOKS

Published by the Penguin Group
Penguin Books Ltd, 27 Wrights Lane, London W8 5TZ, England
Penguin Books USA Inc., 375 Hudson Street, New York, New York 10014, USA
Penguin Books Australia Ltd, Ringwood, Victoria, Australia
Penguin Books Canada Ltd, 10 Alcorn Avenue, Toronto, Ontario, Canada M4V 3B2
Penguin Books (NZ) Ltd, 182–190 Wairau Road, Auckland 10, New Zealand

Penguin Books Ltd, Registered Offices: Harmondsworth, Middlesex, England

This translation first published 1969
13 15 17 19 20 18 16 14 12

Printed in England by Clays Ltd, St Ives plc
Set in Linotype Pilgrim

Contents

Introduction

OF all the major Icelandic sagas, *Laxdæla Saga* has always
stirred the European imagination the most profoundly. More
than any other of the classical prose sagas of medieval Iceland it
is essentially a romantic work; romantic in style, romantic in
taste, romantic in theme, culminating in that most enduring and
timeless of human relationships in story-telling, the love-triangle.
Gudrun Osvif's-daughter, the imperious beauty who married
her lover's best friend against her will and then, in a rage of
jealousy, forced her husband to kill her former lover and forfeit
his own life thereby, is enshrined for all time in the gallery
of great tragi-romantic heroines in world literature.

It was written by an unknown author around the year
1245, as nearly as can be deduced, at a time when the Age of
Chivalry was at its fullest flower in continental Europe, when
knights were dedicated to the service of the Church against
the infidel, and tournaments and courtly love were the standard pastimes of the feudal aristocracy. *Laxdæla Saga* reflects a
European outlook and attitude more than any of the other
major sagas of the thirteenth century; and yet it is also one
of the most essentially Icelandic of all the sagas, the truest of
the Family Sagas proper, a dynastic chronicle that sweeps
from generation to generation for 150 years from the Settlement of Iceland by the Norsemen late in the ninth century. In
this sense, in the care with which the dawn of Iceland's history is recorded and interpreted in saga terms, *Laxdæla Saga*
is also something of a national epic, giving to this young
nation's past a dignity and grandeur which it seemed to lack
in comparison with older and more powerful neighbour-states.

Although *Laxdæla Saga* is best known for the love-story of
Gudrun Osvif's-daughter, it is a much more complex saga than
that; indeed, the 'Gudrun episode' comes relatively late in the
saga (Chapter 32 onwards), and the pattern of the saga in the
earlier chapters is not immediately apparent to the modern
reader – particularly one who is waiting impatiently for Gudrun

to take the stage. And yet it is vitally important to discern and understand this saga pattern, as thirteenth-century audiences would have had no difficulty in doing; the early episodes not only set the scene for the Gudrun tragedy but also give it more texture and meaning, for Gudrun and the men who loved her are caught up in an extraordinary web of conflicting kinships and loyalties. Far from being a series of disconnected episodes, the early action of the saga has an intense bearing on what follows; for *Laxdæla Saga* is a saga of property as well as passion, a story of lands as well as loves, and the great diversity of character and incidents in the early stages are all designed to show how the wealth and property inherited by Gudrun's lover, Kjartan Olafsson, were amassed by his ancestors. It is only when Kjartan's standing is established that the author turns to another branch of the Laxriverdale family, and the two family streams meet in fatal confluence.

It is not easy to find a meaningful analogy for this particular form of saga pattern. Perhaps it could be compared to the course of a long river, starting in a slow trickle and splitting into two streams, but gradually increasing in volume and power as new tributaries swell its waters; these tributaries give the saga-pattern a herring-bone effect in places, for the author often jumps from the main flow to trace a tributary right from its source. When the two major streams converge again the river develops an irresistible current that sweeps everything along with it; the central tragedy forms currents which the characters are helpless to avoid, and which only the strongest can survive. Finally, the saga flows into broader, calmer waters, a serene estuary as the survivors of the tragedy drift tranquilly to their old age and quiet deaths.

Throughout its course, the saga changes in texture in the same way as the nature of a river is determined by the terrain through which it flows. *Laxdæla Saga* begins in the remote past, in a different land, with different customs and different problems; Iceland is then virgin territory, and the river drives its own path where it will as it comes pouring down from the mountains of the pagan, rather mysterious hinterlands of history. With it, it brings the glacial debris of its past, the boulders and silt that it sweeps down into the lusher reaches to create hidden currents and rapids as it moves through a deceptively lyrical, Christianized lowland landscape. Indeed, one of the most memorable aspects of *Laxdæla Saga* is the way in which the style and nature of the story alter subtly as the generations succeed one another.

The saga opens in Norway with a fleeting glimpse of the heroic period of Scandinavia. As King Harald Fine-Hair of Norway consolidates the power of his throne in the second half of the ninth century, the more independent-minded chieftains decide to emigrate. One of them is Ketil Flat-Nose (does his nickname suggest a Lappish origin?); he himself decides to settle in Scotland, but his sons emigrate to newly-discovered Iceland, and it is to Iceland, too, that his strong-willed daughter, Unn the Deep-Minded, eventually comes after some hazardous adventures in Scotland (Chapters 1–5). It is from one of Ketil's sons, Bjorn the Easterner, and from his daughter, Unn the Deep-Minded, that the two main streams of this family chronicle are descended.

In the first section of the saga (Chapters 1–31) the main narrative follows the fortunes of Unn's descendants. Unn is the archetypal pioneer, a forceful matriarch who establishes dynasties in Scotland, Orkney and the Faroe Islands by marrying off her grand-daughters to carefully-chosen suitors. When she comes to Iceland she lays claim to an enormous area of land in the virgin territory of Breidafjord, on the west coast, which she parcels out to her followers with due regard to their social standing, lineage and intrinsic merit (Chapter 6).

To her grandson, Ólaf Feilan, she leaves her own estate of Hvamm (Chapter 7); Olaf Feilan fades from the saga immediately, but three generations later his family line is destined to emerge into the saga again, for his great-grandson, Thorkel Eyjolfsson, becomes the fourth husband of Gudrun Osvif's-daughter (Chapter 68).

It is the family line of another of Unn's grandchildren, Thorgerd, that the saga now follows; for when Thorgerd marries Dala-Koll her dowry is the whole of Laxriverdale (Chapter 5), and it is with the fortunes of the Laxriverdale dynasty, the 'Laxdalers' of the title, that *Laxdæla Saga* is most concerned. Every incident that now follows is seen to have a bearing on the eventual appearance of one of the most illustrious figures in that family, Olaf the Peacock, the father of Kjartan Olafsson.

Dala-Koll is succeeded by his son, Hoskuld Dala-Kollsson (Chapter 7), who quickly establishes himself as a forceful and ambitious chieftain. His widowed mother, Thorgerd, restlessly emigrates to Norway where she marries again and has a son, Hrut Herjolfsson, who is Hoskuld's half-brother (Chapter 8). When she dies, Hoskuld takes possession of her whole estate, and clearly has no intention of allowing his half-brother to claim his rightful share.

Hoskuld, ever anxious to improve his position, looks for a marriage alliance that will add to his wealth and power, and marries the daughter of a wealthy farmer up north (Chapter 9). But his bride, Jorunn, turns out to be a hard woman, steely-tempered and wasp-tongued, and the marriage, despite a litter of children, is loveless. Two sons are introduced – Thorleik Hoskuldsson, who takes after his mother's side of the family, and Bard Hoskuldsson, who is his exact opposite, sweet-natured and generous-hearted.

At this point the saga abruptly turns aside to explore the first of the 'herring-bone' tributaries. A man called Hrapp of Hrapp-stead is briefly introduced, a disagreeable Hebridean (like so many other stock villains in this and other sagas) who is excessively brutal to his neighbours (Chapter 10). He is one of Hoskuld's neighbours in Laxriverdale; but his significance in the saga-pattern is not fully apparent until after his death (Chapters 17–18); for Hrapp's ghost haunts the farm at Hrapp-stead so viciously that the people flee from it. When Hrapp's brother-in-law, Thorstein Black the Wise, attempts to settle there he and all his immediate family are drowned as they are sailing across Breidafjord; and the disaster is attended by an enormous seal with human eyes. . . . Thus, through Hrapp's baleful supernatural activities, the Hrappstead lands remain deserted and ownership falls into the hands of a farmer in another district, Thorkel Fringe, who has no desire to farm them himself (Chapter

18). This is an important sub-theme in the saga; but its significance does not emerge until some time later, when the Hrappstead lands are bought by Olaf the Peacock (Chapter 24). So it is on this haunted estate, its name changed to Hjardarholt but still shadowed by the malignant shade of Hrapp, that Kjartan Olafsson grows up.

Immediately after Hrapp of Hrappstead is first introduced another important sub-theme is begun, with the entry of another of Hoskuld Dala-Kollsson's neighbours, Thord Goddi (Chapter 11). This is an even more tortuous tributary, but it, too, leads towards Olaf the Peacock, as follows: Thord Goddi is married to a mettlesome woman called Vigdis Ingjald's-daughter (a grand-daughter of Olaf Feilan, incidentally, cf. Genealogical Table No. 5); the two of them become involved in giving shelter to a penniless outlaw, Thorolf, who had killed the brother of a powerful local chieftain, Ingjald Saudisle-Priest (Chapter 14). When Ingjald comes to kill the outlaw, Vigdis and her craven husband fall out; Vigdis routs the visitors and divorces her husband for his cowardice. Then Vigdis tries to claim half the marital estate in a divorce settlement; but to prevent her getting her hands on any of his money, Thord Goddi goes to Hoskuld Dala-Kollsson and makes over all his wealth to him in trust for Hoskuld's son, Olaf the Peacock, whom he now takes into fosterage, being childless himself (Chapter 16).

But we have over-run the story in following these two meandering tributaries to the point where they flow into the main narrative stream; for they are digressions from the story of Hoskuld Dala-Kollsson, whom we left in Chapter 9 newly married to Jorunn. Hoskuld now decides to go abroad to fetch timber from Norway with which to build himself a home suited to his stature in the community (Chapter 11). But timber is not, apparently, his only aim, for while he is abroad he buys himself a beautiful young concubine (Chapter 12). Jorunn of the steely temper is little pleased when he brings this domestic acquisition back to Iceland; but her jealousy is only really aroused when it is revealed that the concubine is no mere slave-girl but a lady of impeccable aristocratic birth – Melkorka, the daughter of an Irish king (Chapter 13). Hoskuld, however, is delighted with this revelation, for he always laid great store by wealth and breeding; and now he gives all his love and devotion to the illegitimate son his concubine had borne him – Olaf the Peacock.

When Hoskuld's half-brother, Hrut Herjolfsson, comes to Iceland and claims his share of their mother's estate Hoskuld refuses to hand it over, and a bitter quarrel between the brothers ensues; but the quarrel is settled just short of fratricide (Chapter 19). Hoskuld is now mellowing into old age, and our attention turns to the growing brilliance and renown of Olaf the Peacock, the apple of his father's eye. His mother, Melkorka, is anxious that he should go to Ireland to vindicate his noble lineage, and to provide him with the necessary capital (and to spite Hoskuld) she marries a local farmer, Thorbjorn the Feeble (Chapter 20). Olaf sets off on a triumphant progress abroad, and meets his grandfather in Ireland (Chapter 21). King Myrkjartan fêtes him and flatters him, and even offers him the succession to the throne, but Olaf politely declines and returns to Iceland in a blaze of glory (Chapter 22). Back in Iceland, Hoskuld plans for Olaf an ambitious dynastic marriage into the family of the great warrior-poet, Egil Skalla-Grimsson of Borg. The daughter, Thorgerd, at first refuses to marry a mere concubine's son, but is dazzled and swept off her feet when Olaf turns up to woo her in person (Chapter 23). Olaf now buys the deserted lands of Hrappstead, as was mentioned earlier, and builds himself a handsome manor there, renaming it Hjardarholt (Chapter 23).

In contrast, Olaf's half-brother, Thorleik Hoskuldsson, lives up to the mean strain in his mother's ancestry, and gets involved in a brief flare-up of trouble with his uncle, Hrut Herjolfsson (Chapter 25).

Now Hoskuld Dala-Kollsson dies; on his death-bed, intent to the last on enhancing Olaf's standing, he manages to bequeath a third of the estate to Olaf by a trick – much to the displeasure of Hoskuld's disgruntled legitimate son, Thorleik (Chapter 26). In order to staunch the ill-feeling between them, Olaf magnanimously offers to foster Thorleik's son, Bolli (Chapter 27); so now Bolli Thorleiksson goes to stay at Hjardarholt, where he is brought up with his cousin and foster-brother, Olaf's eldest son, Kjartan Olafsson (Chapter 28).

Now the stage is set for the next generation to take over. Under the benign influence of Olaf the Peacock, Kjartan and Bolli grow up together absolutely devoted to one another, two young men of outstanding prowess and accomplishments; yet of the two, Kjartan always has the edge on Bolli, and Bolli grows up in the shadow of his more brilliant cousin (Chapter 28). With these two, the House of Hoskuld has reached its fullest flower; but two small episodes now cast a shadow of apprehension over this lyrical mood. Olaf the Peacock has a very disagreeable dream, ominously portending that he will see his favourite son drenched in blood one day (Chapter 31); and his daughter, Thurid, marries a rogue Norwegian, Geirmund the Noisy, whom Olaf had reluctantly brought back to Iceland from a voyage abroad (Chapter 29). When that marriage disintegrates, a sword with a curse on it comes into Olaf's family – the sword 'Leg-Biter', which is fated to cause the death of the most brilliant scion of the family; and the sword is given by Thurid to her cousin, Bolli Thorleiksson (Chapter 31). And with these fleeting shivers on the clear, sunlit waters of the river, the first section of the saga ends.

The second section, the core of the whole saga (Chapters 32–56), opens with the entry of the other main dynastic line from Ketil Flat-Nose – the descendants of Bjorn the Easterner: Osvif Helgason of Sælingsdale and his daughter Gudrun. In the same breath we hear of a minor property transaction in which Osvif buys some upland grazing in Sælingsdale on which to pasture his livestock in summer; and that shieling is to be the scene of tragedy later (Chapter 32).

And now one crucial chapter clenches the whole story together, through the medium of a sage, Gest Oddleifsson, who can foretell the future. In the course of one day he utters three prophecies that are to shape the rest of the saga narrative (Chapter 33).

He meets Gudrun, his kinswoman (cf. Genealogical Table No. 5), a beautiful, self-confident young girl of only fourteen or fifteen, who tells him about four strange dreams she has had and asks him to interpret them. In one stroke her whole destiny is laid bare to us (as it was already known to the saga audience) when Gest Óddleifsson predicts that she will have four husbands. Later that day he comes to Hjardarholt at Olaf the Peacock's invitation; Gest has never seen the two cousins, Kjartan and Bolli, before, but now as he watches them swimming with some friends he prophesies with tears in his eyes that one day Bolli will stand over Kjartan's body, and earn his own death thereby. In a third, minor prediction, Gest prophesies that one day he himself and Osvif Helgason will be much closer neighbours (this comes true in Chapter 66, when they are buried in the same grave at Helgafell).

In this pivotal chapter the destinies of Gudrun and Kjartan (who have not yet met) are juxtaposed; and from now on, the saga narrative flows strong and clear as these prophecies are worked out.

Gudrun marries her first husband, much against her will, at the age of fifteen; he is a wealthy but pusillanimous man called Thorvald Halldorsson, whom she divorces after two years (Chapter 34).

Next she marries a man called Thord Ingunnarson; Thord is already married to a fierce-tempered woman called Aud, whom he divorces in order to marry Gudrun (at the cost of a vengeful sword-thrust that mutilates his chest and arm). The marriage between Thord and Gudrun is very happy; but now Thord tangles with a family of evil Hebridean sorcerers (Kotkel and his family), and is drowned by their spells (Chapter 35). Kotkel and his family are eventually wiped out, but not before they have embroiled the luckless Thorleik Hoskuldsson in yet another violent quarrel with his uncle, Hrut Herjolfsson (Chapter 37). The outcome of this is that Thorleik goes abroad for ever, leaving his son Bolli with Olaf the Peacock at Hjardarholt (Chapter 38).

And now Gudrun, with her second marriage over, meets Kjartan Olafsson, who starts making frequent visits to see her at the natural hot-spring baths in Sælingsdale. There is close friendship between their parents, Olaf and Osvif; but Olaf is obscurely uneasy at the growing love between Kjartan and

Gudrun (Chapter 39). And always the faithful Bolli tags along with Kjartan, the inseparable companion who always comes second.

Kjartan is eager to seek fame and fortune abroad. He decides rather abruptly to go to Norway, and asks Gudrun to wait three years for him as his betrothed. Gudrun is put out by the suddenness of his decision and refuses, and they part rather huffily. Kjartan sails off to Norway, accompanied as always by Bolli (Chapter 40). They sail straight into trouble, for the King of Norway, Olaf Tryggvason, is putting tremendous political pressure on Iceland to accept Christianity. Kjartan's almost superhuman accomplishments are readily appreciated by King Olaf, and for the first time Bolli's submerged resentment of his more brilliant cousin breaks to the surface. They and their companions eventually are baptized, but Iceland is still proving stubborn; so King Olaf keeps Kjartan and three other Icelanders hostage in Norway in an attempt to exert more pressure on the leading chieftains of Iceland. Bolli is not held, however; and in the year 1000 (the third year of Kjartan's absence) Bolli returns to Iceland, leaving Kjartan with King Olaf enjoying the favour of the king's sister, Ingibjorg.

The first thing Bolli tells Gudrun when he returns to Iceland is that Kjartan looks as if he intends to settle in Norway, especially in the light of his intimate friendship with Ingibjorg. Then he proposes to Gudrun himself, and eventually Gudrun, grieved by Kjartan's apparent perfidy but much against her will none the less, is pressurized by her father and brothers into marrying Bolli (Chapter 43).

The following year, Kjartan Olafsson returns. News that Iceland had accepted Christianity reached Norway in the spring of the year 1001, and the moment that Kjartan is released by King Olaf he hurries to Iceland, brusquely breaking off his affair with Princess Ingibjorg – who nevertheless shows her regality by giving him an immensely valuable gold-woven head-dress as a wedding-present for Gudrun; and King Olaf gives him a sword which has the power of making him immune to all other weapons for as long as he carries it (Chapter 43). When Kjartan discovers that Gudrun is already married to his foster-brother he shows no outward signs of emotion; and soon he is persuaded to get married himself. His choice falls, casually enough, on Hrefna Asgeir's-daughter (sister of his former partner abroad, Kalf Asgeirsson), a girl as demure and sweet as Gudrun is ambitious and imperious; and to Hrefna he gives the coveted head-dress (Chapter 45).

The fierce jealousies and resentments inherent in this tense situation soon break out, despite Olaf the Peacock's constant efforts to keep the peace. Kjartan rudely snubs a generous gift offered by Bolli; in revenge, Gudrun's brothers steal Kjartan's sword, the sword that would have kept him safe from all weapons. And at a feast, Hrefna's priceless head-dress is also stolen mysteriously. Kjartan gives vent to his fury by humiliating Bolli and Gudrun and her family, by besieging their home for three days and denying them access to the outdoor privy (Chapter 47).

There is now open enmity between the two houses; and after some further spiteful exchanges, Gudrun at last goads Bolli and her brothers into making an attempt on Kjartan's life. They ambush him as he rides home down Svinadale with only two companions. Kjartan fights them off while the reluctant Bolli stands aloof; but when Bolli at last joins in the battle, Kjartan throws down his weapons rather than fight his own foster-brother, and Bolli grimly and silently strikes him dead – with the sword 'Leg-Biter' (Chapter 49).

In a chilling passage, Gudrun gloats over Kjartan's death, and the grief it will cause Hrefna. But Bolli, deeply repenting what he has done, knows her better, and recognizes the frustrated love that has inspired the jealous rage in her breast. Hrefna moves north to her family home, where she dies of a broken heart (Chapter 50).

Olaf the Peacock strives desperately to heal the awful breach that has opened in his family; for three years, until his own death, he manages to secure an uneasy peace. But when his moderating influence is gone, Kjartan's brothers, goaded on by their mother Thorgerd (no less fierce and unforgiving than Gudrun herself), plan their revenge on Bolli. Helped by their uncle, Melkorka's son Lambi Thorbjornsson, and a warrior called Helgi Hardbeinsson, the Olafssons set upon Bolli in the summer shieling that Osvif had once bought, and kill him there (Chapter 55). Gudrun is pregnant at the time; and when one of the killers, Helgi Hardbeinsson, meets her and wipes his bloody spear on her sash, he prophesies that her unborn son will eventually cause his own death in revenge. The following spring, Gudrun gives birth to Bolli Bollason (Chapter 56).

The last section of the saga (Chapters 57–78) tells of the long and complex plans that Gudrun laid to avenge her husband Bolli, and of the final fulfilment of the prophecies. Once again, the author introduces two men in juxtaposition who are going to have a marked effect on Gudrun's destiny – Thorgils Holluson and Thorkel Eyjolfsson (Chapter 57). And now the complexities of kinship become very dense, for Thorgils is himself a descendant of Bjorn the Easterner, and as such is related to Gudrun, as well as to her dead husband, Bolli Thorleiksson, and her dead lover, Kjartan Olafsson; and he is also related, distantly, to Thorkel Eyjolfsson, through Ketil Flat-Nose (cf. Genealogical Table No. 5).

Gudrun has by now moved from Sælingsdale to Helgafell, by exchanging homes with her great friend and mentor Snorri the Priest (Chapter 56). And now Thorgils Holluson begins to pay court to her assiduously. Gudrun is more concerned to have her late husband avenged, and will not even think of remarrying until that is achieved – and certainly not marrying Thorgils Holluson. But when her son, Bolli Bollason, is twelve years old and ready to fulfil his destiny as his father's avenger, Snorri the Priest thinks up an ingenious scheme whereby Thorgils Holluson can be used to further Gudrun's ends. Gudrun makes him an ambiguous promise of marriage on condition that he leads a punitive expedition against one of Bolli's killers, Helgi Hardbeinsson (Chapter 60). Bolli Bollason goes with him, and after a fierce defence Helgi is killed – by Bolli (Chapter 64). Gudrun now explains to Thorgils the ambiguity in her promise of marriage – she had only promised to marry no other man in the land than him, and Thorkel Eyjolfsson, whom Snorri the Priest had already decided should be her fourth husband, was abroad at the time. Thorgils leaves in a rage, and soon Snorri engineers his death to leave the way completely clear for Thorkel Eyjolfsson (Chapter 67).

Gudrun now marries Thorkel, who becomes a great chieftain (Chapter 68). Soon, however, Thorkel goes abroad to fetch timber for a church he intends to build at Helgafell; in Norway the king chides him for arrogance and forecasts that the timber will never be used for church-building (Chapter 74). That prediction comes true when Thorkel is drowned in Breidafjord, after taking part in an abortive attempt to purchase Hjardarholt (the property theme is never long absent in this saga). And so Gest Oddleifsson's four-fold prophecy about Gudrun's marriages is finally fulfilled (Chapter 77).

And now the survivors of this complex dynastic tragedy live out their lives. Bolli Bollason becomes a man of great pomp and magnificence, living in a blaze of chivalric courtliness; he marries Snorri's daughter, Thordis, and inherits his estate in Sælingsdale, the estate that Gudrun and Bolli had once owned. Gudrun's son by her fourth marriage, Gellir Thorkelsson, becomes a man of great influence and piety, and dies on his way home from a pilgrimage to Rome.

And Gudrun herself, after her passion-racked life, becomes a nun and Iceland's first anchoress; when she dies she is very old, and blind, and she is buried at Helgafell.

But before she dies, her son Bolli Bollason comes to see her. He is curious to know one thing about his mother's life: he asks her, 'Which man did you love the most?'

The old widow answers evasively at first, and merely gives a perfunctory catalogue of the qualities of her four *husbands*. But Bolli is insistent, and asks again, 'Which man did you love the most?' And now Gudrun answers, 'I was worst to the one I loved the most.'

It is the final, enigmatic confession of a woman seeking serenity and expiation after a cruelly passionate life; and Bolli is satisfied by it.

'And there this saga ends.'

Such is the bare outline of the 'plot' of the saga, the sequence of events that make up its narrative framework. Summarized in this way, it implies a certain historicity; but the concept of historicity has to be approached rather carefully in the Icelandic sagas. In the past, they have sometimes been treated as literal historical truth, because they could be shown to fit, more or less accurately, into the general context of the known early history of Iceland.

As far as *Laxdæla Saga* is concerned, most of the major characters are undoubtedly historical personages, and many of the major landmarks in their lives are corroborated by other historical sources. The *Icelandic Annals*, for instance, which briefly chronicle outstanding events year by year, record some of the main points of reference:

963	birth of Snorri the Priest (Gudrun's friend)
979	birth of Thorkel Eyjolfsson (Gudrun's fourth husband)
997	King Olaf Tryggvason sends Thangbrand to Iceland
1000	Christianity adopted in Iceland
1003	Kjartan Olafsson killed (Gudrun's lover)
1007	Bolli Thorleiksson killed (Gudrun's third husband)
1026	Thorkel Eyjolfsson drowned
1031	death of Snorri the Priest
1073	death of Gellir Thorkelsson, aged sixty-four (Gudrun's son by her fourth husband)

In addition, *Landnámabók* (Book of Settlements) makes sporadic references to Gudrun's husbands, which corroborate the fact that she was married four times – the central theme of the whole saga:

'The sons of Osvif were outlawed for the killing of Kjartan Olafsson. Osvif's daughter was Gudrun, the mother of Thorleik (Bollason), Bolli (Bollason), and Gellir (Thorkelsson).'

'... Thorvald Halldorsson, who married Gudrun Osvif's-daughter.' (Gudrun's first husband, Chapter 34.)

'... Thord Ingunnarson, who married Gudrun Osvif's-daughter.' (Gudrun's second husband, Chapter 35.)

'... Bolli Thorleiksson, who married Gudrun Osvif's-daughter.' (Gudrun's third husband, Chapter 43.)

'... Bolli Thorleiksson, who married Gudrun Osvif's-daughter.

They had six children.... Gudrun had previously been married to Thord Ingunnarson. Her last husband was Thorkel Eyjolfsson.' (Gudrun's fourth husband, Chapter 68.)

It's not really surprising that *Laxdæla Saga* should be so well informed about Gudrun Osvif's-daughter, for Gudrun was the great-grandmother of Iceland's first vernacular historian, Ari Thorgilsson the Learned (cf. the genealogy in Chapter 78); and it is hard to avoid the conclusion that Ari the Learned (1068–1148) was a major source for Gudrun's life-story. The only extant historical work which can be ascribed to Ari with absolute certainty is *Íslendingabók* (or *Libellus Islandorum*, the Book of Icelanders), which he wrote around the year 1127; but he was in all probability one of the compilers of the original version of *Landnámabók* (Book of Settlements) in the first half of the twelfth century, and it is also thought by some scholars that he was the prime source of information for the entries in the *Icelandic Annals*.

On two occasions in *Laxdæla Saga*, Ari the Learned is specifically cited as a historical source (Chapters 4, 78); but such appeals to historical authority are not unusual in other sagas, and give no indication of the special importance of the family connexion between Gudrun and Ari the Learned for the creation of *Laxdæla Saga*. Gellir Thorkelsson, Gudrun's son by her fourth husband, was the father of Thorkel Gellison, who was Ari's uncle (Chapter 78); and in *Íslendingabók* and *Landnámabók*, Thorkel Gellison is cited more than once as a significant source of information, particularly for Ari's account in *Íslendingabók* about the Icelandic colonists in Greenland (cf. *The Vinland Sagas*, Penguin Classics, 1960, p. 26):

Eirik the Red went out to colonize Greenland fourteen or fifteen years before Christianity came to Iceland, according to what Thorkel Gellison was told in Greenland by a man who had himself gone there with Eirik the Red.

Elsewhere in *Íslendingabók*, Ari refers to him as 'my uncle Thorkel Gellison, who could remember far back'.

Now, according to the saga (Chapter 78), Gudrun Osvif's-daughter lived to be a very old woman, so old that she became blind. If she lived to be ninety, as is not unlikely, she would have died only a very few years before Ari, her great-grandson, was born in 1067; and Ari, according to his own statement, was fostered at Helgafell, Gudrun's home, until the age of six by his grandfather, Gudrun's son Gellir Thorkelsson, who played a prominent part in Icelandic politics in the eleventh century until his death in 1073 (he was a supporter of King Olaf the Saint, King of Norway from 1016 to 1030, who tried unavailingly to gain political control over Iceland). So Ari the Learned was born and raised at Helgafell, the estate which played such an important part in Iceland's early religious history (a monastery was established there in 1184), the house in which his great-grandmother had made her celebrated confession about her love-life to her son Bolli Bollason (Chapter 78) only a few years before Ari's birth. Thereafter, at the time when Ari was beginning to collect material for his historical writings, one of his main informants, his uncle Thorkel Gellison, was living at Helgafell, having taken over the estate on his father's death in 1073. There is yet another strand of genealogy connecting Ari with the story of Helgafell; another of the people cited as important sources of information in *Landnáma-bók* was Snorri the Priest's daughter, Thurid (d. 1112 or 1113), and Snorri had lived at Helgafell before he exchanged homes with Gudrun Osvif's-daughter in the year 1008 (Chapter 56).

This is not the place for a detailed study of the sources of *Laxdæla Saga*, written and oral; much of it would perforce have to be rather speculative. But whatever the specific sources the author used – histories, annals, genealogies, other sagas, oral stories – it is clear that many of the key events in the saga are authentic and not invented, and that despite some serious dis-crepancies in the chronology of the saga which will be dis-cussed later, it fits well enough into the known historical setting created by the early Icelandic historians like Ari the Learned.

In addition, the overall air of historicity in the saga is strengthened by the author's very decided antiquarian tastes. Superficially, this shows in his interest in onomastic anecdotes purporting to give the etymological derivations of place-names :

Dogurdarness and Kambsness (Chapter 5), Budardale (Chapter 13), Gudmundar Isles (Chapter 18), Orrustudale and Trollaskeid (Chapter 19), Haugsgard and Hjardarholt (Chapter 24), Harrastead and Harrabol (Chapter 31), Kjalar Isle, Skjaldar Isle, and Haugsness (Chapter 35), Eldgrimsholt and Skrattavardi (Chapter 37), Brenna (Chapter 38), Sverdskelda (Chapter 46), Bollatoptir (Chapter 55), Staff Isle and Skofnungs Isle (Chapter 76). He often refers to the fact that at the time of writing, traces of old buildings were still visible: the boat-shed built by Hoskuld Dala-Kollsson in Budardale (Chapter 13); Hrut's temple (Chapter 19); Haugsgard, the wall surrounding the burial mound of Thord Goddi (Chapter 24); Skrattavardi, the cairn of the Kotkels (Chapter 37); and the burial mound of Melkorka and Thorbjorn the Feeble (Chapter 38). There are also some references to early farmsteads that had been abandoned by the time the author was writing – Hrappstead (Chapter 9), Melkorkustead (Chapter 13), and Hafratindar (Chapter 49). More generally, he calls attention to customs or situations which no longer obtained at his time – pagan ordeal rituals (Chapter 18), memorial feasts (Chapter 26), outdoor privies (Chapter 47), the fact that there was no church in the Dales when Kjartan Olafsson was killed (Chapter 50), and the wearing of long pin-brooches to fasten cloaks (Chapter 75).

There are recurrent stylistic phrases like 'it is generally agreed' or 'people say that' or 'it is common knowledge'. In addition, there are formal references to other written sources – to Ari the Learned (Chapters 4, 78), to a lost *Thorgil's Saga* (Chapter 67), and to a *Njardvikings' Saga* (Chapter 69).

All this, and the carefully-recorded genealogies common to all the Icelandic Sagas, helps to create a flavour of historicity, of scrupulous attention to historical detail; but apart from the bare outline of events, to what extent can *Laxdæla Saga*, or any of the other Icelandic Sagas, really be called 'historical' in any strict definition of the term?

In *Laxdæla Saga* there are, as we said earlier, serious discrepancies in the chronological scale, particularly in the part alleged to have been played by Bolli Bollason in avenging his father. Bolli was born in the spring after Bolli Thorleiksson's killing in 1007 (Chapter 56); and according to the saga, it was not until he was twelve years old that vengeance was exacted on Helgi Hardbeinsson, one of Bolli Thorleiksson's killers (Chapter 64). Thus, it could not have been before 1020 at the earliest that Gudrun married her fourth husband, Thorkel Eyjolfsson – for the saga states unequivocally that she did not remarry until her third husband had been avenged with blood. But it is quite clear from other sources that Gudrun must have married Thorkel Eyjolfsson very soon after Bolli Thorleiksson's death, for her eldest son by him, Gellir Thorkelsson, was an adult by the year 1026 and was sixty-four years old when he died in 1073; and indeed, the saga itself states that Gellir was twelve years old when he went abroad with his father the year before Thorkel Eyjolfsson was drowned in 1026 (Chapter 74), so that the chronology of the saga is inconsistent with its own account, as well as with the historical facts. It is clear that Gudrun must have married Thorkel Eyjolfsson in the year 1008, the same year that she exchanged homes with Snorri the Priest (Chapter 56); and this date chimes much better with the saga's account of how Gudrun defied Thorkel at their wedding feast by championing Gunnar Thidrandi's-Killer (Chapter 69), for according to the *Story of Gunnar Thidrandi's-Killer*, Thidrandi seems to have been killed not long before that date.

So, obviously, Bolli Bollason could not have played any part in the vengeance for his father's death, and that whole episode seems to have been invented for the purpose of enhancing Bolli Bollason's prestige. Indeed, the whole of the marvellously detailed account of the vengeance wreaked on Helgi Hardbeinsson for the death of Bolli Thorleiksson seems to have no historical basis at all. There is no reference to Helgi Hardbeinsson or his family in any other extant source. And the whole fabric of the story is extremely suspect; it is motivated, in the saga, by the scene after Bolli's killing (Chapter 55), when Helgi Hardbeinsson wipes his bloodied spear-blade on Gudrun's sash and prophesies that the child she is carrying in her womb (Bolli Bollason) will bring about his death one day. But as we have seen, Bolli Bollason could not have taken part in any vengeance for his father. And in 1244, only a very short time

25

before *Laxdæla Saga* itself was written, a very similar incident occurred, as recorded in the contemporary *Sturlunga Saga*: a man called Asbjorn Gudmundsson took part in the killing of a farmer, and when the dead man's wife came up, Asbjorn wiped his bloodied sword on her clothing. It seems very likely that the episode in *Laxdæla Saga* was invented by the author, modelled on this celebrated contemporary event, since it is so closely associated with a prophecy that could not have been made, and with a man who probably never existed. Indeed, the much-admired scene in Chapter 63 when Helgi Hardbeinsson identifies his attackers by the descriptions brought to him by his shepherd is essentially a highly sophisticated *literary* achievement, based on a classic technique of story-telling that stretches all the way back to Homer (*Iliad*, Book III).

There are several other echoes of contemporary events in *Laxdæla Saga* which point to a deliberate manipulation of material for artistic ends, especially the rather complicated succession to the inheritance in the family of Thorstein Black the Wise when they all drowned in a single shipwreck (Chapter 18); there was a very similar legal wrangle in 1178, recorded in *Sturlunga Saga* – and the suspicion that the author of *Laxdæla Saga* may have borrowed this theme is strengthened by the fact that there is no suggestion in any other extant source that Thorstein Black the Wise, or any of his family, died by drowning. The story seems to have been invented in order to explain how the deserted lands of Hrappstead came into the possession of Thorkel Fringe.

Similarly, the many dreams and prophecies which the author uses to tauten the material of his narrative are essentially literary devices that cannot by definition be historically true – whether he himself invented them, or whether some of them had already accreted to various episodes of the story before he worked his material into its present literary form.

Indeed, it sometimes seems as if the more vivid, the more 'real', the more compellingly visualized a scene in an Icelandic Saga is, the less likely it is to be historically 'true'. The only valid 'historicity' in the sagas is not so much what it tells us about the history of Iceland as what it tells us about thirteenth-century attitudes to the history of Iceland. The saga-writers were not trying to write history in our sense of the term; they were trying to create an acceptable image of the past. And like great composers, they took themes, the written or unwritten folk-tunes of the nation's past, so to speak, and orchestrated them with their own literary skill and intellectual interpretations. To understand the historical value of the sagas, we have to understand what history meant to a saga-writer and his thirteenth-century audience.

Laxdæla Saga is strung between two historical poles, the two most significant events in the early history of Iceland – the Settlement, from about 870 onwards, and the Conversion to Christianity in the year 1000. These two major national events form the background of the whole saga age, and permeate most of the major sagas. In *Laxdæla Saga* they form a twin polarity, for the physical demands of the Age of Settlement and the intellectual demands of the Age of Christianity affected the motivation of people in markedly different ways. They thicken the texture of the narrative and give extra meaning to it. In some sagas, like *Njal's Saga*,* for instance, the Conversion is the more important of the two events; the events leading to the Conversion are described at considerable length, and the impact of Christianity on the major characters has a decisive effect on the course and the meaning of the narrative. In *Laxdæla Saga* the Conversion has one decisive effect on the plot, because it is the year that Kjartan Olafsson spends in Norway as a hostage while King Olaf Tryggvason was putting political pressure on Iceland that cost him the chance to win Gudrun's hand in marriage; but apart from that, the impact of the Age of Christianity is not explored so subtly as in *Njal's Saga*. In *Laxdæla Saga* the Age of Settlement is the more meaningful.

We know a great deal about the Age of Settlement as a whole, chiefly from *Landnámabók*, whose extant versions record the names and families of some 400 of the original settlers and brief anecdotes about them. This and other accounts of the

* *Njal's Saga*, translated by Magnus Magnusson and Hermann Pálsson, Penguin Books, 1960.

Settlement may not be entirely reliable; but this was how the Icelandic antiquarians saw the birth of their nation, and, to them, remembering the past was not an idle pastime, but a matter of extreme importance.

In the first place, it had a functional importance. It was necessary to remember how much land was claimed by each settler, and how the land was claimed. Future land-claims would always relate back, through the memory of witnesses, to the various stages of ownership that the land had passed through – who had inherited from whom, how extensive the land was, where the boundaries lay; in *Laxdæla Saga* there is an example of the kind of trouble that could arise over a forgotten or disputed boundary title, when Hrut Herjolfsson inadvertently settled a freed slave on land that actually belonged to his neighbour (Chapter 25). This kind of necessary remembering helped to create a detailed tapestry of the physical landscape of the early settlements, which was further picked out with vivid folk etymologies of how places got their names – this is where Unn the Deep-Minded lost her comb, which is why it is called Kambsness, and this is the headland where she had her breakfast one morning long, long ago, and that is why it is called Dogurdarness (Chapter 5). Such anecdotes tell us nothing about the real life of the early Icelandic pioneers, but they throw an interesting light on the devoted interest that Icelanders of the twelfth and thirteenth centuries took in their ancestors.

Their purpose, like that of so many historians, was to justify the present in terms of the past. This is argued quite explicitly in *Landnámabók*:

It is often said that writing about the Settlements is irrelevant learning, but we think we can all the better meet the criticisms of foreigners when they accuse us of being descended from slaves or scoundrels, if we know for certain the truth about our ancestry. And for those who want to know ancient lore and be able to trace genealogies, it is better to start at the beginning than to come in at the middle. And indeed, all civilized nations want to know about the origins of their own society, and the beginnings of their own race.

In precisely the same frame of mind, Geoffrey of Monmouth

concocted a totally fictitious *History of the Kings of Britain**
in c. 1136 (the same period as the early Icelandic historians
were documenting their own past), inventing for Britain a
respectable past by promoting an obscure British war-leader of
the early sixth century called Arthur to the status of a Christian
Emperor of Europe descended from Rome. No one wants to be
accused of being 'descended from slaves or scoundrels', and
all nations tend to idealize their past. In *Laxdœla Saga* this
idealization is positively romantic; the kings of Norway are
wheeled on to the stage merely to fête and to flatter the
illustrious Icelanders who visit them – Hoskuld Dala-Kollsson,
Hrut Herjolfsson, Olaf the Peacock, Kjartan Olafsson, Bolli
Bollason. Nobility of lineage is given excessive importance and
colours the whole narrative; the saga constantly emphasizes the
splendour and style in which the tenth-century men of Laxriverdale lived, and how they were accepted as men of high
importance in the royal courts of Scandinavia. The author's
admiration for aristocratic genealogy knows no bounds, particularly in the case of Olaf the Peacock; the revelation that
Olaf's mother Melkorka is in reality an Irish princess of the
blood royal and not merely a slave concubine is crucial to the
family's history. Olaf's sumptuous acceptance by his grandfather, King Myrkjartan of the Irish (Chapter 21), is a
triumphant refutation of the lurking sneer about his birth that
breaks to the surface every now and again – from Hoskuld's
wife, Jorunn ('That concubine's son certainly has the wealth
to ensure that his name is long remembered', Chapter 24); from
the girl Olaf wanted to marry, Thorgerd Egil's-daughter ('. . . if
you want to marry me to a concubine's son, no matter how
handsome and flashily dressed he is', Chapter 23); from the
princess Ingibjorg of Norway ('I want the women of Iceland
to see that the woman whose company you have been keeping
in Norway isn't descended from slaves', Chapter 43). What is
really poignant about the author's attitude is that he was
depicting these tenth-century Icelanders as the intimates, if
not quite the equals, of kings at a time when thirteenth-century

* Geoffrey of Monmouth, *The History of the Kings of Britain*,
translated by Lewis Thorpe, Penguin Books, 1966.

Iceland was being relentlessly crushed of its independence by the power-politics of the kings of Norway.

The harsh reality of Iceland's dwindling political independence in the thirteenth century (Iceland was eventually annexed by the crown of Norway in 1262), and the decades of savage internal strife that contributed to it, lent a desperate nostalgia to the image of the pioneering Age of Settlement. Relatively speaking, the birth of the Icelandic nation was very recent. To the twelfth-century historians, the Pagan Age was only three generations away (and easily bridged by reliable memory), and another three generations would take them right back to the beginnings. And these beginnings had been extraordinarily traumatic.

The Age of Settlement stands out in stark contrast to the Viking Age out of which it was born. Elsewhere the Scandinavian intrusions had been brutally disruptive, but in Iceland there had been nothing to disrupt, no long-established civilization to plunder or take over; the country was uninhabited except for a few Celtic monks who had come there in search of solitude, and who fled when the first Norsemen arrived. The newcomers did not even have to face up to the hostility of indigenous natives as their descendants had to do a century later, when they tried to colonize North America and were repulsed by the Red Indians. They were free to carve up the virgin island as they thought fit; and from out of the chaos of the Viking Age behind them, they had the opportunity of establishing a new system of order without interference from other states. They had come for a variety of reasons. Many, like Ketil Flat-Nose and his family (Chapter 2), seem to have believed they were escaping from the tyranny of King Harald Fine-Hair in Norway, and this may well be true – blended perhaps with the hope of being able to make a better livelihood in Iceland ('for they ... heard ... there was excellent land there ... for the taking', Chapter 2). Others were outlaws, forced to leave Norway 'because of some killings', like Eirik the Red and his father (*The Vinland Sagas*).

Whatever their motives for coming, they were a disparate collection of people. Most of them were pagan, but some were already Christian, or had come into close contact with Christianity in the British Isles. Most were of Scandinavian blood, but some were Celtic or of mixed Norse and Celtic blood, first-generation Norsemen from the Scottish islands and Ireland. No one can be sure precisely where they came from, or precisely how mixed a population it was. But the mere fact of not having a common adversary to resist them must have made the problem of organizing the settlers politically into a coherent state all the more difficult. It has been suggested (by the late Barði Guðmundsson) that one reason why the new nation settled down so quickly into an organized state may have been because the bulk of the original settlers perhaps belonged to one particular tribe in Scandinavia (the Heruli?) whose community identity had not been completely lost by the time Iceland was discovered. This tribe would have had distinctive customs that marked them out from other Norwegians and would account for some of the distinctive, non-Norwegian features that have puzzled scholars about the new Icelanders – people who buried their dead instead of cremating them, people with a system of voluntary allegiance to priest-chieftains that was anti-monarchist in spirit, people with a tradition of esoteric 'court-poetry' that was almost exclusively composed by Icelanders, either in Iceland or in royal courts abroad. Such a tribe would have been more reluctant than most to tolerate the increasing centralization of political power in Norway when King Harald Fine-Hair was strengthening his authority over the whole country (cf. Chapter 2). It is certainly a striking theory, but it can be no more than a speculation that attempts to explain the astonishing feat of organization that the early pioneers brought about – a feat that the twelfth- and thirteenth-century antiquarians looked back on with amazement and awe.

As soon as the country was fully settled, despite the fact that it was larger than Ireland, with primitive communications and no village communities and no royal court to provide a focus, a common law was accepted for the whole country. The foundation of the Althing, the General Assembly, in A.D. 930, was a remarkable achievement to come out of that raw, impactual period; what characterized pagan Iceland and early Christian

Iceland above anything else, setting it quite apart from any other medieval European country, was a dynamic veneration for law and order. The early Icelanders owed no allegiance to king or earl; their allegiance was primarily to the concept of law – and it is worth noting that *law*-breakers were sentenced not to death or imprisonment, but to out*law*ry. To be a member of society was at once a privilege and an obligation, and anyone who violated the law of society forfeited his right to remain within that law, within that society; they were banished from Iceland. That was how Iceland protected itself against disruptive elements.

The major flaw in this system was that the state had no executive power to enforce its punishment; that was left to society at large, which in most cases meant in effect the aggrieved party, if it was strong enough. The sagas constantly deal with themes of violence; this was not, as is often assumed, from any admiration for killings and vengeance, but arose from a deep concern about the seriousness of violent action, of taking the law into one's own hands. The saga-writers were interested in exploring these effects; they were more concerned with the motivation and consequences of violence than with the violence itself; death was only important in the effect it had on the people who caused it, and the people who suffered from its consequences.

In the sagas, crime is seen as a crime against society, rather than a crime against individuals; and more often than not it is the outcome of irregular relationships, a crime against the natural order of things. There are a remarkable number of irregular relationships in *Laxdæla Saga*, all of which lead to trouble; failures to 'observe ... kinship properly' – like Hoskuld and Hrut (Chapter 19), and Olaf and Thorleik (Chapter 27); flawed marriages – like that of Thurid and Geirmund which introduces the fatal sword 'Leg-Biter' (Chapter 30), of Hoskuld and Jorunn which introduces Melkorka (Chapter 12), and above all the flawed marriage of Gudrun and Bolli which Gest had prophesied (Chapter 33). The most important moral and ethical concept in early Icelandic society was *drengskapr*, the idea of fairness of conduct; a crime like Bolli's in killing his foster-brother could only come about when he lost – even though only momentarily – his sense of fairness, his sense of propriety of conduct. Anyone who takes up the wrong sort of challenge in the sagas, as a result of responding to the goadings of others, always comes out the loser in the end.

In the sagas it is not the great warriors who are the heroes, the men who could kill most people with fewest strokes; it is the sages, the men of moderation, the men like Njal of Berg-thorsknoll or Olaf the Peacock who understand the awful futility of violence and devote their lives to combating it. There is less real admiration for Kjartan Olafsson, the peerless, than for his father, Olaf the Peacock, the man of peace, the man of wisdom and responsibility who constantly thinks in terms of the good of the whole community : 'He was extremely well-liked, for whenever he intervened in other people's affairs he did it in such a way that everyone was satisfied' (Chapter 24). To him, vengeance was a purely negative attitude – 'Bolli's death would not bring back my son', (Chapter 49) – and it was only after his death that the bitter anti-social hatreds he had striven to keep in check erupted again.

This idealization of the concept of law and order was in some ways no doubt a reflection of the nostalgia of thirteenth-century Icelanders, beset as they were by violence and political treachery on a scale undreamed of in the tenth century. They saw their hard-won freedom, their independent political insti-tutions, being destroyed before their eyes; so it is little wonder that they thought of the tenth century as being more secure, more stable. And the most stabilizing influence, to them, seemed to be the chieftains, many of whom are heavily idealized. Unn the Deep-Minded sets the pattern in *Laxdæla Saga*, a standard of large-mindedness and concern for the community; it was the role of chieftains to protect, to supervise, to give cohesion to society – a role from which the thirteenth-century chieftains had abdicated so disastrously. And so, in retrospect, the thir-teenth-century Christian writers in Iceland seldom felt or expressed rancour towards paganism; indeed, the author of *Laxdæla Saga* goes out of his way to do the opposite – 'Pagans felt their responsibilities no less keenly when performing such ceremonies than Christians do now when ordeals are decreed'. (Chapter 18).

But this tolerant attitude towards paganism, and even approval of the society which practised it, does not conceal the fact that the thirteenth-century authors were keenly aware of the barrier between themselves and the past – the barrier of Christianity. In so far as they were writing 'history', it was a very stylized history, a stylized image of the past that was being held up as a guiding light for later generations; and the very antiquarianism so evident in *Laxdœla Saga* is a measure of this. The thirteenth-century Christian man of learning, as our author undoubtedly was, could know something about the external phenomena of paganism, but he could not know the attitudes, the ethics; he could know details of ritual worship – but he could not know the real relationship between priest and worshipper, for instance, or fully understand the relationship between priest and gods.

Nor, surely, could he know about the emotions and motivations of people who had lived and died two centuries or more earlier. Emotions are ephemeral; the events remain, but they are interpreted in retrospect, subjectively, according to the experience of the individual. And one of the striking aspects of *Laxdœla Saga* which sets it a little apart from the other classical sagas is the extent to which the author describes the actual emotions felt by his characters.

The success of these thirteenth-century interpretations depended to a large extent on the intellectual and emotional capacity of the individual authors, and their own observations of human nature. The saga-writers were highly articulate authors whose intention was to create an atmosphere of actuality, and sagas are judged nowadays by the success with which they achieved this; they are praised for their objectivity, the cool impartiality with which they present events, whether good or bad. In some measure, this objectivity was natural to the learned medieval mind, which saw men not as good or evil but as a sum of actions, a synthesis of many elements both good and bad. Theology classified actions, rather than people; in the sagas, the only thoroughly evil people, the scoundrels like

Hrapp and Kotkel, are symbols rather than characters; the others are a compound of both good and bad, of noble impulses and base motives, of fine and wicked deeds. Here, the book-learning of the thirteenth century helped to broaden the author's natural talents; and *Laxdæla Saga* is above all the product of a sophisticated, keenly-trained European mind.

Mercifully, the Icelandic Sagas have now lost most of their old Germanic glamour. They are now being treated at last as serious medieval literature, shorn of the spurious romanticism so dear to the nineteenth century. Past generations of scholars have often tended to see the sagas as products of the Noble Savage mind, as tribal expressions that realized tribal dreams; others have regarded them as great artistic achievements of the Native Genius, their authors being untutored and uninfluenced by current European ideals and tastes. *Laxdæla Saga* is certainly a home-grown product, sprung from Icelandic soil; but it also has its roots in European civilization, in the civilized medieval mentality of Europe – and one of its purposes, it could be argued, was to Europeanize Iceland's image, to give Iceland a European context.

This can be seen most clearly in the Gudrun–Kjartan–Bolli situation, where three distinct European cultures meet. Gudrun, partly at least, is a product of the heroic Germanic spirit; Kjartan, more complex, is a product of the Celtic medieval Christian spirit – but more than that, he is a composite of conflicting cultures and attitudes, of saint and warrior and knight combined; while Bolli, and more particularly his son Bolli Bollason, represents the European Age of Chivalry (it is only when Bolli finally breaks away from Kjartan in Norway and ceases to play second fiddle to him that he emerges as a character in his own right).

Take Gudrun first. In the native literature, there is a clear model for Gudrun. In the *Edda*, a collection of heroic and mythological poetry, the Nibelungen cycle tells the powerful and tragic story of Brynhild and her lovers. Brynhild, the Valkyrie, loves the peerless hero Sigurd Fafni's-Slayer, but is tricked into marrying the second-best, Sigurd's sworn-brother,

Gunnar, while Sigurd marries Gunnar's sister, Gudrun. Like the Gudrun of *Laxdæla Saga*, Brynhild becomes fiercely jealous when she realizes how she has been tricked, and goads her husband Gunnar into having Sigurd killed (unlike Bolli, he has scruples about actually killing his sworn-brother himself). Brynhild commits suicide after Sigurd's death, and Sigurd's widow now marries Brynhild's brother, Atli, and Atli later kills Gunnar.

The *Edda* situation is obviously rather more intricate than the *Laxdæla Saga* situation, but the core of it is undoubtedly very similar; and there are also some suggestive verbal echoes between the two. The author clearly knew the *Edda* poems; indeed, it would be surprising if he had not known them, for this pagan legacy of heroic poetry was greatly treasured in thirteenth-century Iceland – vellum manuscripts of them were being copied out during that period, particularly the great *Codex Regius*; and Snorri Sturluson, the historian, was working on his *Prose Edda*, in which he retold some of these poems, not long before *Laxdæla Saga* itself was written. But one should beware of making too much of the parallels; our author was bound by historic facts to a certain extent (he could not, for instance, allow Gudrun to commit suicide over Kjartan's death); there were few gaps in the historic framework to give him any room to manoeuvre. We are more concerned with the literary affinities which influenced his interpretation of the emotions involved in the situation. Gudrun's reactions are in essentially the same spirit as those of her pagan ancestress.

Kjartan's career, on the other hand, seems to be envisaged as a Christian victory; and here there are some fascinating parallels with Celtic literature, quite apart from the overtly Christian aspects of his life – the conversion to Christianity by King Olaf Tryggvason in Norway, the strict observance of fasts, and so on. There are some really striking similarities between the death of Kjartan and the death of a sixth-century Irish saint, St Cellach of Killala. Both of them observed a very strict fast throughout Lent (people came from miles around just to look at Kjartan, Chapter 45); both are killed a few days after Easter, by a former friend and kinsman; in both there is an ominous dream on the Wednesday night after Easter (An Brushwood-Belly's dream at Hol, Chapter 48); Cellach is described as being 'poor and feeble' from fasting, and there is a strong suggestion that Kjartan, too, was recuperating from the rigours of a long fast ('He was only slightly wounded, but very weak with exhaustion', Chapter 49).

The parallels seem too close to be mere coincidence, and certainly the manner of Kjartan's death has a flavour of Christian martyrdom about it, for Kjartan achieves the ideal, flawless art of dying a Christian death. But despite the attempt to make him a Christian hero ('He was a man of great humility, and so popular that everyone, man or child, loved him', Chapter 28), Kjartan's actions fell far short of any Christian ideals and sprang rather from a pagan ethic – pride and self-reliance, a fierce concern for his 'honour' if it meant losing face, a capacity for brutal and coarse retaliation against Bolli and Gudrun.

This Christian wash on Kjartan's portrait is by no means the only echo from Celtic literature in the saga. For instance, Hrapp the Hebridean asks to be buried standing upright in his grave under the threshold of his house, 'So that I can keep an even better watch over my house', (Chapter 17); and St Cellach's father, the King of Connacht, had himself buried in just the same way, with his face to the north confronting his enemies, who were unable to attack his kingdom until they had disinterred him and buried him again in Sligo with his face turned downwards. Similarly, Hrut Herjolfsson's foray against Hoskuld Dala-Kollsson's livestock in pursuit of his claim to his mother's estate (Chapter 19), is nothing more nor less than a classic Irish cattle-raid (táin bó) – one of the very few cattle-raids in the Icelandic sagas. And even the colouring of the four horses that Bolli tries to give to Kjartan (Chapter 45) – white, with red ears and red forelock – is a curiously unnatural colour for a horse; but it is a common colouring motif for cows in Irish legends, particularly magic cows. In a saga as deeply concerned with Ireland as Laxdæla Saga is, where a major theme is Kjartan's descent from King Myrkjartan of the Irish, it is hard to think of these echoes as merely accidental, although it would be a mistake to try to define these influences too strictly in terms of specific literary borrowings. They should be seen rather in spatial terms (they could have been brought to Iceland from various sources long before the saga was written) illustrating the author's literary eclecticism.

The third major literary strand is the flavour of courtly chivalry, which is represented at its most thorough in the portrait of Bolli Bollason. These influences were making themselves felt very strongly in Norway and Iceland from the second quarter of the thirteenth century onwards, starting with the translation of *Tristram's Saga* from French into Norse by one Brother Robert (presumably an Englishman?) in 1226 at the behest of King Hakon Hakonsson of Norway (*d.* 1263). A stream of translations followed – *Charlemagne's Saga*, the *Chanson de Roland*, *Le Mantel Mautaillé*, *Elie de Saint Gille*, *Floire et Blanceflor*, Chrêtien de Troyes' *Conte del Graal*, and the *lais* of Marie de France; all these and many others quickly circulated throughout Iceland, and soon inspired a vast number of translations, adaptations, and new compositions in the vernacular, a great torrent of popular literature that continued to be written for several centuries.

All these literary tastes and styles meet in the composition of *Laxdæla Saga* – the clerical religious learning, the courtly literature of chivalry, the antiquarian feeling for history, the sympathy for the old heroic poetry. But there is nothing freakish about the fact that such an author should live and write in thirteenth-century Iceland, combining native traditions and European learning so brilliantly; for thirteenth-century Iceland seemed capable of producing authors of this kind and calibre almost at will. It was a society where opposition between laity and clergy was never sharp, where the same man could be abbot, saga-writer, historian, and Law-Speaker of the Althing (like Styrmir the Learned, who died in 1245), where many of the leading personalities, whether priests or chieftains, belonged to the same great families. Snorri Sturluson, the poet, saga-author, historian and politician (cf. *King Harald's Saga*, Penguin Classics, 1966, Introduction), was brought up in a church school at Oddi, and his foster-brother was a bishop. Ari the Learned was a priest, a chieftain and a historian. Sæmund the Learned, who wrote the first history of Iceland in Latin (now lost), was also a priest, chieftain and historian.

Many Icelanders studied abroad; Sæmund the Learned studied in Paris; Snorri Sturluson's foster-brother studied in England. Medieval Christianity was the great intellectual uniter, and the monasteries were the great repositories of European learning (it is recorded that soon after the monastery of Helgafell was established in 1184, it had a library of no fewer than 120 books).

There was constant traffic and interchange. In the eleventh century alone, there were six foreign bishops in Iceland, one of whom was Irish (Bishop Jon the Irishman); the others were English or German. In the twelfth century there were priests in Iceland with distinctly English names; and the monastery of Thykkvaby had a number of foreign monks on its strength. There were numerous foreign books available, in original or translation. Geoffrey of Monmouth's works, both the *History of the Kings of Britain* and the *Prophecies of Merlin*, were translated into Icelandic by the early thirteenth century, as was a Latin narrative about the destruction of Troy. Abbot Brand Jonsson (d. 1264), of the monastery of Thykkvaby, translated into noble Icelandic prose the celebrated twelfth-century poem *Alexandreis* by the Frenchman Phillipe Gautier de Chatillon. In the middle of the twelfth century, round about 1155, an Icelandic priest called Nikulas Bergsson, abbot of the Benedictine monastery of Thverriver, in Eyjafjord, composed a guide-book for Icelanders visiting Rome and the Holy Land, basing it on his own four-year pilgrimage throughout Europe.

Such was the literary background against which *Laxdæla Saga* was written, with full awareness of European literary and intellectual traditions. Interestingly enough, this awareness is reflected, subconsciously perhaps, in the actual narrative of the saga; it is remarkable how often the impact of foreign culture and foreign attitudes are shown to have a disruptive effect on early Icelandic society. Bolli Bollason says (Chapter 72), 'I have always wanted to travel to southern lands one day, for a man is thought to grow ignorant if he doesn't ever travel beyond this country of Iceland'; but every journey abroad in *Laxdæla Saga* has a momentous effect, in one way or another –

it is Kjartan's absence in Norway, for instance, that loses him both Gudrun and his life. Consider what the saga characters bring back with them – new ideas and new styles, certainly, like Olaf the Peacock and Kjartan Olafsson and Bolli Bollason; cosmopolitan tastes in clothes and weapons; timber for building mansions and churches. But sometimes the weapons have a baleful effect, like the sword 'Leg-Biter', or the kingly gifts turn sour, like the gold-woven head-dress, and inspire only jealousy and hatred. Sometimes the timber is ill-fated, like the timber that Thorkel Eyjolfsson brought back to build a new church at Helgafell. Sometimes the people who are brought back play a crucial part in the lives of the characters, like Hoskuld's Melkorka, or Olaf's Geirmund the Noisy. It is almost as if the author, knowing the impact that Norway was having on Iceland's internal politics in the thirteenth century, counterpoints his literary Europeanism with an uneasy recognition of the dangerously dynamic effect that foreign influence can have on a small, self-reliant community – the small, idealized, vulnerable society of early Iceland which he evoked so nostalgically.

We have talked throughout of 'the author' of *Laxdæla Saga*, with the familiarity of long acquaintance. And yet he is totally unknown. No one can even guess who he might have been, although it seems inevitable from the evidence of the saga itself that he must have been a Breidafjord man, a descendant, no doubt, of the Laxriverdale dynasty; and that he must have been intimately connected either with Hjardarholt, the estate that plays so important a part in the early sections of the saga, or Helgafell, which came to have such an important place in Iceland's religious history (Chapter 66). The closest we can come to him, in fact, is a little scrap of manuscript, known as D2, which was salvaged from a bookbinding; this fragment, one worn and somewhat damaged leaf of vellum, which covers Kjartan's return to Iceland after his stay in Norway (Chapters 43–4), has been dated *c.* 1250 – much the oldest of the surviving manuscripts, and therefore very close indeed to the original manuscript of our anonymous author.

Apart from this, we know nothing of him – except that he

existed, and that he stamped his genius unmistakably and distinctively on his work. *Laxdæla Saga* is not, to our minds, so rich and profound a work as *Njal's Saga*; but it is great and remarkable none the less, a magnificent achievement in the great body of Icelandic literature of which he was so clearly aware. The grand design of the saga is astonishingly dense yet supple, using all the sophisticated literary techniques of saga-writing to impose a masterly coherence on his sprawling material. The whole structure of the saga is constantly tautened by the use of dreams and prophecies and supernatural portents that haunt the reader's memory while they await their fulfilment; and the generations are punctuated by careful descriptions of betrothals and marriages and funerary feasts (indeed love and marriage play an extraordinarily pervasive and multifaceted part throughout the whole saga).

There is about it the air of a pageant – a style that luxuriates in descriptions of ornate occasions, an emphasis on emotion that is akin to mime rather than method acting, a certain repetitiveness of phrasing, a surface glitter. There are any number of superbly visualized scenes, tableaux almost: Melkorka talking to her baby son on a sunlit morning (Chapter 13), Gest Oddleifsson watching the innocent swimmers who are to become central figures in the family tragedy (Chapter 33), the shepherd describing to Helgi Hardbeinsson the circle of men eating breakfast before coming to kill him (Chapter 63). There is a sense of grandeur, of the grandiose, almost, that grows stronger as generation succeeds generation and gives the climacteric tragedy of Gudrun–Kjartan–Bolli a horror and a pity that such brilliance and beauty and prowess should be so cruelly destroyed.

Sometimes one feels the portraits to be overdrawn – Bolli Bollason, in particular, seems to be only a glittering but empty husk of a character (but then, he is never really allowed the chance to come alive); but the superlatives are a distinctive feature of the author's style, and the air of lyricism contrasts effectively with the grim tensions gathering below the surface. And at the end of the saga we are left with the memory of an unforgettable gallery of varied and intensely individual people, the men and women who lived and died in Laxriverdale, both stupid and clever, noble and base, aggressive and peaceful, humble and arrogant, brave and cowardly, generous and mean, obstinate and compliant.

But dominating them all is Gudrun Osvif's-daughter, lovely and imperious, as fierce in hatred as in love, proud, vain, jealous, and infinitely desirable. Like all great women, she remained an enigma all her life; and long after her death we can still argue about her, and admire her, and care about her; and wonder still who it was she really loved the most.

Scotland, 1967

Note on the Translation

THIS translation is based on the standard edition of *Laxdæla Saga* in the Íslenzk Fornrit series (vol. 5, Reykjavik, 1934), edited by Professor Einar Ólafur Sveinsson of the University of Iceland. The text is based on the vellum *Möð.uvallabók* codex which was written early in the fourteenth century. We have added chapter headings of our own.

The saga has been translated into English on four previous occasions: by Mrs Muriel A. C. Press (The Temple Classics, 1899), by Robert Proctor (Chiswick Press, 1903), by Thorstein Veblen (New York, 1925), and most recently, by A. Margaret Arent (University of Washington Press, 1964). The earlier translations were deliberately archaic and mannered in style (like the opening sentence of Proctor's incredibly inaccurate version, 'Ketil Flatneb hight a man, the son of Bjorn Roughfoot; he was a mighty hersir in Norway and of great kin.'); Miss Arent's translation is in a more graceful modern idiom, with a useful Introduction and notes, which must have opened many readers' eyes to the real quality of the saga. We frequently found it a source of inspiration, although we did not always agree with her interpretation of the text, and gladly acknowledge our debt to her.

As in our previous translations in the Penguin Classics series (*Njal's Saga, The Vinland Sagas, King Harald's Saga*), we have relegated the genealogical material (in italics) to the footnotes, where it does not impede the flow of the narrative. Where a particular genealogy seemed to us worth special notice, we have added notes of our own to call attention to it; in particular, we have noted the parts played by the characters in this saga in other Icelandic Sagas, for *Laxdæla Saga* is deeply rooted in the great mass of medieval Icelandic literature. The genealogical implications are extremely complex and deserve careful study; and we have provided a number of charts to guide the reader through the maze.

There is also a Chronological Table to give the reader an

43

outline context for the events of the saga; and as usual there is a Glossary of the more important characters in the saga. The maps were prepared by William Blaik, based on the maps in the Íslenzk Fornrit edition.

M.M.
H.P.

LAXDÆLA SAGA

1. Ketil Flat-Nose

THERE was a man called Ketil Flat-Nose, who was the son of Bjorn Buna. Ketil was a powerful and well-born lord in Norway; he lived in Romsdale, in Romsdale Province, which lies between Sunnmore and Nordmore.

Ketil Flat-Nose was married to Yngvild, the daughter of Ketil Wether, a man of great distinction. They had five children. Their sons were Bjorn the Easterner and Helgi Bjolan. One daughter was called Thorunn Hyrna; she was the wife of Helgi the Lean.[1] The second daughter was called Unn the Deep-Minded; she was the wife of Olaf the White.[2] The third daughter was called Jorunn Wisdom-Slope.[3]

1. *Helgi the Lean was the son of Eyvind the Easterner and of Rafarta, the daughter of King Kjarval of Ireland.*
This Kjarval has been identified with King Cearbhall of Ossory, who died c. 888 according to Irish annals.

2. *Olaf the White was the son of Ingjald, the son of King Frodi the Valiant, who was killed by Earl Sverting and his sons.*
Olaf the White has been identified with a great Norse viking whom the Irish annals call Amhlaibh Conung (King Olaf), who dominated Ireland in the third quarter of the ninth century.
Unn the Deep-Minded plays a part in several other sagas, including *The Vinland Sagas* (Penguin Classics, 1965). In some sources she is called Aud, not Unn.

3. *Jorunn Wisdom-Slope was the mother of Ketil the Fisher, who was the first settler at Kirkby. He was the father of Asbjorn, the father of Thorstein, the father of Surt, the father of Sighvat the Law-Speaker.*
Sighvat Surtsson was Law-Speaker at the Althing, 1076-83. For an account of the Althing, the Icelandic General Assembly, see *Njal's Saga*, Penguin Classics, 1960. pp. 18–19.

2. Flight from Norway

IN the latter years of Ketil's life, King Harald Fine-Hair rose to such power that neither provincial kings nor other men of stature could prosper in Norway or retain their rank and title without his sanction.[1] When Ketil learned that King Harald was intending to subject him to the same treatment as other chieftains, who had been forced to become the king's vassals and had been denied compensation for fallen kinsmen, he summoned his own kinsmen to a meeting and addressed them thus:

'You are all aware of our past dealings with King Harald, and there is no need to recount them here; our more urgent task is to try to solve the problems that face us now. I have reliable reports of King Harald's hostility towards us, and I am sure we need look for no mercy from that quarter. It seems to me that there are only two courses open to us: either to flee the country, or else be killed off each in his own place. I would much prefer to end my days as my forefathers have done, but I have no wish to commit you to such dangers on my decision alone, for I know the temper of my kinsmen and friends: I know that you would not wish to forsake me, whatever hazard there might be in standing by me.'

Ketil's son, Bjorn, replied: 'I can make my own intentions

1. According to the early Icelandic historians, King Harald ruled as a king for about seventy years, from c. 859 to 928; he died c. 931 at the age of eighty. Before King Harald's time, Norway consisted of a number of petty kingdoms (of one of which he was a ruler), which he succeeded in uniting under a single crown, probably c. 880. His struggle for supremacy in Norway seems to have forced many leading Norwegians to leave the country and settle in Scotland and Iceland. The origin of his nickname, 'Fine-Hair', is explained in the Kings' Sagas as follows: as a young man, Harald had sworn never to cut or comb his hair until he had conquered all Norway, and when he eventually achieved his aim and was freed of his pledge, everyone realized for the first time what a fine head of hair he had.

clear at once: I want to follow the example of other eminent men and leave this country. I cannot see how it would benefit me to sit at home waiting for King Harald's slaves to hound us off our lands or put us all to death.'

This was considered bravely spoken, and there was loud approval. And so it was settled that they should leave the country, for Ketil's sons urged it strongly and no one spoke against it. Bjorn and Helgi wanted to go to Iceland, for they claimed to have heard tempting reports of it; they said that there was excellent land there to be had for the taking, with an abundance of stranded whales and plenty of salmon, and good fishing-grounds all the year round.

But Ketil said, 'That fishing-place will never see me in my old age.'

Then he declared his own intentions: he preferred to go west across the sea to Scotland because, he said, he thought it was good living there. He knew the country well, for he had raided there extensively.

3. Ketil's sons in Iceland

AFTER that, Ketil held a splendid feast; it was then that he gave his daughter Thorunn Hyrna in marriage to Helgi the Lean, as was written earlier. Then he made ready for his voyage from Norway west across the sea; his daughter Unn the Deep-Minded and many others of his kinsmen went with him.

That same summer Ketil's sons and their brother-in-law Helgi the Lean sailed for Iceland. Bjorn Ketilsson made land in the west, in Breidafjord; he sailed in along the southern side of the bay until he reached another fjord that branched off from it. There was a steep hill on the headland to the east, and an island lay close inshore. Bjorn said they would stop there for a while. He went ashore with a few men and roamed along the beach. The mountains came almost down to the sea, and Bjorn thought it a good place to live. Nearby in a creek he found the pillars of his high-seat washed ashore, and now they all felt they had been guided to the site of their new home.[1] Bjorn then took possession of all the land between Staf River and Hraunfjord, and built his home at the place which has been called Bjarnarhaven ever since.

He was known as Bjorn the Easterner.[2]

Helgi Bjolan made land in the south of Iceland and took possession of the whole of Kjalarness between Kollafjord and Hvalfjord; he lived at Esjuberg till old age.

Helgi the Lean made land in the north and took possession of the whole of Eyjafjord between Sigluness and Reynisness; he made his home at Kristness.[3]

1. These carved wooden pillars flanked the seat of honour and, according to tradition, were often brought by the early settlers from their old homes in Norway. They were symbols of the luck of the house, and the settlers would often put them overboard within sight of land and build their new homes at the spot where they were washed ashore. For instance, Iceland's first settler, Ingolf Arnarson, built his home at Reykjavik, site of the present capital, when his high-seat pillars were discovered there several years after he first arrived in Iceland.

2. *Bjorn the Easterner was married to Gjaflaug, the daughter of Kjallak the Old; their sons were Ottar and Kjallak. Kjallak had a son called Thorgrim (the father of Killer-Styr and Vermund), and a daughter called Helga; she was married to Vestar of Eyr, the son of Thorolf Bladder-Bald, the first settler at Eyr, and their son was Thorlak, the father of Steinthor of Eyr.*
There is considerable confusion in the early Icelandic sources about when Ketil Flat-Nose and the various members of his family left Norway; but according to *Eyrbyggja Saga*, Bjorn the Easterner came to Iceland in A.D. 884. The same source explains his nickname as follows: Bjorn had been fostered in Sweden, and when the rest of the family emigrated to the Hebrides, he remained behind in the east. When he later rejoined his kinsmen in the west he refused to embrace the Christian faith, as the others had done by then, and was given this nickname to emphasize his alien, non-Western attitude.

3. *From Helgi the Lean and Thorunn Hyrna stems the Eyfirding kin.* Although Christianity was not officially adopted in Iceland until the year A.D. 1000, some of the original settlers in the Age of Settlement (870–930) were Christians. 'Kristness', the name given by Helgi the Lean to his farm, is one of the few extant Christian

4. Unn the Deep-Minded

KETIL FLAT-NOSE made land in Scotland and was well received by men of rank there, for he was famous and of noble birth; they invited him to stay there on his own terms. Ketil settled there with all his kinsmen except his grandson Thorstein the Red.[1]

Thorstein went to war at once. He raided far and wide throughout Scotland and was everywhere victorious. Later he made a treaty with the Scots and became king over the half of Scotland they ceded to him.[2] The Scots did not honour the treaty for long; they treacherously broke their truce with him and he was killed in Caithness, according to the account of his death by Ari Thorgilsson the Learned.[3]

Unn the Deep-Minded was also in Caithness when Thorstein lost his life. When she learned that her son had been killed she realized that she had no further prospects there, now that her father, too, was dead. So she had a ship built secretly in a forest, and when it was completed she loaded it with valuables and prepared it for a voyage. She took with her all her surviv-

---

place-names dating from the earliest days of the Settlement. It is said of Helgi (in *Landnámabók*, the Book of Settlements) that he was only half Christian, however: 'He believed in Christ, but invoked Thor during sea-voyages and in times of stress.'

1. Thorstein the Red was the son of Unn the Deep-Minded and Olaf the White.

2. *Thorstein was married to Thurid Eyvind's-daughter, the sister of Helgi the Lean.*

3. Ari the Learned (1067–1148) was the first Icelandic historian to write in the vernacular. He wrote *Íslendingabók* (Book of Icelanders) in *c.* 1125, a brief historical survey of the Icelandic state, and in all probability he also contributed largely to the earliest version of *Landnámabók* (Book of Settlements), an account of all the principal settlers in Iceland and their descendants. But the particular source referred to here is no longer extant. Ari's authority is cited again in Chapter 78, where his genealogy is also traced back to the heroine of this saga, Gudrun Osvif's-daughter.

ing kinsfolk; and it is generally thought that it would be hard to find another example of a woman escaping from such hazards with so much wealth and such a large retinue. From this it can be seen what a paragon amongst women she was.

Unn had with her many outstanding men of noble birth. There was a man named Koll, and he was one of the most distinguished of Unn's company, mainly because of his lineage; he was a chieftain by rank. Another of those who went with Unn was called Hord; he too was of noble birth, and a man of distinction.

When all was ready, Unn sailed for Orkney. Here she stayed for a short while and gave away in marriage her grand-daughter Groa, one of Thorstein the Red's daughters.[1]

Then Unn sailed for the Faroe Islands, where she also made a brief stay and gave away in marriage another of Thorstein's daughters, called Olof.[2]

5. Unn in Iceland

UNN now prepared her departure from the Faroe Islands and announced to her companions that she was going to Iceland. She had with her Olaf Feilan, Thorstein the Red's son, and those of Thorstein's daughters who were still unmarried. She put out to sea and had a good voyage, and made land in the south of Iceland at Vikrarskeid; the ship was wrecked there, but there was no loss of life or cargo.

1. *Groa was the mother of Grelod, the wife of Earl Thorfinn, the son of Earl Turf-Einar, the son of Earl Rognvald of More; their son was Hlodver, the father of Earl Sigurd, the father of Earl Thorfinn the Mighty. All the Orkney earls stem from this line.*
The long history of the dynasty of the Norse earls of Orkney is told in *Orkneyinga Saga*, which was written in Iceland *c.* 1200.

2. *From Olof stems the greatest family line in the Faroe Islands, known as the Gotuskeggjar kin.*
One of the Icelandic Sagas, *Færeyinga Saga*, describes events in the Faroe Islands during the late tenth and early eleventh centuries. It is thought to have been written early in the thirteenth century.

Unn then went to visit her brother Helgi Bjolan with a company of twenty. When she arrived, Helgi came out to welcome her, and invited her and nine of her companions to stay with him. She replied indignantly that she had not suspected him of being so mean-minded, and left at once; she was now going to visit her brother Bjorn the Easterner in Breidafjord. When Bjorn heard she was on her way he went out to receive her with a large company and welcomed her warmly, and invited her to stay with all her companions; for he knew his sister's nature. She was highly pleased and thanked him for his generosity. She stayed there all winter and was entertained most hospitably, for there was no lack of provisions and no sparing of expense.

In the spring she sailed across Breidafjord and went ashore on a headland, where she and her companions ate their morning meal; since then it has been known as Dogurdarness.[1] It juts out from Medalfellstrand. From there she sailed in along Hvamms-fjord and went ashore on another headland, where she made a brief stay. Here she lost her comb, and the place has been called Kambsness ever since.

After that, Unn went round all the Breidafjord Dales and took possession of as much land as she pleased. Then she sailed right up to the head of the fjord, and there her high-seat pillars had been washed ashore. She now thought it had been clearly shown where she should build her home.

She had a farm built at this place, which has been known as Hvamm ever since, and there she settled.

In the same spring that Unn built her home at Hvamm, Koll married her grand-daughter Thorgerd, one of Thorstein the Red's daughters. Unn bore the cost of the wedding-feast. She gave the whole of Laxriverdale as Thorgerd's dowry, and Koll built his home to the south of Lax River.

Koll was a person of great consequence. Their son was called Hoskuld.[2]

1. Literally, 'Breakfast-ness'.
2. Hoskuld Dala-Kollson; he also plays a significant part in the early stages of *Njal's Saga*. Hoskuld's father, Koll, became known as Dala-Koll after he moved to Lax River, in the Breidafjord Dales.

6. Unn gives land

AFTER that, Unn made grants of her land to several other people.

To Hord she gave the whole of Hordadale as far as Skraumuhlaups River. He made his home at Hordabolstead; he was a man of great distinction and fine progeny.[1]

Unn said to her men: 'Now you shall have the reward for your labours; there is no shortage now of the means with which to repay you for your service and goodwill. As you all know, I have given freedom to the man called Erp, the son of Earl Meldun;[2] it has never been my wish that a man of such high birth should be called a slave.'

Thereupon she granted him Saudafellslands, between Tungu River and Mid River.[3]

To Sokkolf she granted Sokkolfsdale, and he lived there till old age.

Another of her freed slaves was called Hundi, a Scotsman by birth; to him she gave Hundadale.

The fourth of her slaves was called Vifil; and to him she granted Vifilsdale.[4]

1. *Hord's son was Asbjorn the Wealthy, who lived at Asbjarnarstead in Ornolfsdale. Asbjorn married Thorbjorg, the daughter of Midfjord-Skeggi; their daughter was Ingibjorg, the wife of Illugi the Black, who were the parents of Hermund and Gunnlaug Serpent-Tongue. That family line is known as the Gilsbekking kin.*
The romantic and tragic life-story of Gunnlaug Serpent-Tongue, the poet, is told in *Gunnlaug's Saga.*
2. 'Meldun' (*Mael-Dúin*) is a familiar Celtic name, but this Earl Meldun has never been identified. He was probably some sort of chieftain in the west of Scotland whose son was taken prisoner by Thorstein the Red during his campaigns against the Scots (Chapter 4).
3. *Erp's children were Orm, Asgeir, Gunnbjorn, and Halldis, who was the wife of Alf of the Dales.*
4. Vifil was the grandfather of Gudrid Thorbjorn's-daughter, who married Thorfinn Karlsefni, the Icelandic merchant who attempted

Thorstein the Red's fourth daughter was called Osk; she was the mother of Thorstein Black the Wise, who discovered the principle of the intercalary week.[1]

Thorstein the Red's fifth daughter was called Thorhild; she was the mother of Alf of the Dales.[2]

Thorstein the Red's sixth daughter was called Vigdis.[3]

7. Unn's last feast

OLAF FEILAN was the youngest of Thorstein the Red's children. He was a handsome man, big and powerful and splendidly accomplished. Unn held him in higher regard than all other men, and made it known publicly that Olaf was to inherit everything at Hvamm after her death.

Now Unn was growing weary with old age. She summoned Olaf Feilan and said to him, 'I have been thinking, kinsman, that you ought to establish yourself and take a wife.'

Olaf agreed readily, and said he would rely on her guidance.

'I have had it in mind,' said Unn, 'that your wedding-feast should be held towards the end of this summer, for that is the best time for getting all the necessary provisions; I am sure that

---

to colonize North America just after the year 1000: cf. *Eirik's Saga*, in *The Vinland Sagas*.

1. In early times, the Icelanders reckoned 364 days, or fifty-two weeks, in the year, and thus the year was a day and a quarter short. The year was divided into two seasons of equal length – summer and winter; and as time went by the Icelanders realized that the year was too short, as the calendar year was no longer matching the solar year. At Thorstein Black's suggestion, an intercalary week was added to the summer season every seventh year, soon after the middle of the tenth century.

2. *There are many who trace their lineage to Alf of the Dales. His daughter was Thorgerd, the wife of Ari of Reykjaness, the son of Mar, the son of Atli, the son of Ulf the Squint-Eyed and of Bjorg Eyvind's-daughter, the sister of Helgi the Lean; from them stems the Reyknessing kin.*

3. *From Vigdis stems the Hofdi kin in Eyjafjord*

our friends will be coming in large numbers, because I intend this to be the last feast I shall hold.'

'That is a generous offer,' said Olaf. 'But I shall only marry a woman who will deprive you of neither wealth nor authority.'

That autumn Olaf Feilan married Alfdis, and the wedding-feast was held at Hvamm. Unn went to great expense over it, for she invited many eminent people far and wide from other districts. She invited her brothers Bjorn the Easterner and Helgi Bjolan, who each came with a large company. Dala-Koll came too, her grandson-in-law, and Hord of Hordadale and many other important people. The feast was attended in great numbers, but even so there were not nearly as many as Unn had invited, for the people of Eyjafjord had a long way to travel.

By now, old age was weighing heavily upon Unn; she never rose before noon and always went early to bed. She allowed no one to come and consult her between the time she went to bed in the evening and the time she was dressed again; and she would give an irate reply if anyone asked about her health.

On the day of the wedding, Unn stayed in bed longer than usual but she was up by the time the guests arrived. She came out to receive them and welcomed her kinsmen and friends most graciously, saying that it was proof of their affection that they had travelled so far to be present – 'I mention in particular Bjorn and Helgi, but I want to give thanks to all of you who have come here today.'

Then she walked into the dining-hall followed by a large company. And when the hall was filled with guests, everyone marvelled at the magnificence of this feast.

Then Unn said, 'I call upon you, my brothers Bjorn and Helgi and all my other kinsmen and friends, to witness – that this house, and everything in sight that goes with it, I am now giving to my grandson Olaf Feilan to own and to administer.'

Thereupon she rose to her feet and said that she was now retiring to her bed-chamber; she urged them all to enjoy themselves in whatever way each thought best, and ordered ale to be served to the whole company. It is said that Unn was tall and stoutly-built. She walked briskly down the length of the hall, and those present remarked on how stately she still was.

There was drinking all that evening until it was thought time to go to bed. Next morning Olaf Feilan went to his grandmother's bedroom. When he entered, Unn was sitting propped up against the pillows; she was dead. Olaf went back into the hall and announced the news; everyone thought it most impressive how Unn had kept her dignity to her dying day.

Now the feast combined the celebration of Olaf's wedding and Unn's funeral. On the last day of the feast, Unn's body was carried to the burial mound that had been prepared for her. She was laid in a ship inside the mound, and a load of treasure was laid there with her. Then the burial mound was closed.[1]

Olaf Feilan, with the assent of those of his kinsmen who were present at the feast, now took over the full ownership and management of Hvamm. When the feast ended, he gave magnificent parting gifts to the most distinguished of the guests.

Olaf became a great and powerful chieftain, and lived at Hvamm till old age. He and Alfdis had four children – Thord Gellir,[2] Thora,[3] Helga,[4] and Thordis.[5]

---

1. Ship-burials of this kind seem to have been a fairly common practice in pre-Christian Scandinavia, and five small ones have been excavated in Iceland. The most celebrated examples that archaeologists have brought to light are the Gokstad and Oseberg ships in Norway, and the Sutton Hoo ship-burial in East Anglia with its magnificent hoard of treasure.

2. *Thord Gellir married Hrodny, the daughter of Midfjord-Skeggi; their sons were Eyjolf the Grey, Thorarin Foal-Brow, and Thorkel Kuggi.*

Thord Gellir played a prominent part in Iceland's early political history and is mentioned in many other sagas. Two of his grandsons, Thorkel Eyjolfson (son of Eyjolf the Grey) and Thorstein Kuggason (son of Thorkel Kuggi) figure largely in later chapters of *Laxdæla Saga*.

3. *Thora was the wife of Thorstein Cod-Biter, the son of Thorolf Moster-Beard; their sons were Bork the Stout and Thorgrim, the father of Snorri the Priest.*

Snorri the Priest (d. 1031) figures in many Sagas, especially *Eyrbyggja Saga* and *Njal's Saga*, and also later in this Saga (Chapter 36 onwards).

4. *Helga was the wife of Gunnar Hlifarson. Their daughters were*

While Olaf was living at Hvamm, his brother-in-law Dala-Koll fell ill and died. Hoskuld Dala-Kollsson was still very young when his father died, but he was older in ability than in years, a handsome and capable youth. Hoskuld inherited all his father's estate, and the farm now came to be called after him and was known as Hoskuldstead. He quickly became well-liked in his own right, for he was given every support by his kinsmen as well as by the friends his father Dala-Koll had made.

His mother, Thorgerd Thorstein's-daughter, was still a young and very beautiful woman at the time. After Dala-Koll's death she could find no happiness in Iceland and told her son Hoskuld she wanted to go abroad with her share of the estate. Hoskuld said he was distressed that they should part, but added that he would no more oppose her wishes in this than in anything else. He bought her a half-share in a ship lying at Dogurdarness, and Thorgerd went on board with a large cargo of valuables. Then she put out to sea and had a good voyage to Norway.

Thorgerd had strong family ties in Norway and many kinsmen of noble birth. They welcomed her warmly and offered her anything she cared to accept from them. Thorgerd was pleased, and told them that it was her intention to settle there in Norway. She had not been a widow for long before a suitor asked for her hand, a man called Herjolf. He was a landowner by rank, and was wealthy and highly respected. Herjolf was a big, powerful man, not at all handsome but very imposing in appearance, and exceptionally skilled in arms.

When the marriage-offer was made it was Thorgerd's right, as a widow, to give her own answer, and with the full approval of her kinsmen she did not refuse the proposal. So Thorgerd married Herjolf and went off with him to his home, and they came to love one another dearly. Thorgerd quickly proved

Jofrid, who was married first to Thorodd Tungu-Oddsson and then to Thorstein Egilsson; and Thorunn, who was the wife of Herstein, the son of Thorkel Blund-Ketilsson.

5. Thordis was the wife of Thorarin Ragi's-brother, the Law-Speaker.

Thorarin was Law-Speaker at the Althing, 950–69. His brother, Glum, was the second of Hallgerd's husbands in Njal's Saga.

what an exceptionally capable woman she was, and Herjolf was considered to have enhanced his prestige and standing greatly by winning such a wife as Thorgerd.

8. Hrut Herjolfsson

HERJOLF and Thorgerd had not been married long before a son was born to them. The child was sprinkled with water and given the name Hrut. As he grew up he quickly became big and strong; he was exceptionally well-built, tall and broad-shouldered, slim-waisted and straight-limbed. He was extremely handsome, taking after his grandfather Thorstein the Red, or Ketil Flat-Nose, and quite outstanding in all accomplishments.

Herjolf fell ill and died, and this was considered a great loss. After that, Thorgerd yearned to return to Iceland to visit her son Hoskuld, for she loved him above all others; meanwhile Hrut stayed behind in Norway with his kinsmen, well cared for. Thorgerd sailed off to Iceland and went to visit her son Hoskuld in Laxriverdale. He gave her a good welcome. She was very wealthy and she stayed with Hoskuld for the rest of her life.

A few years after her return she fell ill and died, and was laid in a burial mound. Hoskuld took over all the inheritance, although half of it properly belonged to his brother, Hrut Herjolfsson.

9. Hoskuld marries

AT that time the ruler of Norway was Hakon, the foster-son of King Athelstan.[1] Hoskuld Dala-Kollsson was a member of his

1. King Hakon the Good was the son of Harald Fine-Hair, and according to Icelandic reckoning he was King of Norway from 933 to 961. His boyhood was spent in England at the court of King Athelstan of Wessex (925–39).

court and used to spend alternate winters at home in Iceland and with King Hakon. His name was renowned in Norway as well as in Iceland.

There was a man called Bjorn, who lived in Bjarnarfjord; he was the first settler there, and the fjord is named after him. Bjarnarfjord cuts into the coast to the north of Steingrimsfjord, separated from it by a neck of land. Bjorn was a wealthy man, of noble birth; his wife was called Ljufa, and they had a daughter called Jorunn.

Jorunn was a good-looking, imperious woman of exceptional intelligence; she was considered the best match in all the West-fjords.

Hoskuld had heard about this woman, and also that her father Bjorn was the most notable farmer in the Strands. So he rode from home with nine companions and went to visit Bjorn in Bjarnarfjord; he was well received there, for Bjorn had heard good reports of him. Hoskuld then made an offer of marriage. Bjorn welcomed the proposal, and said he thought his daughter could marry no better, but left it to her to decide. When Jorunn was consulted she replied, 'Everything we have heard about you, Hoskuld, would make us wish to give you a favourable answer, for we believe that the woman who marries you would be well provided for. However, my father shall have the final word, for I shall consent to whatever he wishes in this.'

The long and the short of it was that Jorunn was betrothed to Hoskuld with a large dowry; the wedding was to be held at Hoskuldstead. With that, Hoskuld rode off home and remained there until it was time for the wedding. Bjorn arrived for the feast from the north with a handsome company; a large number of kinsmen and friends invited by Hoskuld were already there to greet them. It was a magnificent feast, and when it was over, each left for his own home in warm friendship and with suitable gifts.

Jorunn stayed behind at Hoskuldstead and took charge of the household with Hoskuld; it was soon apparent from all her ways that she would be sensible and capable and accomplished in many respects, but always rather large-tempered. Hoskuld and

Jorunn got on well together, but they were usually rather reserved with one another.

Hoskuld now became a great chieftain. He was powerful and wealthy, and robust in his dealings; he was considered in no way a man of less account than his father Dala-Koll had been.

Hoskuld and Jorunn had not been married long before children were born to them. Their eldest, a son, was called Thorleik. They had another son, called Bard. Their daughters were Hallgerd (later nicknamed Long-Legs), and Thurid. They were all promising children.[1]

Thorleik was big and powerful and very handsome, but taciturn and brusque in his manner; people thought he showed in his nature that he would not turn out to be a peaceable man. Hoskuld always said that he would very much take after the Strands side of the family.

Bard Hoskuldsson was also manly in appearance and powerful and intelligent; he showed signs of taking more after his father's side of the family. As he grew up he was good-natured and well-liked, and Hoskuld loved him most of all his children.

Hoskuld's prestige and standing were now in their fullest flower. At about this time he gave his sister Groa in marriage to Veleif the Old; their son was Dueller-Bersi.

10. Killer-Hrapp

THERE was a man called Hrapp who lived in Laxriverdale on the north side of the river, opposite Hoskuldstead. The farm then became known as Hrappstead; it is derelict now.

Hrapp was the son of Sumarlidi, and was known as Killer-Hrapp. He was Scottish on his father's side, whereas all his mother's family came from the Hebrides, and Hrapp had been born and brought up there. He was a big, strong man who would never yield to anyone, whatever the opposition; and

1. Hallgerd Long-Legs is one of the central characters in *Njal's Saga*. She had three husbands, and was responsible for the deaths of all of them; her third husband was Gunnar of Hlidarend.

because he was so overbearing, as has just been written, and refused to pay compensation for his misdeeds, he fled to Iceland and bought the land he was now farming.

His wife was called Vigdis Hallstein's-daughter, and they had a son called Sumarlidi. Vigdis was the sister of Thorstein Black the Wise, who was mentioned previously, and who was then living at Thorsness. Sumarlidi was being fostered there, and was a most promising youth.

Thorstein Black had been married, but his wife was now dead. He had two daughters; one was called Gudrid, and the other Osk.

Gudrid was married to Thorkel Fringe,[1] who lived at Svignaskard; he was a great chieftain and a sage.

Osk was married to a Breidafjord man called Thorarin, a sturdy and well-liked man; he was living with his father-in-law, for Thorstein Black was an old man by then and greatly in need of their care.

Hrapp did not endear himself to most people. He was aggressive towards his neighbours, and let them know he would make life very difficult for them if they regarded anyone as being superior to him. So all the farmers got together and went to see Hoskuld Dala-Kollsson and told him their troubles. Hoskuld told them to let him know if Hrapp did them any harm – 'for he isn't going to rob me of either men or money.'

11. Thord Goddi

A MAN called Thord Goddi was living in Laxriverdale to the north of the river, at a farm which has been known as Goddastead ever since. He was a very wealthy man, and had bought the land he now farmed; he had no children. He was one of Hrapp's neighbours, and often suffered at his hands; but Hoskuld looked after him and saw to it that he did not lose his farm.

Thord Goddi had a wife called Vigdis Ingjald's-daughter, a grand-daughter of Olaf Feilan; she was a niece of Thord Gellir on

1. *Thorkel Fringe was the son of Ore-Bjorn.*

her father's side, and of Thorolf Red-Nose of Saudafell on her mother's side. Thorolf Red-Nose was a man of great courage and ample resources, and his kinsmen always looked to him to champion them. Vigdis had been given in marriage to Thord Goddi more for his money than his support.

Thord had a slave called Asgaut whom he had brought with him to Iceland. Asgaut was a big, capable man; but though he was called a slave there were few freeborn men who could call themselves his equal, and he knew well how to serve his master. Thord had several other slaves, but this is the only one whose name is recorded here.

There was a man called Thorbjorn, known as Thorbjorn the Feeble, who lived in Laxriverdale at the next farm above Goddastead; he was a huge, powerful man. Thorbjorn was wealthy, chiefly in gold and silver, but he was never very free with his money to others.

Hoskuld Dala-Kollsson felt that there was only one flaw in his own splendour: he thought his home was not so fine a building as he would have wished. So he bought from a Shetlander a ship that was lying in the Blondu Estuary. He made this ship ready and announced that he was going abroad, leaving Jorunn to look after the estate and the children.

They put out to sea and had favourable winds; they made Norway rather to the south and landed in Hordaland at the place where the town of Bergen now stands, and laid up the ship. Hoskuld had a host of kinsmen there, although they are not mentioned here by name.

King Hakon was in residence at Oslo Fjord at the time, but Hoskuld did not go to see him, for his kinsmen welcomed him with open arms. The winter passed uneventfully.

12. The concubine

It so happened early next summer that King Hakon went on a naval expedition east to the Brenn Isles for a royal assembly which, in accordance with the laws, had to be held every third summer to secure continuing peace in the realm; these meetings were convened by the Scandinavian kings to deal with matters of mutual concern. To attend them was considered a festive occasion, and people flocked to them from practically every known country.

Hoskuld Dala-Kollsson wanted to attend the assembly and launched his ship, since he had not been to see the king during the winter; and besides, it was an important trading market.

There were huge crowds at the assembly that year and there was a great deal of celebration, with drinking and games and every form of entertainment. Nothing of any great moment took place. Hoskuld met many of his kinsmen from Denmark there.

Then one day when Hoskuld was on his way out to enjoy himself with some companions, he noticed a gaily-decorated tent standing apart from the other booths. He went over to it and entered; inside he found a man dressed in costly clothing and wearing a Russian hat. Hoskuld asked him his name.

'My name is Gilli,' he replied, 'and most people realize who I am when they hear my nickname: I am called Gilli the Russian.'

Hoskuld said he had often heard him spoken of, for he was said to be the wealthiest man the guild of merchants had ever known – 'So no doubt you can offer us whatever we want to buy?'

Gilli asked them what they were looking for. Hoskuld replied that he wanted to buy a slave-girl – 'if you have one for sale.'

'You're not trying to embarrass me, are you, by asking for something you don't expect me to have?' said Gilli. 'I wouldn't be too sure of that.'

Hoskuld could see a curtain drawn right across the booth. Gilli lifted it up, and Hoskuld now saw that there were twelve women sitting behind it. Gilli invited him to go through and have a look to see if he wanted to buy any of them. Hoskuld went through. The women were all sitting in a row across the booth, and he inspected them carefully. The one sitting right at the edge of the tent caught his eye; she was shabbily dressed, but Hoskuld thought her beautiful, from what he could see.

'How much would that woman cost, if I wanted to buy her?' he asked Gilli.

'You'd have to pay three marks of silver for her,' replied Gilli.

'That's rather a high price you're charging for a slave-girl, surely?' said Hoskuld. 'It's three times the normal price.'[1]

'You're quite right,' said Gilli, 'I value her more highly than the rest. You can have any one of the eleven others for only one mark of silver, and leave this one with me.'

'Let me see first how much silver there is in this purse at my belt,' said Hoskuld, and asked Gilli to fetch the scales while he looked in his purse.

Then Gilli said, 'I don't want to cheat you over this, Hoskuld. The woman has one serious defect, and I want you to know of it before we clinch a deal.'

Hoskuld asked what it was.

'The woman is a mute,' said Gilli. 'I've tried every way of coaxing her into speech, but I've never got a word out of her. I'm quite convinced she cannot speak.'

'Bring out your scales,' said Hoskuld, 'and we'll see how much there is in this purse.'

Gilli did so; and when they weighed the silver it came to three marks precisely.

Then Hoskuld said, 'So it seems we have a deal on our hands after all. Here's the money, and I'll take the woman. I must say you've dealt most fairly over this, for you certainly didn't try to deceive me in any way.'

With that, Hoskuld went back home to his booth. And that night he slept with the woman.

Next morning when they were getting up, Hoskuld said to her, 'Gilli the Wealthy wasn't very generous with the clothes he gave you to wear; but I suppose it was harder for him to clothe twelve than for me to clothe only one.'

He opened one of his chests and took out some fine clothing

---

1. If the normal price for a concubine was one mark of refined silver, it was equivalent to the value of four milch cows; if the silver was unrefined, the price was equivalent to two milch cows.

and gave it to her; and everyone remarked that fine clothes certainly suited her well.

Later, when the rulers had finished debating the matters which the law required, the assembly was brought to a close. Hoskuld then went to see King Hakon and greeted him respectfully, as was his due. The king looked at him and said, 'We would have accepted your greeting even if it had come somewhat earlier, Hoskuld; but still, we do so now.'

13. Olaf the Peacock born

AFTER that, the king received Hoskuld most cordially and invited him aboard his ship – 'and stay with us as long as you want to remain in Norway,' he said.

'Accept my thanks for your invitation,' replied Hoskuld, 'but I have much to do this summer. The main reason for my long delay in coming to your court was that I was trying to obtain some building-timber.'

The king asked him to bring his ship to Oslo Fjord, and there Hoskuld stayed with the king for a while. The king gave him a cargo of timber and had it loaded onto his ship.

Then the king said to Hoskuld, 'We shall not detain you here with us for any longer than you wish, but we shall find you hard to replace.'

He accompanied Hoskuld to his ship and said, 'I have always found you a man of honour; and now I have a feeling that this is the last time you will sail from Norway while I am ruler here.'

He drew from his arm a bracelet of gold weighing one mark and gave it to Hoskuld, and as a further gift he gave him a sword valued at half a mark of gold.[1]

Hoskuld thanked the king for the gifts and all the honour he

1. An ounce of gold (one eighth of a mark) was worth a mark of refined silver at this time, and a mark of silver was equivalent to the price of about four milch cows. So the bracelet was worth thirty-two cows, and the sword sixteen cows – princely gifts indeed.

had bestowed on him. Then he embarked and put out to sea for Iceland. They had favourable winds and made land in the south, then sailed west round Reykjaness and up past Snæfellsness, and on into Breidafjord. Hoskuld landed at the mouth of Lax River and had the cargo unloaded there; he had the ship itself laid up farther up river, where he built a boat-shed for it whose ruins are still to be seen there. He put up some booths there, and the place is therefore called Budardale.

He had the timber taken home – an easy task, for it was not far to go – and then he rode home with a few companions and was given a good welcome, as was to be expected. His estate had prospered during his absence.

Jorunn asked who the woman with him was.

Hoskuld replied, 'You'll probably think I'm being sarcastic – but I don't know her name.'

'It can only be one of two things,' said Jorunn : 'Either the stories I've been hearing are untrue – or else you will have talked to her long enough to ask her for her name.'

Hoskuld said he would not try to deny it, and told her the truth. He asked that the woman should be well treated, and said he wanted her to stay there as a member of the household.

'I'm not going to quarrel with this concubine you've brought home from Norway,' said Jorunn, 'however unpleasant her presence might be; and anyway that's obvious if she's both deaf and dumb.'

After his return to Iceland, Hoskuld slept with his wife every night and had nothing to do with his concubine. However it was apparent to everyone that she was a woman of character and breeding, and certainly no simpleton.

Late that winter Hoskuld's concubine gave birth to a son. Hoskuld was summoned and the child was shown to him; and it seemed to him, as it did to others, that he had never seen a more handsome or noble-looking child. Hoskuld was asked what the boy was to be called; he wanted the name to be Olaf, for his uncle Olaf Feilan had died shortly before.

Olaf was a peerless child, and Hoskuld loved him dearly.

Next summer Jorunn said that the concubine would have to do some work or else go. Hoskuld told the woman that she was to wait upon Jorunn and himself, and look after her child as well. By the time the boy was two years old he could speak perfectly and was running about on his own like a child of four.

It so happened one morning that Hoskuld was out of doors seeing to his farm; it was a fine day, and the dawn sun was shining. He heard the sound of voices and went over to the stream at the foot of the sloping homefield. There he saw two people he knew well: it was his son Olaf, and the boy's mother. He realized then that she was not speechless at all, for she was talking busily to the child. Hoskuld now went over to them and asked her what her name was, and told her there was no point in concealing it any longer. She agreed, and they sat down on the slope of the homefield.

Then she said, 'If you want to know my name, I am called Melkorka.'

Hoskuld asked her to tell him more about her family.

'My father is called Myrkjartan, and he is a king in Ireland,' she said. 'I was taken captive and enslaved when I was fifteen.' [1]

Hoskuld said she had kept silent for far too long over such a noble lineage. Then he went back into the house and told Jorunn what he had discovered while he was out. Jorunn said she had no way of knowing whether the woman was telling the truth, and that she had little liking for mystery folk, and they discussed it no further. Jorunn was certainly no kinder to Melkorka after this, but Hoskuld was rather more friendly.

A little later, when Jorunn was going to bed, Melkorka helped her off with her shoes and stockings and laid them on the floor; Jorunn picked up the stockings and started beating her about the head with them. Melkorka flew into a rage and struck her on the nose with her fist, drawing blood. Hoskuld came in and separated them. After that he sent Melkorka away and gave her a place to live in farther up Laxriverdale; this farm has been

1. Myrkjartan: Irish *Muircheartach*. There was no High King of Ireland called Muircheartach during this period, but there were several petty kings and princelings of that name; a number of attempts have been made to identify this Myrkjartan with one or other of them, but none has been proved conclusively.

known as Melkorkustead ever since. It is derelict now. It is on the south side of the river. Melkorka made her home there, and her son Olaf went with her; Hoskuld supplied everything that was needed for the farm.

As Olaf grew up it was quickly apparent that he would be a paragon of good looks and courtesy.

14. Hall of Saud Isles

THERE was a man called Ingjald who lived in the Saud Isles, which lie out in Breidafjord; he was known as Ingjald Saudisle-Priest, a man of considerable wealth and importance. He had a brother called Hall, a big, strapping young man; Hall had small means, and most people considered him a wastrel. The two brothers seldom saw eye to eye, for Ingjald thought that Hall made little attempt to conform to the ways of successful men, while Hall for his part blamed Ingjald for not trying to improve his position.

There is a fishing-station in Breidafjord called the Bjarn Isles; there are a number of islets in this group, and they were very productive. At that time people used to go there in great numbers for the fishing, and many were stationed there all the year round. Sagacious people thought it very important that men in such fishing-stations should get on well together, for it was believed that fishing-luck would desert them if they quarrelled; and most people were careful to respect this.

One summer, it is said, Hall, the brother of Ingjald Saudisle-Priest, came to the Bjarn Isles to do some fishing. He got himself a place in a boat with a certain Thorolf who came from Breidafjord and was practically a penniless vagrant, but a brisk fellow for all that. Hall stayed there for some time, and thought himself much superior to all the others. One evening when Hall and Thorolf had landed and were about to divide the catch, Hall demanded that he should both divide and take the first choice, for he thought himself the better man. Thorolf refused to surrender his rights and became very abusive. Words were exchanged, and neither would give way; then Hall snatched up a gaff lying nearby and tried to drive it into Thorolf's head, but people intervened and restrained him. Hall was in a rage but could do nothing this time, and the catch was left undivided. Thorolf went away that evening and Hall, because of his superior standing, took possession of the whole catch, including Thorolf's share. Then he engaged another man in Thorolf's place and went on fishing as before.

Thorolf resented all this bitterly, and felt he had been humiliated in his dealings with Hall. He remained in the islands, and was determined to put right the injustice that had been forced on him; but Hall had no fears for his own safety, because he was sure that no one would dare to try to challenge him so near his own home.

One fine day Hall went out fishing in the boat with two others. The fish were biting well that day, and as they rowed back in the evening they were in high spirits. Thorolf had been keeping watch on Hall's movements during the day and was lying in wait for him at the landing-place that evening when they came in to land. Hall was rowing in the bows, and now he jumped overboard to make the boat fast; but as he waded ashore Thorolf was there to meet him, and struck at him at once. The blow caught Hall on the neck, just above the shoulder, and his head flew off. Thorolf turned and made off, while Hall's companions ran over to the dead man.

News of the killing spread quickly through the islands and caused a great stir, for Hall was a man of noble birth even though he had never enjoyed much luck.

Thorolf now tried to get away from the islands, for he had no hope that anyone would shelter him after such a grave deed, nor had he any kinsmen there whom he could expect to protect him, whereas there were powerful men not far away, such as Hall's brother, Ingjald Saudisle-Priest, who would be certain to seek his life. He managed to get a passage over to the mainland. He travelled in great stealth and nothing is known of his journey until he arrived one evening at Goddastead: Thord Goddi's wife, Vigdis, was distantly related to him, which was why he had gone there, and he had already heard how the land lay there – that Vigdis was a much more forceful person than her husband.

As soon as he arrived that evening, Thorolf went to see Vigdis and told her of his troubles, and asked her for protection. Vigdis replied as follows: 'I shall not disown our kinship, and in my opinion you are none the worse a man for what you have done; but it seems to me that anyone who harbours you would be risking life and property, considering the importance of those who will be taking action over this killing. My husband Thord is not much of a hero,' she went on, 'and we women always lack foresight in our expedients, particularly if there is anything at stake; but I cannot bring myself to refuse to give you any help now that you have come here expecting it.'

She took him to a storehouse and told him to wait inside for her, and put a lock on the door. Then she went to Thord and said, 'A visitor has come here for the night; he is called Thorolf, and is a distant kinsman of mine. He might need to stay here a bit longer, if you have no objections.'

Thord said he did not much care to have people staying with them, but Thorolf could rest there for a day provided he had no trouble on his hands; otherwise he would have to leave at once.

'I have already invited him to stay overnight,' said Vigdis, 'and I have no intention of going back on my word, even though he isn't everybody's friend.'

Then she told Thord that Hall had been killed and that Thorolf, the man who had just arrived, was the killer. Thord grew angry at this and said he knew for certain that Ingjald would make him pay dearly for the shelter that Thorolf had already been given – 'considering that the man is already behind locked doors in this house.'

'Ingjald won't make you pay anything for giving Thorolf shelter for one night,' said Vigdis, 'because Thorolf is going to stay here all winter.'

'That's how to get me into really serious trouble,' said Thord. 'I am utterly opposed to letting a man of such ill-luck stay here.'

But Thorolf spent the winter there, nevertheless.

Word of this reached Ingjald, whose responsibility it was to

71

take action over his brother's killing. Late in the winter he made ready for a journey to the Dales, launched a boat, and set off with eleven others on board. They sailed before a strong north-westerly wind and landed at Laxriver Mouth the same evening. They hauled the boat ashore and went straight to Goddastead, where their arrival had not been unexpected, and were given a good welcome.

Ingjald took Thord aside for a talk and told him the purpose of his visit; he said he had heard that Thorolf, his brother's killer, was there. Thord protested that it was quite untrue. Ingjald told him not to deny it – 'and let us now make a deal: you hand him over to me without forcing me to use violence, and I shall give you these three marks of silver I have here. And furthermore, I shall waive the charges you have brought upon yourself by harbouring Thorolf.'

Thord found the money very tempting, as well as the promise that the charges he had feared would cost him so dearly would be waived. 'I won't breathe a word about our talk to anyone,' he said. 'But this will be our bargain, nonetheless.'

After that they slept until the night was nearly over and there was only an hour left until dawn.

15. Vigdis takes over

INGJALD and his men got up and dressed.

Vigdis asked Thord what he and Ingjald had been talking about the night before. Thord said they had talked about many things, and had agreed to have the house searched on condition that they should be cleared if Thorolf was not to be found there – 'So I have now sent my slave Asgaut to take Thorolf away,' he added.

Vigdis said she did not much care for lies, and that she disliked having Ingjald snooping about her house, but told Thord to have it his own way. Ingjald then searched the house, but failed to find Thorolf. At that moment Asgaut returned, and Vigdis asked him where he had left Thorolf.

'I took him to our sheep-sheds, as Thord told me to do,' replied Asgaut.

Vigdis said, 'Could anything be more handy for Ingjald on his way back to the boat? I'm not going to risk the chance that they didn't hatch this plan together last night. I want you to set off at once and take Thorolf away as quickly as you can. You are to escort him to Thorolf Red-Nose at Saudafell. If you do as I tell you, you will be well rewarded; I shall give you your freedom, and enough money to take you wherever you want to go.'

Asgaut agreed to this and went back to the sheep-sheds, where he met Thorolf and told him they had to leave as quickly as possible. It was just then that Ingjald was riding away from Goddastead, determined to get full value for his money. When the farm was behind them they saw two men coming towards them – Asgaut and Thorolf. This was early in the morning and there was still very little daylight. Asgaut and Thorolf now found themselves trapped, with Ingjald on one side and Lax River on the other. The river was in full spate, with huge banks of ice on either side and a powerful current in the middle; it was a fearful river to cross.

Thorolf said to Asgaut, 'We seem to have only two courses open to us: one is to wait for them here at the river and defend ourselves for as long as our strength and our courage hold out – although the chances are that it won't take them long to destroy us. The alternative is to tackle the river, but that too is not without its dangers.'

Asgaut left it to him to decide, and said he would not abandon him now – 'whatever course you choose to take.'

'Let's take to the river, then,' said Thorolf. They did so, and stripped off their heavy clothing. Then they went down over the ice-bank and plunged into the water; and because they were hardy men and were fated to live longer, they got across the river and on to the ice-bank on the far side.

No sooner had they got across than Ingjald and his companions reached the other side of the river. Ingjald said to his men, 'What do we do now? Shall we attempt the river or not?'

They said it was up to him to decide and that they would

rely on his judgement, but in their opinion the river was impassable. Ingjald said he agreed – 'and we shall have to turn away.'

When Thorolf and Asgaut saw that Ingjald and his men were not going to tackle the river they wrung out their clothes and got ready to continue their journey. They walked all day and arrived at Saudafell towards evening. They were given a good welcome there, for there was always an open door at Saudafell.

That same evening Asgaut went to Thorolf Red-Nose and told him the whole story behind their visit, and that his kinswoman Vigdis was sending him this man for protection. He told him everything that had happened between her and Thord Goddi, and then delivered the tokens she had sent to Thorolf.

Thorolf Red-Nose replied, 'I'm not going to disown these tokens, and I shall certainly look after this man as she asks. I think Vigdis has acted very honourably, and it's a great pity that such a woman should be married to such a wretch. As for you, Asgaut, you can stay here for as long as you wish.'

Asgaut said he would not be staying very long. Thorolf Red-Nose took in his namesake and made him a member of his household. Asgaut parted from them in great friendship, and then set off for home.

Meanwhile, Ingjald had turned back to Goddastead after his parting with Thorolf. By that time, at the request of Vigdis, men from the neighbouring farms had arrived at Goddastead, no fewer than twenty of them. When Ingjald arrived he called Thord out and said to him, 'You have treated us dishonourably, Thord, for we have every reason to believe that you helped the man to escape.'

Thord said the accusation was untrue. All their plotting was now exposed, and Ingjald demanded the return of the money he had given Thord.

Vigdis was present at their conversation, and said they had both got what they deserved; she told Thord not to keep the money – 'because,' she said, 'you earned it dishonourably.'

Thord told her to have it her own way. Vigdis went indoors to a chest that belonged to Thord and there, at the bottom, she found a heavy purse. She took the purse and went out with it to Ingjald, and told him to take his money. Ingjald cheered up at this and held out his hand for it. Vigdis raised the purse and struck him on the nose with it, drawing blood; she accompanied this with a stream of derisive words, adding that he would never get the money back, and told him to clear off.

Ingjald realized he had no choice but to go away at once, and so he did; he did not break his journey until he reached home, ill-pleased with his trip.

16. Thord Goddi fosters Olaf

ASGAUT arrived home about this time. Vigdis gave him a good welcome and asked if they had been well received at Saudafell. He was pleased about it and told her of the outspoken words that Thorolf Red-Nose had used. Vigdis was delighted.

'You have carried out your task faithfully and well, Asgaut,' she said, 'and you shall now know at once what reward you have earned: I give you now your freedom, and from this day onward you shall be called a free man. In addition you shall have the money which Thord accepted for the life of my kinsman Thorolf. This money will now be in better hands.'

Asgaut thanked her handsomely for the gift.

In the summer Asgaut took passage abroad in a ship putting out from Dogurdarness. They had strong winds and the voyage did not take long. They landed in Norway, and from there Asgaut travelled south to Denmark, where he settled and was considered a man of mettle. And that is the last we hear of him.

After all the plotting between Thord Goddi and Ingjald Saudisle-Priest to contrive the death of her kinsman Thorolf, Vigdis now showed her animosity: she declared herself divorced from Thord Goddi and went to her kinsmen and told them what she had done. Her uncle, Thord Gellir, who was head of the Hvamm family, was very displeased at this, but there the matter rested.[1]

1. A woman in early Iceland had legal rights far in advance of any other European society of the time. She had absolutely equal rights

75

Vigdis had brought with her from Goddastead nothing but her own personal belongings. The men of Hvamm now let it be known that they intended to claim half of Thord Goddi's estate. When Thord heard this he became very alarmed and rode at once to see Hoskuld Dala-Kollsson to tell him of his troubles.

'You have often been scared before,' said Hoskuld, 'but never with better reason.'

Thord then offered Hoskuld money for his help, and said he would not be sparing with it.

Hoskuld said, 'Everyone knows you would never let anyone else benefit from your money of your own free will.'

'It's quite different now,' said Thord, 'for I want you to take charge of all my wealth. I also want to offer to foster your son Olaf and leave him everything when I die, for I have no heirs here in Iceland and I think my money would then be in better hands than if Vigdis and her kinsmen got it into their clutches.'

Hoskuld accepted this offer, and made a binding agreement on these terms.

Melkorka was displeased over it, for she thought the fosterage too lowly. Hoskuld said she was not looking at it the right way : 'Thord is old and childless, and all his money will go to Olaf on his death. And you can go and visit him whenever you like.'

Thord then took Olaf, who was seven years old at the time, into his care and soon became devoted to him.

When the pursuers in the suit against Thord Goddi heard about this they realized that the money would now be much more difficult to claim. But Hoskuld sent handsome gifts to

---

in marriage, and could obtain a divorce merely by declaration; if her grounds for this action were judged to be valid, she could claim half of the marital estate. There were many recognized grounds for divorce, including incompatibility, non-consummation of marriage (cf. Unn and Hrut Herjolfsson in *Njal's Saga*), and even the wearing of clothes properly belonging to the opposite sex (cf. chapter 34). Her status as a spinster was also protected; it was a punishable offence to compose love-songs to a woman, because this was regarded as compromising her honour and therefore her marital prospects.

Thord Gellir and asked him not to take offence at what had happened, for they had no legal claim on Thord Goddi for the money. He pointed out that Vigdis had not brought any valid charges against Thord Goddi which could justify her desertion : 'Thord was none the worse a man for seeking some means of ridding himself of someone who had been thrust upon him and was as prickly with guilt as a juniper bush.'

When this message from Hoskuld, together with the generous gifts, reached Thord Gellir he was mollified and said he thought the money had come into good hands now that it was in Hoskuld's care. Thord accepted the gifts and there the matter rested, although their friendship was not as warm now as before.

Olaf grew up with Thord Goddi and became tall and strong. He was so handsome that his equal was nowhere to be found. When he was twelve years old he rode to the Assembly, and people from other districts thought it worth their while to come just to see how exceptionally well-built he was. Olaf's weapons and clothing were in keeping with this, so that he stood out from all other men.

Thord Goddi's circumstances improved greatly after Olaf came to live with him.

Hoskuld gave Olaf a nickname and called him 'the Peacock', and the name stuck.

17. Killer-Hrapp dies

IT is said of Killer-Hrapp that he became more and more brutal; he molested his neighbours so relentlessly that they could scarcely hold their own against him. But from the time that Olaf grew up, Hrapp could get no hold over Thord Goddi.

Hrapp's nature remained unchanged even when his strength began to fail with the onset of old age and he had to take to his bed. He then summoned his wife and said to her, 'I have never been prone to ill-health, and it seems more than likely that this illness will put an end to our life together. So when I am dead

I want my grave to be dug under the living-room door, and I am to be placed upright in it under the threshold, so that I can keep an even better watch over my house.'

Hrapp soon died and all his instructions were carried out, for Vigdis did not dare do otherwise. And difficult as he had been to deal with during his life, he was now very much worse after death, for his corpse would not rest in its grave; people say he murdered most of his servants in his hauntings after death, and caused grievous harm to most of his neighbours.[1] The farm at Hrappstead had to be abandoned and Vigdis, Hrapp's widow, went west to her brother Thorstein Black the Wise, who looked after her and her property.

And now, as so often before, people went to see Hoskuld Dalla-Kollsson and told him of all the trouble Hrapp was causing, and asked him to do something about it. Hoskuld agreed. He went over to Hrappstead with several men and had Hrapp's body dug up and taken to a spot far removed from any paths or pastures. After this, Hrapp's hauntings abated a little.

Sumarlidi, Hrapp's son, inherited all his property, which was both extensive and valuable. Sumarlidi started farming Hrappstead the following spring, but when he had been there for a short time he went mad, and died soon afterwards.

His mother Vigdis then inherited all these possessions, but she refused to go near the Hrappstead lands; so Thorstein Black took charge of all the inheritance. Thorstein was advanced in years by this time, but still very robust and healthy.

1. In Icelandic folk-lore ghosts were not simply the insubstantial spirits of the dead, but the corpses themselves, the un-dead dead, which rose from their graves to terrorize the living by physical violence. The classic example in the sagas is the ghost of Glam, with whom Grettir fought an epic battle in *Grettir's Saga*. Ghosts could also assume different shapes, like the seal in Chapter 18.

18. Thorstein Black drowns

IN the district of Thorsness at this time, two of Thorstein Black's kinsmen, Bork the Stout and his brother Thorgrim, were gaining authority; it soon became plain that these brothers wanted to be the biggest and most important men there.[1] When Thorstein Black became aware of this he wanted to avoid any clashes with them, so he made it known that he intended to move house and settle at Hrappstead, over in Laxriverdale.

After the spring Assembly, Thorstein made ready to leave. His livestock were being driven round by the coast. Thorstein manned a boat and embarked with a party of eleven, including his daughter Osk and son-in-law Thorarin and their daughter Hild, who was then three years old.

Thorstein ran into a strong southwesterly wind. They sailed into an area of currents and into a tide-race known as Kolkistustraum, the strongest of all the currents in Breidafjord. They had difficulty making progress, chiefly because the tide was on the ebb and the wind unfavourable; the weather was squally, gusting fiercely during showers but windless between them. Thorarin was at the helm with the sail-braces slung round his shoulders, because there was little room in the boat; the cargo consisted mainly of chests piled up high. They were in the narrows, but the boat could make little headway because of the raging current against them; then they drove onto a submerged reef, but without wrecking the boat.

Thorstein ordered the sail to be struck as quickly as possible and then told his men to use poles to push the boat off. They tried this but failed, because the water on either side was so deep that the poles could not reach bottom; so they had to wait for the tide to rise, and meanwhile the water was ebbing away from under the boat.

1. These two brothers also play a part in *Eyrbyggja Saga* and in *Gisli's Saga*, which relates the story of how Thorgrim was killed by his own brother-in-law, and how Bork the Stout, having married the widow, tried to avenge the killing.

Throughout the day they saw an enormous seal swimming in the current; it circled the boat all day. It had huge flippers, and everyone thought its eyes were those of a human. Thorstein told his men to harpoon the seal, but all their attempts failed.

Then the tide began to rise; but just as the boat was about to be refloated, a violent gust of wind broke upon them and the boat heeled over. Everyone on board was drowned, except for one man called Gudmund who was washed ashore with some timber at a place which has been known as the Gudmundar Isles ever since.

Thorstein Black's other daughter, Gudrid, who was married to Thorkel Fringe, now fell heir to the estate left by her father.

News of the drowning of Thorstein Black and the others spread far and wide.

Thorkel Fringe at once sent for this man Gudmund, the sole survivor; and when they met, Thorkel made a secret deal with him to give an account of the drownings in the way that Thorkel dictated. Gudmund agreed to do this, and then Thorkel asked him in the presence of witnesses to describe what had happened. So now Gudmund said that the first to drown was Thorstein Black, followed by his son-in-law Thorarin; this would make little Hild the heir, for she was Thorarin's daughter. Then he said that the girl was the next to die, followed by her mother Osk (who would have inherited from her daughter), and that Osk was the last to drown. This meant that the estate should all revert to Thorkel Fringe, for his wife Gudrid was heir to her sister Osk.

Thorkel Fringe and his friends spread this story about; but Gudmund had previously given a different account, and Thorarin's kinsmen found the story rather dubious and said they would refuse to accept it without proof. They claimed that half of the estate was theirs, but Thorkel maintained that it all belonged to him alone and demanded that the issue be put to ordeal, according to custom.

The ordeal practised at that time was submission under turf: a strip of turf was cut loose from the soil, with both ends left anchored to the ground, and the man who was to be subjected to the ordeal had to pass under the turf.[1]

Thorkel Fringe himself had some misgivings as to whether the drownings really had taken place in the order that Gudmund and he had declared : pagans felt their responsibilities no less keenly when performing such ceremonies than Christians do now when ordeals are decreed.[2] The one who passed under the turf was cleared of guilt if the turf did not fall on him. So Thorkel made an arrangement with two men to be present and pretend to quarrel over something while the ordeal was being performed, and to disturb the turf so obviously that everyone could see that they had caused it to fall.

After that the man who was to undergo the ordeal came forward, and as soon as he was underneath the turf these two men came to blows beside it, as arranged, and fell to the ground, and the turf collapsed as was only to be expected. People rushed to separate them, which was not difficult, for they had not been fighting seriously. Thorkel asked for a verdict by consensus on the outcome of the ordeal, and all his men claimed that it would have turned out well if no one had interfered.

So Thorkel Fringe took possession of all the movable property, but the farm at Hrappstead became derelict.

1. There were various forms of 'ordeal' used in pre-Christian Iceland, such as the handling of hot iron, or walking on hot metal. In the turf-ordeal, a long strip of turf was cut in a semi-circle and loosened from the earth; with the ends still anchored, it was raised into a precarious arch under which the person concerned, or someone delegated to take his place, had to pass without bringing the arch down. Passing under the turf was also part of the rites of swearing blood-brotherhood, accompanied by the mingling of blood into the soil. (Cf. *Gisli's Saga,* Chapter 6.)

2. According to the Icelandic Annals, ordeals were abolished in Iceland in 1248, the year after they were abolished in Norway by Cardinal William of Sabena (the Lateran Council of 1215 had already forbidden members of the clergy to take part in them). This reference suggests that *Laxdæla Saga* must have been written before the year 1248.

19. Hrut demands his share

THE saga now returns to Hoskuld Dala-Kollsson : his standing
was high, and he was a great chieftain. He had in his custody a
great deal of money which properly belonged to his half-brother,
Hrut Herjolfsson, and many people said that Hoskuld's wealth
would be severely trimmed if he were to pay out in full Hrut's
share of their mother's estate.

Hrut was a retainer of King Harald Gunnhildarson,[1] who held
him in high esteem, mainly because of his outstanding courage
in all hazards. Queen Gunnhild had so great a regard for him
that she considered no one at court his equal in converse or
anything else. Whenever comparisons were made and men's
merits discussed, it was obvious to everyone that Gunnhild
thought it mere stupidity or envy for any other man to be
compared with Hrut.

Because Hrut had a large estate to claim in Iceland, and
distinguished kinsmen to visit, he was eager to go there. When
he was ready to leave, the king gave him a ship as a parting gift
and said that Hrut had proved himself a true man.

Gunnhild accompanied Hrut to the ship and said, 'There is no
need to say in whispers that I have found you a man of great
distinction, for in prowess you are equal to the best in the land,
and much their superior in intelligence.'

She gave him a gold bracelet and bade him farewell; then
she drew her mantle over her head and walked quickly back
to her residence.[2]

Hrut went on board his ship and put out to sea. He had
favourable winds and made land in Breidafjord. He sailed up to

1. According to Icelandic reckoning, Harald Gunnhildarson
(Harald Grey-Cloak) was King of Norway from 960 to 975. His
mother, Queen Gunnhild, was the widow of Eirik Blood-Axe.
2. In *Njal's Saga* (Chapters 3–4) Hrut's relationship with Queen
Gunnhild is described more explicitly. The nymphomaniac queen
laid a spell on him that ruined his first marriage to Unn.

the islands and from there through Breidasound; he landed at Kambsness and put down the gangway.

News of the ship's arrival spread quickly, and also that Hrut Herjolfsson was the captain; but it brought little joy to Hoskuld, and he did not go to meet Hrut.

Hrut hauled the ship ashore and made it secure, and there he built his farm, which has ever since been known as Kambsness. Then he rode to see Hoskuld to claim his inheritance from his mother. Hoskuld said he owed him nothing, since their mother had not been penniless when she left Iceland and met Herjolf. Hrut was displeased at this and rode back home. All Hrut's kinsmen, apart from Hoskuld, showed him due respect. Hrut lived at Kambsness for three years and continued to claim the money from Hoskuld at Assemblies and other lawful meetings; he presented his case well, and most people agreed that he had justice on his side. But Hoskuld argued that Thorgerd had married Herjolf without his consent as her legal guardian. And there the matter rested.

That autumn Hoskuld went to a feast given by Thord Goddi. When Hrut heard about this he rode to Hoskuldstead with eleven men, where he rounded up twenty head of cattle and drove them away with him, leaving the same number behind. Then he sent a message to Hoskuld to tell him where to look for his cattle. Hoskuld's servants seized their weapons at once and sent word to their neighbours for help; and then, fifteen strong, they rode off as fast as they could. Hrut and his men were unaware of the pursuit until they had almost reached the farm at Kambsness; they dismounted at once, tethered their horses, and made for a nearby gravel-bank where Hrut said they would make a stand. He said that even though his lawsuit against Hoskuld was making little progress, he would never let it be said that he had fled before Hoskuld's slaves.

Hrut's companions pointed out that they would be outnumbered, but Hrut said he did not care – the others would fare all the worse the more of them there were.

The Laxriverdale men jumped off their horses and made ready for battle. Hrut urged his men not to heed the odds, and then rushed into the attack. He was wearing a helmet. with a drawn sword in one hand and a shield in the other. He was exceptionally skilled in arms, and he was now so ferocious that few could keep up with him. Both sides fought bravely for a while, but the Laxriverdale men soon found that they were no match for Hrut, for he now killed two men in a single onslaught. With that, the Laxriverdale men begged for quarter, which Hrut willingly accorded them. Four of Hoskuld's servants were dead by then, and all the survivors were wounded.

Hrut now went home. He himself was somewhat wounded, but his men only slightly or not at all, for he had borne the brunt of the fighting. The place where they fought has been known as Orrustudale[1] ever since.

After this, Hrut had the cattle slaughtered.

As soon as Hoskuld heard of the raid he gathered men in haste and rode home. He arrived there at the same time as his servants, who told him of their sorry expedition. Hoskuld was enraged at this, and said he was not going to tolerate any more robberies and killings from Hrut. He gathered forces all that day.

Then his wife Jorunn went to see him and asked him what he was planning. He replied, 'I'm not planning anything much, but I would dearly like to give people something better to talk about than the killing of my servants.'

Jorunn said, 'What a monstrous idea, to want to kill someone of your brother's standing! Some people would say that Hrut wouldn't have been unjustified if he had seized these cattle even sooner. He has now shown that he no longer intends to be deprived like some bastard of what is after all his birthright. He will certainly not have decided to pit himself against you now unless he were sure he could rely on help from people of importance; I have been told that secret messages have been passing between him and Thord Gellir, which I don't think should be ignored: Thord would like nothing better than to lend his support in so clear-cut a case. You know perfectly well, Hoskuld, that ever since the dispute between Thord Goddi and Vigdis, Thord Gellir and you haven't been on such friendly terms as before, even though you managed at

1. Literally, 'Battle Valley'.

the time to avert the enmity of those kinsmen by sending gifts; and I'm sure, Hoskuld,' she went on, 'that they still feel that you and your son Olaf are depriving them of their proper rights over it. In my opinion you would be better advised to make an honourable offer to your brother Hrut, for a hungry wolf will have his prey, as the saying goes. I'm sure that Hrut will respond favourably, for he is said to be a sensible man; he will no doubt recognize that this solution would do credit to you both.'

Hoskuld calmed down considerably at Jorunn's words, for it seemed to him that what she said was very reasonable. Then mutual friends of the brothers acted as intermediaries, carrying conciliatory messages from Hoskuld to Hrut. Hrut received them well and said that he certainly wanted to come to terms with Hoskuld. He said he had always been concerned to observe their kinship properly, provided that Hoskuld was willing to grant him his due; he also said he was willing to recompense Hoskuld for the wrongs that he, for his own part, had done him.

So now these issues between the brothers Hoskuld and Hrut were finally settled, and from then on they lived in good kinship.

Hrut busied himself with his farm and soon became a man of importance. He seldom intervened in any matters, but when he did take a hand he wanted to have his own way. He moved house, and lived till old age at the farm now known as Hrutstead; in the homefield he had a temple whose traces can still be seen. The place is now called Trollaskeid, and the highway passes through it.

Hrut married a woman called Unn, the daughter of Mord Fiddle; but Unn left him, and that was the cause of the conflict between the men of Laxriverdale and the men of Fljotshlid.[1]

1. The full story of this conflict is told in *Njal's Saga*: after Hrut's marriage to Unn was blighted by the witchcraft of Queen Gunnhild, Unn's father failed to recover the dowry back from Hrut and later she enlisted the help of Gunnar of Hlidarend, who eventually forced Hrut to pay up.

His second wife was Thorbjorg Armod's-daughter.

Hrut married a third time, but the name of his third wife is not recorded. Hrut had sixteen sons and ten daughters by these two wives. It is said that Hrut went to the Althing one summer accompanied by fourteen of his sons; this is mentioned here because it was considered a sign of great splendour and power. All his sons were accomplished men.

20. Melkorka marries

HOSKULD now remained quietly at home, as old age began to overtake him; his sons had reached full manhood by then.

Thorleik Hoskuldsson took over the farm at Kambsness, and Hoskuld paid out to him his share of the estate. After that, Thorleik married a woman called Gjaflaug.[1] It was a distinguished match; Gjaflaug was a beautiful but very arrogant woman, and Thorleik was aggressive and very bold. There was little warmth between Thorleik and his uncle, Hrut.

Bard Hoskuldsson stayed at home with his father; he was no less in charge of the farm than Hoskuld was.

Hoskuld's daughters do not concern this story much, but they had many descendants.

Olaf Hoskuldsson was also fully grown now, and was the most handsome man people had ever set eyes on; he always wore the finest clothing and weapons.

Olaf's mother, Melkorka, lived at Melkorkustead, as was written before. Hoskuld was now paying less attention to her affairs than he had done previously, and said he thought they were just as much her son Olaf's concern as his own. Olaf said he would look after her himself as well as he possibly could. Melkorka felt that Hoskuld was behaving disgracefully towards her, and she determined to do everything she could to annoy him.

The man who had given Melkorka most help with the running

1. *Gjaflaug was the daughter of Arnbjorn Sleitu-Bjarnarson and Thorlaug Thord's-daughter of Hofdi.*

of her farm had been Thorbjorn the Feeble; he had made her an offer of marriage soon after she went to live at Melkorkustead, but Melkorka had rejected the proposal.

There was a ship lying at Bordeyri in Hrutafjord. The captain, a man called Orn, was one of King Harald Gunnhildarson's retainers.

Melkorka had a talk with her son Olaf next time they met, and told him she wanted him to go abroad to visit his highborn kinsmen – 'for it is quite true, as I have told you, that Myrkjartan is my father and that he is king of the Irish. You can easily get a passage on the ship at Bordeyri.'

'I have spoken about this to my father,' said Olaf, 'but he isn't in favour of it; and as for money, my foster-father's wealth lies more in land and livestock than in ready Icelandic wares.'[1]

Melkorka replied, 'I don't want to have you called a concubine's son any longer, and if it's only the lack of means that you feel stands in the way of your going, then I would go so far as to marry Thorbjorn the Feeble if that will enable you to travel; for I'm sure he would supply whatever wares you think you will require, if he can gain my hand in return. And this will have the additional advantage of displeasing Hoskuld on two accounts, when he comes to hear both that you have gone abroad, and that I have got married.'

Olaf told his mother to have it her own way. Then he spoke to Thorbjorn and told him he needed a loan of wares from him, and a big one at that.

'You can only have it on condition that I get Melkorka's hand in marriage,' replied Thorbjorn, 'in which case I would regard my money as being just as much yours as your own is.'

Olaf said they would settle on these terms. They discussed all the necessary details, and agreed to keep it all a secret.

Hoskuld suggested to Olaf that he should ride to the Althing with him, but Olaf said he was too busy on the farm to go – he

1. Icelanders going abroad would take wares with them to be traded for ready cash. The principal exports from Iceland in those days were wool, tweed, sheepskins, hides, cheese, tallow, falcons and sulphur.

wanted to fence off a pasture near Lax River for his lambs. Hoskuld was very pleased that Olaf was busying himself with the farm.

So Hoskuld left for the Althing, and preparations were now made for the wedding at Lambastead. Olaf alone decided the terms of the marriage contract. Olaf took out of the undivided estate thirty hundreds[1] in wares, which were not to be paid back. Bard Hoskuldsson attended the wedding and knew about all the arrangements.

After the wedding-feast was over, Olaf rode off to the ship and met Orn the captain and took passage with him. But before Olaf and Melkorka parted she gave him a fine gold ring and said, 'My father gave me this ring as a teething gift, and I expect he will recognize it when he sees it.' She also gave Olaf a knife and a belt, and asked him to give them to her nurse – 'I'm sure she won't disown these tokens.' And Melkorka added, 'I have fitted you out for leaving home as best I could, and I have taught you to speak Irish, so it will make no difference what part of Ireland you land in.'

And with that they parted.

As soon as Olaf arrived at the ship a favourable wind sprang up, and they put out to sea at once.

21. Olaf in Ireland

WHEN Hoskuld came home from the Althing and heard what had happened he was very displeased, but since his own family were involved he was soon pacified and accepted the situation.

Olaf and his companions had a good voyage, and reached Norway. Orn urged Olaf to visit the court of King Harald, saying that the king bestowed honours on men who were by no means more accomplished than Olaf was. Olaf said he would

1. The *hundred* (in fact 120) refers to ells of woollen homespun cloth, and was a common unit of measure. Thirty 'hundreds' at this time were equivalent in value to a herd of nearly forty milch cows, or a flock of 240 sheep (cf. also *Njal's Saga*, Chapter 2).

do as Orn suggested. So Olaf and Orn went to the court and were well received there. The king at once accepted Olaf on account of his kinsmen, and invited him to stay with him.

Gunnhild bestowed many favours on Olaf when she discovered that he was Hrut Herjolfsson's nephew; but there were some who said that she enjoyed talking to Olaf whether he had any family connexions or not.

As the winter passed, Olaf became moody, and Orn asked him what was troubling him. Olaf said, 'I have a voyage I must make west across the sea, and it means a great deal to me that you should help me in undertaking that journey this summer.'

Orn begged Olaf not to insist on it, because he knew of no ships that would be sailing west that year. During their conversation Queen Gunnhild joined them and said, 'This is something I have never heard you doing before – you are having an argument.'

Olaf greeted Gunnhild warmly, but did not drop the subject. Orn now left them, and Olaf and Gunnhild continued the conversation. Olaf told her what he wanted to do, explaining how much the voyage meant to him; he said he knew for a fact that King Myrkjartan was his grandfather.

Then Gunnhild said, 'I shall provide you with the means for this voyage, so that you may travel in such style as you wish.'

Olaf thanked her for her promise.

Gunnhild now had a ship prepared, and hired a crew, but asked Olaf to decide how many men he would like to take with him on the voyage. Olaf fixed the number at sixty, adding that he thought it imperative to choose men who were more like warriors than merchants. She agreed to that. Orn was the only member of Olaf's company who is mentioned by name. They were all well equipped.

King Harald and Gunnhild accompanied Olaf to the ship, and said they would add their own good luck to the friendship they had already bestowed on him; King Harald said that this was no hardship, for they thought Olaf the most promising man to have come from Iceland during their reign. Then the king asked Olaf how old he was.

'I am eighteen years of age now,' replied Olaf.

'Men like you are indeed exceptional,' said the king, 'for you are still only little more than a boy. You must come to us again as soon as you return.'

Then the king and Gunnhild wished him farewell. Olaf and his men boarded their ship and put out to sea at once. They had poor weather that summer, with dense fogs and hardly any wind, and what little there was of it was unfavourable. They drifted about all over the ocean, and most of the men on board lost all sense of direction. At last the fog lifted and the wind began to blow, so they hoisted sail. But now an argument arose about the direction in which Ireland lay, and they could not agree on it. Orn maintained one thing, but most of the others contradicted him and said he was utterly confused, and that the majority should decide. The question was finally referred to Olaf, and Olaf said, 'I want only the shrewdest to decide; in my opinion the counsel of fools is all the more dangerous the more of them there are.'

When Olaf had spoken, the matter was accepted as settled, and after that Orn took charge of the navigation. They sailed for some days and nights, and always with very little wind. Then one night the watchmen jumped up and shouted to them all to wake up at once; they said they could see land ahead so close that the prow had almost struck it. The sail was up, with a very light breeze. They all got up immediately, and Orn told them to sheer away from the shore if they possibly could.

Olaf said, 'There's no chance of that, for I can see breakers everywhere astern. Lower sail at once! We can decide what to do when daylight comes and we recognize what country this is.'

They put out anchors, which caught bottom at once. During the night there was much discussion about where they were, but as soon as it was daylight they recognized that this was Ireland.

Orn said, 'I don't think we have landed at a good place, for this is far from the harbours and market-towns where foreigners are supposed to have safe-conduct; and here we are, left high and dry like sticklebacks on a beach. I think I'm right in saying that under Irish law they can confiscate all our goods, for they claim everything as flotsam even when the sea has ebbed less from a ship than it has here.'

Olaf said it would not come to that – 'but I have noticed a crowd of people gathering ashore; the Irish are very interested in the arrival of our ship. During the ebb-tide today I saw that there is an estuary round behind the headland which doesn't empty completely at low tide; so if the ship isn't damaged we will lower the boat and tow the ship into it.'

There was a bottom of clay where they had been lying at anchor, and none of the planking of the ship had been damaged. They moved the ship into the estuary and cast anchor there.

Later that day a great crowd of people came down to the beach. Then two men came rowing out to the ship in a boat. They asked who were the masters of the ship, and Olaf answered them, speaking in Irish as they had done. When the Irish realized that these were Norsemen, they cited their laws and told them to surrender their goods, in which event no harm would befall them until the king had judged their case.

Olaf replied that this was the law only when merchants had no interpreters with them – 'but I can tell you truthfully that these are peaceful men; nevertheless we will not yield without putting up a fight.'

At that the Irish raised a war-cry and waded out into the sea to try to drag the ship ashore with the crew on board. The water was no deeper than their armpits, or the waists of the tallest ones; but the pool in which the ship lay was so deep that no one could touch bottom. Olaf told his men to get their weapons out and line the gunwales of the ship from stem to stern. They stood so close that their shields overlapped all round the ship, with a spear-head jutting out from below every rim.

Olaf walked forward to the prow. He was wearing a coat of mail, and had a gilded helmet on his head. He was girded with a sword whose pommel and guard were embossed with gold, and in his hand he held a barbed spear, chased and beautifully engraved. Before him he carried a red shield on which a lion was traced in gold.

When the Irish saw this battle-array they were frightened, and realized that this would not be such an easy prize as they had thought. So the Irish fell back and gathered into a huddle. A great murmur of unease broke out among them, for it now seemed obvious to them that this was a warship and that many more ships might be on the way. They sent word hurriedly to the king, who was conveniently attending a feast not far away. The king rode at once with his following to the ship, which was lying well within hailing distance from the shore. The Irish had shot at them many times, but Olaf and his men had not been injured. Olaf was standing there in the accoutrements already described, and people marvelled at the splendour of the ship's captain. But when Olaf's men saw the great company of cavalry approaching in all its bravery they fell silent, for they thought that here were heavy odds to deal with. When Olaf heard the murmur of unease among his crew he told them to be of good heart – 'for the outlook is more hopeful for us now; it is their king, Myrkjartan, that the Irish are greeting.'

They rode up so close to the ship that each could hear what the other said. The king asked who was in command of the ship. Olaf gave his name, and asked who the gallant knight was whom he was addressing.

'My name is Myrkjartan,' he replied.

'Are you the king of the Irish?' asked Olaf.

The other said he was. Then the king asked him the news, and Olaf dealt skilfully with all his questions. Then the king asked where they had sailed from and whose men they were; and after that he questioned Olaf more closely about his lineage than he had done before, for he realized that this man was proud and would not answer more than he was asked.

Olaf said, 'You shall know that we put out from Norway, and that these men on board this ship are retainers of King Harald Gunnhildarson. As for my lineage, my lord, I can tell you that my father lives in Iceland; he is called Hoskuld, and is a man of noble birth. But of my mother's kin I expect that you will have seen more than I, for my mother is called Melkorka, and I have been told in good faith that she is your daughter, my lord; and that is why I have undertaken so long a journey.

And now it means a great deal to me to hear what answer you give to what I have said.'

The king made no reply, and conferred with his men. The wisest of them asked him what truth there might be in the story that this man had told. The king replied, 'It is quite obvious that this Olaf is a man of noble birth, whether he is our kinsman or not, and also that he speaks exceptionally good Irish.'

After that the king stood up and said, 'Now I shall give my answer to your words. I shall grant safe-conduct to you and all your men; but as for the kinship you claim with us, we shall have to go into that further before I give my reply.'

The gangway was now put out and Olaf and his companions came ashore. All the Irish marvelled at their warrior-like bearing. Olaf greeted the king respectfully and took off his helmet and bowed to him, and the king received him cordially. Then they talked together, and Olaf presented his case anew in a long and eloquent speech. He ended by saying that he was wearing on his finger a gold ring which Melkorka had given him when they parted in Iceland – 'and she told me, my lord, that you had given it to her as a teething gift.'

The king took the ring and looked at it, and his face went very red. Then he said, 'The token is genuine, and is made all the more remarkable by the fact that you bear so close a family resemblance to your mother that one could easily recognize you from that alone. And because of all this I shall certainly acknowledge our kinship, Olaf, and let all those present who can hear me be witnesses to this. In addition, I wish to invite you with all your companions to my court; the honour you will be accorded there will depend on how worthy a man I find you when I have put you further to the test.'

After that the king ordered them to be given horses, and appointed men to secure their ship and take care of their goods. Then the king rode to Dublin, where it caused a great stir that the king's grandson should now be with him – son of the daughter who had been taken captive so long ago when she was fifteen years old.

But no one was more affected by the news than Melkorka's

nurse, who was now bedridden, stricken with grief and old age. Yet she needed no crutches when she came to meet Olaf.

The king said to Olaf, 'Here now is Melkorka's nurse, and she will want to hear from you everything about her.'

Olaf welcomed the old woman with open arms and put her on his knee, and told her that her foster-child was enjoying a good life in Iceland. Then he gave her the knife and the belt, and the old woman recognized them and wept for joy. She said that Melkorka's son was an exceptional man – 'and no wonder, for he comes of good stock!' The old woman was hale and hearty all that winter.

The king was seldom at peace, for at that time there was constant warfare in the British Isles, and throughout the winter he repelled attacks by vikings and raiders. Olaf and his men were on the king's ship, and whoever came up against them found them rather a formidable company to deal with. The king used to consult Olaf and his men on all decisions, for he found Olaf to be both shrewd and resolute in all hazards.

Late that winter the king held an assembly which was attended in great numbers. The king rose to his feet and addressed them thus : 'You are all aware that last autumn a man arrived here who is my daughter's son, and is also of noble descent on his father's side. I have found Olaf to be a man of such prowess and accomplishments that we do not have his equal here. And so I want to offer him my kingdom after my death, for Olaf is better fitted to rule than my own sons.'

Olaf thanked him for this offer with great eloquence and skill, but said that he did not care to risk how Myrkjartan's sons would take it after their father's death. He said it was better to have a brief honour than a lasting shame. He said he wanted to go back to Norway as soon as it was safe to sail across the sea, and that his mother would know little happiness if he did not return. The king left the decision to Olaf, and after that the assembly was brought to a close.

When Olaf's ship was ready the king accompanied him to it and gave him a spear inlaid with gold and an embossed sword and many other treasures. Olaf asked leave to take Melkorka's nurse with him, but the king said there was no need for that, and so she did not go. Olaf and his men embarked, and he and the king parted in the warmest friendship. After that they put out to sea; they had favourable winds, and reached Norway. Olaf's journey to Ireland brought him great renown. They hauled their ship ashore, and Olaf got horses and went with his companions to visit King Harald.

22. Olaf returns

OLAF HOSKULDSSON arrived at the court of King Harald, where the king gave him a good welcome, and Gunnhild an even better one; they urged him effusively to come and stay with them. Olaf accepted the invitation, and he and Orn joined the king's court. The king and Gunnhild bestowed so much honour on Olaf that no foreigner had ever enjoyed such privileges from them before. Olaf gave the king and Gunnhild many rare treasures he had acquired out west in Ireland. At Christmas, King Harald gave Olaf a set of scarlet clothes.

Olaf stayed there quietly all winter. Late next spring the king and Olaf had a talk. Olaf asked the king's leave to go to Iceland that summer – 'for I have noble kinsmen to visit there,' he said.

'It would please me more,' replied the king, 'if you were to settle here with us, and have whatever position you yourself desire.'

Olaf thanked the king for the honour he was offering him, but said he preferred to go to Iceland, unless it were against the king's wishes.

Then the king said, 'We shall not make an issue of this, Olaf. You shall go to Iceland this summer, for I can see you have set your heart on it; and you are not to have any trouble or worry over your preparations, for I shall take care of all that.'

And with that they ended their conversation.

King Harald had a ship launched in the spring, a fine large merchant-ship. The king had it fitted out with full rigging, and loaded it with timber. When the ship was ready the king summoned Olaf and said to him, 'This ship is yours, Olaf, for I do not want you to sail from Norway this summer as someone else's passenger.'

Olaf thanked the king handsomely for his generosity. Then he made ready for the voyage, and when he was ready and the wind was favourable he put out to sea. King Harald and he parted on terms of warmest affection. Olaf had a good voyage that summer, and sailed his ship to Bordeyri in Hrutafjord.

News spread quickly of the ship's arrival and the name of her captain. Hoskuld was delighted when he heard that his son had returned, and rode north at once with some men to Hrutafjord, where father and son had a joyful reunion. Hoskuld invited Olaf to come and stay with him, and Olaf accepted. Olaf laid up his ship, and his goods were taken south. When all this had been seen to, Olaf rode south with eleven companions home to Hoskuldstead. Hoskuld welcomed his son fondly, and his brothers and all his other kinsmen also received him warmly, but none more so than Bard.

Olaf's voyage brought him great renown, and now his true lineage was made known: that he was the grandson of Myrkjartan, king of the Irish. This was soon known throughout the country, as was the honour that had been bestowed on him by the great men he had visited. Olaf had also brought home with him a great deal of wealth. He spent the winter with his father.

Melkorka soon came to see her son Olaf, and Olaf greeted her affectionately. She asked him many questions about Ireland, first about her father and her other kinsmen, and Olaf told her everything she wanted to know; but it was not long before she was asking if her nurse was still alive, and Olaf said she certainly was. Then Melkorka asked why he had not done her the pleasure of bringing her to Iceland.

'The people in Ireland didn't want me to take your nurse away from there, mother,' replied Olaf.

'I suppose so,' she said, but it was obvious that she was very upset about it.

Melkorka and Thorbjorn the Feeble had a son, who was

called Lambi. He was a tall, powerful man, and resembled his father in appearance as well as temperament.

When Olaf had spent one winter in Iceland, and spring came, he and his father discussed plans for his future.

Hoskuld said, 'I should like you to take a wife, Olaf, and then take over your foster-father's farm at Goddastead, where there is still plenty of wealth. You could then run it under my guidance.'

'I haven't given this much thought before,' said Olaf. 'And I don't know where the woman is to be found who would make a lucky catch for me. You must realize that I shall be aiming high in my choice of a wife. However, I'm sure you wouldn't have raised this question unless you had given some thought to a solution.'

'You're quite right,' said Hoskuld. 'There is a man called Egil Skalla-Grimsson[1] who lives at Borg, in Borgarfjord. Egil has a daughter called Thorgerd. This is the woman for whose hand I intend to ask on your behalf, for she is the best match in all Borgarfjord and even farther afield. Besides, your position would be greatly strengthened by a marriage-alliance with the men of Myrar.'

Olaf said, 'I shall rely on your guidance in this matter, for this match would be greatly to my liking if it can be brought about. But you must realize, father, that if this proposal is made and nothing comes of it, I shall be very displeased.'

'We shall take that risk and make the proposal, then,' said Hoskuld.

Olaf left the decision to him. Time now passed until the Althing was due. Hoskuld made ready to go there, and had a large following. His son Olaf went with him. They tented their booths. The Althing was well attended, and Egil Skalla-Grimsson was among those present. Everyone who saw Olaf remarked on how handsome and distinguished-looking he was. He was well accoutred in weapons and clothing.

1. The eponymous hero of *Egil's Saga*, and the greatest of all the Icelandic warrior-poets.

23. Olaf marries

ONE day Hoskuld and his son Olaf left their booth and went to see Egil. Egil gave them a good welcome, for he and Hoskuld were well acquainted. Hoskuld now made the offer of marriage on behalf of Olaf, and asked for the hand of Thorgerd; she was also present at the Althing.

Egil received the offer favourably, saying that he had heard good reports of both father and son: 'I also know, Hoskuld,' he said, 'that you are of noble birth and highly esteemed, and that Olaf's voyage has brought him great renown; and it's not surprising that such men are ambitious to marry well, for he lacks neither looks nor lineage. But still, I must discuss this with Thorgerd herself, for no man shall marry her against her will.'

Hoskuld said, 'I would indeed like you to talk this over with your daughter, Egil.'

Egil said he would do that, and went to see Thorgerd, and they had a talk together.

'There is a man called Olaf Hoskuldsson, who is now one of the most famous men in Iceland,' said Egil. 'His father Hoskuld has made an offer of marriage and asked for your hand on his son's behalf. I have told them that it depends on your decision, and now I want to know your answer; but in my opinion the answer is an easy one, for this would make a distinguished match.'

'I have often heard you say that you love me best of all your children,' replied Thorgerd, 'but now it seems to me that you cannot really mean it, if you want to marry me off to a concubine's son, no matter how handsome and flashily dressed he is.'

'You're not so well informed in this as you are in other matters,' said Egil. 'Haven't you heard that he is the grandson of Myrkjartan, the king of the Irish? He is of much nobler descent on his mother's side than on his father's – which in itself would make a good enough match for us.'

But Thorgerd would not be convinced, and they could not see eye to eye over it.

Next day Egil went to Hoskuld's booth, and Hoskuld gave him a good welcome. They talked together and Hoskuld asked how the marriage-proposal had gone. Egil was disappointed over it and told him everything that had happened. Hoskuld said this looked far from hopeful – 'but I know you have done your best,' he said.

Olaf was not present at their conversation, and Egil now went away. Later Olaf asked what had become of the marriage-proposal, and Hoskuld told him that Thorgerd for her part was delaying it.

Olaf said, 'I told you before, father, that I would be angry if it brought me any humiliation. It was your idea rather than mine that this proposal should be made at all; but now I shall see to it that the matter doesn't rest there. It's certainly true, as the saying goes, that wolves prey on another's trust.[1] We shall go over to Egil's booth at once.'

Hoskuld told him to have it his own way. Olaf put on the scarlet clothes that King Harald had given him; on his head he put the gilded helmet, and in his hand he carried the embossed sword that King Myrkjartan had given him. He and Hoskuld now went to Egil's booth with Hoskuld in front and Olaf immediately behind him.

Egil gave them a good welcome and Hoskuld sat down beside him, but Olaf remained standing and looked around. He saw a woman seated on the dais in the booth; she was beautiful and distinguished, and was wearing fine clothes. Olaf was sure this must be Thorgerd, Egil's daughter. He walked over to the dais and sat down beside her; Thorgerd greeted this man and asked who he was.

Olaf told her his own name and his father's. 'You must think it very bold of the concubine's son to dare to sit beside you and try to talk to you,' he said.

1. The taunt is made all the sharper by the implied pun on Hoskuld's name: *Höskuldr* means, literally, 'Grey-Head', and the colour-word *höss* is particularly associated with the greyness of wolves.

'You no doubt think you have done more daring deeds than talking to women,' replied Thorgerd.

Then they began talking, and they talked together all that day, and no one could overhear what they were saying. Before they parted, Egil and Hoskuld were called over, and Olaf's marriage-proposal was raised anew; and this time Thorgerd left the decision to her father. The matter was now easily settled, and the betrothal took place at once. In deference to the men of Laxriverdale it was conceded that the bride should be brought to them; the wedding was to take place at Hoskuldstead seven weeks before winter.

After that Egil and Hoskuld parted. Father and son rode home to Hoskuldstead; they remained there for the rest of the summer, and everything was quiet.

Then the preparations for the wedding-feast at Hoskuldstead were made and nothing was stinted, for means were plentiful. The guests arrived at the appointed time. The men of Borgarfjord attended in great numbers, including Egil and his son Thorstein Egilsson. With them came the bride, and a select following from that district. Hoskuld had a great number of guests waiting to welcome them. The feast was magnificent, and when it was over the guests were given gifts when they left. Olaf gave Egil the sword that King Myrkjartan had given him, and Egil's face lit up at the gift. The feast had been uneventful, and now all the guests went home.

24. Hjardarholt

OLAF and Thorgerd lived at Hoskuldstead and came to love one another dearly. It was obvious to everyone that she was an exceptional woman. She was not an interfering person as a rule, but whenever she did take a hand she insisted on having her own way. That winter, Olaf and Thorgerd were alternately at Hoskuldstead or with Olaf's foster-father at Goddastead.

In the spring Olaf took over the farm at Goddastead. That summer Thord Goddi fell ill and then died. Olaf had a mound raised over him on the tongue of land that juts out into Lax River and is called Drafnarness; the mound is surrounded by a wall which is known as Haugsgard.

Soon many people began to flock to Olaf, and he became a great chieftain. Hoskuld was not envious of this, for he always wanted Olaf to be consulted in all matters of importance.

Olaf's estate was the outstanding farm in Laxriverdale.

There were two brothers staying with Olaf, both of whom were called An; one was known as An the White, and the other as An the Black. There was a third man called Beinir the Strong. They were Olaf's smiths, and they were all stalwart men.

Thorgerd and Olaf had a daughter who was called Thurid.

The lands which had belonged to Killer-Hrapp were all lying empty, as was written earlier. Olaf thought they were well situated, and one day he suggested to his father that they should send messengers to Thorkel Fringe with an offer to buy from him the lands at Hrappstead and the other properties included in the estate. This was easily arranged and the deal was clinched, for Thorkel realized that it was better to have a bird in the hand than two in the bush. The agreement was that Olaf was to pay three marks of silver for the land, which was an excellent bargain, for the lands were rich and extensive and very productive, with good salmon-fishing and seal-hunting as well, and plenty of woodland.

Some distance above Hoskuldstead, to the north of Lax River, a clearing had been cut in the wood, and you could be sure of finding Olaf's livestock always gathered there, in good weather or bad. One autumn Olaf had a farmhouse built in that same clearing, using timber hewn from the forest as well as driftwood. It was a magnificent building. It stood empty throughout the winter, but in spring Olaf moved in. Before he moved house he herded together all his livestock, which had multiplied vastly – no one in Breidafjord was richer in livestock at that time. Olaf then sent word to his father to stand outside at Hoskuldstead and watch his train as he moved to his new home, and invoke a benison upon it. Hoskuld agreed to do this.

Olaf now made his arrangements: first in the line were driven the shyest of the sheep, followed by the milch ewes and cows; next came the barren cattle, with the pack-horses bringing up the rear. The farmhands were placed so as to prevent the animals straying from a straight line. In this way, the van was reaching the new farm just when Olaf was riding out of Goddastead, and there was no gap anywhere in the line.

Hoskuld was standing out of doors with his men; and now Hoskuld wished his son wealth and well-being in this new farm – 'and I have a feeling that this will be so, and that his name will be long remembered.'

His wife Jorunn retorted, 'That concubine's son certainly has the wealth to ensure that his name is long remembered!'

Just as the servants had unloaded the pack-horses, Olaf came riding in. Then he said, 'Now I shall satisfy your curiosity over the question that has been discussed all winter, as to what this farm is to be called: its name is to be Hjardarholt.'[1]

Everyone thought this name fittingly chosen in view of the purpose the place had previously served. Olaf now organized the farm at Hjardarholt; it soon became very prosperous, and nothing was ever lacking there.

Olaf's reputation now grew in stature, and there were many reasons for this. He was extremely well-liked, for whenever he intervened in other people's affairs he did it in such a way that everyone was satisfied. His father helped him in every way to gain prestige; and Olaf also had a great asset in his alliance with the men of Myrar. Olaf was considered the noblest of all Hoskuld's sons.

The first winter that Olaf lived in Hjardarholt he had many servants and farmhands, each of whom had his particular work to do. One of them tended the barren cattle, and another the milch cows. The byre was out in the woods some distance away from the farmhouse.

One evening the man who tended the barren cattle came to Olaf and asked him to get someone else to see to the beasts – 'and give me some other work to do.'

'I want you to keep on with the work you've been doing,' replied Olaf.

The man said he would rather leave than do that.

1. The name means, literally, 'Herd's-wood'.

'Then you really must think there's something the matter,' said Olaf. 'I shall go with you this evening when you tie up the cattle, and if I think you have any excuse for this I shan't blame you in any way. But otherwise you'll be made to suffer for it.'

Olaf took his gold-inlaid spear which the king had given him, and set out with the farmhand. There was light snow on the ground. They came to the byre, which was open, and Olaf told the man to go in first – 'and I'll drive the cattle in behind you, and you tie them up'.

The farmhand went to the door, and before Olaf knew it the man came leaping back into his arms. Olaf asked him why he was so terrified. He replied, 'Killer-Hrapp is standing in the door of the byre and he tried to catch hold of me, but I've had enough of wrestling with him.'

Olaf now went to the door and thrust at Hrapp with his spear. Hrapp grabbed the socket of the spear with both hands and wrenched it so sharply that the shaft snapped. Then Olaf tried to rush Hrapp, but Hrapp sank into the ground where he had been standing, and that was the end of their encounter: Olaf was left with the shaft, and Hrapp had the spear-head. Olaf and the farmhand now tied up the cattle, and after that they went back home. Olaf told the man that he would not blame him for having complained.

Next morning Olaf went to the place where Hrapp had been buried, and had him dug up. Hrapp's corpse was still undecayed, and Olaf found his spear-head there. After that he had a pyre built, and Hrapp was burned on it and his ashes were carried out to sea. From that time on no one ever suffered any harm from Hrapp's hauntings.

25. Thorleik and Bard Hoskuldsson

Now we must tell something of Hoskuld's other sons.

Thorleik Hoskuldsson had been a great sea-going merchant and stayed with people of rank when he was on his trading voyages, before he settled down as a farmer. He was considered a man of great note. He had also been on viking raids, where he had proved himself a man of courage.

Bard Hoskuldsson had also been a sea-going merchant and had been highly thought of wherever he went, for he was a true and upright man and very temperate in all things. Bard married a Breidafjord woman called Astrid, who came of a good family.[1]

Hrut Herjolfsson gave freedom to one of his slaves called Hrolf, together with a little property and a house near the boundary between his own land and Hoskuld's. The boundary line was so close to Hrutstead at this point that Hrut's people miscalculated and inadvertently settled the freedman on Hoskuld's land. The freedman prospered and quickly became wealthy there. Hoskuld was extremely annoyed that Hrut had settled the freedman right under his nose, and asked the freedman to pay him for the land he was farming – 'for it belongs to me.'

The freedman went to see Hrut to tell him of his talk with Hoskuld. Hrut told him to ignore it, and not to pay Hoskuld any money. 'I've no idea,' said Hrut, 'to which of us the land actually belonged.'

So the freedman went home and stayed on at his farm just as before. A little later Thorleik Hoskuldsson, with his father's approval, went over to the farm and seized the freedman there and put him to death; Thorleik then claimed possession, on his own and his father's behalf, of all the wealth the freedman had amassed.

Hrut heard about this, and he and his sons were furious. Many of his sons were fully grown by then, and this family group was considered very formidable as opponents. Hrut consulted the law over this case to find out how he should pro-

1. *Bard had a son called Thorarin, and a daughter called Gudny, who married Hall, the son of Killer-Styr, and from whom a great many people are descended.*
Killer-Styr is the eponymous hero of *Killer-Styr's Saga* (which is also known as *Heidarviga Saga*), and plays an important role in *Eyrbyggja Saga*.

ceed, but when the matter was investigated by legal experts, their verdict went against Hrut, chiefly on the ground that Hrut had settled the freedman on Hoskuld's land without his permission and the freedman had then made his money there; consequently, Thorleik had killed him on his and his father's own property. Hrut was ill-contented with the result, but there the matter rested.

After that, Thorleik built a farm at the boundary between Hoskuld's land and Hrut's; that farm is known as Kambsness. Thorleik farmed there for some time, as has already been said.

Thorleik had a son by his wife; the boy was sprinkled with water and given the name of Bolli. He soon grew up to be a most promising young man.

26. Hoskuld Dala-Kollsson dies

HOSKULD DALA-KOLLSSON fell ill in his old age, and sent for his sons and other kinsmen. When they arrived, Hoskuld said to the brothers Bard and Thorleik, 'I have caught some sickness, and since I have never been prone to ill-health I think this will bring about my death. Now as you know, you were both born in wedlock, and are therefore entitled to all the estate I leave. But I also have a third son, who is illegitimate. I now want to request you brothers to grant Olaf the right to share the estate equally with you, one third to each.'

Bard answered first and said he would do as his father wished – 'for I expect that Olaf will do me all the more honour the wealthier he is.'

Then Thorleik said, 'It is far from my wish that Olaf be given the right of inheritance. Olaf is wealthy enough as it is. You, father, have given him many of your treasures already, and for a long time you have favoured him at our expense. I shall certainly not surrender my birth-rights readily.'

Hoskuld said, 'But you will not, I hope, deny me the lawful right to give twelve ounces to my son, considering how high-born he is on his mother's side?'

Thorleik agreed to that. Then Hoskuld called for the gold bracelet which King Hakon had given him (it weighed one mark – eight ounces), and the sword which the king had given him, which was worth half a mark of gold (four ounces); and these he gave to his son Olaf, and with them the family good luck; he added that this did not mean he was unaware that the family luck had passed to him already. Olaf accepted the treasures and said he would take the risk of how Thorleik would like it. Thorleik was very annoyed at this, and felt that Hoskuld had treated him in an underhand way.[1]

Olaf said, 'I shall not give up the treasures, Thorleik, for you consented to such a gift in the presence of witnesses, and I shall take the risk of whether I can hold on to them.'

Bard said he wanted to abide by his father's wishes.

After that, Hoskuld died and his death was considered a great loss, particularly by his sons and all their kinsmen and friends. His sons had a stately mound built for him, but only a very few valuables were buried with him.

When the funeral was over, the brothers began to discuss arrangements for a memorial feast in honour of their father, for such was the custom in those days. Then Olaf said, 'I don't think this feast should be held in too much of a hurry if it is to be as magnificent as is fitting, since the autumn is now far advanced and the necessary provisions are hard to obtain. Besides, most people would find it difficult to attend the feast in autumn, particularly those who have far to come, and it is more than likely that many of those whom we should most want to attend wouldn't be able to come. I suggest that I should undertake to invite the guests to this feast, at the Althing next summer; and I shall bear one third of the cost.'

The brothers agreed to this, and Olaf went home. Thorleik and Bard divided the estate between them. Bard got the lands and property, which was the wish of most people, for he was

1. By law, a man could bequeath to an illegitimate child a maximum of 'twelve ounces' without the permission of the legitimate heirs. In this context, the 'ounce' was assumed to be an ounce of silver; but Hoskuld tricks his sons by giving Olaf twelve ounces of gold – eight times the value of silver.

the better liked; Thorleik got most of the goods and chattels. The brothers Olaf and Bard got on well together, but Olaf and Thorleik were on rather unfriendly terms.

The winter now passed and summer came, and soon the Althing was due. The Hoskuldssons made ready to attend the Althing. It was obvious at once that Olaf would be the most prominent of the brothers. When they arrived at the Althing they put up their booth and furnished it in fine style.

27. Hoskuld's memorial feast

ONE day when people were gathered at the Law Rock, Olaf stood up and asked for a hearing. First he told them of the death of his father: 'Many of those present today were his kinsmen or friends, and it is the wish of my brothers that I invite all of you chieftains to a memorial feast in honour of our father Hoskuld, for most of the notable men here had family ties with him. Let it also be known that none of the more important people shall leave the feast without gifts. We also want to invite all the farmers and anyone else who wishes to accept, rich or poor, to attend a fortnight's feast at Hoskuldstead ten weeks before winter.'

When Olaf had finished his speech there was loud approval, and everyone considered his gesture a magnificent one. When Olaf returned to the booth he told his brothers what he had in mind; they were none too pleased, and thought he had gone rather too far. When the Althing was over the brothers rode home.

The summer passed, and the brothers prepared for the feast. Olaf supplied his third of the cost without stint, and the feast was furnished with the finest provisions. Great stores were laid in, for a host of guests was expected. And when the feast began, it is said that most of the important people who had promised to attend were present. There was such a throng that it is generally agreed that the guests numbered no fewer than one thousand and eighty; this was the second largest feast ever held in Iceland, second only to the funeral feast the Hjaltasons gave in honour of their father's memory, when there were about 1440 guests.[1]

Hoskuld's memorial feast was magnificent in every respect, and greatly enhanced the prestige of the brothers, but Olaf was considered the foremost of them. He shared with his brothers equally the cost of the gifts, and all the most important people were given one.

When most of the guests had gone, Olaf had a talk with his brother Thorleik and said, 'As you are aware, kinsman, there has been little love lost between us in the past, but now I want to suggest that we observe our kinship better. I know you disliked it when I accepted the treasures my father gave me on his deathbed. If you still feel you have been wronged in this, I want to regain your goodwill by fostering your son: for he who fosters another's son is always said to be the lesser man.'

Thorleik received this well and said, as was true, that it was an honourable offer. So Olaf now took Thorleik's son Bolli, who was three years old at the time. The brothers parted with the greatest affection, and Bolli went with Olaf home to Hjardarholt. Thorgerd received the boy well, and Bolli was brought up there, and was loved no less than their own children.

28. Kjartan and Bolli

OLAF and Thorgerd had a son. The boy was sprinkled with water and given a name. Olaf had him called Kjartan, after Myrkjartan, his own grandfather.

Bolli and Kjartan were much of an age.

Olaf and Thorgerd had many other children. The sons were called Steinthor and Halldor and Helgi and Hoskuld; Hoskuld

1. Thorvald and Thord Hjaltason belonged to a distinguished family in the north of Iceland. Their father, Hjalti Thordarson, was one of the original settlers in Iceland, and the memorial feast his sons held after his death is described in *Landnámabók* (Book of Settlements).

was the youngest of the Olafssons. The daughters were called Bergthora and Thorgerd and Thorbjorg. They were all promising children as they grew up.

At that time, Dueller-Bersi was living at a farm called Tongue, in Saurby. He went to see his cousin Olaf Hoskuldsson, and offered to foster his son Halldor. Olaf accepted the offer, and Halldor went home with Bersi; he was one year old at the time.

That same year Bersi fell ill, and was bedridden for most of the summer. It is said that one day the people at Tongue were out hay-making, and the two of them, Bersi and Halldor, were left alone in the house. Halldor was lying in his cradle; then the cradle fell and the boy tumbled out of it on to the floor. Bersi was unable to get to him; and then Bersi said :

> 'Here we both lie
> In helplessness,
> Halldor and I,
> Both powerless.
> Age afflicts me
> And infancy you;
> It'll get better for you
> But not for me.'

Later, people came in and picked Halldor up off the floor. Bersi recovered from his illness. Halldor grew up there, and became a tall, sturdy man.

Kjartan Olafsson grew up at home at Hjardarholt. He was the most handsome man ever to have been born in Iceland. He had a striking face, with regular features, beautiful eyes, and a fair complexion. His hair was long and fine as silk, falling in curls. He was tall and strong, just as his grandfather Egil Skalla-Grimsson had been, and Thorolf.[1] Kjartan was better proportioned than any other man, and everyone who saw him marvelled at him; he was also better skilled in arms than most, extremely dextrous, and exceptionally good at swimming. He surpassed all others in all accomplishments; yet he was a man of great

1. Thorolf was Egil's brother, and was killed in England at the Battle of Vínheiðr – probably Brunanburh, in 937 (*Egil's Saga*, Chapter 53).

humility, and so popular that everyone, man or child, loved him. He was cheerful by nature, and generous with money. Olaf loved Kjartan most of all his children.

His foster-brother Bolli was a tall man. He was second only to Kjartan in prowess and all accomplishments. He was strong and handsome in appearance, courteous and very warrior-like, and had a taste for the ornate. The foster-brothers were very fond of one another.

And now Olaf remained quietly at home for a good many years.

29. Geirmund marries Thurid

ONE spring Olaf told Thorgerd he intended to go abroad – 'and I want you to look after the estate and the children.'

Thorgerd said it was not much to her liking, but Olaf insisted. He bought a ship which was lying at Vadil, in the west, and sailed abroad that summer, and brought his ship to Hordaland.

A man called Geirmund the Noisy lived there, near the coast, a rich and powerful man and a great viking; he was a very unruly man but had now settled down and was a retainer of Earl Hakon the Powerful.[1]

Geirmund went down to the ship and soon realized who Olaf was, for he had heard about him before. Geirmund invited Olaf to come and stay with him with as many men as he wished. Olaf accepted the offer and went there with five of his men; the rest of the crew got lodgings elsewhere in Hordaland. Geirmund was a good host to Olaf; he had an impressive house and kept a large household, and there was plenty of entertainment all winter.

When winter was drawing to a close, Olaf told Geirmund that

1. Earl Hakon Sigurdsson (Hakon the Powerful) ruled Norway from 975 to 995, according to Icelandic reckoning. He overthrew King Harald Gunnhildarson and his mother, Queen Gunnhild, to gain the throne; he was succeeded by King Olaf Tryggvason (995–1000), cf. Chapter 40.

his reason for coming to Norway was to obtain timber for building a house – and that it was essential he should get timber of good quality.

Geirmund replied, 'Earl Hakon has the best forests, and I know for certain that if you went to see him,' his forests would be at your disposal, for the earl gives a good welcome to visitors who are much less well-accomplished than you, Olaf.'

In the spring, Olaf set out to visit Earl Hakon. The earl gave him a cordial welcome and invited him to stay with him as long as he wished. Olaf told the earl the reason for his journey : 'I wish to request your leave, my lord, to cut building-timber from your forests.'

'We would not grudge it even if you filled your whole ship with our timber,' said the earl, 'and you must accept it as a gift, for we feel it is not every day that men like you come from Iceland to visit us.'

When they parted, the earl gave him an axe inlaid with gold, a most valuable treasure; and they parted in the greatest affection.

Meanwhile Geirmund the Noisy had secretly disposed of his lands, for he was planning to go to Iceland that summer on Olaf's ship; but he let no one know about it. Olaf knew nothing until Geirmund had loaded his goods on board the ship; it amounted to a considerable fortune.

'You wouldn't be travelling on my ship if I had known of this before,' said Olaf, 'for I think there are people in Iceland who would be better off if they never set eyes on you. But since you're already here with so much wealth, I cannot bring myself to drive you away like a stray dog.'

'I'm not going to be left behind.' said Geirmund, 'for all your big talk; I've every intention of paying my own passage.'

With that they embarked and put out to sea. They had a good voyage and made land in Breidafjord. They put out the gangway at Laxriver Estuary. Olaf had the timber unloaded, and hauled the ship into the shed his father had built.

Olaf invited Geirmund to stay with him.

That summer Olaf had a hall built at Hjardarholt, larger and finer than anyone had ever seen before. The wainscoting and ceiling were adorned with fine carvings depicting the old legends; the craftsmanship was so superb that people thought the hall even more magnificent when the wall-hangings were not up.

Geirmund was taciturn and brusque with most people as a rule. He always went around in a scarlet tunic with a grey fur-cloak over it, a bearskin cap on his head, and a sword in his hand. It was a magnificent weapon; the pommel and guard were made of walrus ivory, without any silver, but the blade was very sharp and there was never any rust on it. He called this sword 'Leg-Biter', and he never let it out of his sight.

Geirmund had not been there long before he fell in love with Olaf's daughter, Thurid; he asked Olaf for her hand in marriage, but Olaf rejected the proposal. Geirmund then bribed Thorgerd with money to help him achieve his ends. Thorgerd accepted the money, for it was no small sum; then she raised the question with Olaf, and said that in her opinion their daughter could not make a better marriage – 'for he is a great warrior, and wealthy and generous.'

'I won't oppose you in this any more than anything else,' said Olaf, 'although I would be happier if Thurid married some other man.'

Thorgerd went away, well pleased with this outcome, and told Geirmund how matters stood. He thanked her for her help and resolution. Geirmund now renewed his proposal of marriage, and this time it was accepted without demur. After that, Geirmund and Thurid were betrothed, the wedding to take place at Hjardarholt late that winter. The feast was attended by many guests, for the hall had been completed by then.

One of the guests at the feast was Ulf Uggason, who composed a poem about Olaf Hoskuldsson and the carved legends depicted in the hall, and this poem he recited at the feast; it is called the 'House Lay', and is an excellent poem.[1]

1. This poem, *Húsdrápa*, belongs to a well-established genre of Old Norse poetry, in which the poet describes visual representations of myths and heroic legends. Several verses of Ulf's 'House Lay' are still extant, in *Snorri's Edda*; they describe some of the scene-

Olaf rewarded him generously for the poem. He also gave splendid gifts to all the most important people who had attended the feast. Olaf was thought to have increased his prestige by this feast.

30. Geirmund and Thurid part

THE marriage between Geirmund and Thurid was not particularly happy, and they were both to blame for that. For three years Geirmund stayed at Hjardarholt with Olaf, but then he wanted to get away and announced that he was going to leave Thurid there and also their daughter, Groa, who was just a year old; but he refused to leave any money behind for them.

Thurid and her mother were furious over this, and told Olaf.

'What's the matter now, Thorgerd?' said Olaf. 'Is the Norwegian not so generous now as he was that autumn when he wanted to become your son-in-law?'

They got nowhere with Olaf, for he was a very peaceable man; he also said the child should remain there until she was old enough to take care of herself.

When Geirmund left, Olaf gave him the merchant-ship with all its fittings. Geirmund thanked him warmly and said it was a most generous gift. Then he made the ship ready, and put out from Laxriver Estuary before a light north-easterly breeze; but the wind dropped as soon as they got as far out as the islands. He lay at anchor off Oxen Island for a fortnight, without being able to get away.

It was about that time that Olaf had to leave home to see to his driftage.[1] Then his daughter called some of the servants

carvings in Olaf's hall at Hjardarholt, including Baldur's funeral, the swimming contest between Heimdall and Loki, and Thor's fight with the World-Serpent.

Ulf Uggason is also mentioned briefly in *Njal's Saga*, and a stanza by him is quoted there (Chapter 102).

1. Although Iceland, according to the early historians, was said to have been well-wooded when the first settlers arrived, the 'woods'

and told them to accompany her. She also took the child with her. There were ten of them in all. They launched Olaf's ferry-boat, and Thurid told them to row and sail down Hvammsfjord. When they reached the islands she told them to lower the dinghy they had on board. Thurid got into the dinghy with two of the men, and told the others to look after the ferry until she returned.

She took the child in her arms and told the men to row across the channel to Geirmund's ship. Then she took a gimlet out of the locker in the prow and handed it to one of her companions, telling him to get into the ship's tow-boat and bore a hole in it so that it would be useless if it were needed in a hurry. Then she had herself put ashore, still carrying the child in her arms. It was now sunrise. She walked up the gangway and on to the ship. All the crew were asleep. She went over to the hammock in which Geirmund was sleeping. His sword, 'Leg-Biter', was hanging from a peg. Thurid laid the little girl, Groa, in the hammock, seized hold of 'Leg-Biter', and took it away with her. Then she left the ship and went back to her companions.

The baby now began to cry, and Geirmund woke up. He sat up and recognized the child, and realized who must have done this. He jumped to his feet and reached for his sword, but could not find it, as was only to be expected. He went over to the gunwale and saw Thurid and her companions rowing away from the ship. Geirmund called to his men and told them to jump into the tow-boat and row after them. They did so, but when they had gone only a short distance the dark-blue sea came pouring in, and they turned back to the ship.

Then Geirmund called out to Thurid and asked her to come back and return the sword 'Leg-Biter' – 'and take your daughter with you and have as much money as you want.'

---

were mostly dwarf birch and unsuitable for building purposes. To make up for this scarcity of timber, driftwood was used to supplement imports from Norway (cf. Chapter 24, where Olaf Hoskulds-son used driftwood as well as forest-timber in the building of Hjardarholt); and driftage rights were a valuable asset which could be sold or rented to inland farmers.

'How badly do you want your sword back?' said Thurid.

'I'd much rather lose a fortune than lose my sword,' replied Geirmund.

'Then you shall never have it back,' said Thurid. 'You have treated us disgracefully, and you will never see me again.'

Geirmund said, 'There will be no luck for you in taking that sword away.'

She said she would take that risk.

'Then I lay this curse upon it,' said Geirmund. 'May this sword bring about the death of the man in your family who would be the greatest loss, and may it come about in the most atrocious way.'

After that, Thurid went home to Hjardarholt. Olaf had returned home by then, and he disapproved strongly of what she had done; but there the matter rested.

Thurid gave the sword 'Leg-Biter' to her cousin Bolli, for she loved him no less than her own brothers. Bolli carried the sword for a long time thereafter.

Geirmund and his companions now got a favourable wind and put out to sea, and reached Norway in the autumn. One night they foundered on a submerged reef off Stad, and Geirmund and all his crew perished. And that is the last we hear of Geirmund.

31. Olaf's dream

OLAF HOSKULDSSON remained at home in high esteem, as was written before.

There was a man called Gudmund Solmundsson, who lived at Asbjarnarness, north in Vididale. Gudmund was a wealthy man. He asked for Thurid's hand in marriage, and won her with a large dowry. Thurid was an intelligent woman, large-tempered and capable in every respect. Their sons were called Hall and Bardi and Stein and Steingrim; their daughters were called Gudrun and Olof.

Olaf's second daughter, Thorbjorg, was a very beautiful woman, of ample build; she was called Thorbjorg the Stout She was married west in Vatnsfjord to an excellent man called Asgeir Knattarson.[1]

Thorbjorg was later married to Vermund Thorgrimsson, and they had a daughter called Thorfinna, who was the wife of Thorstein Kuggason.

Olaf's third daughter, Bergthora, was married west in Djupafjord to a man called Thorhall the Priest.[2]

Olaf the Peacock had many valuable beasts among his livestock. He had a magnificent ox called Harri, dapple grey in colour, and bigger than any other cattle. He had four horns: two of them were large and well-placed, the third stood straight up in the air, and the fourth grew out of his forehead and curled down below his eyes; he used this horn for breaking ice. He used to scrape the snow with his hooves, like a horse, to get at the grass.

One very severe winter the ox went away from Hjardarholt to a place in the Breidafjord Dales which is now known as Harrastead. There he stayed throughout the winter with sixteen other cattle, and found grazing for them all. In the spring the ox returned to the home pastures to a place known as Harrabol, on the Hjardarholt estate.

When Harri was eighteen years old his ice-breaker fell off, and that same autumn Olaf had him slaughtered. Next night

1. *Their son was Kjartan, the father of Thorvald, the father of Thord, the father of Snorri* [d. 1194], *the father of Thorvald. From them stems the Vatnsfirding kin.*
Thorvald Snorrason (d. 1228) was the son-in-law of the great Icelandic historian Snorri Sturluson (1179-1242). Snorri wrote *Heimskringla* (History of the Kings of Norway), and compiled *Snorri's Edda*, a textbook on poetics. It has also been suggested that he was the author of *Egil's Saga* (cf. *King Harald's Saga*, Penguin Classics, 1966, Introduction).

2. *Thorhall was the son of Oddi Yrarson. Their son was Kjartan, the father of Smith-Sturla, who was the foster-father of Thord Gilsson, the father of Sturla.*
This Sturla, Hvamm-Sturla as he was called, was Snorri Sturluson's father.

Olaf dreamed that a woman came to him; she was big and angry-looking.

'Are you asleep?' said the woman.

Olaf said he was awake.

'You are asleep, but that makes no difference,' said the woman. 'You have had my son killed and returned him to me mutilated; and for that you shall live to see your own son drenched in blood by my doing, and I shall choose the one whom I know you would least want to lose.'

With that she vanished. Olaf woke up, and thought he could still see a glimpse of her. He was greatly disturbed by the dream and told it to his friends, but no one could interpret it to his liking. He preferred to listen to the interpretations of those who said it had been a false dream he had dreamed.

32. Gudrun Osvif's-daughter

THERE was a man called Osvif Helgason.[1] He was a great sage, and lived at Laugar in Sælingsdale. The farm at Laugar lies to the south of Sælingsdale River, opposite Tongue.

1. *Osvif's father, Helgi, was the son of Ottar, the son of Bjorn the Easterner, the son of Ketil Flat-Nose, the son of Bjorn Buna* (cf. Chapter 1). *Osvif's mother was called Nidbjorg, the daughter of Kadlin, the daughter of Ganger-Hrolf, the son of Oxen-Thorir, who was an excellent chieftain east in Oslo Fjord; he was so called because he owned three islands with 80 oxen on each, and he gave one island with all its oxen to King Hakon the Good. This gift became very renowned.*

Ganger-Hrolf (*Göngu-Hrólfr*, known as Rollo in French sources) was the Norwegian viking who founded the Norman dynasty in France. He captured Rouen late in the ninth century and was eventually granted the dukedom of Normandy by King Charles the Simple of France in 911. His nickname, Ganger (the Walker), alludes to the fact that he was too huge and heavy for any horse to carry. In nearly all other Icelandic sources, including *Heimskringla* (History of the Kings of Norway), Ganger-Hrolf is said to be the son not of Oxen-Thorir but of Earl Rognvald of More in Norway (cf. the

Osvif's wife was called Thordis, the daughter of Thjodolf the Short. One of their sons was called Ospak, another Helgi, the third Vandrad, the fourth Torrad, and the fifth Thorolf. All the Osvifssons were stalwart men.

Their daughter was called Gudrun, and she was the loveliest woman in Iceland at that time, and also the most intelligent. Gudrun Osvif's-daughter was a woman of such courtliness that whatever finery other women wore, they seemed like mere trinkets beside hers. She was the shrewdest and best-spoken of all women; and she had a generous disposition.

A woman called Thorhalla the Gossip lived at Osvif's farm; she was distantly related to him. She had two sons, called Odd and Stein. They were brawny men, and did much of the hard work on Osvif's estate. They were great tale-bearers, as was their mother, and were not much liked; but the Osvifssons thought very highly of them.

The farmer over at Sælingsdale Tongue was called Thorarin, the son of Thorir Sæling. He was a capable farmer; he was a big, strong man, and owned good lands, but not much livestock. Osvif wanted to buy some land from him, because he himself was short of land but had a lot of livestock. So the outcome was that Osvif bought from Thorarin all the land he owned on both sides of the valley from Gnupaskard to Stakkagill; the land there is rich and fertile. Osvif ran a shieling for grazing livestock there.[1] He always kept a large household, and lived in the most splendid style.

There is a farm west in Saurby called Hol, and two brothers

---

genealogy of the Orkney earls descended from Groa Thorstein's-daughter, Chapter 4). A fictitious and highly entertaining *Ganger-Hrolf's Saga* was written in Iceland in the fourteenth century, but has no bearing on the life of the historical Rollo.

1. Transhumance, the custom of moving livestock seasonally to different pastures, was common to many mountainous countries including Scotland, Norway and Switzerland. The 'shieling' (cf. Norwegian *sæter*, Swiss *chalet*) refers both to the summer grazing as well as to the hut built to accomodate the herdsmen and dairy-maids. This particular shieling on Osvif's estate later becomes the setting for the central tragedy of the saga (Chapter 55).

lived there with their brother-in-law. The brothers, who were well-born men, were called Thorkel Whelp and Knut. The brother-in-law who shared the farm with them was called Thord, and he was known as Ingunnarson, after his mother.[1]

Thord was handsome and vigorous, a man of great ability and a very skilled lawyer. He was married to Aud, the sister of Thorkel and Knut; she was neither attractive nor accomplished, and Thord had little love for her. He had married her mainly for money, for there was much wealth there. The farm had flourished from the time that Thord had come to help the brothers run it.

33. Gudrun's dreams

A MAN called Gest Oddleifsson lived west at Hagi in Barda-strand. He was a great chieftain and a very wise man, and prescient in many ways. All the most important people were his friends, and many came to him for advice.[2]

Gest used to ride to the Althing every summer, and would always spend a night at Hol. On one of these occasions, when Gest had spent the night at Hol on his way to the Althing as usual, he left there early in the morning, for he had a very long way to go – he planned to arrive that evening at Thykkvawood, the home of his brother-in-law Armod Thorgrimsson; Armod was married to Gest's sister, Thorunn, and their sons were called Ornolf and Halldor.

Gest rode east from Saurby, and after a day's ride he arrived at the baths at Sælingsdale, where he rested for a while.[3] Gudrun

1. *Thord's father was Glub Geirason.*
People in Iceland sometimes used their matronymic, particularly if the father died when they were very young.

2. Gest Oddleifsson is mentioned in many sagas, including *Njal's Saga* (Chapter 103), where his conversion to Christianity is described. In all sources he is depicted as a benevolent sage who could see into the future.

3. Osvif's farm was called *Laugar* (literally, 'Baths'), and derived its name from the hot-springs there; these 'baths' were open-air pools

Osvif's-daughter came to the baths and welcomed her kinsman Gest warmly; he returned her greeting affectionately and they fell into conversation, for both of them were intelligent and fluent talkers.

Later that day Gudrun said, 'I should like you, kinsman, to come to our house tonight with all your companions. This is also my father's wish, though he allowed me the privilege of bringing you this invitation; and he also sends word that he wants you to stay here with us every time you are travelling this way.'

Gest was gratified and said it was a generous invitation, but that he would be riding on as he had planned.

Gudrun said, 'I have had many dreams this winter, and there are four dreams in particular which have disturbed me greatly; but no one has interpreted them to my satisfaction, although I'm not just asking for wishful interpretations of them.'

'Tell me your dreams,' said Gest. 'It may be that I can make something of them.'

Gudrun said, 'I dreamed I was outside, standing near a stream. I was wearing a head-dress on my head, but I felt that it didn't become me, and so I was anxious to change it. A lot of people warned me not to, but I paid no attention to that and tore the head-dress from my head and threw it into the stream; and that was the end of that dream.'

Gudrun went on, 'At the beginning of my second dream, I dreamed I was standing by a lake, and it seemed to me that a silver ring appeared on my hand, and I was sure the ring was mine. It seemed to become me extremely well, and I thought it a wonderful treasure and was determined to keep it forever. But when I least expected it, the ring slipped off my hand into the lake and I never saw it again. This loss I felt much more keenly than I would have expected from losing a mere ring; and with that I woke up.'

'That was no less of a dream,' was all that Gest said.

Gudrun went on, 'In my third dream I dreamed I was wearing

---

of natural hot water which were used for laundry as well as personal ablutions, not only by members of the household but also by neighbours.

a gold ring on my hand, and it seemed to me the ring was mine and that it made up for my previous loss. I had the feeling that I would enjoy this ring longer than the other one; but it didn't seem to become me all that much better, to the extent that gold is more precious than silver. Then I seemed to stumble and tried to steady myself with my hand, and the gold ring struck against a stone and broke in two, and the two pieces seemed to bleed. What I felt now was more like grief than mere regret for a loss. Then it occurred to me that there might have been some flaw in the ring, and when I looked at the pieces I thought I could see many other flaws in them, and yet I felt sure that the ring would have stayed whole if I had looked after it better; and with that, this dream came to an end.'

'The dreams are not drying up,' said Gest.

Gudrun went on, 'In my fourth dream I dreamed I was wearing on my head a helmet of gold set with many precious stones, and this treasure seemed to be mine. The only fault I could find with it was that it seemed rather too heavy, for I could scarcely cope with it and had to tilt my head under it. I didn't blame the helmet for that and had no intention of parting with it; but the helmet toppled off my head into the water of Hvammsfjord, and after that I woke up. And now all the dreams are told.'

Gest answered, 'I can see clearly what these dreams signify, but you will find it all rather monotonous, for I shall interpret them all in much the same way.

'You will have four husbands, and I suspect that when you marry the first one it will not be a love-match for you. When you dreamed that you were wearing a large head-dress on your head, and that it ill became you, this means that you will have little love for him. And when you took it off and threw it into the water, this means that you will leave him. That's why people say that something is "thrown to the sea" when a person discards something without getting anything in return.'

Gest went on, 'In your second dream you dreamed you had a silver ring on your hand; this means that you will be married to a second husband, an excellent man whom you will love dearly but only enjoy for a short time. I wouldn't be surprised if you were to lose him by drowning; and that's all I shall make of that dream.

'In your third dream you dreamed you had a gold ring on your hand; this means that you will have a third husband, but he will not excel your second husband to the same extent that you think this metal rarer and more precious than silver. I have the feeling that there will have been a change of faith by that time, and that this husband of yours will have embraced this new faith, which we think is much the more exalted. You dreamed that the ring broke in two, partly through your own carelessness, and that you saw blood coming from the two pieces; this means that your husband will be slain. You will then be able to see more clearly the flaws that were in that marriage.'

Gest went on, 'In your fourth dream you dreamed you were wearing on your head a helmet of gold set with precious stones, and you found it heavy to bear; this means that you will have a fourth husband. He will be the greatest chieftain of them all, and he will dominate you completely. And when you thought it toppled into Hvammsfjord, this means that he will encounter that same fjord on the last day of his life. And I shall make no more of that dream.'

Gudrun flushed deep red while the dreams were being interpreted, but did not utter a word until Gest had finished. Then she said, 'You would have found me rosier prophecies if I had given you material for them; but accept my thanks none the less for interpreting my dreams. Yet it's a grave thought, if all this is to come to pass.'

Then Gudrun repeated her invitation that he should stay there for the rest of the day, and said that he and Osvif would have many profound things to discuss.

'I must ride on as I had planned,' replied Gest. 'But you must give my greetings to your father, and tell him also from me that the time will come when he and I shall be much closer neighbours, and we shall have plenty of time for talking then if we are allowed to talk together.'

With that, Gudrun went home and Gest rode on his way. At the fence of the homefield at Hjardarholt he met one of Olaf's servants, who invited Gest to the house at Olaf's request. Gest said he would like to see Olaf that day, but would spend the night at Thykkvawood.

The servant went home at once and gave Olaf the message. Olaf had some horses fetched, and rode to meet Gest with several companions. They met at Lja River. Olaf welcomed him warmly and invited him to his house with all his following. Gest thanked him for the invitation and said he would ride home with him to see his house, but would stay the night with Armod. Gest stayed only a short while, but looked all over the house and admired it, and said that nothing had been spared for it.

Olaf accompanied Gest as far as Lax River. The foster-brothers, Kjartan and Bolli, had been out swimming there during the day; this was a sport in which the Olafssons always took the lead. There were many young men from other farms swimming there too. As the company rode up, Kjartan and Bolli came running out of the water, and they were almost fully dressed by the time Gest and Olaf got there. Gest looked at all the young men for a while, and then told Olaf which one was Kjartan, and which Bolli, too, and then he pointed out with his spear-shaft each of the sons of Olaf and named by name all those who were there. There were many other fine-looking men there who had just come from the swimming and were sitting on the river-bank beside Kjartan and Bolli; but Gest said he could not discern the family resemblance to Olaf in any of those young men.

'No one can exaggerate your wisdom, Gest,' said Olaf. 'You can pick out people you have never seen before and name them. But now I want you to tell me which one of these young men will be the greatest?'

'That will turn out much in accordance with your own affections,' replied Gest. 'Kjartan will be the most highly thought of, for as long as he lives.'

Then Gest spurred his horse and rode away. A little later Gest's son, Thord the Short, rode up to his side and said, 'What's the matter, father? Why are you shedding tears?'

'It will do no good to say it,' replied Gest, 'but I can't bring myself to keep silent over something that will happen in your time. It will not surprise me if Bolli one day stands over Kjartan's body and earns his own death thereby; and that is a terrible thing to know about such fine young men.'

With that they rode on to the Althing, which was uneventful that year.

34. Gudrun's first marriage

THERE was a man called Thorvald, who was the son of Halldor Garpsdale-Priest. He lived at Garpsdale, in Gilsfjord. He was a wealthy man, but no hero. At the Althing he asked for the hand of Gudrun Osvif's-daughter, who was fifteen years old at the time. The proposal was received not unfavourably, but Osvif said that his terms would make it clear that Thorvald and Gudrun were not of equal standing. Thorvald spoke meekly, and said it was a wife he was asking for, not money. So Gudrun was betrothed to Thorvald, and Osvif alone decided the terms of the marriage contract; it was stipulated that Gudrun should be in charge of their money as soon as they were sharing the same bed, and be entitled to one half of all the estate, no matter how long or little their marriage lasted. Thorvald was also to buy precious things for her, so that no woman of comparable wealth should own finer jewellery than Gudrun; but the value of the estate was not to be affected by such outlays.

People now rode home from the Althing. Gudrun was not consulted about all this, and she showed the strongest displeasure; but there the matter rested.

The wedding took place at Garpsdale in late summer. Gudrun had little love for Thorvald, and was hard to please in the buying of valuables. In all the Westfjords there were no jewels so costly that Gudrun did not consider them her due, and she repaid Thorvald with animosity if he failed to buy them, however expensive they might be.

Thord Ingunnarson made himself very friendly with Thorvald and Gudrun, and spent a lot of time with them, and there was much talk about an affair between Thord and Gudrun.

On one occasion Gudrun asked Thorvald to buy some gift for

her. Thorvald said she showed no moderation, and slapped her on the face.

At that, Gudrun said, 'You have now given me what every woman wants above all – good colouring; and you have taught me to stop bothering you for things.'

That same evening, Thord arrived. Gudrun told him how she had been insulted, and asked him how she should repay it.

Thord smiled and said, 'I have a good solution for this. Make him a shirt with such a wide neck-opening that by wearing it he gives you grounds for divorcing him.'[1]

Gudrun raised no objection to this, and they dropped the subject. That same spring Gudrun declared herself divorced from Thorvald and went home to Laugar. After that there was a division of the whole estate, and Gudrun got a half of it; it had increased in value by then. They had been together for two years.

That same spring Ingunn, Thord's mother, sold her farm in Kroksfjord and went west to Skalmarness; her farm has been known as Ingunnarstead ever since.[2]

At that time a man called Hallstein the Priest was living at Hallsteinsness, on the west side of Thorskafjord. He was a powerful man, but rather unpopular.

35. Gudrun's second marriage

THERE was a man called Kotkel, who had only recently arrived in Iceland. His wife was called Grima. Their sons were Hallbjorn Sleekstone-Eye and Stigandi. These people had come from the Hebrides. They were all extremely skilled in witchcraft and were great sorcerers. Hallstein the Priest took them into his

1. According to early Icelandic law, it was ground for divorce if the husband wore effeminate clothing; normally, men wore high-necked shirts, whereas women's dresses were very *décolleté*. The same applied if a woman wore masculine clothing (cf. Chapter 35).

2. *Ingunn had been married to Glum Geirason, as was written before.*

care and settled them at Urdir in Skalmarfjord; their presence there was not well liked.

That summer, Gest Oddleifsson went to the Althing, and went by boat to Saurby as was his custom. He stayed overnight at Hol in Saurby. The people there lent him horses as usual. Thord Ingunnarson now joined Gest on his journey, and they came to Laugar in Sælingsdale. Gudrun Osvif's-daughter rode to the Althing too, and Thord Ingunnarson accompanied her.

One day when they were riding across Blaskogaheath in fine weather, Gudrun said, 'Is it true, Thord, that your wife Aud always wears breeches with gores in the crutch, like a man's, and cross-garters almost down to her shoes?'

He said he had not noticed it.

'There can't be much truth in the story, then,' said Gudrun, 'if you haven't noticed it. But why, then, is she known as Breeches-Aud?'

'I don't imagine she has been called that for very long,' said Thord.

Gudrun said, 'It will matter much more to her if she keeps that name for a long time to come.'

After that, people arrived at the Althing; nothing much happened there. Thord spent a lot of time in Gest's booth, always talking to Gudrun.

One day Thord Ingunnarson asked Gudrun what the penalty was for a woman who always wore breeches like a man's.

Gudrun replied, 'The same penalty applies to women in a case like that as to a man who wears a neck-opening so wide that his nipples are exposed : both are grounds for divorce.'

Then Thord said, 'Would you advise me to declare myself divorced from Aud here at the Althing, or back in my own district where I can get support from others? For those who are likely to feel offended by this are proud-minded people.'

Gudrun answered after a while, 'Only idlers wait till evening.'

Thord jumped to his feet at once and went to the Law Rôck, where he named witnesses and declared himself divorced from Aud, on the ground that she wore gored breeches like masculine women do. Aud's brothers were greatly annoyed, but there the matter rested. Thord rode from the Althing with the Osvifssons.

When Aud heard the news she said:

> *'I'm glad I know*
> *I've been abandoned.'*

After that, Thord rode west to Saurby with eleven men for the division of the estate, and everything went smoothly, for Thord did not quibble about how the money was divided. Thord drove a large number of livestock east to Laugar. Then he asked for the hand of Gudrun; there was no difficulty in reaching agreement with Osvif, and Gudrun raised no objection. The wedding was to take place at Laugar ten weeks before winter. It was a magnificent feast.

The marriage between Gudrun and Thord was happy.

The only reason why Thorkel Whelp and Knut did not bring an action against Thord Ingunnarson was that they could not get any support for it.

Next summer the men of Hol had their shieling in Hvammsdale; Aud was at the shieling too. The men of Laugar had their shieling in Lambadale, which cuts west into the mountains off Sælingsdale. Aud asked the boy who looked after their sheep how often he met the shepherd from Laugar. He said they met all the time, as was to be expected, since there was only a ridge separating the two shielings.

Aud then said, 'Go and see the shepherd from Laugar today and find out for me who are at the shieling and who are staying at home on the farm; and remember to speak respectfully about Thord, as you should.'

The boy promised to do as she asked. In the evening when the boy came back, Aud asked him what he had to report.

'I've heard news which will please you,' said the shepherd. 'There's now a wide floor between Thord's bed and Gudrun's, for she is up at the shieling and he is toiling hard at housebuilding: Osvif and he are the only men at home on the farm.'

'You have done well to find this out,' she said. 'Have two horses ready saddled at bedtime.'

The shepherd did as she told him, and a little before sunset Aud mounted her horse, and she was certainly wearing breeches then. The shepherd rode the other horse and could scarcely keep up with her, so furiously did she spur her horse. She rode south across Sælingsdale Heath and did not pull up until she reached the fence of the homefield at Laugar. There she dismounted and told the shepherd to look after the horses while she went to the house. Aud went up to the door, and found it open. She went into the living-room and over to the bed-closet in which Thord lay sleeping. The door of the bed-closet had been pulled to, but the bolt was not fastened. She went into the bed-closet; Thord lay on his back, sound asleep. She woke him up, and he turned on his side when he saw that a man had come in; Aud drew a short-sword and lunged at him with it, wounding him severely; the sword caught his right arm and gashed him across both nipples. So fierce was the thrust that the sword stuck fast in the bed-boards.

With that, Aud went back to her horse and jumped into the saddle, and rode back home.

Thord tried to jump to his feet after he received the wounds but could not, for he was weakened by loss of blood. Osvif now woke up and asked what had happened, and Thord said he had been wounded. Osvif asked him if he knew who had done it, and got up and bandaged his injuries. Thord said he thought it had been Aud. Osvif offered to ride after her; he said she probably had not brought many men with her, and that her punishment would not be in doubt. Thord would not hear of it on any account, saying that she had only done what she had to.

Aud got back home about sunrise, and her brothers asked her where she had been. Aud said she had been to Laugar, and told them what she had gone there to do. They were pleased about it, but said she had probably not done enough.

Thord was in bed with his injuries for a long time. His chest wounds healed well, but he never recovered the full use of his arm.

All was quiet that winter. In the following spring, Ingunn, Thord's mother, came east from Skalmarness, and he received her well. She said she wanted to place herself under Thord's care, for Kotkel and his wife and sons were making life unbearable with their thieving and sorcery, and enjoyed the protection of Hallstein the Priest.

Thord wasted no time, and said he was going to bring these thieves to justice even though it meant offending Hallstein. He set off at once with nine companions; Ingunn also went with him. He took a boat from Tjaldaness, and sailed west to Skalmarness. Thord had all his mother's goods brought down to the boat, but the livestock were to be driven round by the heads of the fjords. There were twelve of them altogether in the boat, including Ingunn and another woman.

Thord now went to Kotkel's farm with his nine men. Kotkel's sons were not at home. Thord then summonsed Kotkel and Grima and their sons for witchcraft and theft, on pain of outlawry. He referred this case to the Althing, and then returned to the boat.

When Thord had sailed a short distance from land, Hallbjorn Sleekstone-Eye and Stigandi returned home, and Kotkel told them what had happened. The brothers were furious at this and said that no one had ever openly challenged them before so aggressively. Then Kotkel erected a large ritual-platform and they all climbed onto it; there they chanted potent incantations – these were magic spells. And presently a tempest arose.

Thord Ingunnarson and his companions, who were still at sea, realized that the storm was directed against him. The ship was driven west beyond Skalmarness. Thord showed great courage and seamanship. People on shore saw him throw all the cargo overboard, everything heavy except the people themselves. Those ashore had hopes that Thord would now be able to make land, for he had passed the point where the reefs were worst. But then a breaker reared up near the shore, where no one had ever known this to happen before; the breaker struck the ship so violently that it overturned at once. Thord and all his companions were drowned there, and the ship was smashed to pieces.

The keel was washed up at a place which has since been known as Kjalar Isle. Thord's shield was washed up on an island called Skjaldar Isle. Thord's body and the bodies of his companions were soon washed ashore, and a mound was raised over them at a place which has been called Haugsness ever since.

36. Kotkel in Laxriverdale

THE news spread far and wide, and was everywhere condemned; everyone felt that death was the only proper end for people who performed the kind of sorcery that Kotkel and his family had done.

Gudrun was deeply grieved at Thord's death. She was with child then, and her time was near. Soon she gave birth to a boy; he was sprinkled with water and named Thord.

At that time Snorri the Priest was living at Helgafell. He was a kinsman and friend of Osvif's, and Gudrun and her family always looked to him for support.

Snorri the Priest accepted an invitation to Laugar. Gudrun then told him of her troubles, and he said he would give his support when he thought the time right; and as a solace to Gudrun, he offered to foster her child. Gudrun accepted that, and said she would rely on his foresight. This boy, Thord, was known as Thord Cat.[1]

After that, Gest Oddleifsson went to see Hallstein the Priest and gave him the choice of sending the sorcerers away – or else, he said, he would kill them, however belatedly. Hallstein chose quickly and ordered them to leave at once and not to stop anywhere west of Dalaheath, adding that they deserved better to be killed.

Kotkel and his family went away, and the only belongings they took with them were four stud-horses. The stallion was black; he was a big, handsome animal, and experienced at fighting.[2] There is nothing told of their journey until they came to

1. *Thord Cat was the father of the poet Stuf.*
Gudrun's grandson, Stuf, was one of the many Icelandic poets who were members of the court of King Harald Hardradi of Norway (d. 1066). There is an entertaining account of Stuf's first encounter with King Harald in *Stuf's Story*. Some of his poetry is quoted in *King Harald's Saga*.
2. Horse-fighting was a popular sport in early Iceland. Two stallions were pitted against one another, spurred on by their

Thorleik Hoskuldsson at Kambsness. Thorleik offered to buy the horses off them, for he could see they were outstanding animals.

'You can have them on one condition,' said Kotkel. 'In return for the horses, you must find us a place to stay here in this neighbourhood.'

'Isn't that rather a high price to pay for the horses?' said Thorleik. 'I've heard that you have trouble on your hands in this district.'

'You must mean the men of Laugar,' said Kotkel.

Thorleik said he did.

Then Kotkel said, 'Our quarrel with Gudrun and her brothers isn't at all what you've been told. People have been heaping slanders on us without cause; as far as that's concerned, you're quite safe to take the horses. From all we've heard about you, we won't be at the mercy of the people in this district if we have your protection.'

Thorleik now changed his attitude, for he thought the horses were excellent animals, and Kotkel pleaded his cause cleverly. So Thorleik took the horses, and gave Kotkel and his family a place to live at Leidolfstead in Laxriverdale, and supplied them with livestock.

The men of Laugar came to hear of this, and the Osvifssons wanted to attack Kotkel and his sons at once. But Osvif said, 'We must follow Snorri the Priest's advice and leave this task to others, for it won't be long before Kotkel's neighbours will have fresh complaints against them, and Thorleik will have to bear the brunt of that, as he deserves. Many of those who have sided with him before will soon become his enemies. But if no one else has driven them out of the district or put them to death within the next three years, I shall not discourage you then from doing Kotkel and his family any harm you like.'

Gudrun and her brothers agreed to this.

Kotkel and his family did little work to support themselves, yet they needed to buy neither hay nor food for the winter. Their presence there was much resented, but no one dared to annoy them for fear of Thorleik.

handlers wielding goads. These sporting occasions all too often ended in brawls and blood-feuds – cf. *Njal's Saga*, Chapter 59.

37. Kotkel's death

AT the Althing one summer, Thorleik Hoskuldsson was sitting in his booth when a tall man came walking in. He greeted Thorleik, who returned the greeting and asked this man his name and where he came from. He said he was called Eldgrim and that he lived in Borgarfjord, on a farm called Eldgrimstead, which stands in the valley that cuts west into the mountains between Mull and Grisartongue. That valley is now called Grimsdale.

'I've heard tell that you're no coward,' said Thorleik.

'I've come to see you,' said Eldgrim, 'because I want to buy from you those valuable stud-horses which Kotkel gave you last year.'

'The horses are not for sale,' replied Thorleik.

Eldgrim said, 'I am offering you an equal number of stud-horses in exchange, and so much more besides that people will say I'm paying you double price for the horses.'

'I'm no huckster,' said Thorleik, 'and you'll never get the horses, even if you offer treble the price.'

Eldgrim said, 'It's no exaggeration to say that you're a proud and stubborn man. I only hope you'll be forced to part with them one day, and for a much less generous price than the one I've just offered you.'

Thorleik flushed dark at these words and said, 'You'll have to come much closer, Eldgrim, before you bully me out of these horses.'

'You think it impossible that you'd ever be beaten by me,' said Eldgrim. 'But this summer I shall come and take a look at the horses – and then we'll see which of us keeps them after that.'

'Keep your promise,' said Thorleik, 'but don't offer me unfair odds.'

They talked no more about it. Those present remarked that these two would get what they deserved. Then people went home from the Althing, and there the matter rested.

Early one morning at Hrutstead, the farm of Hrut Herjolfsson, a man happened to go outside. When he came back in, Hrut asked him if he had anything to report. The man said he had nothing to report except that he had seen someone riding across the shallows up to where Thorleik's horses were – 'and there the man dismounted and rounded them up.'

Hrut asked where the horses were.

The farmhand said, 'They were keeping close to their usual pasture, grazing in your meadows down below the fence.'

'My nephew Thorleik has certainly never been very particular where he grazes his beasts,' said Hrut, 'so I think it hardly likely that the horses are being driven away on his orders.'

With that, Hrut jumped to his feet. He was in his drawers and wearing a shirt, and now he threw on a grey fur-cloak. He took hold of a gold-inlaid halberd which King Harald Grey-Cloak had given him. He stalked out of the house and saw a man driving the horses down below the fence. Hrut went to meet him, and saw that it was Eldgrim who was driving the horses. Hrut greeted him, and Eldgrim returned the greeting, but rather tardily. Hrut asked him where he was going with the horses.

'I won't try to hide it from you,' replied Eldgrim, 'even though I'm aware of the kinship between you and Thorleik: I've come to fetch these horses, and I don't intend him ever to see them again. I have kept the promise I made him at the Althing, and have come for the horses alone and unaided.'

'It's no great achievement to take the horses away while Thorleik is asleep in his bed,' said Hrut. 'The only way to carry out the deal you made would be to see him before you leave the district with the horses.'

'Go and warn Thorleik if you want to,' said Eldgrim, 'for as you can see I left home so equipped that I would be only too pleased if Thorleik and I happened to meet.' And with that he brandished the barbed spear he was holding. He had a helmet on his head and was girded with a sword, and carried a shield at his side; and he was wearing a coat of mail.

'I'd rather try something else than go over to Kambsness,' said Hrut, 'for I am heavy of foot. But I won't allow my nephew

Thorleik to be robbed if I can help it, even though there's little love lost between us.'

'Do you mean you're going to try to take the horses away from me?' said Eldgrim.

Hrut replied, 'I shall give you other stud-horses if you will let these go, though they may not be quite as good as these ones.'

'That's all very well, Hrut,' said Eldgrim, 'but now that I've got my hands on Thorleik's horses you won't take them off me, either with bribes or threats.'

Then Hrut replied, 'I think the choice you're making will be the worst for both of us.'

Eldgrim now tried to get away, and spurred his horse; and when Hrut saw this he raised his halberd and drove it between Eldgrim's shoulder-blades so hard that the coat of mail burst open at the impact and the halberd came out through his chest. Eldgrim fell dead from his horse, as was only to be expected. Hrut then covered up the body; the place is called Eldgrimsholt, and lies to the south of Kambsness.

Hrut now rode down to Kambsness and told Thorleik what had happened. Thorleik was enraged over it and felt he had been greatly insulted by Hrut's action, whereas Hrut felt he had done him a great favour. Thorleik said that not only had Hrut's motives been bad, but that no good would come of it in return. Hrut said that Thorleik must do as he pleased, and they parted on unfriendly terms.

Hrut was eighty years of age when he killed Eldgrim, and his prestige was greatly enhanced by it.

Thorleik thought no more highly of Hrut for all the credit he gained from this deed, for he was in no doubt that he himself would have got the better of Eldgrim if they had fought it out, considering how little it had taken to overcome him. So Thorleik went to see his tenants, Kotkel and Grima, and asked them to do something to humiliate Hrut. They took this up eagerly and said they would be delighted to do it. Thorleik then went back home.

A few days later, Kotkel and Grima and their sons set off from home at night-time. They climbed on to the roof of Hrut's house and made great incantations there. When the spells began, the people inside were at a loss to make out what was going on, but sweet was the singing they heard. Hrut alone recognized what these sounds meant and forbade anyone to look outside that night. 'Everyone who can must stay awake,' he said, 'and no harm will come to us if we do as I tell you.'

Yet they all fell asleep. Hrut stayed awake the longest, but in the end he slept too.

One of Hrut's sons was called Kari; he was then twelve years old, and was the most promising of all Hrut's sons. Hrut loved him dearly. Kari slept little or not at all, for it was against him that this sorcery was directed. He began to feel very restive, and eventually he got up and went to look outside; he walked into the spells, and fell down dead at once.

Hrut and his household woke up next morning and found the boy missing; he was discovered lying dead a short distance from the door. Hrut felt the loss very deeply, and had a mound raised over his son.

After that he rode to see Olaf Hoskuldsson and told him what had happened. Olaf was furious over it and said it had been very foolish to let such wicked people as Kotkel and his family live so close to them; he also said that Thorleik had chosen an evil part for himself in his dealings with Hrut, but added that it had gone much further than Thorleik could have intended. Olaf said that Kotkel and his wife and sons must be put to death immediately – 'however belatedly'.

Olaf and Hrut set out with fifteen men. When Kotkel and his family saw people riding to their house they fled up into the mountains. Hallbjorn Sleekstone-Eye was captured there and a bag was pulled over his head. Some of the men were left there to guard him while the others chased after Kotkel and Grima and Stigandi farther into the mountains. Kotkel and Grima were captured on the ridge between Haukadale and Laxriverdale, and were stoned to death there. A cairn of stones was heaped over their bodies, and the remains of it are still to be seen there; the place is called Skrattavardi.[1]

Stigandi escaped south over the ridge into Haukadale, and there they lost him.

1. Literally, 'Devils' Cairn'.

Hrut and his sons took Hallbjorn Sleekstone-Eye down to the sea, launched a boat and rowed with him some distance out from land; then they removed the bag from his head, and tied a stone round his neck. Hallbjorn turned his gaze towards the land, and the look in his eyes was far from pleasant.

Then Hallbjorn said, 'It was not a lucky day for our family when we came to this Kambsness and met with Thorleik. And now I lay this curse,' he went on, 'that Thorleik will enjoy little happiness there from this day on, and that all his successors at Kambsness will inherit nothing but trouble there.'

This curse is considered to have been very effective.

Then they drowned him and rowed back to land.

A little later Hrut went to see his nephew Olaf Hoskuldsson and told him he was not going to put up with matters as they stood between Thorleik and himself, and asked him to give him men to make an attack on Thorleik.

'It is not proper for you kinsmen to come to blows,' replied Olaf. 'Admittedly Thorleik has been the cause of a great deal of misfortune; but I would rather try to make peace between you, for you have always been patient in waiting for your due.'

'There can be no question of a settlement,' said Hrut. 'The breach between Thorleik and myself will never be healed, and if I had my way there would no longer be room for both of us to live in Laxriverdale.'

'You will not find it feasible to go further against Thorleik than I will allow,' said Olaf, 'and if you do, it is not unlikely that the valley will meet the mountain.'[1]

Hrut then realized that Olaf would not be budged, and went home very displeased. Things were quiet now, on the surface at least, for the rest of the year.

1. This phrase is evidently an allusion to *Isaiah* xl, 4: 'Every valley shall be exalted, and every mountain and hill shall be made low.' Olaf, the man of humility, is telling Hrut, the man of pride, that if he insists on action, his pride will be humbled by the force of Olaf's humility.

38. Stigandi is killed

MEANWHILE, Stigandi became an outlaw and caused a great deal of trouble.

There was a man called Thord, who lived at Hundadale. He was wealthy, but of little account. That summer it so happened that the ewes at Hundadale began to yield very little milk. People noticed that the woman who was looking after the ewes had acquired a lot of valuable things, and also that she would often disappear for hours on end without anyone knowing where she had been. Thord forced a confession out of her, and in her terror she admitted that a man often came to see her. 'He is a tall man,' she said, 'and I find him very handsome.'

Thord asked how soon this man was due to meet her again, and she said she thought it would be soon.

After that, Thord went to see Olaf and told him that Stigandi must be somewhere nearby, and asked him to go there with his men to capture him. Olaf wasted no time and went over to Hundadale, where the bondwoman was brought to him for questioning. Olaf asked her where Stigandi's hideout was. She said she did not know. Olaf offered to pay her if she would help them lay hands on Stigandi, and then she agreed.

That same day, as she was herding her ewes, Stigandi came to her. She welcomed him affectionately and offered to search his hair for lice. He laid his head in her lap, and soon fell asleep. Then she slipped away from under his head and went to Olaf and his men, and told them what she had done so far.

They made for Stigandi, and told one another that he must not be allowed to do what his brother had done and have the chance of putting his evil eye on anything. So they took a bag and pulled it over his head. Stigandi woke up at this but offered no resistance, for he was only one against many. There was a tear in the bag, and Stigandi could glimpse the hillside on the opposite side of the valley. It was a fine stretch of land, rich with grass; but suddenly it was as if a whirlwind came and turned the whole sward upside down, so that no grass has ever grown there since. The place is still called Brenna.[1]

After that they stoned Stigandi to death, and covered his body with a cairn. Olaf kept his word to the bondwoman and gave her her freedom, and she went with him home to Hjardarholt.

Hallbjorn Sleekstone-Eye was washed up from the sea soon after he was drowned. The place where he was buried is called Knarrarness; but he did not rest quietly in his grave.

A man called Thorkel the Bald was living at Thykkvawood, where his father had farmed before him. He was a very brave man, and extremely strong. One evening a cow went missing at Thykkvawood, and Thorkel and his farmhand went to look for it. It was after sunset, but there was bright moonlight. Thorkel said that they should search separately, and once he was by himself he thought he saw the cow on a hillock in front of him; but when he came closer it turned out to be no cow, but Hallbjorn Sleekstone-Eye. They charged one another fiercely; Hallbjorn gave ground, and when Thorkel was least expecting it, Hallbjorn slipped out of his grasp and sank into the ground. After that, Thorkel went home; the farmhand had found the missing cow and had already arrived. From then on, Hallbjorn Sleekstone-Eye gave no further trouble.

Both Thorbjorn the Feeble and Melkorka were now dead, and they rest in the same mound in Laxriverdale. Their son, Lambi Thorbjornsson, took over the farm. He was a great warrior, and was very wealthy. Lambi was more highly thought of than his father had been, because of his mother's family ties. He and Olaf were on good brotherly terms.

The winter after Kotkel's execution passed, and in the spring the brothers Olaf and Thorleik met. Olaf asked if Thorleik intended to stay on at his farm. Thorleik said he would.

'I have a request to make of you,' said Olaf. 'I want to ask you to start a new life, Thorleik, and go abroad. You will be considered a worthy man wherever you go. I think that our uncle, Hrut, feels himself deeply slighted by what you have done to him, and I would rather not risk having you living so

1. Literally, 'The Burnt Place'.

close to one another any longer. Hrut has strength on his side; his sons are self-willed men and great warriors. Because of our kinship, I would be in a very difficult position if you two kinsmen of mine were to fight in earnest.'

'I have no fears of being unable to hold my own against Hrut and his sons,' said Thorleik, 'and I would never leave the country on that account. But if it matters so much to you, Olaf, and you think it would put you in a difficult position, I will do as you ask; for I was never happier than when I was abroad. I also know that you will care for my son Bolli none the worse though I am far away; and Bolli is the one I love above all others.'

'You are doing the best thing if you do this for me,' said Olaf. 'And I shall certainly care for Bolli in the same way as I have always done, and hold him in no less love than I do my own sons.'

After that the two brothers parted with the warmest affection. Thorleik now sold up his estate and invested his money in going abroad. He bought a ship which was lying at Dogurdarness. And when everything was ready he embarked with his wife and all his dependants. The ship had a good voyage, and they reached Norway in the autumn. From there, Thorleik went south to Denmark, for he did not feel happy in Norway; most of his friends and kinsmen there were dead, and some had been banished from the country. After that, Thorleik went to Gotaland. It is generally agreed that Thorleik did not have to struggle against old age, but was considered a man of great worth for as long as he lived. And that is the last we hear of Thorleik Hoskuldsson.

39. Kjartan and Gudrun

AT that time there was much talk in the Breidafjord Dales about the quarrel between Hrut and Thorleik, and of how much Hrut had suffered at the hands of Kotkel and his sons. And now Osvif spoke to his daughter Gudrun and her brothers, and asked them to call to mind whether they would have been better off if they had imperilled their own lives against such hellhounds as Kotkel and his family.

Gudrun said, 'No one can be misguided, father, with you to guide him.'

Olaf now lived on his estate in high esteem, and all his sons were at home with him, as well as their cousin and foster-brother, Bolli. Kjartan was by far the most prominent of Olaf's sons; he and Bolli loved one another the most, and Kjartan never went anywhere without Bolli.

Kjartan often went to the baths at Sælingsdale, and it always so happened that Gudrun was at the baths too. Kjartan enjoyed talking to her, for she was both intelligent and fluent. It was common talk that of all the young people of that time, Kjartan and Gudrun were the best matched.

There was also great friendship between Olaf and Osvif and they frequently exchanged visits, and the friendship was in no way lessened by the growing affection between the younger people.

On one occasion Olaf spoke to Kjartan and said, 'I don't know why I always feel so uneasy when you go over to Laugar and talk to Gudrun. It's not because I don't think Gudrun superior to all other women, and she is the only woman I look upon as an equal match for you; but I have the feeling, although I don't want to make it a prophecy, that we kinsmen are not fated to reap any luck from our dealings with the people of Laugar.'

Kjartan said he did not want to do anything against his father's wishes, if it was within his power, but said he was sure that things would turn out better than his father thought.

Kjartan continued his visits as before; and Bolli always went with him.

And so this year passed.

40. Kjartan and Bolli abroad

THERE was a man called Asgeir the Hot-Head, who lived at Asgeirsriver in Vididale. His father, Audun Shaft, had been the first member of this family to come to Iceland, and the first man to settle in Vididale.[1]

Asgeir the Hot-Head had five children. His sons were called Audun[2] and Thorvald[3] and Kalf. All these brothers were promising young men. Kalf Asgeirsson was at this time engaged in trading, and was considered an excellent man.

Asgeir had a daughter called Thurid; she was married to Thorkel Kuggi, the son of Thord Gellir, and their son was Thorstein Kuggason.

Asgeir's second daughter was called Hrefna; she was the loveliest woman in the north, and everyone was fond of her.

Asgeir was a man of great consequence.

On one occasion it is said that Kjartan Olafsson set off on a journey south to Borgarfjord; there is nothing to tell of his journey until he arrived at Borg, the home of his uncle Thorstein Egilsson. Bolli went with him, for so great was the love between these foster-brothers that they were never happy unless they were together. Thorstein welcomed Kjartan with great warmth, and said it would please him the more the longer he stayed. So Kjartan remained at Borg for some time.

1. *Audun Shaft had another son, called Thorgrim Hoary-Head, the father of Asmund, the father of Grettir.*
Grettir Asmundsson, the outlaw, is the eponymous hero of *Grettir's Saga*, one of the most moving and tragic of all the Icelandic sagas.

2. *Audun was the father of Asgeir, the father of Audun, the father of Egil, who married Ulfeid, the daughter of Eyjolf the Lame; and their son was Eyjolf, who was killed at the Althing.*

3. *Thorvald was the father of Dalla, the wife of Bishop Isleif, and their son was Bishop Gizur.*
Bishop Isleif Gizurarson (1006–80), the son of Gizur the White (cf. Chapter 41), was the first native bishop of Iceland; he was succeeded by his son, Bishop Gizur Isleifsson (1042–1118).

That summer there was a ship lying in the estuary of Gufu River; the owner of that ship was Kalf Asgeirsson, who had been staying with Thorstein Egilsson over the winter. Kjartan told Thorstein in private that the main reason why he had come south was that he wanted to buy a half-share in Kalf's ship – 'for I am eager to go abroad'; and he asked Thorstein what he thought of Kalf. Thorstein said that in his opinion Kalf was a good man. 'It's not surprising, kinsman,' said Thorstein, 'that you are eager to see the way other people live. Your journey will turn out to be remarkable one way or another. It matters a great deal to your kinsmen how your journey turns out.'

Kjartan said it would surely go well. Then he bought a half-share in Kalf's ship and they became equal partners in it. Kjartan was to come to the ship in the tenth week of summer. Kjartan was given gifts when he left Borg; and then he and Bolli rode home.

When Olaf heard about this new venture he felt that Kjartan had decided on it rather hastily, but said he would not interfere.

Soon afterwards, Kjartan rode to Laugar and told Gudrun that he was going abroad.

Gudrun said, 'This is a very sudden decision, Kjartan.' And she made further remarks which left Kjartan in no doubt that she was displeased about it.

'Don't let yourself be upset over this,' said Kjartan. 'I will do anything else that would make you happy.'

'Keep that promise,' said Gudrun, 'for I can tell you at once what I want.'

Kjartan asked her to do so.

Gudrun said, 'I want to go abroad with you this summer, and that would make up for your hasty decision; for I am not happy here in Iceland.'

'That's out of the question,' said Kjartan. 'Your brothers haven't settled down yet and your father is an old man, and they wouldn't have anyone to look after them if you leave the country. So wait for me instead for three years.'

Gudrun said she would make no such promise, and they could not see eye to eye over it; with that they parted, and Kjartan rode back home.

That summer Olaf rode to the Althing. Kjartan accompanied his father on the way east from Hjardarholt as far as North-riverdale, where they parted. From there Kjartan rode to the ship, and his cousin Bolli went with him. There were ten Ice-landers in all who went with Kjartan, and they were all so fond of him that none would leave him. With this company Kjartan arrived at the ship. Kalf Asgeirsson gave them a good welcome. Kjartan and Bolli were taking a valuable cargo abroad with them.

They now made their preparations for sailing, and as soon as the wind was favourable they put out and sailed down Borgar-fjord before a light breeze, and so out to sea. They had a good voyage and made land in Norway to the north, near Trondheim. They sailed in to Agdaness, where they met some people and asked the news.

They were told that there had been a change of rulers in Norway. Earl Hakon was dead, and King Olaf Tryggvason had succeeded him, and the whole of Norway had come under his sway.[1] King Olaf had ordered a change of faith in Norway, but the people were by no means agreed on it.

Kjartan and his companions brought their ship in to Trond-heim. There were many Icelanders of high standing in Norway at that time; and three ships lying at the quayside all belonged to Icelanders.

One ship was owned by Brand the Generous;[2] another be-longed to Hallfred the Troublesome-Poet;[3] and the third was

1. Olaf Tryggvason was king of Norway from 995 to 1000. During his reign he is said to have converted five countries to Christianity – Norway, Iceland, Shetland, Orkney, and the Faroe Islands. His turbulent life is described in Snorri Sturluson's *Heimskringla*, Odd Snorrason's *King Olaf's Saga*, and several other sources.

2. *Brand the Generous was the son of Vermund Thorgrimsson.* This Brand is mentioned in several Icelandic sources; his legendary generosity is exemplified in the brief *Brand's Story*, where his liberality is put to the test by King Harald Hardradi of Norway. Brand was a descendant of Bjorn the Easterner (cf. Genealogical Tables).

3. Hallfred the Troublesome-Poet is the eponymous hero of *Hall-fred's Saga*. As a poet he is chiefly remembered for his love lyrics.

owned by two brothers called Bjarni and Thorhall.[1] All these men had intended to sail to Iceland that summer, but the king had laid an embargo on their ships because they refused to accept the new faith he was proclaiming.

All the Icelanders gave Kjartan a good welcome, particularly Brand the Generous, for they knew one another well already. The Icelanders all met in council, and all agreed that they would reject the new faith that the king was proclaiming; and all those who have just been mentioned formed a league.

Kjartan and his companions brought their ship up to the quayside and unloaded it, and disposed of the cargo.

King Olaf was in residence in Trondheim. He was informed of the ship's arrival, and that there were many important men aboard.

One fine day in the autumn people went from the town to swim in the river Nid. Kjartan and his men saw this, and Kjartan said to his companions that they too should go and enjoy some swimming that day. And so they did.

There was one man from the town who surpassed everyone at this sport and Kjartan asked Bolli if he would like to pit himself against this townsman.

'I don't think I'm a match for him,' replied Bolli.

'I don't know what has happened to your mettle,' said Kjartan. 'So I shall have to try myself.'

'You can if you like,' said Bolli.

Kjartan now plunged into the river and made for this man who was the best swimmer, and forced him under water at once and held him there for a while before letting go of him. No sooner had they come to the surface than this man seized hold of Kjartan and pulled him down, and they stayed under for what seemed to Kjartan a very reasonable time. They surfaced for a

---

and a number of stanzas in which he described his conversion to Christianity. His nickname reflects the difficulty that King Olaf Tryggvason had in converting him. According to his saga, Hallfred was drowned at sea and is buried on the island of Iona, in the Hebrides.

1. *Bjarni and Thorhall were the sons of Skeggi of Breidriver, in Fljotshlid.*

second time, and still they exchanged no words. Then they went under for a third time and now they stayed down much longer than before. Kjartan was no longer sure how this game would end, and felt that he had never been in such a tight corner before. At last they came to the surface and swam ashore.

Then the townsman said, 'Who are you?'

Kjartan told him his name.

'You are a good swimmer,' said the townsman. 'Are you as good at other sports as this one?'

Kjartan replied, after a pause, 'Out in Iceland it was said that other sports were comparable. But that isn't saying much now.'

'That depends on whom you have been competing with,' said the townsman. 'Why don't you ask anything about me?'

'I don't care what your name is,' said Kjartan.

The townsman said, 'You are not only highly accomplished but you are arrogant as well. But you shall know my name nevertheless, and against whom you have been swimming. I am King Olaf Tryggvason.'

Kjartan made no reply, and turned to go. He was wearing a scarlet tunic, but had no cloak on. The king was almost fully dressed by then; he called to Kjartan and told him not to leave in such a hurry. Kjartan turned back, but rather slowly. The king took off his own fine cloak and gave it to Kjartan, and said he must not go back to his men without a cloak. Kjartan thanked the king for the gift, and went over to his companions and showed them the cloak. They were not too pleased about it, for they felt Kjartan had put himself too much in the king's power.

Things were now quiet for a while. In the autumn the weather worsened, with severe frost and cold. The pagans said that it was no wonder that the weather was misbehaving: 'It's all because of the king's innovations and this new faith of his that the gods are angry.'

The Icelanders all stayed in the town together that winter, and Kjartan was very much their leader. The weather improved, and people then flocked into the town at the king's command. A number of people in Trondheim had accepted Christianity by then, but there were far more, however, who opposed it. One day the king held an assembly in the town out at Eyrar, and preached the Christian faith in a long and eloquent address. The Trondheim people were there in a great mob, and offered to do battle with the king in reply. The king warned them to remember that he had dealt with much heavier odds in his time than fighting against the rabble of Trondheim. At this the peasants lost heart and surrendered to the king unconditionally, and a good many people were baptized there and then. After that the assembly was brought to a close.

That same evening the king sent spies to the lodgings where the Icelanders were staying, and told them to find out what they were talking about. When the spies arrived, there were loud voices to be heard from within.

Kjartan was asking Bolli, 'How willing are you, cousin, to accept the faith that the king is preaching?'

'I am not at all willing,' said Bolli, 'for this faith of theirs seems to me very feeble.'

'Didn't you think the king was making threats against those who refuse to submit to his will?' asked Kjartan.

'The king certainly left us in no doubt at all that they would be very harshly dealt with,' said Bolli.

'I refuse to be any man's lackey,' said Kjartan, 'as long as I can still stand upright and wield my weapons. I think it craven to be caught like a lamb in a pen or a fox in a trap. Instead, if one has to die anyway, I would much prefer to achieve something first that would long be remembered.'

'What is it you want to do?' asked Bolli.

'I won't try to hide it,' said Kjartan. 'I want to burn the king in his house.'

'No one could call that craven,' said Bolli, 'but in my opinion it could never succeed. The king is a man of great luck and good fortune; and he keeps careful guard both day and night.'

Kjartan said that courage could fail even the bravest of men. Bolli retorted that it remained to be seen whose courage would need challenging; but many of those present now protested that this was idle talk. When the king's spies had heard all this they went away and reported the whole conversation to the king.

Next morning the king called an assembly, and all the Icelanders were summoned to attend. When the assembly had begun, the king rose to his feet and thanked those people for attending who wished to be his friends and had embraced the new faith. Then he summoned the Icelanders to an audience. He asked if they would accept baptism, but they made little response. The king said they were choosing the course that would do them least good – 'and which of you was it who thought it such a good idea to burn me in my house?'

Then Kjartan said, 'You probably think that the man who suggested it wouldn't have the courage to admit it; but you are seeing him now, right here.'

'I do see you indeed,' said the king, 'and you certainly do not lack ambition. But you are not fated to stand over my dead body; and you have given me ample cause to ensure that you cannot threaten to burn any more kings alive for wanting to teach you a better faith. But since I am not sure whether you meant this in earnest, and since you have now admitted it like a man, you shall not be put to death for it. It may also well be that you will keep your faith all the better for having spoken more against it than the others. I can also see that it would make all the difference to your crews, and that they will accept the faith on the day that you are baptized of your own free will. Moreover I think it likely that your kinsmen and friends will pay careful heed to the message you bring them when you get back to Iceland. I have a feeling, Kjartan, that you will have a better faith when you leave Norway than you had when you arrived. Go now from this meeting, in peace, wherever you want to go; I shall not force you to become Christians on this occasion, for God has said that he does not wish anyone to come to him under duress.'

There was loud approval at the king's speech, particularly from the Christians; but the pagans left it to Kjartan to reply as he thought fit.

Then Kjartan said, 'We wish to thank you, sire, for giving us your peace; this is the most likely way of tempting us to accept your faith, by disregarding our serious offences against you and speaking with such kindness even when you have us so utterly in your power. But I shall only accept this new faith in Norway to the extent that I shall have little reverence for Thor next year when I go back to Iceland.'

Then the king said, with a smile, 'It is obvious from Kjartan's bearing that he feels more confidence in his own strength and weapons than he does in Thor and Odin.'

With that, the assembly was brought to a close.

Later on, a number of people urged the king to force Kjartan and his men to accept the faith, and said they thought it unwise to have so many pagans near him. The king replied angrily, and said he thought there were plenty of Christians who did not conduct themselves so well as Kjartan and his men did: 'And for such men I am prepared to wait a long time.'

The king had many useful works done that winter: he had a church built, and the town greatly enlarged. This church was completed by Christmas.

Now Kjartan said that they should go close enough to the church to see the ceremonies of this faith which the Christians held; and many of the people agreed that this would be excellent sport. So Kjartan and Bolli and their companions went over to the church, and with them went Hallfred the Troublesome-Poet and many of the other Icelanders. The king was preaching the faith to the people in a long and eloquent sermon, and the Christians applauded him warmly.

When Kjartan and the others returned to their lodgings an argument broke out about how the king had impressed them on this occasion which the Christians called their second most important festival: 'For the king said, as we all heard, that on this night was born that Lord in whom we are to believe if we bow to the king's wishes.'

Kjartan said, 'The first time I set eyes on the king, I was so impressed by him that I realized at once that he was a man of outstanding qualities, and this has been confirmed on every occasion I have seen him since in public. But never have I been so impressed by him as I was today, and now I am sure that all our welfare depends on our believing that he whom the king proclaims is the true God. The king cannot be any the more eager for me to accept this faith than I now am to be baptized; and the only thing that prevents me from going at once to see the king is the lateness of the hour, for the king will be at table now, and it would take all day if all of us are to be baptized together.'

Bolli responded well to this, and said he would do as Kjartan decided.

Their conversation was reported to the king before the tables had been cleared, for he had spies in all the lodgings of the pagans. The king was overjoyed at the news and said, 'Kjartan has proved the old saying that holy days are always luckiest.'

Early next morning as the king was on his way to church, Kjartan met him in the street with a large following. Kjartan greeted the king with the greatest courtesy and said he had urgent business with him. The king returned the greeting cordially and said he knew exactly what the business was – 'and you will find it very easily taken care of.'

Kjartan asked that there should be no delay in getting to some water, and said that a great deal of it would be required. The king replied with a smile : 'Yes, Kjartan,' he said, 'I don't think your demands would make us disagree even though you tried to drive a rather harder bargain.'

Then Kjartan and Bolli and all their crew were baptized, and a great many others as well. This was on the second day of Christmas, before Mass. Then the king invited Kjartan and Bolli to his Christmas feast. It is generally agreed that it was on this day that Kjartan gave his allegiance to King Olaf, after doffing his baptismal robes, and Bolli too.

Hallfred the Troublesome-Poet was not baptized that day, for he stipulated that the king himself should be his godfather; and the king agreed to do that the following day.

Kjartan and Bolli stayed with King Olaf for the rest of the winter. The king esteemed Kjartan above all other men for his lineage and prowess, and it is common knowledge that Kjartan was so well-liked that no one at the court envied him; and everyone agreed that Kjartan's peer had never come from Iceland.

Bolli too was a man of great valour, and was highly thought of by good men.

The winter passed, and in the spring those who intended to make voyages made their preparations.

41. Hostages in Norway

KALF ASGEIRSSON went to see Kjartan and asked him what he planned to do that summer.

Kjartan replied, 'I was hoping that we might sail to England, for that is a good trading centre for Christians now. But I should like to see the king first before making a final decision, for he wasn't much disposed to let me go when we spoke about it in the spring.'

With that, Kalf went away and Kjartan went to see the king and greeted him courteously. The king received him cordially, and asked him what he and his companions had been discussing. Kjartan told him what was uppermost in their minds, and added that he had come to see the king in order to ask his leave for the journey.

The king replied, 'I will only grant you leave, Kjartan, on condition that you go to Iceland this summer and compel the people there to accept Christianity, either by force or persuasion. But if you think this too hazardous a mission, I will not release you on any account, for in my opinion you are better suited to serve royalty than to become a trader.'

Kjartan chose rather to stay with the king than to go to Iceland and preach the faith there. He said he did not want to come into conflict with his own kinsmen – 'and moreover, the chances are that my father and other chieftains in my family will be no more reluctant to bow to your will if I remain in your power enjoying high favour.'

The king said, 'That is a wise and noble decision.'

The king gave Kjartan a complete outfit of newly-made clothes of scarlet cloth. They suited him well, for it is said that King Olaf and Kjartan were of the same height and build when they were measured.

King Olaf sent his court priest, Thangbrand, to Iceland. Thangbrand brought his ship to Alptafjord, and stayed the winter with Hall of Sida at Thvattriver, where he preached the faith with bland words and harsh measures; he killed the two men who opposed him most. Hall of Sida accepted the faith in the spring, and he and his household were baptized on the Saturday before Easter; thereafter Gizur the White[1] and Hjalti Skeggjason and many other chieftains accepted baptism, but there were far more who opposed it; and soon there was open hostility between pagans and Christians.

Some of the chieftains made a plan to kill Thangbrand and all those who supported him; in the face of this threat, Thangbrand fled back to Norway. He went to see King Olaf and told him what had happened during his mission, and added that he was convinced that Christianity would never take root in Iceland. The king was furious at this, and vowed that many Icelanders would suffer for it unless they came to their senses of their own accord.

At the Althing that summer, Hjalti Skeggjason was sentenced to outlawry for blasphemy against the gods; the prosecution was brought by Runolf Ulfsson of Dale, in the Eyjafells district, who was a great chieftain.[2]

That same summer, Gizur the White and Hjalti Skeggjason sailed abroad to Norway, and went at once to see King Olaf. The king received them cordially and said they had done well; he invited them to stay with him, and they accepted.

Runolf of Dale's son, Sverting, had been in Norway that winter and was planning to go to Iceland that summer; his ship was at the quayside ready to cast off, waiting for a favourable wind. The king forbade him to leave, and said that no ships would be allowed to go to Iceland that summer. Sverting went to see the king and pleaded with him; he asked for leave to go, and said

1. Both Gizur the White and Hall of Sida play an important part in *Njal's Saga*. It was Gizur who led the attack on Gunnar of Hlidarend. Gizur's son, Isleif, was the first native bishop of Iceland (cf. Chapter 40). Hall of Sida was one of the chief peace-makers after the Burning of Njal.

2. The conversion of Iceland to Christianity in the year 1000, and the stirring events that led up to it, are described more fully in *Kristni Saga*. and in *Njal's Saga* (Chapters 100–105). The incident at the Althing of 999, mentioned here. arose when Hjalti Skeggjason lampooned the goddess Freyja in a verse.

it mattered a great deal to him that his ship should not have to be unloaded. The king was angry and replied, 'It is good for the idolater's son to have to stay where he likes it least.'

So Sverting went nowhere.

The winter passed uneventfully. Next summer the king sent Gizur the White and Hjalti Skeggjason to Iceland to preach the faith anew; but he kept four Icelanders behind as hostages: Kjartan Olafsson, Halldor (the son of Gudmund the Powerful), Kolbein (the son of Thord Frey's-Priest), and Sverting (the son of Runolf of Dale).[1]

Now Bolli decided to go to Iceland with Gizur and Hjalti. He went to see his cousin Kjartan and said, 'I am now ready to leave; I would willingly wait for you another year if you were any more likely to be free to travel next summer than you are now. But as far as we can see, the king isn't going to release you on any account; and it is also my honest belief that you are giving little thought to the pleasures that Iceland has to offer while you are sitting and talking with Ingibjorg, the king's sister.'

Ingibjorg was staying at King Olaf's court at the time, and was the loveliest woman in all Norway.

Kjartan said, 'Don't say such things. But give my greetings to my kinsmen, and also to my friends.'

42. Bolli returns

WITH that, Kjartan and Bolli parted. Gizur and Hjalti sailed from Norway and had a good voyage. They reached the Vestmanna Islands in time for the Althing and went from there to

1. Gudmund the Powerful of Modruvellir was one of the most influential chieftains in Iceland at the turn of the tenth century. He figures prominently in several sagas, including *Njal's Saga*.

Kolbein Thordarson was the brother of Flosi Thordarson of Svinafell, the chieftain who was responsible for the burning of Njal and his sons in *Njal's Saga*; and Runolf of Dale also played a part in the events leading to the burning of Njal.

the mainland, where they held meetings and talks with their kinsmen. Then they went to the Althing, where they preached the faith in long and eloquent speeches; and after that, the whole of the people of Iceland accepted the faith.

Bolli rode from the Althing to Hjardarholt with his uncle, Olaf, who had received him with great affection. Soon after he returned home, Bolli amused himself by riding over to Laugar, and was given a good welcome there. Gudrun asked carefully about his travels – and then about Kjartan. Bolli answered all her questions very readily; he said there was nothing much to tell about his own travels – 'but as for Kjartan, there is truly excellent news to tell of him, for he is at the court of King Olaf enjoying more prestige there than any other man. But it wouldn't surprise me if we in this country were to see little of him for the next few years.'

Gudrun then asked if there was any particular reason for that, apart from the friendship between Kjartan and the king. So Bolli told her the rumours about the attachment between Kjartan and the king's sister, Ingibjorg, and said he was inclined to think that the king would rather give Ingibjorg to him in marriage than let Kjartan go, if it came to that.

Gudrun said that this was good news – 'for Kjartan can only be truly fulfilled if he wins a good wife.'

With that she dropped the subject abruptly and walked away, her face deeply flushed. But other people doubted if she really thought the news as good as she pretended.

Bolli stayed at home at Hjardarholt that summer. He had gained great prestige from his travels, and all his kinsmen and friends were proud of his prowess. He had also brought back a great deal of wealth. He often went to Laugar, and talked to Gudrun.

On one occasion, Bolli asked Gudrun how she would answer if he were to propose to her.

Gudrun replied quickly, 'There's no point in discussing it, Bolli; I will never marry any other man as long as I know Kjartan is alive.'

'Then I think you will have to stay single for a good many years,' said Bolli, 'if you're going to wait for Kjartan. He could easily have entrusted me with some message for you if it had mattered all that much to him.'

They discussed it a little further but could not see eye to eye over it. Then Bolli rode home.

43. Gudrun's third marriage

A LITTLE later, Bolli had a talk with his uncle, Olaf, and said, 'I am beginning to feel that I would like to settle down and get married. I think I have now reached full manhood. I should like to have the benefit of your support, in word and in deed, for you will carry much weight with most of the people concerned.'

Olaf answered, 'Most women would be considered well married if they had you as a husband. But I suppose you wouldn't have raised this if you hadn't already decided where it should end.'

Bolli said, 'I am not going outside the district to look for a wife when the prospects are so good near at hand. I want to ask for the hand of Gudrun Osvif's-daughter. She is now a woman of great renown.'

Olaf replied, 'This is the one thing I would never wish to have a hand in. You know just as well as I do, Bolli, all the talk there was about the love between Kjartan and Gudrun. But if this matters all that much to you, I shall not try to stand in your way if you and Osvif come to an agreement on it. But have you discussed this with Gudrun at all?'

Bolli said he had mentioned it only once, and that she had not shown much interest – 'but I expect that Osvif will have the greatest say in the matter.'

Olaf told him to go about it as he pleased. Soon afterwards, Bolli set off with Olaf's sons, Halldor and Steinthor. There were twelve of them in all, and they rode over to Laugar, where Osvif and his sons gave them a good welcome. Bolli said he wished to speak to Osvif, and then he made his marriage-offer for the hand of his daughter, Gudrun.

Osvif replied: 'As you know, Bolli, Gudrun is a widow, and

she therefore has the right to give her own answer; but I shall urge it strongly.'

Osvif then went to see Gudrun and told her that Bolli Thorleiksson had arrived: 'He is asking for your hand in marriage, and the decision is now yours. But I can let you know my own wishes at once: Bolli would not be rejected if I had my way.'

'You are being rather hasty over this,' said Gudrun. 'Bolli raised this matter with me once before and I tried to put him off. My mind is still unchanged.'

Then Osvif said, 'Most people would say you are speaking more from pride than prudence if you refuse a man like Bolli. But as long as I live, I shall continue to give guidance to you my children in all matters where I can see more clearly than you.'

And since Osvif took so firm a stand over this, Gudrun for her part did not give an outright refusal, despite all her reluctance. Her brothers also urged it strongly, for they thought that an alliance with Bolli would be of great advantage to them. The long and the short of it was that the betrothal took place, and the wedding was arranged for the beginning of winter.

With that, Bolli rode home to Hjardarholt and told Olaf what had been arranged. Olaf showed no enthusiasm for it.

Bolli stayed at home until it was time to go to the wedding. He invited his uncle, Olaf, to attend; Olaf was reluctant to accept, but yielded eventually to Bolli's entreaties. The feast at Laugar was magnificent.

Bolli stayed on there over the winter. There was little love in their marriage on Gudrun's part.

When summer came, and ships were able to sail, the news reached Norway that Iceland had been converted to Christianity. King Olaf was overjoyed at the news and gave all the men he had kept as hostages leave to sail away to Iceland or wherever else they wished to go.

Kjartan Olafsson, who acted as spokesman for all the hostages, said, 'Accept our warmest thanks. The choice we make is to go to Iceland this summer.'

Then King Olaf said, 'We shall not go back on our word, Kjartan, but we meant this more for the others than for you, for we consider, Kjartan, that you have been staying here more as a friend than a hostage. I would be happy if you did not insist on going out to Iceland, even though you have distinguished kinsmen there, for you have the chance of taking a position here in Norway such as cannot be found anywhere in Iceland.'

Then Kjartan replied, 'May our Lord reward you for all the honour you have done me since I came into your power. But I hope that you will grant leave to me no less than to those others you have been holding here for some time.'

'So be it,' said the king, but added that it would be hard to find a man without rank or title to compare with Kjartan.

Kalf Asgeirsson had been in Norway that winter; he had arrived there from England the previous autumn with the ship and wares he shared with Kjartan. And now that Kjartan had been given leave to go to Iceland, he and Kalf made their preparations for the voyage.

When the ship was all ready, Kjartan went to see Ingibjorg, the king's sister. She welcomed him warmly and made room for him to sit beside her, and they talked together. Then Kjartan told Ingibjorg that he was about to leave for Iceland.

Ingibjorg replied, 'We suspect, Kjartan, that it is your own wilfulness and not the promptings of others that has made you decide to leave Norway for Iceland.'

After that they had little to say to one another.

Ingibjorg now turned to a casket that stood beside her, and took from it a white head-dress embroidered with gold; she gave it to Kjartan and said it would be good enough for Gudrun Osvif's-daughter to wrap around her head : 'You shall give her this head-dress as a wedding gift, for I want the women of Iceland to see that the woman whose company you have been keeping in Norway isn't descended from slaves.'

The head-dress lay in a velvet bag; it was a most costly treasure.

'I shall not see you on your way,' said Ingibjorg. 'Now farewell and luck go with you.'

Kjartan stood up and embraced her, and everyone believed they felt their parting deeply.

Kjartan now went away and saw the king, and told him he

was ready to leave. King Olaf and a crowd of people accompanied him down to the ship, which was lying at the quayside with one gangway still out.

Then the king spoke up and said, 'Here is a sword, Kjartan, which I want you to accept as a parting gift. Let this sword never leave your side, for I believe that no weapon will ever bite into you as long as you bear this sword.'

It was a magnificent weapon, and richly ornamented. Kjartan thanked the king eloquently for all the honour and privileges he had bestowed on him during his stay in Norway.

Then the king said, 'I want to ask you, Kjartan, to keep your faith well.'

With that, the king and Kjartan parted with great affection, and Kjartan went on board his ship. The king gazed after him and said, 'They have been allotted a dire destiny, Kjartan and his kin, and there is no altering their fate.'

44. Kjartan returns

KJARTAN and Kalf now put out to sea. They had favourable winds and the voyage did not take long; they made land at Hvit River in Borgarfjord.

News of Kjartan's arrival spread far and wide. His father Olaf and other kinsmen heard of it and were greatly pleased. Olaf rode at once from the Dales south to Borgarfjord, and father and son had a joyful reunion. Olaf invited Kjartan to his home with as many of his companions as he wished to bring. Kjartan accepted gratefully, and said it was the only place in Iceland where he wanted to stay. Olaf then rode back home to Hjardarholt, while Kjartan remained at the ship for the summer. He now heard about Gudrun's marriage and showed no sign of emotion at the news, although many people had been feeling apprehensive about it.

Kjartan's sister, Thurid, and her husband Gudmund Solmundsson came to the ship, and Kjartan gave them a good welcome. Asgeir the Hot-Head also came to see his son Kalf, and with him came his daughter Hrefna; she was the loveliest of women.

Kjartan invited his sister Thurid to have anything she pleased from his wares, and Kalf said the same to Hrefna. Kalf now opened up a large chest and told them to have a look inside.

During the day a sudden gale blew up, and Kjartan and Kalf rushed out to secure the ship; when they had finished they went back to the booths. It was Kalf who entered first. Thurid and Hrefna had by now turned out most of the contents of the chest. Just then, Hrefna pulled out the head-dress and unfolded it; what a wonderful treasure it was, they said. Hrefna wanted to try on the head-dress; Thurid thought it a good idea, so Hrefna put it on.

Kalf saw her doing this, and said there had been a mistake and told her to take it off at once – 'for this is the only thing that Kjartan and I do not own in common.'

At these words, Kjartan entered the booth. He had heard what they had been saying and joined in at once, and said it did not matter. Hrefna was sitting there, still wearing the head-dress. Kjartan looked closely at her and said, 'I think the head-dress becomes you very well, Hrefna; and I also think it would be best for me to own both, head-dress and maiden alike.'

Then Hrefna said, 'Everyone thinks you will be in no hurry to get married, but will win any woman you ask.'

Kjartan said it would not matter much what woman he married, but added he would let no one keep him waiting long for an answer: 'I can see this attire suits you well, and it is fitting that you should become my wife.'

Hrefna now took off the head-dress and gave it back to Kjartan, who put it away.

Gudmund and Thurid invited Kjartan to come north and visit them next winter, and Kjartan promised he would come.

Kalf Asgeirsson went north with his father. Kjartan and he now dissolved their partnership, and everything was done in full amity and agreement.

Kjartan now rode from the ship west to the Dales with eleven companions. He arrived home at Hjardarholt, where everyone was glad to see him. In the autumn he had his wares brought west from the ship. The eleven men who had accompanied him to the Dales all stayed at Hjardarholt that winter.

Olaf and Osvif still kept up their old custom of inviting one another to a feast alternately each autumn. This autumn the feast was to be at Laugar, and Olaf and all the people of Hjardarholt were to attend it.

Gudrun now said to Bolli that she felt he had not told her the whole truth about Kjartan's returning to Iceland. Bolli replied that he had told her what he believed to be true at the time. Gudrun had little to say about this, but it was obvious that she was very displeased, and most people thought she was still yearning for Kjartan even though she tried to hide her feelings.

Time passed, until the autumn feast at Laugar was due. Olaf made ready to go, and asked Kjartan to come with him. Kjartan said he would stay at home and look after the farm. Olaf begged him not to be offended with his own kinsmen: 'Don't forget, Kjartan, that you have loved no man so much as your foster-brother Bolli; and it is my wish that you come. You cousins will soon make it up once you meet one another again.'

Kjartan did as his father asked. He brought out the scarlet clothes which King Olaf had given him at their parting, and dressed himself in all his finery. He girded on the sword the king had given him. On his head he wore a gilded helmet, and at his side a red shield with the Holy Cross emblazoned in gold, and he carried a spear with a gold-inlaid socket. All his men wore coloured clothing. There were more than twenty all told in the company. They set out from Hjardarholt and rode all the way to Laugar, where a great many people had gathered already.

45. Kjartan marries

BOLLI and the Osvifssons came out to receive Olaf and his company, and gave them a good welcome. Bolli went up to Kjartan and embraced him, and Kjartan accepted his greeting. After that they were shown into the house Bolli was very cheerful with them, and Olaf responded very well to that, but Kjartan was rather distant.

The feast went off well.

Bolli had some stud-horses which were considered exceptionally fine. The stallion was a big, handsome animal, and had never been beaten in a fight; he was a white horse, with red ears and a red forelock. Three mares went with him, all of the same colouring as the stallion. Bolli wanted to give these horses to Kjartan; but Kjartan said he had no interest in horses, and refused to accept them. Olaf begged him to accept the horses – 'for this is a magnificent gift.' But Kjartan flatly refused.

On that note they parted, with little warmth. The men of Hjardarholt went home, and all was now quiet.

Kjartan was rather moody that winter, and people got very few words out of him. Olaf thought it a great pity.

After Christmas that winter, Kjartan and his eleven companions prepared for a journey to the north. They rode on their way until they arrived at Asbjarnarness in Vididale, where Kjartan was made welcome with the greatest warmth and affection. The house there was magnificent.

Gudmund's son, Hall, was then about twenty years old, and took much after his Laxriverdale kinsmen; everyone agrees that there has never been a more valiant man in the whole of the Northern Quarter.

Hall Gudmundsson received his uncle Kjartan with great affection. Presently, games were arranged at Asbjarnarness, and people flocked to them from far and wide throughout the area; some came from the west from Midfjord and from Vatnsness, and others from Vatnsdale and even as far away as Langadale. There was a great crowd of people there, and everyone remarked on what a paragon among men Kjartan was.

Then the games began. Hall was in charge of them, and he invited Kjartan to join in the play : 'We would like you, uncle, to show us your courtesy in this.'

Kjartan replied, 'I have not been training much for sports of late, for other matters occupied us at King Olaf's court; but I don't want to refuse you just for this once.'

Kjartan now got ready to play, and all the strongest men

available were matched against him.[1] The game went on all day, but no one could stand up to Kjartan in strength or agility.

And in the evening when the game was brought to a close, Hall Gudmundsson rose to his feet and said, 'It is my father's wish that all those who have come a long way should be invited to stay the night as our guests and continue the games tomorrow morning.'

This was considered a princely invitation, and there was loud approval.

Kalf Asgeirsson was present at the games; he and Kjartan were devoted to one another. Kalf's sister, Hrefna, was also there, dressed in all her finery. In all, there were more than 120 people who spent the night at the farm.

Next morning, sides were made up for the game; this time, Kjartan sat by and watched. His sister Thurid came over to talk to him and said, 'I am told, Kjartan, that you have been rather reserved all winter, and people are saying that you are still yearning for Gudrun; their reason for thinking this is that there is no longer any affection between you and your cousin Bolli, despite all the love there has always been between you. Do now the only proper thing : don't take this so much to heart, and don't begrudge your kinsman a good match. We think it would be best for you to get married, as you yourself said last summer, even though Hrefna isn't entirely an equal match for you – for such a match couldn't be found anywhere in Iceland.

'Her father, Asgeir, is a noble man of good family. He has plenty of wealth, too, to make this match attractive, and his other daughter is married to a distinguished man. You have told me yourself that Kalf Asgeirsson is a man of great valour, too. And they live in great splendour.

'I would like you to have a talk with Hrefna, and I'm sure you will find that her looks are matched by her wits.'

1. The game referred to here seems to have been some sort of ball-game that was normally played on ice, with a wooden ball and heavy clubs. The exact rules are no longer known, but from references in early sources it is clear that the game demanded as much physical strength as skill.

Kjartan received all this well, and said there was much in what she had said. After that a meeting with Hrefna was arranged, and they talked together for the rest of the day.

That evening, Thurid asked Kjartan how Hrefna's conversation had impressed him. He said he was pleased with her, and that she seemed to be an outstanding woman in every respect as far as he could see.

Next morning, messengers were sent to Asgeir to ask him to come to Asbjarnarness. This matter was then brought up, and Kjartan asked for the hand of Hrefna Asgeir's-daughter. Asgeir responded favourably, for he was a shrewd man and was well aware what an honour was being offered. Kalf urged the matter strongly, too: 'I want nothing to be stinted in this,' he said.

Hrefna, for her own part, did not refuse either, and asked her father to make the decision. A full agreement was now reached and duly witnessed.

Kjartan insisted on having the wedding feast at Hjardarholt. Asgeir and Kalf made no demur, so it was decided that the wedding was to take place at Hjardarholt after the fifth week of summer. With that, Kjartan rode home, laden with gifts. Olaf was very pleased at the news, for Kjartan was now much more cheerful than he had been before he left home.

Kjartan observed a strict fast throughout Lent, which was without precedent in this country, for it is said that he was the first man to have dry-fasted in Iceland.[1] People thought it so remarkable that Kjartan could live for so long without meat that they travelled long distances just to look at him. In the same way, Kjartan surpassed all men in every other respect.

When Easter was over, Kjartan and Olaf made preparations for a great feast. Asgeir and Kalf came from the north at the appointed time, with Gudmund and Hall and a company of sixty in all; a great number of people invited by Kjartan and Olaf were there already to greet them. It was an excellent feast, and it lasted for a whole week.

Kjartan gave Hrefna the head-dress as a wedding gift, and this gift caused quite a stir, for no one there was so cultured or

1 The 'dry fast' consisted of fish, whale, bread, vegetables, nuts and fruit, but no meat, butter or dairy produce.

so wealthy that he had ever seen or owned such a treasure. According to well-informed people, there were eight ounces of gold woven into the head-dress.

Kjartan was very cheerful at the feast and entertained everyone with his talk and tales of his travels. People marvelled at the striking events he had to relate, for he had been a long time in the service of that most excellent chieftain, King Olaf Tryggvason.

When the feast came to an end, Kjartan chose handsome gifts for Gudmund and Hall and other important people. Kjartan and his father gained great renown from this feast.

Kjartan and Hrefna came to love one another dearly.

46. Theft

OLAF and Osvif remained good friends despite the ill-feeling that had arisen between the young people.

That summer, a fortnight before winter, Olaf held a feast. Osvif had also announced a feast at the very beginning of winter. They invited one another to attend with as many men as each thought proper to his dignity. It was Osvif's turn to go to Olaf's feast first, and at the appointed time he came to Hjardarholt, and with him came Bolli and Gudrun and the Osvifssons.

Next morning, as the women were walking through the hall, one of them asked in what order they were to be seated. At that moment Gudrun was passing the bed-closet in which Kjartan usually slept; Kjartan was inside, dressing, and was putting on a scarlet tunic. And now, before anyone else had time to reply, Kjartan called out to the woman who had been asking about the seating arrangements, 'Hrefna is to sit in the high-seat, and she is always to be placed first as long as I am alive.'

But before this it was Gudrun who had always been given the high-seat at Hjardarholt and everywhere else.

Gudrun heard this and looked at Kjartan and coloured, but said not a word.

Next day Gudrun told Hrefna to put on the head-dress and let people see the most valuable treasure that had ever come to Iceland. Kjartan was nearby, although not right beside them, and overheard what Gudrun said, and was quicker than Hrefna to reply:

'She is not to wear the head-dress at this feast,' he said, 'for I think it more important that Hrefna should own this great treasure than that the guests should feast their eyes on it on this occasion.'

The autumn-feast that Olaf was giving was to last for a week.

Next day, Gudrun asked Hrefna in private to show her the head-dress. Hrefna agreed to do so; and later that day they went out to the storehouse in which valuables were kept. Hrefna opened a casket and brought out a velvet bag, and from it she took the head-dress and showed it to Gudrun. Gudrun unfolded the head-dress and gazed at it for a while, but made no comment about it, either good or bad. Then Hrefna put it away again, and they went back to their places at the feast.

The entertainment continued. On the day the guests were leaving, Kjartan was busy arranging for horses for those who had far to go, and taking care of each one's needs for the journey. While he was attending to these matters, he had not been carrying the sword which the king had given him, although usually he never let it out of his sight. But when he came back to his place where he had left the sword he now found it missing. He went at once to tell his father about this loss.

'We must go about this as quietly as possible,' said Olaf. 'I shall get men to keep a check on each group that rides away.'

He did so. An the White was to ride with Osvif's party and keep an eye on anyone who might leave the group or lag behind. They rode up to Ljarwoods and past the farms in the Skogar district, where they made a halt and dismounted. While the others were resting at Skogar, Thorolf Osvifsson left with a few men and disappeared for a time into some brushwood.

An the White accompanied the whole party as far as Lax River, which flows out of Sælingsdale, and then said he would turn back. Thorolf said it would have been no loss if he had not come at all.

Light snow had fallen the previous night, so that footprints could easily be traced. An rode back to Skogar and followed Thorolf's tracks to a swamp, or bog. He groped around in the mire with his hand and felt the pommel of a sword. An wanted to have witnesses with him for this, and rode to fetch Thorarin of Sælingsdale Tongue, and Thorarin went back with An to retrieve the sword. An then brought the sword to Kjartan, who wrapped it in a cloth and put it away in a chest. The place where Thorolf and his men hid the sword has been called Sverdskelda ever since.

This was all kept very quiet. The scabbard of the sword was never found again; and Kjartan valued the sword less after this than he had done before.

Kjartan was very embittered by all this, and did not want to let the matter rest there.

But Olaf said, 'Don't take this too much to heart. They have played you an ugly trick, but you yourself have not come to any harm. We mustn't make a laughing-stock of ourselves by making a quarrel out of this, when there are friends and kinsmen involved.'

So as a result of his father's entreaties Kjartan let the matter drop.

After that, Olaf got ready to attend the feast at Laugar at the beginning of winter, and told Kjartan he must come too. Kjartan did not want to go, but eventually promised to do so at his father's request.

Hrefna was also to go, and she wanted to leave the head-dress behind. But Thorgerd, her mother-in-law, said, 'When are you ever going to use that wonderful treasure, if it's kept hidden in a chest whenever you go to feasts?'

'Most people would say,' replied Hrefna, 'that I am likely to visit places where there are fewer people to envy me than at Laugar.'

'We don't lay great store by people who spread gossip of that kind,' said Thorgerd.

And so because Thorgerd urged it so strongly, Hrefna took the head-dress with her, and Kjartan raised no objection when he realized how his mother felt about it. After that they all set off and arrived at Laugar in the evening, where they were given a good welcome.

Thorgerd and Hrefna handed over their dresses to be taken care of. But next morning when the women went to fetch their clothing, Hrefna looked for the head-dress and it had disappeared from the place where it had been put. A thorough search was made, but it was nowhere to be found. Gudrun said the chances were that the head-dress had been left behind at home, or that Hrefna had packed it so carelessly that it had fallen out on the way.

Hrefna now told Kjartan that the head-dress had disappeared. He replied that it was a delicate matter and they had to be cautious in these circumstances, and asked her to do nothing about it; then he told his father what had happened.

Olaf said, 'As before, I should still like you to ignore this incident and let it pass. I shall make discreet inquiries about it myself, for I would do anything to prevent a breach between you and Bolli. "Whole flesh is easier to dress than wounds", my son,' he said.

'We all know, father,' replied Kjartan, 'that you would like everyone to come well out of this affair. But I'm not sure that I myself care to be worsted like this by the people of Laugar.'

On the day that the guests were to depart, Kjartan spoke up and said, 'I call on you, cousin Bolli, to show yourself more willing to treat us properly from now on than you have done hitherto. I'm making no secret of this, for it is already common knowledge that certain things have disappeared around here which we believe have found their way into your keeping.

'In the autumn, when we held a feast at Hjardarholt, my sword was taken; that has now been recovered, but not the scabbard. And now once again a treasure which is considered very valuable has disappeared here. I now want both of them back.'

Bolli replied, 'We are not guilty of the charges you make against us, Kjartan. We would have expected anything of you but to accuse us of theft.'

'We believe,' said Kjartan, 'that those who were involved in this plot are so close to you that you could make amends for them if you so wanted. You have provoked us far enough. We have put up with your hostility for a long time, but now I declare we shall endure it no longer.'

Then Gudrun replied to his speech, and said, 'You are stirring up a fire, Kjartan, which would be better kept damped down. Even if you are right in saying that there are people here who have seen to it that the head-dress should disappear, I reckon they have only taken what by right was theirs. You can believe whatever you please about what has become of it; but I myself won't grieve if the head-dress has now been taken care of in such a way that Hrefna's looks will have little benefit of it from now on.'

With that they parted, rather bleakly, and the people of Hjardarholt rode back home. There were no more invitations, but everything was quiet on the surface. No trace of the head-dress was ever found again, but many people believed that Thorolf Osvifsson had burned it at the request of his sister Gudrun.

Early that winter, Asgeir the Hot-Head died, and his sons took over his estate.

47. Kjartan retaliates

AFTER Christmas that winter, Kjartan gathered forces and got sixty men together. He did not tell his father the purpose of his expedition, and Olaf himself asked little about it. Kjartan took with him tents and provisions, and rode off on his way until he came to Laugar. He told his men to dismount, and ordered some of them to look after the horses and others to pitch the tents.

In those days it was the custom to have the privy outside, some distance away from the farmhouse itself, and such was the arrangement at Laugar.

Kjartan now seized all the doors of the house and refused to allow anyone to go outside; and for three days he forced them all to stay indoors without access to the privy. After that he rode back home to Hjardarholt, and his followers dispersed to their own homes. Olaf was very displeased over this venture, but Thorgerd said there was no reason to fault it, for the men of Laugar had brought it, or even worse, upon themselves.

Then Hrefna said, 'Did you talk to anyone at Laugar, Kjartan?'

'There was little enough of that,' he replied. But he added that he and Bolli had exchanged a few words.

Then Hrefna said, with a smile, 'I've been told for a fact that you and Gudrun talked together; and I've even heard how she was dressed – that she was wearing the head-dress, and that she looked very well in it.'

Kjartan flushed deep red, and it was obvious to everyone that he was furious at her teasing. 'I saw nothing of what you have described, Hrefna,' he said. 'And Gudrun needs no head-dress to look better than any other woman.'

At that, Hrefna dropped the subject.

The men of Laugar were furious and thought the incident a much greater humiliation and disgrace than if Kjartan had killed one or two of their men. The Osvifssons were angriest of all about it, but Bolli tried to calm them down. Gudrun had the least to say about it, but from what little she did say people doubted whether anyone else felt it more bitterly than she did.

There was now open enmity between the men of Laugar and the men of Hjardarholt.

Late in the winter Hrefna gave birth to a child; it was a boy, and he was named Asgeir.

Thorarin of Sælingsdale Tongue let it be known that he wanted to sell the Tongue lands – both because he was short of money, and also because he was well aware of the growing ill-feeling between people in the district, and he was a close friend of both sides. Bolli wanted to buy himself a farm, for the Laugar people had plenty of livestock but little land. On Osvif's advice, Bolli and Gudrun rode over to Tongue; they thought it would be very convenient to acquire land so close to their own estate, and Osvif told them not to let any trifles stand in the way of an agreement. Gudrun and Bolli discussed the deal with Thorarin, and they came to terms on what the price should be and also on how it was to be paid; and so the bargain was struck between them. But the agreement was not duly witnessed, for there were not sufficient people present to fulfil the requirements of the law. After that, Bolli and Gudrun rode back home.

When Kjartan heard what had happened, he rode at once with eleven men over to Tongue and arrived there early in the day. Thorarin welcomed him warmly and invited him to stay; Kjartan said he would be riding back the same evening, but would be stopping there for a while. Thorarin asked him the reason for his visit.

Kjartan said, 'My reason for coming here is to discuss a sale of land which you and Bolli have arranged, for it is not my wish that you sell this land to Bolli and Gudrun.'

Thorarin said that anything else would be awkward for him – 'for the price Bolli has promised me for the land is a very good one, and is to be paid at once.'

'You will lose nothing if Bolli doesn't buy the land,' said Kjartan, 'for I shall buy it at the same price; and you will do yourself no good by going against what I want done, for you will find out that I intend to have my own way in this district, and I will be trying to oblige others more than the people of Laugar.'

Thorarin replied, 'I am feeling now that "mighty is the master's word". But I would very much prefer that the deal agreed between Bolli and myself should stand.'

'I don't call it a proper sale of land if it isn't duly witnessed,' said Kjartan. 'You can now do one of two things: either sell me the land here and now on the same terms as you agreed with others, or else farm the land yourself.'

Thorarin chose to sell him the land, and this time the agreement was witnessed at once. After the purchase Kjartan rode home.

News of this spread throughout the Breidafjord Dales, and the people of Laugar heard about it that same evening. Then Gudrun said, 'It seems to me, Bolli, that Kjartan has given you a harsher choice than he offered Thorarin: either that you leave this district with little honour, or else that you confront him and prove yourself rather less faint-hearted than you have been hitherto.'

Bolli made no reply, and walked away at once.

Everything was now quiet for the rest of Lent.

On the Tuesday after Easter, Kjartan rode from home with one companion, An the Black. They arrived at Sælingsdale Tongue that same day; Kjartan wanted Thorarin to ride with him west to Saurby to arrange the transfer of debts to him, for Kjartan had a great deal of money outstanding there. But Thorarin was away at another farm, so Kjartan stayed there for a while, waiting for him.

That same day, Thorhalla the Gossip came to Tongue. She asked Kjartan where he was going. He told her he intended to go west to Saurby.

'Which route are you taking?' she asked.

Kjartan replied, 'I shall ride by way of Sælingsdale on my way west, and Svinadale on my way back.'

She asked him how long he would be.

'I shall probably ride back on Thursday,' he replied.

'Will you do me a favour?' she asked. 'I have a kinsman out west at Hvitadale, in Saurby, who has promised me half a mark's worth of homespun cloth, and I should like you to collect it for me and bring it back with you.'

Kjartan promised to do this.

Then Thorarin returned, and set off with them. They rode west across Sælingsdale Heath and arrived that evening at Hol, in Saurby, where Aud and her brothers lived; Kjartan was given a good welcome there, for they were all good friends.

Thorhalla the Gossip came home to Laugar that same evening. The Osvifssons asked her if she had met any people that day. She said she had met Kjartan Olafsson. They asked her where he was going. She told them what she knew – 'and never has he looked more gallant than now; it's not surprising that such men should consider everything so much beneath them.' She went on, 'It was obvious to me that Kjartan enjoyed nothing better than talking about his purchase of land from Thorarin.'

Gudrun said, 'Kjartan can well afford to be as bold as he pleases, for it has been proved that no matter what insult he thinks up, there is no one who dares stand up to him.'

Bolli and the Osvifssons were all present at this exchange between Gudrun and Thorhalla. Ospak and his brothers made little comment apart from their usual disparaging remarks about Kjartan. Bolli pretended not to hear, as he always did when people spoke ill of Kjartan, for he used to remain silent or else contradict what was said.

48. Ambush

KJARTAN spent the Wednesday after Easter at Hol, and there was much entertainment and merry-making there.

That night, An the Black was very restless in his sleep, so they woke him up. They asked him what he had been dreaming.

'A horrible woman came at me and dragged me to the edge of the bed,' he replied. 'She had a huge knife in one hand and a trough in the other. She plunged the knife into my breast and ripped my whole belly open, and pulled out all my entrails and stuffed brushwood in their place. Then she went away.'

Kjartan and the others laughed aloud at the dream and said he ought to be called An Brushwood-Belly. They caught hold of him and said they wanted to feel if there was any brushwood in his stomach.

Then Aud said, 'There's no need to make so much fun of this. I suggest that Kjartan should either stay here longer, or else, if he insists on going, he should take a larger company with him than he had on his way here.'

Kjartan said, 'You must take everything An Brushwood-Belly tells you very seriously when he sits around chatting with you all day, if you regard whatever he dreams as revelation. But dream or no dream, I am leaving as I had previously planned.'

Kjartan set off early on the Thursday after Easter, and with him, at Aud's insistence, went Thorkel Whelp and his brother Knut. There were twelve of them in all who accompanied Kjartan on his way.

Kjartan called in at Hvitadale and collected the homespun cloth for Thorhalla the Gossip as he had promised. Then he rode south down Svinadale.

Over at Laugar, in Sælingsdale, Gudrun rose early as soon as the sun was up. She went to the room where her brothers were sleeping, and shook Ospak. Ospak and his brothers woke up at once; and when he saw it was his sister he asked her what she wanted, to be up so early in the morning. Gudrun said she wanted to know what they were planning to do that day. Ospak said they would be having a quiet day – 'for there isn't much work to be done just now.'

Gudrun said, 'You would have had just the right temper if you had been peasants' daughters – you do nothing about anything, whether good or bad. Despite all the disgrace and dishonour that Kjartan has done you, you lose no sleep over it even when he rides past your door with only a single companion. Men like you have the memory of hogs. It's obviously futile to hope that you will ever dare to attack Kjartan at home if you haven't the nerve to face him now when he is travelling with only one or two companions. You just sit at home pretending to be men, and there are always too many of you about.'

Ospak said she was making too much of this, but admitted that it was difficult to argue against her. He jumped out of bed at once and dressed, as did all the brothers one after another; then they made ready to lay an ambush for Kjartan.

Gudrun now asked Bolli to go with them. Bolli said it would not be right for him to do that because of his kinship with Kjartan, and he recalled how lovingly Olaf had brought him up.

'That's perfectly true,' said Gudrun. 'But you don't have the luck to be able to please everybody; and if you refuse this journey, it will be the end of our marriage.'

And at Gudrun's promptings, Bolli remembered all his resentment against Kjartan, and he armed himself quickly. There were nine of them in all: the five Osvifssons were there – Ospak, Helgi, Vandrad, Torrad and Thorolf; the sixth was Bolli, and the seventh was Gudlaug, Osvif's nephew, a very promising young man; and then there were Odd and Stein, the sons of Thorhalla the Gossip.

They rode over to Svinadale, and dismounted beside a ravine called Hafragill. There they tethered their horses and sat down to wait. Bolli was silent all day, and lay on the brink above the ravine.

When Kjartan and his companions had come as far south as Mjosyndi, where the valley begins to widen out, Kjartan said that Thorkel Whelp and his men ought to turn back. Thorkel said they would ride on to the end of the valley. When they had gone south past the shieling known as Nordursel, Kjartan again told the brothers Thorkel Whelp and Knut not to come any farther – 'That thief Thorolf isn't going to laugh at me for not daring to go my way without a crowd.'

Thorkel Whelp replied, 'We will do as you ask, and not ride any farther. But we will always regret it if we are not with you and you are in need of men today.'

Then Kjartan said, 'My cousin Bolli will never be a party to a plot against my life; and if the Osvifssons try to ambush me, there's no knowing which side would live to tell the tale, even though the odds were rather against me.'

And with that, the brothers and their men rode back west.

49. Kjartan's death

KJARTAN rode south down the valley with his two companions, An the Black and Thorarin.

There was a man called Thorkel, who lived at Hafratindar in Svinadale; the farm is now deserted. He had gone to see to his horses that day with his shepherd-boy. They caught sight of both parties – the men of Laugar lying in ambush, and Kjartan and his two companions riding down the valley. The boy said they should go and warn Kjartan, for it would mean good luck for them if they could avert the terrible events which were about to take place.

'Hold your tongue!' said Thorkel of Hafratindar. 'Are you so stupid as to think you can save someone's life if he is fated to die? To tell you the truth, they can do one another as much harm as they please for all I care. I think it a much better idea to find a place where we can get a good view of the encounter and enjoy the sport without danger to ourselves. Everyone keeps praising Kjartan for being more skilled in arms than anyone else; I reckon he's going to need all his skill now, for as we can see the odds against him are very heavy.'

And so, of course, Thorkel had his way.

Kjartan and his companions came riding down towards Hafragill.

Meanwhile, the Osvifssons had begun to suspect why Bolli had chosen for himself the one spot where he could easily be seen by anyone approaching from the north. They discussed it among themselves and decided that Bolli was not to be trusted. So they climbed up to him and started wrestling and rolling about with him, and took hold of his legs and dragged him down the slope.

Kjartan and his companions came up quickly, for they were riding hard; and when they had passed south of the ravine they caught sight of the ambush and recognized the men.

Kjartan jumped off his horse at once and turned to face the Osvifssons. There was a huge boulder standing nearby, and there Kjartan said they would make their stand. As the others made for them, Kjartan hurled his spear and struck Thorolf's shield just above the handle, driving the shield against him; the spear went right through the shield and Thorolf's upper arm, severing the biceps. Thorolf dropped the shield, and his arm was useless for the rest of the fight.

Then Kjartan drew his sword – but he was not carrying the sword the king had given him. The Thorhollusons set upon Thorarin, for that was the task allotted to them. It was a fierce struggle, for Thorarin was a powerful man and they were no weaklings themselves, and it was hard to know which side would get the better of the other.

Gudlaug and the Osvifssons made for Kjartan, so there were five of them against two, Kjartan and An the Black. An put up a stout defence and was always trying to cover Kjartan. Bolli stood aloof with the sword 'Leg-Biter'. Kjartan's blows were hard but his sword was of little use, and he was always having to put it under his foot to straighten it. The Osvifssons and An the Black now suffered some wounds, but Kjartan had still not been wounded. Kjartan fought with such courage and agility that the Osvifssons had to give ground, and they turned on An instead; and now An fell, having fought for some time with his entrails coming out. At the same moment, Kjartan hacked off Gudlaug's leg at the thigh, and that was enough to kill him.

Now the four Osvifssons threw themselves at Kjartan again, but Kjartan defended himself so bravely that he never yielded an inch before them.

Then Kjartan said, 'Why did you ever leave home, cousin Bolli, if you intended to stand by idle? You would be better now to give your help to one side or the other and find out how well "Leg-Biter" can do.'

Bolli pretended not to hear. And now, when Ospak realized that they could not overcome Kjartan on their own, he urged Bolli in every way he could, telling him that he surely would not want to live with the shame of having promised them his help in a fight and then not given it. 'Kjartan bore hard enough on us before, when we had done much less to provoke him,' he added, 'and if he gets away this time, you, Bolli, like us, will face the direst consequences before long.'

So Bolli drew 'Leg-Biter', and turned on Kjartan.

Then Kjartan said to Bolli, 'It is an ignoble deed, kinsman, that you are about to do; but I would much rather accept death at your hands, cousin, than give you death at mine.'

And with that, Kjartan threw down his weapons, and made no attempt to defend himself; he was only slightly wounded, but very weak with exhaustion.

Bolli made no reply to Kjartan's words, but dealt him his death-blow all the same. Then Bolli caught him as he fell, and Kjartan died in Bolli's lap. At once Bolli repented bitterly of what he had done.

Bolli now declared that he himself had done the killing, and sent the Osvifssons back to Laugar, while he and Thorarin stayed behind with the bodies. When the Osvifssons returned home they told what had happened. Gudrun seemed pleased at the news. Thorolf's arm was dressed but it took a long time to heal, and gave him trouble for the rest of his life.

Kjartan's body was taken home to Sælingsdale Tongue

Bolli then rode home to Laugar and Gudrun went out to meet him. She asked him how late in the day it was. Bolli said it was around noon of that day. Then Gudrun said, 'Morning tasks are often mixed: I have spun yarn for twelve ells of cloth and you have killed Kjartan.'

Bolli replied, 'This luckless deed will live long enough in my mind without you reminding me of it.'

'I do not think it luckless,' said Gudrun. 'It seems to me that you had more prestige the year that Kjartan was in Norway than now when he has ridden roughshod over you since he came back to Iceland. But last of all, what I like best is that Hrefna will not go laughing to bed tonight.'

Then Bolli said, in sudden fury, 'I doubt if she will turn any paler at the news than you, and I suspect you would have been less shocked if I had been left lying on the field of battle and Kjartan had lived to tell the tale.'

Gudrun now saw how angry Bolli was, and said, 'Don't say such things, for I am deeply grateful to you for what you have done. I now know for certain that you will do anything to please me.'

The Osvifssons went into hiding in an underground chamber that had been secretly prepared for them. The Thorhollusons were sent off to Helgafell to tell Snorri the Priest what had happened and to ask him to send immediate help and support against Olaf the Peacock and the others whose duty it would be to take action over the killing of Kjartan.

Over at Sælingsdale Tongue, something remarkable happened on the night after the killing: An the Black, whom everyone had thought to be dead, sat up. Those who were keeping vigil over the bodies were frightened and thought it a great marvel. But An said to them, 'I beg of you in God's name not to be afraid of me, for I have been alive all the time and never even lost consciousness until a swooning sleep came over me. Then I dreamt of the same woman as before; and in my dream she now took the brushwood from my belly and put my entrails back instead, and at this change I felt much better.'

An's wounds were now dressed, and he recovered completely; from then on he was known as An Brushwood-Belly.

When Olaf Hoskuldsson heard the news, he was deeply affected by Kjartan's killing, although he bore it with fortitude. His sons wanted to attack Bolli at once and destroy him.

'Far from it,' said Olaf. 'Bolli's death would not bring back my son. I loved Kjartan above all others; but I could not bear to see any harm befall Bolli. I see a much more fitting task for you: go after the Thorhollusons, who have been sent off to Helgafell to gather forces against us; any punishment you see fit to mete out to them will please me.'

The Olafssons set off at once and boarded a ferry-boat belonging to Olaf. There were seven of them in all and they rowed away down Hvammsfjord, pulling as hard as they could. There was a slight breeze in their favour, and they rowed with the sail up until they reached Skor Isle; they paused there briefly to ask about people's movements. Soon afterwards they saw a boat coming across the fjord from the west, and recognized at once the men on board; it was the Thorhollusons. Halldor Olafsson and his companions made for them immediately. There was no resistance offered, for the Olafssons leapt on to their boat and attacked them at once. Stein Thorholluson and his brother Odd were seized and beheaded over the side

The Olafssons then turned for home, and their expedition was thought highly enterprising.

50. Action over Kjartan

OLAF went to meet Kjartan's body. He sent messengers south to Borg to tell Thorstein Egilsson what had happened, and also that he wanted Thorstein's support for the prosecution of the case; he said that if important people joined forces with the Osvifssons against them, he wanted to have everything well in hand.

He sent the same message north to Vididale to his son-in-law Gudmund Solmundsson and to the Asgeirssons, adding that he had charged all those who had taken part in the attack on

Kjartan with his killing, apart from Ospak Osvifsson, who was already an outlaw over a woman called Aldis.[1]

Olaf had referred the manslaughter action to the Thorsness Assembly.

He had Kjartan's body brought home, and a tent raised over it, for at that time no church had yet been built in the Dales.

As soon as Olaf learned that Thorstein Egilsson had wasted no time and gathered a large force, and that the men of Vididale had done the same, he himself mustered men from all over the Dales; it was a huge company, and he now sent this whole force off to Laugar and told them: 'It is my wish that you defend Bolli, if he needs it, no less loyally than you serve me, for I suspect that the men from the other districts feel they have a score of their own to settle with Bolli, and they will soon be upon us.'

When this had been arranged, Thorstein Egilsson and his men, and also the men of Vididale, arrived; and they were all wild with anger. Hall Gudmundsson and Kalf Asgeirsson were the most vehement in urging that they should attack Bolli and hunt down the Osvifssons who, they said, could not possibly have left the district as yet. But since Olaf strongly urged restraint, messages of conciliation were exchanged between the two sides. There were no difficulties as far as Bolli was con-

1. *Aldis was the daughter of Dueller-Ljot of Ingjaldssand. She and Ospak had a son called Ulf, who later became King Harald Sigurdsson's Marshal; he married Jorunn Thorberg's-daughter, and their son was Jon, the father of Erlend the Flabby, the father of Archbishop Eystein.*

King Harald Sigurdsson of Norway was the Harald Hardradi who invaded England in 1066 and was killed by King Harold of England at the Battle of Stamford Bridge on 25 September, three weeks before the Battle of Hastings (see *King Harald's Saga*).

Ulf Ospaksson, the king's Marshal, is mentioned there as one of King Harald's staunchest supporters; he died just before the invasion of England.

Ulf's great-grandson, Archbishop Eystein Erlendsson, was Archbishop of Trondheim, in Norway, from 1161-88. The archbishopric of Trondheim then embraced Shetland, Orkney, the Hebrides, the Faroe Islands, Iceland and Greenland as well as all Norway.

cerned, because he invited Olaf himself to arbitrate on his behalf; and Osvif found he was in no position to object, for he had not received any support from Snorri the Priest.

A peace-meeting was arranged at Ljarwoods, and the whole case was put unconditionally into Olaf's hands: the fines and sentences of outlawry for Kjartan's killing were to be meted out wholly at Olaf's discretion. Then the peace-meeting was brought to a close. On Olaf's advice, Bolli did not attend the peace-meeting. The terms of the settlement were to be announced at the Thorsness Assembly.

With that, the men of Myrar and the men of Vididale rode back to Hjardarholt.

As consolation for Hrefna, Thorstein Kuggason offered to foster Asgeir, Kjartan's son.

Hrefna went north with her brothers. She was filled with grief but bore herself always with courtesy and was gracious of speech to everyone. Hrefna took no other husband after Kjartan. She lived only a short time after her return to the north, and it is said that she died of a broken heart.

51. Settlement

KJARTAN'S body rested for a week at Hjardarholt.

Thorstein Egilsson had had a church built at Borg. He took Kjartan's body home with him, and Kjartan was buried at Borg. The church had only recently been consecrated, and was still hung with white.

Soon it was time for the Thorsness Assembly. The actions against the Osvifssons were now heard, and they were all sentenced to outlawry. Money was put up to secure them a passage abroad, and they were forbidden to return to Iceland for as long as any of the Olafssons, or Asgeir Kjartansson, were alive. No compensation was to be paid for Osvif's nephew, Gudlaug, because he had taken part in the ambush and attack on Kjartan; and Thorolf Osvifsson was to receive no redress for the wounds he had suffered.

Olaf refused to have Bolli prosecuted, but asked him to put up damages on his own behalf instead. Halldor and Steinthor and the other Olafssons were greatly displeased at this, and said that life would be very hard to bear if Bolli remained in the same district as themselves; but Olaf said that everything would be in order as long as he was alive.

There was a ship lying at Bjarnarhaven belonging to a man called Audun Fetter-Hound. Audun was at the Assembly, and said, 'The chances are that these men will find themselves no less outlawed in Norway than here, if Kjartan's friends are still alive.'[1]

But Osvif said, 'Your prediction, Fetter-Dog, will not come true, for my sons will be held in high esteem by men of rank, while you, Fetter-Hound, will fall into the hands of trolls before this summer is out.'

Audun Fetter-Hound sailed abroad that summer and his ship was wrecked off the Faroe Islands. All lives on board were lost, so Osvif's prophecy was thought to have been very effective.

The Osvifssons went abroad that summer, and none of them ever returned.

Olaf the Peacock gained great prestige as a result of these court actions, for having been so firm where it was called for – in the case of the Osvifssons – whereas he had shielded Bolli because of their kinship. Olaf thanked his men warmly for their support.

On Olaf's advice, Bolli bought the estate at Sælingsdale Tongue.

It is said that Olaf lived for three years after Kjartan was killed. After Olaf's death his sons shared out the property. Halldor took over the farm of Hjardarholt, and their mother, Thorgerd, stayed there with him. Thorgerd was filled with hatred for Bolli, and felt that he had cruelly repaid his fosterage.

1. There is a reference to this incident in *Gunnlaug's Saga* (Chapter 5), where it is made clear that Audun Fetter-Hound refused to give the Osvifssons a passage abroad.

52. Thorkel's reward

IN the spring, Gudrun and Bolli took over the farm at Sælings-dale Tongue, and it soon became a fine estate. A son was born to them. He was baptized, and named Thorleik; he was quickly handsome and precocious.

Halldor Olafsson was living at Hjardarholt, as has already been written; he was very much the leader of the brothers.

In the spring of the year that Kjartan had been killed, Thorgerd Egil's-daughter had placed a boy, a distant kinsman of hers, with Thorkel of Hafratindar; the boy looked after the sheep there for the summer. Like other people he was greatly grieved at Kjartan's death; but he could never speak of Kjartan in Thorkel's presence, for Thorkel always spoke slightingly of Kjartan and said he had been yellow and cowardly, and he would often mimic the way that Kjartan had taken his death-blow. The boy found this hard to bear, and went to Hjardarholt and told Halldor and Thorgerd and begged them to take him in. Thorgerd told him to stay on at Hafratindar for the rest of the summer. The boy said he could not face staying there any longer – 'and you wouldn't ask me to, if you knew how much I have to bear.'

Thorgerd's heart was softened by his tale of woe, and she said that she, for her part, was quite willing to take him in.

Halldor said, 'Pay no attention to the boy; he's nothing.'

'The boy himself doesn't matter,' said Thorgerd. 'But Thorkel has behaved disgracefully in every way, for he knew of the ambush the men of Laugar were laying for Kjartan and refused to warn him, and used their encounter for his own sport and amusement instead; and moreover, he has been very abusive ever since. It's beyond all hope that you brothers will ever seek vengeance when the odds are not in your favour, if you cannot even repay scoundrels like Thorkel for what they have done.'

Halldor had little to say to that, but told Thorgerd to engage the boy if she liked. A few days later, Halldor rode off from home with several men. He went to Hafratindar and surprised Thorkel in his house. Thorkel was led outside and killed, and met his death like a coward. Halldor refused to allow any looting there, and with that he went back home. Thorgerd was pleased at this deed, and thought the gesture better than nothing.

All was quiet on the surface that summer, but there was a great coldness between Bolli and the Olafssons. The brothers were utterly implacable towards Bolli, whereas he gave in to his kinsmen whenever he could do so without diminishing himself; for he was a man of great pride. Bolli kept a large household and lived in considerable style, for there was no lack of wealth.

Steinthor Olafsson lived at Donustead in Laxriverdale. He married Thurid Asgeir's-daughter, who had previously been the wife of Thorkel Kuggi. Their son was called Steinthor, and was known as Gro-Slappi.

53. Thorgerd and her sons

TOWARDS the end of the winter after the death of Olaf the Peacock, Thorgerd Egil's-daughter sent word to her son Steinthor Olafsson, asking him to come to see her. When they met she told him she wanted to go west to Saurby to see her friend Aud. She told Halldor to come too. There were five of them in all.

Halldor rode beside his mother. They rode on until they came opposite the farm of Sælingsdale Tongue. Then Thorgerd turned her horse towards the farm and asked, 'What is this farm called?'

'As if you didn't know already, mother!' replied Halldor. 'This farm is called Tongue.'

'And who lives here?' she asked.

'You know that too, mother,' he replied.

Thorgerd snorted. 'Yes, I certainly know!' she said. 'I know that Bolli lives here, your brother's killer. And you are remarkably unlike your noble kinsmen if you don't want to avenge such a brother as Kjartan was. Your grandfather, Egil Skalla-

Grimsson, would never have behaved like this. It is cruel to have such craven sons; and I for one believe it would have suited you better to have been your father's daughters and been married off. The old saying, "to every family its flaw", is certainly borne out here, Halldor. To my mind this was Olaf's greatest misfortune, that he blundered so badly in begetting his sons. I am speaking to you, Halldor, since you think yourself the leader of your brothers. And now we shall turn back, for my main reason for coming here was to remind you of this, in case you had forgotten.'

'We could never put the blame on you, mother,' said Halldor, 'if it should ever slip our minds.'

Halldor had little else to say, but his heart swelled with hatred against Bolli.

The winter passed, and summer came; soon it was time for the Assembly. Halldor and his brothers announced that they would be attending it. They rode there with a large following, and tented the booth which Olaf had owned. The Assembly was quiet and uneventful.

The sons of Gudmund Solmundsson from up north in Vididale were also present at this Assembly. Bardi Gudmundsson was then eighteen years old, a big, powerful man. The Olafssons gave their nephew Bardi a pressing invitation to come home with them (Hall Gudmundsson was abroad at the time). Bardi accepted their invitation, for all these kinsmen were very fond of one another. So Bardi rode west from the Assembly with the Olafssons. They came home to Hjardarholt, and Bardi stayed there for the rest of the summer.[1]

54. Plans are laid

HALLDOR now told Bardi in private that he and his brothers intended to make an attack on Bolli, for they could no longer endure their mother's taunts. 'I won't try to hide it from you,

1. Bardi Gudmundsson plays an important part in *Grettir's Saga* and *Killer-Styr's Saga*.

Bardi, that the main reason for inviting you here was that we wanted to have your help and support in this.'

Bardi replied, 'To violate a settlement with one's kinsmen would be widely condemned; and in the second place I think it would be very difficult to get at Bolli. He always has a number of men about him, and is himself a great warrior; and he's never at a loss for shrewd counsel with Gudrun and Osvif at his side. All things considered, it seems to me a very difficult matter to tackle.'

'There's no need at all to exaggerate the difficulties,' said Halldor. 'I wouldn't have raised this matter now if we hadn't been fully committed already to seeking vengeance on Bolli, and I'm sure that you, kinsman, will not shrink from joining in with us.'

'I know you would think it improper of me to shirk it,' replied Bardi. 'Nor shall I, if I cannot dissuade you from it.'

'You are doing the best thing,' said Halldor, 'as was only to be expected of you.'

Bardi said they would have to go about it with great care. Halldor said he had heard that Bolli had sent his men away, some north to Hrutafjord to his ship, the others out along the strands. 'I'm also told that Bolli is at the shieling in Sælingsdale with only the farmhands who are doing the hay-making there. I'm sure we shall never get a better chance of dealing with Bolli than now.'

And so Halldor and Bardi resolved that this was what they would do.

There was a man called Thorstein the Black who lived in Hundadale, in the Breidafjord Dales, an intelligent and wealthy man. He had been Olaf the Peacock's friend for a long time. Thorstein had a sister called Solveig, who was married to a man called Helgi Hardbeinsson. Helgi was a big, powerful man; he was a great trader and had just returned to Iceland from abroad, and was staying with his brother-in-law, Thorstein the Black.

Halldor sent word to Thorstein the Black and his brother-in-law Helgi, and when they arrived at Hjardarholt, Halldor told them his plan and how they were going to carry it out, and asked them to join in the expedition.

Thorstein disapproved of the idea – 'For it is a tragedy that you kinsmen should keep on killing each other off. There are few enough men of Bolli's stature left in your family now.'

But no matter what Thorstein said, it was of no avail.

Halldor sent word to his uncle, Lambi Thorbjornsson, and when he arrived, Halldor told him of his intentions. Lambi came out strongly in favour of the scheme. Thorgerd, too, urged them on fiercely to make the journey, saying that she could never feel that Kjartan had been avenged until Bolli had paid with his life.

After that they prepared to set out. In the company were the four Olafssons – Halldor and Steinthor, Helgi and Hoskuld; the fifth was Bardi Gudmundsson, the sixth was Lambi Thorbjornsson, the seventh Thorstein the Black, the eighth his brother-in-law Helgi Hardbeinsson, and the ninth An Brushwood-Belly.

Thorgerd also went with them. They tried to dissuade her, saying that this was no journey for a woman. But she insisted on going – 'For I know you well enough, my sons, to realize that you will need spurring on.'

So they let her have her way.

55. Bolli's death

THEY rode off from Hjardarholt, nine of them, with Thorgerd making the tenth. They rode north along the foreshore and reached Ljarwoods during the small hours of the night; they did not pause until they came to Sælingsdale early in the morning.

In those days there were thick woods in the valley. Bolli was staying at the shieling there, as Halldor had been told; the shieling stood near the river at a place now called Bollatoptir. There is a long ridge of high ground stretching from above the shieling down to Stakkagill; between this ridge and the mountainside there is a large meadow, called Barm, where Bolli's farmhands were working.

Halldor and his companions rode past Oxnagrof, and then across Ranar Plain and came out on to Hamar Meadow, which lies across the river from the shieling. They knew that there were some men still at the shieling; so they dismounted, and planned to wait until the farmhands had left the shieling for their work.

Bolli's shepherd had gone up the mountainside early that morning to see to the sheep. He caught sight of the men in the woods and the tethered horses; and he suspected that people who travelled so stealthily would not be on a peaceful mission. He ran towards the shieling at once, taking the shortest way, in order to warn Bolli of their presence.

Halldor Olafsson was very keen-sighted. He saw the boy running down the mountainside making for the shieling. He told his companions that it must be Bolli's shepherd – 'and he must have caught sight of us. We shall have to cut him off and stop him getting word to the shieling.'

They did as he suggested. An Brushwood-Belly outran the others and managed to catch the boy. He lifted him off the ground and flung him down so violently that the boy's back-bone snapped.

Then they rode over to the shieling; it consisted of two huts, the sleeping-quarters and the dairy.

Bolli had risen early that morning to arrange the day's work, and had gone back to bed after the farmhands had gone out, and now only Bolli and Gudrun were left in the shieling. They were awakened by the noise of the visitors dismounting, and then they heard them debating which of them should be the first to go into the shieling and attack Bolli.

Bolli recognized Halldor by his voice, and several of his companions. He told Gudrun to go away from the shieling, saying that this was not an encounter she would be likely to enjoy. Gudrun said she thought that nothing would happen there which she should not be allowed to watch, and added that it could do Bolli no harm to have her by his side. Bolli insisted on having his own way, however, and so Gudrun left the shieling; she went down the slope to the stream that flowed there, and began washing her linen.

Bolli was now alone in the shieling. He took his weapons and put on a helmet; he carried a shield in one hand and the sword 'Leg-Biter' in the other. He had no coat of mail.

Halldor and his companions were still debating what to do,

for no one was eager to enter the shieling. Then An Brushwood-Belly said, 'There are those among us who are closer in kinship to Kjartan than I, but no one remembers better than I how Kjartan met his death. When I was being carried home to Tongue, more dead than alive, after Kjartan had fallen, my one thought was that I would gladly do Bolli some harm if ever I had the chance. So I shall be the first to enter the shieling.'

Thorstein the Black said, 'That was bravely spoken, but it would be more sensible not to rush into this recklessly. We must proceed warily, for Bolli will not stand there idle when he is being attacked. He may be short of help now, but you can expect him to put up a fierce defence, for he is a strong and skilful warrior, and the sword he has is a very reliable weapon.'

Now An Brushwood-Belly burst into the shieling with his shield over his head, the narrow end pointing forward. Bolli struck at him with 'Leg-Biter', slicing through the tail end of the shield and cleaving his skull to the shoulders. An died instantly.

Then Lambi Thorbjornsson went in. He held a shield in front of him and carried a drawn sword. At that moment, Bolli was pulling 'Leg-Biter' out of An's body, and his shield had slipped to one side. Lambi now lunged at Bolli's thigh and wounded him severely. Bolli struck back at Lambi's shoulder and the sword ripped down his side; Lambi could take no further part in the battle, and his arm gave him trouble for the rest of his life.

Just then, Helgi Hardbeinsson went into the shieling; he was carrying a spear with a blade eighteen inches long and an iron-bound shaft. When Bolli saw it he threw down his sword and grasped his shield in both hands, and went towards the door to meet Helgi. Helgi thrust at Bolli with the spear; it went right through the shield and through Bolli himself. Bolli fell back against the wall. And now the rest of them, Halldor and his brothers, came rushing into the shieling; Thorgerd, too, came in.

Bolli said, 'It's safe now for you brothers to come a little closer than you have done so far.' And he said he did not think his defence would last very long now.

It was Thorgerd who answered him, and said there was no

need to shrink from dealing with Bolli thoroughly; she told them to finish off their work. Bolli was still standing up against the wall of the shieling, clutching his tunic tightly to stop his entrails falling out. Steinthor Olafsson now sprang at him and swung a great axe at his neck just above the shoulders, and the head flew off at once.

'May your hands prosper,' said Thorgerd, and added that Gudrun would now have some red hairs to comb for Bolli.

With that they left the shieling.

Gudrun now came walking up from the stream and went over to talk to Halldor and the others. She asked them how their encounter with Bolli had gone. They told her what had happened. Gudrun was wearing a tunic with a tight-fitting woven bodice, and a tall head-dress, and round her waist she had tied a fringed sash with dark blue stripes.

Helgi Hardbeinsson went up to her and took one end of the sash and wiped the blood off the spear with which he had run Bolli through.

Gudrun looked at him, and smiled.

'That was an evil and cruel thing to do,' said Halldor.

Helgi told him not to grieve over it – 'For I have the feeling,' he said, 'that under this very sash lies the one who will take my life.'

With that they took to their horses and rode away. Gudrun accompanied them on foot for a while, talking to them, and then she turned back.

56. Gudrun moves to Helgafell

HALLDOR'S companions remarked that Gudrun could not have been much affected by Bolli's death since she had come to see them off and had talked to them as if they had done nothing to distress her.

Halldor replied, 'I don't think Gudrun is unaffected by Bolli's death. Rather, I think she came to see us off because she wanted to know precisely who the men were who took part in this expedition. It's no exaggeration to say that Gudrun surpasses all other women in courage and resolution. It's only to be expected that Gudrun should take Bolli's death to heart, for men like him are truly a great loss, even though we kinsmen didn't have the good luck to be able to live together in peace.'

They rode back home to Hjardarholt.

News of Bolli's death quickly spread far and wide, and was thought very serious; he was deeply mourned.

Gudrun sent word at once to Snorri the Priest, for she and Osvif placed all their trust in him. Snorri wasted no time and went to Sælingsdale Tongue with sixty men. Gudrun was glad to see him. He offered to try to bring about a settlement, but Gudrun was reluctant to accept compensation for Bolli's death on behalf of her son, Thorleik.

'I think, Snorri, that the best help you can give me,' she said, 'is to exchange homes with me, so that I don't have to live in the same district as the people of Hjardarholt.'

At that time Snorri was heavily involved in disputes with the men of Eyr,[1] and he said he would agree to the exchange because of his friendship with Gudrun – 'but you will have to remain at Tongue for another year,' he added.

Snorri now got ready to leave, and Gudrun gave him fine gifts. Snorri rode back home to Helgafell, and the rest of the year was quiet, on the surface at least.

During the winter after Bolli's death, Gudrun gave birth to a child. It was a boy, and he was named Bolli. He quickly became tall and handsome, and Gudrun loved him very much.

When the winter had passed and it was spring again, the exchange of houses between Snorri and Gudrun took place as they had planned. Snorri moved to Sælingsdale Tongue, and lived there for the rest of his life.

Gudrun went to Helgafell with her father Osvif, and they built up an excellent estate there. Gudrun's sons, Thorleik and Bolli, grew up there; Thorleik was four years old when his father Bolli was killed.

1. Snorri's long quarrels with the men of Eyr are described in *Eyrbyggja Saga*. However, according to that source, he had made peace with them several years before this.

57. Thorgils Holluson and Thorkel Eyjolfsson

THERE was a man called Thorgils Holluson,[1] who lived at a farm called Tongue, in Hordadale. He was a big, handsome man, very arrogant and overbearing in most people's eyes. There was little love lost between him and Snorri the Priest, who thought him meddlesome and vain.

Thorgils was always finding pretexts for visiting the western part of the district. He was always coming to Helgafell and offering to help Gudrun with her affairs. She received his offers politely, but no more.

Thorgils invited her son, Thorleik Bollason, to come and stay with him, and the boy spent much of his time at Tongue in Hordadale, where he learned law from Thorgils, who was an outstanding lawyer.

At that time a man called Thorkel Eyjolfsson was engaged in trading voyages. He was a man of great renown and noble lineage, and a great friend of Snorri the Priest. He always stayed with his cousin Thorstein Kuggason whenever he was in Iceland.

One time when Thorkel had a ship lying at Vadil, on Bardastrand, it so happened that the son of Eid of As was killed in Borgarfjord by the sons of Helga of Kropp; the man who did the actual killing was called Grim, and his brother Njal was drowned in Hvit River soon afterwards. Grim was outlawed for the killing, and took refuge in the mountains while he was under the sentence of outlawry. He was a big, powerful man. Eid was very old when this happened, so the case was not followed up any further; but Thorkel Eyjolfsson was severely criticized for failing to pursue it to the limit.[2]

1. *His mother was Halla, the daughter of Gest Oddleifsson; Thorgils was known by his mother's name because she lived longer than his father, whose name was Snorri, the son of Alf of the Dales.*

2. Thorkel was a kinsman of Eid of As (Eid's sister was his grandmother) and since he was the most powerful and prominent member of the family, it was Thorkel's duty to take action over the

Next spring, when Thorkel Eyjolfsson had made his ship ready, he sailed south across Breidafjord; there he got himself a horse and rode alone over to As without a halt to see his kinsman Eid, who welcomed him gladly. Thorkel told him he had come because he wanted to hunt down Grim, his outlaw, and he asked Eid if he had any knowledge of where his hideout might be.

'I don't like the idea of this,' replied Eid. 'I think you're taking a very great risk in this, tackling a hellhound like Grim. But if you insist on going, you must take a number of men with you, so that you will have the situation well under control.'

'I don't think it much of an achievement,' said Thorkel, 'to attack a lone man with a large force; but I should like you to lend me the sword "Skofnung",[1] for I'm sure I could then overcome one single outlaw, no matter how capable he is.'

'It's up to you,' said Eid. 'But it wouldn't surprise me if you live to regret this wilful decision. But since you feel you are doing this for my sake I shall not refuse your request, for I think "Skofnung" will be in good hands when you have it. Such is the nature of the sword, however, that the sun must never shine on its hilt, and it must never be drawn in the presence of a woman. If someone is wounded by the sword, the wound will never heal unless it is rubbed with the healing-stone that goes with the sword.'

Thorkel said he would bear all this carefully in mind, and took the sword. He asked Eid to tell him the way to Grim's hideout. Eid said he thought Grim was most likely to have his hideout up north in Tvidægra, beside Fiski Waters. Thorkel now rode north into the moors, following the route Eid had pointed out to him; and when he had travelled deep into the moors he saw a hut near a big lake, and made for it.

---

killing. The killer had flouted the sentence of outlawry by not leaving the country, so the victim's family could kill him with impunity – and were expected to do so, if honour was to be satisfied.

1. The sword 'Skofnung' was said to have been originally owned by the legendary King Hrolf Kraki of Denmark (cf. Chapter 78), and been rifled from his burial mound by Midfjord-Skeggi, the father of Eid of As. The sword also plays a part in *Kormak's Saga*.

58. Thorkel and Grim

WHEN Thorkel reached the hut, he saw a man sitting at the lakeside beside the mouth of a stream, fishing. He had a cloak over his head.

Thorkel dismounted and tethered his horse at the wall of the hut. Then he walked down to the lake where the man was sitting. Grim saw his shadow on the water and jumped quickly to his feet. Thorkel was very close to him by then and struck at him; the blow caught Grim on the arm just above the wrist, but it was not a very deep wound. Grim threw himself at Thorkel at once and grappled with him; the difference in strength quickly told, and Thorkel fell, with Grim on top of him.

Grim now asked him who he was; Thorkel replied that it was none of his business.

'Things have turned out rather differently than you expected,' said Grim. 'Your life is now in my hands.'

Thorkel said he would not beg for mercy – 'for this has turned out lucklessly for me.'

Grim said that his own misfortunes were great enough without adding to them. 'You are destined for something other than meeting your death in this encounter with me. I'm going to give you your life, and you can repay me in whatever way you like.'

They both got up and walked over to the hut. Thorkel saw that Grim was growing weak from loss of blood, so he took 'Skofnung's' healing-stone and rubbed it on the wound; then he bound it to the arm, and all the pain and swelling disappeared at once.

They spent the night there. Next morning Thorkel made ready to leave, and asked Grim if he wanted to come with him; Grim agreed readily. Thorkel headed west at once and did not go to see Eid; he made no halt until he arrived at Sælingsdale Tongue.

Snorri the Priest welcomed him warmly. Thorkel told him that his expedition had turned out badly. But Snorri said it had turned out well – 'Grim looks a man of good luck to me, and I want you to treat him generously when you part. And now, my friend, my advice to you is that you should give up trading and settle down and find yourself a wife, and become a chieftain as befits your lineage.'

'Your advice has often turned out well for me,' said Thorkel. And he asked Snorri if he had considered which woman he should propose to.

'You should propose to the woman who is the best match there is,' said Snorri. 'Gudrun Osvif's-daughter.'

Thorkel said it was true that it would be an excellent match. 'But I am discouraged by her temper and wilfulness. She will want to have her husband Bolli avenged; Thorgils Holluson seems to be involved with her in that, and this would probably not be much to his liking. But apart from that, Gudrun pleases me.'

'I shall see to it that you come to no harm from Thorgils,' said Snorri. 'And as regards the vengeance for Bolli, I think it very likely that something will have been done about that before this year is out.'

'It may well be that these are not idle words,' said Thorkel. 'But the vengeance for Bolli seems no more likely now than it has been before, unless some very important people can be involved in it.'

Snorri said, 'I should like you to go abroad once more this summer. Then we'll see what happens.'

Thorkel agreed to do so, and with that they parted. Thorkel went west across Breidafjord to his ship. He took Grim aboard with him; they had a good voyage that summer and made land in the south of Norway.

Thorkel then said to Grim, 'You are well aware of the circumstances that brought us together, and there's no need to go into that now; but I should like to part company with you on a happier note than seemed likely at first. I have found you a man of courage, and for that reason I want to send you on your way as if I had never had any quarrel with you. I shall give you as much merchandise as you require to join a guild of good merchants. But don't try to settle in the north of this country, for many of Eid's kinsmen are traders, and they bear you a strong grudge still.'

Grim thanked him for his words, and said he could never have asked for as much as Thorkel was offering. When they parted, Thorkel gave him an ample supply of merchandise, and many people said that he had been extremely generous.

Grim then went east to Oslo Fjord and settled there. He was considered a man of great stature; and that is the last we hear of Grim.

Thorkel spent the winter in Norway, and was thought a man of great account. He was extremely wealthy and very ambitious.

And now we must leave this matter for a while and take up the story again in Iceland, to hear what was happening there while Thorkel was abroad.

59. Vengeance is planned

LATE that summer, Gudrun Osvif's-daughter left home on a journey east to the Dales, and rode to Thykkvawood. At that time her son Thorleik was staying alternately at Thykkvawood with Halldor and Ornolf Armodsson and at Tongue in Hordadale with Thorgils Holluson.

That same evening she sent word to Snorri the Priest that she wanted to see him urgently the following day. Snorri wasted no time and set off at once with one companion to Haukadale River. There is a crag called Hofdi on the north side of the river; it is in the Lækjarwood lands, and it was there that Gudrun had arranged for them to meet.

They both arrived at almost the same time. Gudrun had one companion with her, too – her son, Bolli Bollason; he was twelve years old by then, but just as mature in mind and body as many who had already reached full manhood. He was carrying 'Leg-Biter'.

Snorri and Gudrun began talking at once, while Bolli and Snorri's companion sat up on the crag and kept an eye on people's movements in the district. When Snorri and Gudrun had exchanged news, Snorri asked her what fresh turn of events had happened to make her send for him in such haste.

'To be honest, the matter I'm going to raise is just as fresh as it was when it happened twelve years ago,' said Gudrun. 'I want to talk about the vengeance for Bolli – and that will come as no surprise to you, for I have been reminding you of it from time to time. I might also mention that you have promised to help me achieve it if I would only wait with patience. But now it's obviously futile to hope that you will pay any heed to our cause. I have now waited as long as my temper can stand; but I would still like to have the benefit of your advice as to where the vengeance should land.'

Snorri asked what she had in mind.

'It is my wish that the Olafssons do not all escape unscathed,' said Gudrun.

Snorri said he would forbid any attack on important people in the district – 'people who are near kin to men who would pursue their vengeance to the limit. It's high time these family feuds came to an end.'

'Then we must attack Lambi Thorbjornsson and kill him,' said Gudrun. 'That would get rid of the most malevolent of them all.'

'Lambi certainly deserves to be killed,' said Snorri, 'but I don't think Bolli would be avenged that way. The disparity between the two men would not be properly taken into account in any peace settlement if their deaths were to be balanced against each other.'

'It may well be that we can't even the score fully with the men of Laxriverdale,' said Gudrun, 'but now someone must pay, and pay dearly, whatever dale he lives in. So now let's turn to Thorstein the Black, for no one has chosen a more wicked part in this affair than he.'

'Thorstein's guilt is exactly the same as that of any of those who took part in the attack on Bolli but did not land a blow on him. But surely you are ignoring the men on whom vengeance would be much more fitting, in my opinion – those, in fact, who actually killed him, like Helgi Hardbeinsson.'

'That's true,' said Gudrun, 'but I cannot bear to think that all those for whom I have always cherished so much hatred are to be left in peace.'

'I see a solution for that,' said Snorri. 'Lambi and Thorstein the Black will have to join in with your sons – that would be a fitting ransom for them to pay. But if they refuse, I shall try no further to save them from whatever punishment you care to mete out to them.'

'How are we to go about persuading these men you mentioned to join in?' asked Gudrun.

'That's up to those who are to lead the foray,' said Snorri.

'I'm sure we can rely on your good guidance as to who is to be in charge of it and lead it,' said Gudrun.

Then Snorri smiled, and said, 'You yourself have already picked the man for that.'

'You mean Thorgils Holluson?' said Gudrun.

Snorri said yes.

'I've discussed this with Thorgils already,' said Gudrun, 'and there's nothing more to be said about it, because he made one condition I wouldn't even consider: Thorgils was quite willing to avenge Bolli, but only if he could win my hand in return. And since that's out of the question, I would never ask him to undertake this mission.'

'I can solve that problem for you,' said Snorri, 'because I don't grudge Thorgils this mission. Promise him marriage by all means, but only in the sense that you will marry no other man in this country than Thorgils; and that promise you will be able to keep, because Thorkel Eyjolfsson is not in this country at present, and he is the man I want you to marry.'

'Thorgils is bound to see through this trick,' said Gudrun.

'He certainly won't see through it,' said Snorri, 'for Thorgils is better known for his impulsiveness than his shrewdness. You must make the agreement with only a few witnesses present; have his foster-brother Halldor Armodsson there, but not Ornolf, for he is the cleverer of them. And you can blame me if it doesn't work.'

With that, Gudrun and he ended their conversation and bade one another farewell. Snorri rode back home, and Gudrun returned to Thykkvawood.

Next morning, Gudrun rode from Thykkvawood with her sons. As they were riding west along Skogarstrand, they noticed some people riding hard behind them and catching up on them fast; it was Thorgils Holluson. They greeted one another warmly, and rode together to Helgafell that same day.

60. Gudrun's plotting

A FEW days after Gudrun returned home, she summoned her sons to have a talk with her in her kitchen-garden. When they arrived they saw that some linen clothes had been laid out on the ground, a shirt and a pair of drawers; they were heavily stained with blood.

Gudrun said, 'These very clothes you see before you here challenge you to avenge your father. I shall not waste many words on this, for there is little hope that you will be moved by mere words if you do not heed such tokens and reminders as these.'

The brothers were greatly moved by what Gudrun said, but replied that they had been too young to seek revenge and had been leaderless; they said they had not known how to make plans for themselves or for others – 'but we have certainly not forgotten our loss.'

Gudrun said she felt they were far more interested in sports and horse-fights. And with that they went away.

That night the brothers could not sleep. Thorgils noticed this and asked them what the matter was. They told him of the talk they had had with their mother, and said they could no longer endure their own grief and their mother's taunts.

'We want to seek revenge,' said Bolli. 'We have now reached the age when people would start reproaching us if we sit and do nothing.'

Next day Thorgils and Gudrun had a talk. Gudrun spoke up and said, 'It seems to me, Thorgils, that my sons can no longer bear to stand by idly like this and not seek vengeance for their father. The main reason for the delay has been that I thought

Thorleik and Bolli too young before now to get involved in killings; but there has been ample reason for doing something about it long before this.'

'There's no point in discussing this with me,' said Thorgils, 'for you have flatly refused to marry me. But I'm still of the same mind as when we talked about it earlier; if I can gain your hand in marriage, I wouldn't shrink from killing one or even both of those who had most to do with Bolli's death.'

'I'm sure that Thorleik thinks no one better fitted than you to be the leader,' said Gudrun, 'if there's work to be done that de-mands some courage. But I shall not try to hide it from you that the boys intend to go after that berserk Helgi Hardbeinsson, who sits on his farm in Skorradale and has no fears for his safety.

'I don't care whether his name is Helgi or anything else,' said Thorgils, 'for I don't think it beyond me to deal with Helgi or any other man. As far as I'm concerned there's nothing more to say, provided that you promise in the presence of witnesses to marry me if I carry out this vengeance with your sons.'

Gudrun said she would keep any promise she made, even if there weren't many witnesses present; and she said that this would be the terms of their agreement.

She asked to have his foster-brother Halldor Armodsson and her own sons called in. Thorgils asked for Ornolf to be present as well. Gudrun said there was no need for that – 'I have more doubts about Ornolf's loyalty to you than you yourself seem to have.' So Thorgils let her have her way.

Now Gudrun's sons joined her and Thorgils, and Halldor came with them. Gudrun explained to them: 'Thorgils has promised to lead my sons in an attack on Helgi Hardbeinsson to avenge Bolli. In return, Thorgils has stipulated that he should get my hand in marriage. I now declare in front of you as witnesses that I promise to marry no other man in this country except him, and I don't intend to marry abroad.'

To Thorgils this seemed acceptable enough, and he did not see through it. With that they ended their talk. It was now fully agreed that Thorgils was to undertake this mission. He got ready to leave Helgafell with Gudrun's sons; they rode off to the Dales, and went first home to Tongue in Hordadale.

61. Thorstein and Lambi

THE local Assembly at Leidarholm was held the next Sunday, and Thorgils rode to it with his following. Snorri the Priest was not present, but the Assembly was well attended.

During the day, Thorgils asked to see Thorstein the Black and said to him, 'As you are well aware, you took part in the attack with the Olafssons when Bolli was killed; and you have never made any amends to his sons for that. Even though it happened a long time ago, I don't expect that Thorleik and Bolli will have forgotten the men who took part in that attack. Now, the brothers feel it wouldn't be right for them to take vengeance on the Olafssons, because of their kinship; so now they intend to turn for revenge against Helgi Hardbeinsson, for it was he who dealt Bolli his death-wound. We want to ask you, Thorstein, to take part in this expedition with the brothers, and thus secure peace and a settlement for yourself.'

Thorstein replied, 'It isn't proper for me to be party to a plot against Helgi, my own brother-in-law. I would much rather buy peace with as much money as is considered right and honourable.'

'I don't think the brothers want to make money out of this,' said Thorgils. 'Don't deceive yourself, Thorstein; there are only two choices open to you: either to join in on this expedition, or else face the direst consequences as soon as they have a chance of dealing with you. I myself would like to see you take the first choice, despite your obligations to Helgi; in such a dilemma, everyone must fend for himself.'

'Will the same choice be offered to any of the others who are involved in this quarrel with Bolli's sons?' asked Thorstein.

'Lambi will be given the same choice,' said Thorgils.

Thorstein said he would feel better about it if he was not to be the only one in this.

After that, Thorgils called Lambi Thorbjornsson to see him, and told Thorstein to stay and listen.

'I want to put the same point to you, Lambi, that I've been

discussing with Thorstein,' said Thorgils. 'What amends are you prepared to make to the Bollasons for the complaints they have against you? – for we know for a fact that you actually wounded Bolli. In addition you are all the more guilty because it was you who urged the most strongly that Bolli should be killed; but on the other hand you had the best reason for it, next to the Olafssons.'

Lambi asked what demands would be made on him. Thorgils replied that he would be given the same choice as Thorstein – to join in with the brothers Thorleik and Bolli.

'I think this an evil price to pay for peace, and cowardly at that,' said Lambi. 'I have no wish to take part in this.'

Then Thorstein the Black said, 'It's not quite so simple, Lambi, to refuse it out of hand like this; for there are important people involved in this, people of stature who have felt for a long time that they've been deprived of their rights. Bolli's sons, I'm told, are very promising men and extremely ambitious, and they have every cause to want vengeance. We can hardly expect to escape scot-free after such a grave deed. Besides, people will put most of the blame on me, because of my kinship with Helgi; and I'm quite sure that most people would sacrifice anything sooner than their own lives. One must always deal with the most urgent problems first.'

Lambi replied, 'It's easy to see what you want, Thorstein. And I think it's best that you have your own way if you think it's so simple, for we have been comrades in misfortune for a long time. But I want to make this stipulation, however, if I join in: that my nephews the Olafssons are to be left unmolested if the vengeance against Helgi is achieved.'

Thorgils agreed to this on behalf of the Bollasons. And so it was settled that Thorstein and Lambi should join in with Thorgils on the expedition; and they all agreed to meet at Tongue in Hordadale early on Tuesday. With that they parted, and Thorgils rode home to Tongue that evening.

Soon it was time for those who were to accompany Thorgils on the expedition to come and meet him as agreed; and before sunrise on the Tuesday morning Thorstein and Lambi arrived at Tongue. Thorgils gave them a good welcome.

62. Spying out the land

THORGILS now made ready to leave home, and they rode up along Hordadale. There were ten of them in all. Thorgils Holluson was the leader; in the company were Bolli's sons, Thorleik and Bolli; the fourth was their half-brother, Thord Cat; the fifth was Thorstein the Black, the sixth Lambi; Halldor and Ornolf were seventh and eighth, and Svein and Hunbogi the Strong, the sons of Alf of the Dales, were ninth and tenth. All of them were good warriors.

They made their way to Sopanda Pass and across Langavatnsdale, and then crossed Borgarfjord. They forded North River at Eyja Ford and Hvit River at Bakka Ford, a short distance downstream from Bær. Then they rode through Reykjardale and across the ridge into Skorradale, and so up through the woods near the farm at Vatnshorn. Here they dismounted. It was now very late in the evening.

The farm at Vatnshorn stands a short distance away from the lake, on the south side of the river. Thorgils told his men they would wait there overnight – 'And I shall go over to the farm and try to find out whether Helgi is at home. I'm told he usually keeps only a few people about him but is always on his guard and sleeps in a sturdy bed-closet.'

His companions told him to go ahead. Thorgils now changed his clothes; he took off his blue cloak and put on a coarse grey cowled smock. He went over to the farm, and when he had almost reached the house he saw a man coming towards him.

When they met, Thorgils said, 'You will think it very stupid of me to ask, friend – but what district am I in, and what farm is this, and who lives here?'

'You must be a remarkably ignorant and stupid man,' came the reply, 'if you've never heard of Helgi Hardbeinsson, the great warrior and chieftain.'

Thorgils now asked how hospitable Helgi was to strangers and people in dire need of help who came to his door.

'That's an easy one to answer truthfully,' said the man. 'Helgi is exceptionally generous at giving people shelter, and in every other way.'

'Is Helgi at home now?' asked Thorgils. 'I'd like to put his hospitality to the test.'

The other asked him what kind of trouble he was in.

'I was outlawed at the Assembly this summer,' replied Thorgils, 'and now I need the protection of someone who is strong and fearless. In return I'd offer him my support and service. Take me to the house to see Helgi.'

'I can certainly take you to the house,' he said, 'and you're welcome to stay here overnight; but you won't see Helgi, because he's not at home.'

Thorgils asked where he was.

'Helgi is at his shieling at Sarp,' he replied.

Thorgils asked where it was, and how many men were with him. The man replied that Helgi's son, Hardbein, was there, and two other men, outlaws whom Helgi had taken in. Thorgils asked him to show him the quickest way to the shieling – 'for I want to see Helgi as soon as I can, to put my case to him.'

The house-servant pointed out the way, and with that they parted. Thorgils returned to the wood to his companions, and told them what he had found out about Helgi. 'We shall stay here for the night, and not make for the shieling until morning.'

They did as he said. Next morning Thorgils and his companions rode up through the wood until they were quite close to the shieling. Thorgils told them to dismount there and have their breakfast. They did so, and stayed there for a while.

63. Helgi and his shepherd

Now we must tell what was happening at the shieling where Helgi was staying with the men already mentioned.

Early that morning, Helgi told his shepherd to search the woods near the shieling and keep an eye open for any movements or anything else he might see worth reporting – 'for I had dreams during the night.'

The boy did as he was told. He was away for a while and when he came back Helgi asked if he had seen anything to report.

'I saw something which I'm sure is worth telling,' said the boy.

Helgi asked what it was. The boy said he had seen a number of men – 'and I think they're from outside the district.'

'Where were they when you saw them?' asked Helgi. 'And what were they doing? Did you notice what they were wearing or what they looked like?'

'I wasn't so frightened that I didn't pay attention to such details,' said the boy, 'for I knew you'd ask about them.'

He went on to say that they were not far away from the shieling, and were eating their breakfast. Helgi asked if they were sitting in a circle, or in a line side by side; the boy said they were sitting in a circle, on their saddles.

'Now tell me what they looked like,' said Helgi. 'I want to see if I can guess who they might be.'

The boy said, 'There was one man there sitting on a painted saddle, wearing a blue cloak. He was big and manly, balding at the front and with prominent teeth.'

'I recognize that man clearly from your description,' said Helgi. 'You were looking at Thorgils Holluson, from out west in Hordadale. But what can that warrior be wanting with us?'

The boy went on, 'Next to him there was a man sitting on a gilded saddle. He was wearing a scarlet tunic, and had a gold bracelet on his arm and a gold-embroidered band tied round his head. This man had flaxen hair falling in curls down to his shoulders; he was fair complexioned, with a crooked nose slightly tilted at the tip, and he had very fine eyes – blue and sharp and never still. He had a broad forehead and full cheeks. His hair was cut in a fringe above the eyebrows. He was a well-built man, broad-shouldered and barrel-chested, with beautiful hands and powerful arms. His whole bearing was courteous, and all in all I can say that I've never seen so gallant-looking a man. He looked young, too, for his beard hadn't started growing. He seemed to me to be bursting with grief.'

'You've observed this man very carefully,' said Helgi. 'He

must be a remarkable man indeed, but I don't think I've ever set eyes on him. But I shall have a guess at who he is; I think it must have been Bolli Bollason, for I'm told he's a very promising young man.'

The boy went on, 'Then there was a man sitting on an enamelled saddle. He was wearing a lime-green tunic, and had a large gold ring on his finger. He was very handsome, and looked to be still a young man. He had a fine head of auburn hair; and he, too, was a most courteous-looking man.'

'I think I know the man you've just been describing,' said Helgi. 'It must be Thorleik Bollason. What a sharp and clear-headed lad you are!'

The boy said, 'Next to him sat a young man wearing a blue tunic and black breeches with his tunic tucked inside his belt. He had a straight nose, fair hair, and regular features; he was slimly built and courteous.'

'I recognize that man,' said Helgi. 'I saw him when he was very young. That must be Thord Thordarson, the foster-son of Snorri the Priest. What a very gallant company they have, these men from the west. Is there more to come?'

The boy went on, 'Next there was a man sitting on a Scottish saddle; he was very swarthy, with black hair and a greying beard; not at all handsome, but very warrior-like. He had on a grey pleated cloak.'

'I know very well who that is,' said Helgi. 'It's Lambi Thorbjornsson from Laxriverdale; but I can't see what he's doing in this company.'

The boy said, 'Next there was a man sitting on a pommelled saddle, wearing a blue cowled cloak and with a silver bracelet on his arm. He had a country look about him, and past the prime of life, with dark and very curly chestnut hair. He had a scar on his face.'

'The tale is growing much more ominous now,' said Helgi. 'That must have been my brother-in-law Thorstein the Black you saw, and it strikes me as very odd indeed that he should be in this company, for I would never pay him such a visit. What more is there to come?'

The boy replied, 'Then there were two men sitting there. They were much alike, middle-aged I should think, and very stalwart-looking, red-haired and freckled but handsome none the less.'

'I can easily tell who these men are,' said Helgi. 'They're Thorgils' foster-brothers, Halldor and Ornolf Armodsson. What a reliable lad you are! Are all the men you saw now accounted for?'

'I've not much to add now,' said the boy. 'Next to them sat a man facing outwards from the circle. He wore a corselet of plate mail and a steel helmet with a brim a hand's-breadth wide. On his shoulder he hefted a gleaming axe whose edge must have been eighteen inches long. He had a dark complexion and dark eyes, and looked every inch a viking.'

'I can recognize that man easily from your description,' said Helgi. 'That was Hunbogi the Strong, the son of Alf of the Dales. I find it hard to understand what these men want, coming here with such a select company.'

The boy went on, 'Next to this powerful-looking man there was yet another man; he had dark auburn hair, a broad, ruddy face with bushy eyebrows, and he was above average in height.'

'You don't need to say any more,' said Helgi. 'That was Hunbogi's brother, Svein. We'd better not be caught off guard by these men, for I have a feeling they'll be paying me a visit before they leave the district; there are men in that company who would have called our encounter timely if it had taken place much sooner.

'The women here in the shieling must now put on men's clothing at once and get the horses that are near the shieling and ride off as fast as they can home to the farm. It could be that the people who are lurking nearby will be unable to tell whether the riders are men or women. We need only to gain a little time to get more men here, and then there's no telling which side will have the better chance.'

The women rode off in a group of four.

Thorgils had a suspicion that their presence might have been spotted, and he told his men to mount up and set out as quickly as they could. They went to their horses; but before they had mounted, a man came riding openly towards them. He was a

205

small, brisk man with eyes that darted about in all directions, and he was riding a lively horse. He greeted Thorgils familiarly. Thorgils asked him his name and kin, and where he came from. He said his name was Hrapp, and that he was from Breidafjord on his mother's side – 'and that was where I grew up. I'm called Killer-Hrapp, and as that name implies, I'm not an easy man to deal with despite my lack of inches. On my father's side I come from the south, where I've been staying for the last few years. It's a stroke of luck, Thorgils, finding you here, for I was intending to go and see you anyway, even though that would have been rather difficult for me; I've some trouble on my hands, for I've fallen out with my employer. He treated me badly, and as my name implies I won't put up with that sort of abuse from anyone. So I just went for him. I don't think I did him much harm, or any at all, but I didn't stay long enough to find out, for I felt safer the sooner I got up on this horse I stole from him.'

Hrapp did a lot of talking, and asked few questions; but he soon found out that they were planning to attack Helgi. That seemed to please him very much, and he said they would not need to look for him in the rear.

64. Helgi Hardbeinsson dies

THORGILS and his men set off at a gallop as soon as they had mounted, and rode out of the woods. They caught sight of four people riding away from the shieling, also going at full gallop. Some of Thorgils' companions now said they should ride off in pursuit of them at once.

But Thorleik Bollason replied, 'Let's go to the shieling first and find out who are there, for I rather doubt that these people are Helgi and his men; they look more like women to me.'

Most of them disagreed with him. But Thorgils said that Thorleik should have the final say, for he knew that Thorleik was exceptionally keen-sighted. So they now headed for the shieling. Hrapp galloped off in front of them brandishing the puny spear he was carrying, thrusting and lunging with it and saying that now was the time to put oneself to the test.

Before Helgi and his men were aware of what was happening, Thorgils and his men had surrounded the shieling. They barred the door and took up their weapons.

Hrapp leapt straight up on to the roof of the shieling and asked if the old fox was at home.

Helgi replied, 'You'll soon find out that the one who lives here can be savage enough and knows how to bite so close to his den.' And with that he thrust his spear out through the roof-opening and right through Hrapp; Hrapp fell off the spear to the ground, dead.

Thorgils told the others to go warily and be on their guard against these mishaps – 'for we have all the means we need to take the shieling and Helgi too, now that he's inside, for I think there are very few men in there with him.'

The shieling was built with one main roof-beam whose ends rested on the two gable-walls and projected out beyond them. The turf on the roof was only a year old, and had not grown together yet. Thorgils now told some of his men to take hold of the ends of the roof-beam and put all their weight on them, so that the beam itself would break or else the rafters would cave in; and he told the others to guard the door, in case those inside tried to break out.

There were four people inside the shieling with Helgi: his son Hardbein (who was then twelve years old), the shepherd, and the two outlaws who had come to him that summer; they were called Thorgils and Eyjolf.

Thorstein the Black and Svein, the son of Alf of the Dales, stood guard at the door while the rest of them tried to tear the roof off the shieling. They had divided themselves into two groups for the task; Hunbogi the Strong and the Armodssons took one end of the roof-beam, and Thorgils, Lambi and the Bollasons took the other. They all heaved hard at the beam, and it snapped in the middle.

At that moment, young Hardbein thrust out with his halberd through the gap where the door had burst open; the blow struck Thorstein the Black on his steel helmet, and the point went through and into his forehead; it was a terrible wound. Then Thorstein said, in all truth, that there was certainly someone at home, all right.

Now Helgi Hardbeinsson himself sprang out through the door so boldly that those who were closest gave ground; but Thorgils was standing nearby and swung at him with a sword; the blow caught him on the shoulder and wounded him severely. Helgi, who was carrying a wood-axe, turned on him and said, 'The old one still isn't afraid to face weapons!' And he hurled the axe at Thorgils; it caught him on the leg and made a great wound.

When Bolli saw this he rushed at Helgi with 'Leg-Biter' in his hand and ran him through with it; and that was Helgi's death-wound.

Helgi's two followers and Hardbein now came running out of the shieling. Thorleik Bollason set on Eyjolf, who was a powerful man; Thorleik struck at him with his sword. The blow landed on his thigh just above the knee and took his leg off, and Eyjolf fell down dead.

Hunbogi the Strong rushed at the other outlaw, Thorgils, and swung at him with his axe; the blow landed on his back and sliced him in two at the waist.

Thord Cat was standing nearby when young Hardbein came running out, and wanted to set on him at once. But when Bolli saw this he rushed over and said that Hardbein was not to be harmed: 'There is to be no infamy committed here; Hardbein is to be given quarter.'

Helgi had another son, whose name was Skorri; he was being fostered at a farm called England in southern Reykjardale.

65. Gudrun's double-dealing

AFTER this, Thorgils and his men rode away; they crossed the ridge into Reykjardale, where they announced the killings. Then they rode back west the same way they had come, and did not break their journey until they reached Hordadale. There they told the story of their expedition; it became renowned far and wide, for it was thought a great achievement to have felled such a champion as Helgi Hardbeinsson.

Thorgils thanked his companions well for having come with him, as did Bolli and Thorleik Bollason. And with that, the men who had accompanied Thorgils dispersed. Lambi Thorbjornsson rode west to Laxriverdale, and called in first at Hjardarholt where he gave his kinsmen, the Olafssons, a detailed account of what had happened in Skorradale. They were angry with him for taking part in it and heaped abuse on him; they said he had shown himself to be more of the blood of Thorbjorn the Feeble than of King Myrkjartan of the Irish. Lambi was furious at their remarks and said it was most unseemly of them to upbraid him – 'for I have saved you all from being killed.' After that they had little to say to one another, for they were all even angrier than ever. Lambi then rode home to his farm.

Thorgils Holluson rode out to Helgafell accompanied by the Bollasons and his foster-brothers Halldor and Ornolf. They arrived at Helgafell late in the evening, when all the people were in bed. Gudrun rose and told her household to get up and wait upon the visitors. She came into the room and greeted Thorgils and all the others and asked them their news.

Thorgils returned Gudrun's greeting. He had taken off his cloak and laid aside his weapons, and was sitting with his back against the pillars; he was wearing a russet tunic with a broad silver belt round his waist. Gudrun sat down on the bench beside him. Then Thorgils spoke this verse:

> 'We called on Helgi's homestead
> And left the ravens feasting;
> Accompanied by Thorleik
> We stained our weapons crimson.
> Three warriors we felled there,
> All of them great fighters,
> Towering like oak-trees;
> Vengeance is done for Bolli.'

Gudrun asked them in detail about everything that had happened on their journey, and Thorgils told her all she wanted to

know. Gudrun said the whole expedition had been most effec
tively carried out, and asked them to accept her thanks.

After that they were served with food, and when they had
eaten their fill they were shown to bed. They slept for the rest
of the night.

Next day, Thorgils went to see Gudrun and said, 'As you are
aware, Gudrun, I have now carried out the task you asked me
to undertake, and I think I can say it was carried out most
thoroughly. I'm also sure I haven't done all this for nothing; you
will recall what you promised me in return, and I think I'm
now fully entitled to my prize.'

'It's not so long since we had our talk that it could have
slipped my memory,' said Gudrun. 'I have every intention of
fulfilling everything I promised you; but how exactly do you
recall the terms of our agreement?'

Thorgils said she no doubt remembered it herself.

'I think I promised you,' said Gudrun, 'that I wouldn't marry
any other man in this country than you. Do you disagree with
that?'

Thorgils said she remembered it correctly.

'It's as well,' said Gudrun, 'that there's no difference in our
recollection of it. So now I won't prolong this any further for
you; I don't think I'm destined to become your wife. I believe
I would be keeping to every word of our agreement if I marry
Thorkel Eyjolfsson, for he is not here in this country at present.'

Thorgils flushed very red and said, 'I know all too well where
this comes from, for I have always felt the brunt of cold
counsels from that quarter : I know that this is Snorri's doing.'

He jumped to his feet in a towering rage and broke off the
conversation; he went out to his companions and told them he
was leaving.

Thorleik was displeased that Thorgils should have been
offended in this way, but Bolli took his mother's part over it.
Gudrun said she would give Thorgils good gifts to placate him;
but Thorleik said it would be no use – 'for Thorgils is much too
proud a man to demean himself for trifles of that sort.'

Gudrun said Thorgils would have to console himself at home
in that case.

Thorgils now rode away from Helgafell with his foster-brothers; he arrived back home at Tongue in Hordadale extremely discontented with his lot.

66. Osvif dies

THAT winter Osvif fell ill and died, and this was considered a great loss, for he had been a great sage. Osvif was buried at Helgafell, for Gudrun had had a church built there.

That same summer Gest Oddleifsson fell ill; and as his illness grew worse, he called for his son, Thord the Short, and said, 'I have the feeling that this illness will mean the parting of the ways for us. I want to be buried at Helgafell, for that place will become the greatest in these parts. I have often seen a light shining there.'[1]

After that, Gest died. The winter had been very cold, with thick ice everywhere, and Breidafjord was frozen over so far out that no ship could leave from Bardastrand. Gest's body was laid out for two days at Hagi; on the following night such a gale sprang up that all the ice was driven from the shore, and next day the weather was fair and calm. Thord took ship and put Gest's body on board, and sailed south across Breidafjord the same day, arriving at Helgafell in the evening. Thord was given a good welcome, and stayed there overnight.

Next morning Gest's body was laid to rest; he was buried in the same grave as Osvif Helgason. So Gest's prophecy came true, that they would one day be much closer neighbours than when the one had been living in Bardastrand and the other in Sælingsdale.

Thord the Short went back home as soon as he was ready. The very next night a wild storm blew up, and all the ice was driven back up to the shore again; and for the rest of the

1. This is an allusion to the fact that a monastery was later established at Helgafell in 1184; it lasted until the Reformation, c. 1550. The third abbot of Helgafell, Abbot Ketil Hermundsson (1217-20), was Gudrun's great-great-great-grandson (cf. Chapter 78, n. 3, p. 237).

winter, no ships could cross Breidafjord. It was considered most remarkable that the weather had thus allowed Gest's body to be ferried over, when no other crossings had been possible, before or after.

67. Thorgils Holluson killed

THERE was a man called Thorarin, who lived at Langadale. He was a chieftain, but not a very powerful one. He had a son called Audgisl, a brisk and vigorous man.

Thorgils Holluson took the chieftaincy away from Thorarin and his son, which they thought a great humiliation. Audgisl went to see Snorri the Priest and told him of this injustice, and asked him for help. Snorri answered him cordially, but without committing himself in any way, and said, 'This Hollu-lout is getting very ambitious and vain nowadays. Will Thorgils never meet anyone who dares to stand up to him? He's a big, powerful fellow, of course, but even men of his size have been helped to their graves before now.'

And when Audgisl left, Snorri presented him with an inlaid axe.

In the spring, Thorgils Holluson and Thorstein the Black went south to Borgarfjord and offered compensation to Helgi Hardbeinsson's sons and other kinsmen. They came to terms over it, and an honourable settlement was arranged. Thorstein paid out two-thirds of the compensation for the killing, and Thorgils was to pay over the remaining third at the next Althing.

That summer, Thorgils rode to the Althing; and when they reached the lava-field at Thingvellir, they saw a woman come walking towards them. She was an enormous creature. Thorgils rode to meet her, but she turned away and said:

> 'Beware, beware,
> You men of prowess;
> Always be on guard
> Against Snorri's wiles.
> But none's wary enough;
> Snorri's too wise.'

Then she went on her way.

Thorgils said, 'It seldom happened, when things boded well, that you were leaving the Althing when I was arriving there.'[1]

Thorgils now rode on to the Althing and went to his own booth. All was quiet at the Althing to begin with. Then one day people had their clothes hanging out to dry; Thorgils had a blue cowled cloak spread out on the wall of the booth, and this cloak was heard to say :

> 'Hanging wet upon the wall,
> Cloak knows of a plot;
> Wet it will be evermore –
> Cloak knows two plots to come.'

This was considered a great marvel.

Next day Thorgils crossed the river to hand over the compensation due to Helgi Hardbeinsson's sons. He sat down on the lava outcrop above the booths; his foster-brother, Halldor Armodsson, and several other people were with him. Helgi's sons arrived for the meeting, and Thorgils began to count out the silver.

Audgisl was walking past at that moment, and just when Thorgils had counted 'Ten', Audgisl struck at him; and all those present thought they heard the head say 'Eleven' as it flew off his shoulders. Audgisl ran off towards the Vatnsfjord booth, but Halldor ran after him at once and struck him down dead in the doorway of the booth.

The news that Thorgils had been killed reached Snorri the Priest's booth. Snorri said, 'You must have misheard it; it will have been Thorgils Holluson who did the killing.'

The man replied, 'All the same, his head flew off his shoulders.'

1. This is an indication that Thorgils is about to die: The woman is his *fylgja*, his 'fetch', the personification of his luck, or guardian-spirit. Fetches often manifested themselves before death or at other times of crisis. Elsewhere in the sagas, these fetches are said to have passed on from one member of the family to another.

'Then perhaps it's true after all,' said Snorri.

A settlement was reached over these killings, as is told in *Thorgils Holluson's Saga*.[1]

68. Gudrun's fourth marriage

IN the summer that Thorgils Holluson was killed, a ship put in at Bjarnarhaven; it belonged to Thorkel Eyjolfsson, who was now so wealthy that he owned two merchant ships. His other ship put in at Bordeyri, in Hrutafjord. Both ships were laden with timber.

When Snorri the Priest heard of Thorkel's arrival he rode down to the ship at once. Thorkel received him with great warmth; he had a good supply of drink on board, and it was served without stint. They had a lot to talk about. Snorri asked for news from Norway, and Thorkel gave him a vivid account of everything. Snorri told him in return what had been happening in Iceland during his absence abroad.

'It seems to me a good idea,' said Snorri, 'as I suggested before you went abroad, that you should now retire from trading and settle down quietly, and obtain the wife we talked about then.'

'I know what you're driving at,' replied Thorkel, 'and I feel just the same about it now as I did when we talked it over previously, for I don't want to deny myself such an excellent match if it can be arranged.'

'I'm very ready and willing to make the proposal on your behalf,' said Snorri. 'The two obstacles which you felt stood in the way of your marrying Gudrun have now been removed: Bolli has been avenged, and Thorgils has been disposed of.'

Thorkel said, 'Your plans run deep, Snorri; and I shall certainly turn my mind to this.'

Snorri stayed at the ship for several days. Then they took a

1. This saga is now lost, but it was probably one of the sources used by the author of *Laxdæla Saga* – although it presumably portrayed Thorgils in a more sympathetic light then he appears here.

ten-oared boat which lay alongside the ship, and made ready to leave. There were twenty-five in all, and they went to Helgafell.

Gudrun gave Snorri a most cordial welcome, and they were entertained lavishly. When they had been there for a night, Snorri asked Gudrun for a talk, and said, 'The position is that I have made this journey on behalf of my friend, Thorkel Eyjolfsson, who is here with me as you know; and the purpose of his visit is to make you an offer of marriage. Thorkel is a man of great distinction, and you yourself know all about his family and prestige. He isn't lacking in wealth, and in my opinion he is the most likely man here in the west to become a leading chieftain, if he sets his mind to it. He has always been held in high esteem here in Iceland, but he is even more greatly respected when he is in Norway amongst men of rank and title.'

Gudrun replied, 'My sons, Thorleik and Bolli, will have the greatest say in this; but you are the third person, Snorri, on whom I rely most for advice in all matters of importance to me, for you have always advised me honestly and well.'

Snorri said he thought it obvious that Thorkel should not be rejected. Then he had Gudrun's sons called in, and discussed the proposal with them. He spoke to them blandly, pointing out what an asset Thorkel would be to them with all his wealth and shrewdness.

Bolli replied, 'My mother will know the answer best herself, and I shall agree to whatever she wishes in this. But I also think we should heed the fact carefully that it is you, Snorri, who are presenting this proposal, for you have done a great deal for us in the past.'

Then Gudrun said, 'We must rely heavily on Snorri's judgement in this matter, for your advice, Snorri, has always served us well.'

Snorri kept pressing the proposal, and the outcome was that it was decided that Gudrun and Thorkel should be joined in marriage. Snorri offered to hold the wedding-feast at his home; this pleased Thorkel – 'For I do not lack the means to make whatever provision for it you think fit.'

But Gudrun said, 'It is my wish that the feast should be held here at Helgafell. I don't shrink from the expense, and I don't want to put Thorkel or anyone else to the trouble.'

'You often show, Gudrun,' said Snorri, 'what an exceptional woman you are!'

So it was agreed that the wedding-feast should take place at Helgafell six weeks before winter. With that, Snorri and Thorkel left; Snorri went home, and Thorkel returned to his ship. He spent the summer alternately at the ship and at Tongue.

Time passed until the wedding was due. Gudrun made great preparations and laid in vast supplies. Snorri the Priest came to the feast with Thorkel; they had nearly sixty people with them, a very select company, and most of them wore brightly-coloured clothing. Gudrun had over a hundred guests waiting to greet them. The brothers, Bolli and Thorleik, went out with the guests who had already arrived to receive Snorri and Thorkel. Snorri and his company were given a splendid welcome; their horses and baggage were seen to, and they were shown into the house. Thorkel and Snorri and their men occupied the upper bench, and Gudrun's guests the lower one.

69. Gunnar Thidrandi's-Killer

THAT autumn, a man called Gunnar Thidrandi's-Killer had been sent to Gudrun for shelter and protection; she had taken him in, and his identity had been kept secret. Gunnar had been outlawed for the killing of Thidrandi Geitisson of Krossavik, as is told in *The Njardvikings' Saga*.[1] He had to stay mostly under cover, for there were many powerful men prosecuting the case.

On the first evening of the wedding-feast, when the guests went down to the water to wash, there was a tall man standing at the lakeside. He was broad-shouldered and barrel-chested, and was wearing a hat. Thorkel asked him who he was, and he gave the first name that occurred to him.

Thorkel said, 'You're not telling the truth; you're more likely

1. This is probably a reference to *The Story of Gunnar Thidrandi's-Killer*, where these events are described in much greater detail.

to be Gunnar Thidrandi's-Killer, judging by his description. And if you're such a champion as people say you are, you wouldn't want to conceal your name.'

'You're being very outspoken about this,' replied Gunnar, 'and I see no reason why I should try to deceive you. You've identified me correctly; what do you intend to do with me?'

Thorkel said he would find out soon enough, and told his men to seize him.

Gudrun was sitting on the dais at the upper end of the hall with some other women; they were all wearing linen head-dresses. As soon as she realized what was happening, she left the bridal bench and called on her men to go to Gunnar's help, and told them to spare no one who offered them any resistance. Gudrun had a much larger force than Thorkel, and the whole situation had now taken a very unexpected turn.

Snorri the Priest now intervened and asked both sides to allay this storm: 'It should be obvious to you, Thorkel, that you mustn't make such an issue of this. You can see for yourself what an exceptional woman Gudrun is, when she gets the better of both of us.'

Thorkel said he had promised Thidrandi's brother, Thorkel Geitisson, to kill Gunnar if he ever turned up in the western districts – 'And Thorkel is a great friend of mine.'

Snorri said, 'You have a much greater obligation now to do as we ask; and for yourself, this is a matter of the utmost importance, for however far you seek, you'll never find such a wife as Gudrun.'

At these words Thorkel realized that Snorri was speaking the truth, and he calmed down; and Gunnar was escorted away that evening.

The feast now went well and in great splendour. When it was over, the guests made ready to leave. Thorkel gave lavish gifts to Snorri and all the other important people. Snorri invited Bolli Bollason to come home with him, and asked him to stay there as long and as often as he liked. Bolli accepted the invitation, and rode home with Snorri to Sælingsdale Tongue.

Thorkel Eyjolfsson now settled at Helgafell and took charge of the estate. It soon became clear that he was no worse at farming than at trading. In the autumn he had the house pulled down, and a new one was built by the beginning of winter; it was a large and imposing building.

Thorkel and Gudrun came to love one another dearly.

The winter passed. In the spring, Gudrun asked Thorkel what he was going to do about Gunnar Thidrandi's-Killer. Thorkel said it was up to her to decide – 'For you took it up so vigorously that you won't be satisfied unless he is sent on his way with all due honour.'

Gudrun said he had guessed correctly. 'I want you to give him a ship,' she said, 'and all the other things he needs.'

Thorkel smiled, and said, 'No one can say you think small, Gudrun, and it wouldn't suit you to be married to a weakling. It isn't in your nature. I shall do as you wish.'

This was now done. Gunnar accepted the gift with great gratitude: 'I could never be wealthy enough to repay you all the great honour you have shown me,' he said.

Gunnar went abroad, and made land in Norway. Later he returned to his own home. Gunnar was very wealthy, and a man of great nobility and stature.

70. Thorleik and Bolli

THORKEL EYJOLFSSON became a great chieftain, and set his mind to winning popularity and respect. He liked to have his own way in his own district, and took part in many lawsuits, although his litigations are not recorded here. Next to Snorri the Priest, he was the most powerful man in Breidafjord during his lifetime.

Thorkel ran his estate well. He had all the buildings at Helgafell enlarged and strengthened. He also laid out the foundations for a new church, and made it known that he intended to go and fetch the timber for it himself.

Thorkel and Gudrun had a son, who was called Gellir. He was a most promising youth from his earliest years.

Bolli Bollason stayed alternately at Tongue and at Helgafell; Snorri the Priest was extremely fond of him. His brother Thorleik stayed at Helgafell. The brothers were both tall, stalwart men, but Bolli was the foremost in all things.

Thorkel was fond of his step-children, and Gudrun loved Bolli most of all her sons.

When Thorleik was twenty years old (Bolli was sixteen then), he told his step-father Thorkel and his mother that he wanted to go abroad: 'I'm tired of sitting at home like a woman; I would like to be provided with the means to travel.'

Thorkel replied, 'I don't think I've ever stood in your way, or Bolli's, since I became a member of the family. I think it very understandable that you are eager to see the way other people live, for I'm sure you'll be considered a man of mettle wherever you find yourself among good men.'

Thorleik said he would not want much money: 'It isn't certain how well I would look after it, for I am young and inexperienced in many ways.'

Thorkel said he could have as much as he wanted.

Thorkel now bought for Thorleik a share in a ship which was lying at Dogurdarness. Thorkel escorted him to the ship, and sent him off well equipped in every way. Thorleik sailed abroad that summer, and his ship made land in Norway. At that time the ruler of Norway was King Olaf the Saint.[1] Thorleik went at once to see King Olaf, who gave him a good welcome; he knew of his family, and invited him to stay with him. Thorleik accepted the invitation; he stayed with the king that winter and became one of his retainers, and the king held him in high esteem. Thorleik was considered a man of great mettle, and remained with King Olaf for several years.

Now we return to Bolli Bollason. In the spring of the year that he was eighteen years old, he told his step-father Thorkel and his mother that he wanted them to pay out his share of his father's estate. Gudrun asked what plans he had in mind, when he was claiming this payment.

Bolli replied, 'It is my wish that a certain woman should be

1. King Olaf Haraldsson (St Olaf) was king of Norway from 1016 to 1030. His life-story is told in Snorri Sturluson's *St Olaf's Saga*.

sought in marriage for me. I would like you, Thorkel, to speak on my behalf and see it through.'

Thorkel asked who the woman was that he wanted to marry.

Bolli answered, 'Her name is Thordis, the daughter of Snorri the Priest. Of all women she is the one I most want to have, and I won't be quick to marry another if I fail to win her. It's very important to me that this match should be achieved.'

Thorkel said, 'You have every right to expect my support in this matter, kinsman, if you think it so important. I expect that Snorri will readily give his consent, for he will realize that he is being made a good offer, when you are the suitor.'

Gudrun said, 'Let me say at once, Thorkel, that I want nothing to be spared to enable Bolli to achieve the match he desires. It is not only because I love him above all others, but also because, of all my children, he has always been the most reliable in carrying out my wishes.'

Thorkel said that he, for his part, had every intention of endowing Bolli generously : 'He deserves it on every account, and I know he will make a very good husband.'

A little later Thorkel and Bolli left home with several companions and rode to Tongue. Snorri gave them a kind and cordial welcome and entertained them most hospitably. Thordis, Snorri's daughter, was at home with her father; she was a lovely and capable woman.

When they had been at Tongue for several days, Thorkel brought up the marriage-offer with Snorri, asking for the hand of his daughter Thordis on behalf of Bolli.

'This is a good offer,' replied Snorri, 'as was to be expected of you, and I would want to give you a favourable answer; for in my opinion Bolli is a most promising young man, and I would think the woman well married who marries him. But it will depend chiefly on what Thordis feels about it, for she shall only marry the man she herself wants.'

The proposal was now put to Thordis, who replied by saying that she would rely on her father's judgement; she added that she would rather marry Bolli, a man from her own district, than some stranger from farther away. When Snorri found that she was not averse to marrying Bolli, the agreement was concluded, and the betrothal took place. Snorri was to hold the wedding-feast at his home, and it was to take place about mid-summer.

After that, Thorkel and Bolli rode back home to Helgafell, and Bolli stayed at home until it was time for the wedding. Thorkel and Bolli then made ready to leave with the companions they had chosen, a large and splendid company. They rode over to Tongue, where they were given an excellent welcome. There was a host of guests there and the feast was a magnificent one. When the feast was over, the guests made ready to leave. Snorri gave fine gifts to Thorkel and Gudrun and to his other friends and kinsmen. Then all of those who had attended the feast returned to their own homes.

Bolli stayed on at Tongue, and he and Thordis quickly came to love one another dearly. Snorri did everything he could to do well by Bolli, and showed him even more kindness than he did his own children. Bolli accepted all this gratefully, and spent that year at Sælingsdale Tongue in high regard.

The following summer a ship put in from abroad at Hvit River. Thorleik Bollason owned a half-share in this ship, and the other half belonged to some Norwegians. When Bolli heard that his brother had returned he rode south to Borgarfjord at once and went to the ship. The brothers had a joyful reunion.

Bolli stayed at the ship for several days. Then the two brothers rode west to Helgafell. Thorkel and Gudrun received them with great warmth, and invited Thorleik to stay the winter with them, which he accepted. Thorleik now stayed at Helgafell for a while before he rode south to Hvit River again to have his ship laid up and his goods brought west. He had gained greatly in both wealth and prestige, for he had become the retainer of that noblest of all men, King Olaf.

He spent that winter at Helgafell, while Bolli remained at Tongue.

71. The feud ends

THAT winter the brothers met constantly and talked together in private, and took no pleasure in sports or other amusements. On one occasion when Thorleik was at Tongue, the brothers talked for days and nights on end. Snorri then suspected that they must be plotting something important, so he went over to join in their conversation. The brothers greeted him well, but dropped the subject abruptly.

Snorri returned their greeting. Then he said, 'What plans are you two hatching, that you have no time to eat or sleep?'

'There aren't any plans,' replied Bolli. 'We're not talking about anything important.'

When Snorri realized that they were trying to hide from him what they had in mind, he suspected even more that they were discussing something which could bring drastic consequences if it were carried out; so he said to them, 'On the contrary, I suspect it is neither gossip nor jokes you have been exchanging all this time, and I don't blame you for that; but be so good as to tell me, and don't hide it from me. The three of us will certainly be no less capable of solving the problem, for I won't stand in the way of anything which will enhance your honour.'

Thorleik found Snorri's response encouraging, and told him briefly that their intention was to attack the Olafssons and make them pay dearly; they said they now lacked nothing to be on equal standing with the Olafssons, since Thorleik was now a retainer of King Olaf, and Bolli was related by marriage to a chieftain of Snorri's stature.

Snorri answered: 'Bolli's death was amply repaid with Helgi Hardbeinsson's life. There has been more than enough of these troubles already, and it's high time an end was made to them.'

Then Bolli said, 'What's this, Snorri? Aren't you so keen to support us now as you made out a little while ago? Thorleik would never have told you of our plans if he had asked my advice first. As to your claim that Bolli was fully avenged by

Helgi's death, everyone knows that compensation was paid for Helgi's killing, but my father's death has never been atoned.'

When Snorri realized that he could not dissuade them, he offered to try to bring about a settlement with the Olafssons rather than have the killings start up anew. The brothers agreed to that. So Snorri now rode to Hjardarholt with several companions. Halldor Olafsson gave him a good welcome and invited him to stay. Snorri said he had to ride back home that evening – 'But I have an urgent matter to discuss with you.'

Then they had a talk, and Snorri made known the purpose of his visit, saying that he had learned that Bolli and Thorleik were no longer content to have their father unatoned for by the Olafssons: 'And now I want to try for a settlement and see whether we cannot put an end to this ill-luck you kinsmen have been sharing.'

Halldor was not averse to this idea and replied, 'I am well aware that Thorgils Holluson and the Bollasons had intended to attack me or my brothers, until you diverted their vengeance elsewhere and made them want to kill Helgi Hardbeinsson instead. You have acted very honourably in this matter, whatever the part you played in previous dealings between us kinsmen.'

Snorri said, 'It matters a great deal to me that my journey here should not be wasted, and that we can achieve what is nearest to my heart – a good and lasting settlement between you kinsmen; for I know well the temper of the people you are dealing with, and I'm sure they will abide faithfully by anything they agree to.'

'If my brothers are also willing,' said Halldor, 'I shall consent to pay compensation for the killing of Bolli, whatever amount those appointed to arbitrate may decide upon. But I want to exempt any outlawry, or any loss of my chieftaincy or my farm, as well as the farms on which my brothers live, and I stipulate that they are to be allowed to own them unmolested whatever the outcome of the case. And each side shall appoint one arbiter.'

'This is a good and generous offer,' said Snorri, 'and Thorleik and Bolli will accept it if they pay any heed to my advice at all.'

With that, Snorri rode home and told the brothers the outcome of his mission, adding that he would abandon their cause completely if they did not agree to these terms. Bolli told him to have it his own way – 'And I want you, Snorri, to arbitrate on our behalf.'

Snorri now sent word to Halldor Olafsson saying that the terms had been accepted, and asking him to appoint someone to arbitrate with him. Halldor chose Steinthor Thorlaksson of Eyr to arbitrate on his behalf. The peace-meeting was to be held at Drangar in Skogarstrand, four weeks after the beginning of summer.

Thorleik Bollason now rode back to Helgafell, and the rest of the winter passed quietly.

As the appointed time for the peace-meeting approached, Snorri arrived with the Bollasons in a party of fifteen. Steinthor Thorlaksson came to the meeting with the same number. Snorri and Steinthor now discussed the case and reached agreement; then they announced the amount of compensation they had awarded. The sum is not recorded here; but it is said that the money was paid in full, and that the settlement was faithfully kept. The money was paid over at the Thorsness Assembly.

Halldor Olafsson gave Bolli a fine sword, and Steinthor Olafsson gave Thorleik a shield, which was also an excellent gift. Thereafter the Assembly was brought to a close, and both sides were thought to have enhanced their prestige over this affair.

72. Partnership

WHEN the settlement between the Bollasons and the Olafssons had been made, and Thorleik Bollason had been back in Iceland for a year, Bolli announced that he intended to go abroad.

Snorri tried to dissuade him and said, 'We think there's a grave risk in how this might turn out for you. If you want to have more responsibilities than you have at present, I shall get you some land and establish you on a farm, and even provide you with a chieftaincy and do all I can to enhance your prestige.

I expect this would be easy, for most people are well disposed towards you.'

Bolli replied, 'I have always wanted to travel to southern lands one day, for a man is thought to grow ignorant if he doesn't ever travel beyond this country of Iceland.'

When Snorri realized that Bolli was determined to go, and that it would be useless to try to dissuade him, he offered him as much money as he needed for his journey. Bolli admitted that he would like to take a great deal of money with him – 'For I don't want to be beholden to any man, neither here nor abroad.'

Then Bolli rode south to Borgarfjord, to Hvit River, and bought the other half-share in Thorleik's ship from the men who owned it. So now the brothers owned the ship jointly. After that, Bolli rode west back home.

Bolli and Thordis had a daughter, who was called Herdis. Gudrun offered to foster her. The child was one year old when she went to Helgafell. Thordis also spent a great deal of time at Helgafell, and Gudrun was very fond of her.

73. Bolli and Thorleik abroad

THE brothers now went to their ship. Bolli took a great deal of money and wares abroad with him. They prepared the ship, and when everything was ready they put out to sea; they did not have favourable winds at first, and they were out at sea for a long time. They reached Norway in the autumn, making land in the north at Trondheim.

King Olaf was in residence at Oslo Fjord, over in the east, where he had made arrangements to spend the winter. When the brothers heard that the king would not be coming north to Trondheim that autumn, Thorleik said he wanted to sail down the coast to visit King Olaf.

Bolli replied, 'I'm not very keen on spending the autumn drifting from one market-town to another; it sounds too tedious and craven for my liking. I'd rather spend the winter in town here. I'm told the king may be coming north in the spring; but if he doesn't come, I won't object then to our going to visit him.'

Bolli had his way in this; so they unloaded their ship and got themselves lodgings in the town. It soon became evident that Bolli was very ambitious and wanted to outdo everyone else. In this he succeeded, for he was generous and open-handed, and soon he was held in high esteem in Norway. He kept a large following in Trondheim that winter, and whenever he went to visit the taverns it was obvious that his own men were better accoutred with clothes and weapons than any others in town. Moreover, he himself paid for all his companions whenever they were drinking, and he was equally liberal and generous in other things. The brothers stayed in Trondheim throughout the winter.

That winter King Olaf was in residence in Sarpsborg, in the east, and now news came that he was not expected to travel north. So, early in spring, the brothers made their ship ready, and sailed down the coast. They had a good voyage and arrived at Sarpsborg, and went to visit King Olaf at once. The king gave a good welcome to his retainer, Thorleik, and his companions; then he asked who the striking man next to Thorleik was.

'He is my brother,' said Thorleik, 'and his name is Bolli.'

'He is certainly an outstanding man,' said the king.

After that the king invited the brothers to stay with him, which they accepted with thanks, and they remained with the king for the rest of the spring. The king was as well disposed towards Thorleik as before, yet he thought much more highly of Bolli, whom he considered to be a paragon among men.

Late in the spring the brothers discussed where they should go now. Thorleik asked Bolli if he wanted to return to Iceland that summer, or whether he wanted to stay longer in Norway.

'I don't intend to do either,' replied Bolli. 'To tell you the truth, when I left Iceland I had no intention that people should hear of me from just next door. I would like you to take over the ship now, kinsman.'

Thorleik thought it a pity that they should part – 'But you will no doubt have your own way in this as in everything else, Bolli.'

They told all this to the king, who said, 'Don't you want to stay longer with us, Bolli? I should much prefer you to stay here with me for a time, and I shall give you the same rank and title as I have bestowed upon your brother.'

Bolli replied, 'I would be very happy to give you my allegiance, sire, but first I want to travel farther, as I had previously planned and as I have always longed to do. But I shall gladly accept your offer if I am destined to return.'

'You must decide for yourself where you want to go, Bolli,' said the king, 'for you Icelanders are self-willed in most matters. But as my last word to you, I want to say that I think you, Bolli, are the most remarkable man to have come from Iceland during my reign.'

When Bolli had received the king's leave, he made ready to sail, and boarded a merchant-ship which was bound for Denmark. He had a great deal of money with him, and several of his comrades accompanied him. He and King Olaf parted in great friendship, and the king gave Bolli handsome gifts. Thorleik stayed behind with King Olaf, while Bolli went on his way south until he arrived in Denmark. He spent the winter in Denmark and was given great honours by important people there. He lived in the same magnificent style as he had done in Norway.

When Bolli had spent one winter in Denmark he continued his travels to other lands, and did not break his journey until he reached Constantinople. He had not been there long before he joined the Varangian Guard; we have not heard of any other Norseman entering the service of the Byzantine Emperor before Bolli Bollason did.[1] He stayed in Constantinople for several years,

1. The Varangian Guard (*Væringjar*) was originally composed almost entirely of Scandinavian warriors, mainly from Sweden, who served as mercenaries in the bodyguard of the Byzantine emperors from the latter part of the tenth century onwards. Perhaps the most celebrated Varangian was King Harald Hardradi of Norway (cf. *King Harald's Saga*, Chapters 3–15). Bolli Bollason certainly could not have been the first Norseman to join the Varangian Guard; the Icelandic Sagas mention several others who were earlier, like for instance Kolskegg Hamundarson, the brother of Gunnar of Hlidarend

and was considered exceptionally valiant in every hazard, and was always in the forefront. The Varangians thought very highly of Bolli during his stay in Constantinople.

74. Thorkel Eyjolfsson abroad

Now we return to Thorkel Eyjolfsson, sitting in Iceland enjoying his chieftaincy. Gellir, his son by Gudrun, grew up at home, and from his earliest years was a manly and well-built youth.

It is said that on one occasion Thorkel told Gudrun of a dream he had had: 'I dreamed,' he said, 'that I had a beard so huge that it extended over the whole of Breidafjord.' He asked her to interpret the dream for him.

Gudrun asked, 'What do you yourself think the dream signifies?'

'It seems obvious to me that it means that my authority will extend over the whole of Breidafjord.'

'That could well be,' said Gudrun. 'But I'm inclined to think it signifies rather that your beard will be dipped into Breidafjord one day.'

That same summer Thorkel launched his ship and prepared it for a voyage to Norway. His son Gellir was twelve years old at the time, and he went abroad with his father. Thorkel made it known that he intended to fetch timber for his church. He put out to sea as soon as he was ready; they had an easy voyage but not a particularly fast one, and made land in the north of Norway.

King Olaf was then in residence in Trondheim. Thorkel went to visit the king at once with his son Gellir. They were well received. Thorkel was held in such high esteem by the king that winter, that it is common talk that the king gave him no fewer than one hundred marks of refined silver.[1] At Christmas the king

---

(*Njal's Saga*, Chapter 81), who went there in A.D. 990, almost twenty years before Bolli Bollason was born.

1. The magnitude of this gift is hard to believe; it would have been equivalent to a herd of some 425 milch cows.

gave Gellir a cloak which was a most choice and magnificent gift.

That winter King Olaf had a timber church built in the town; it was a magnificent minster, and all the materials were carefully chosen.

In the spring the timber which the king had given Thorkel was brought down to the ship. It was fine timber in both size and quality, for Thorkel had kept a close eye on it. Early one morning when the king was out of doors with a few companions he saw a man up on top of the church that was being built there. He was very surprised at this, for it was earlier in the morning than was usual for the carpenters to be up. The king now recognized the man; it was Thorkel, busy measuring all the largest timbers – the cross-beams, the sills, and the pillars.

The king went over to him at once and said, 'What's going on there, Thorkel? Are you thinking of cutting the timber you are taking to Iceland according to the measurements of this church?'

'That is right, sire,' said Thorkel.

Then King Olaf said, 'Trim a yard off every beam, and that church of yours will still be the largest ever built in Iceland.'

Thorkel replied, 'You can keep your timber if you think you have given too much, or if you're wanting to have it back; but I shall not trim it by even a foot. I have both the enterprise and the means to get myself some other timber elsewhere.'

Then the king said, with great restraint: 'You are a very remarkable man, Thorkel; but now you are getting above yourself, for it is sheer effrontery for a peasant's son to vie with us. It's not true that I begrudge you the timber – if you are destined to build a church with it; for it will never be large enough to contain all your arrogance. But I have the feeling that people will have little benefit from this timber, and that you will be most unlikely to build anything with it at all.'

With that they ended their conversation. The king walked away, and it was obvious that he was offended by the way Thorkel had refused to heed what he had suggested. Yet the king did not show his feelings in public; and he and Thorkel parted in great affection.

Thorkel went on board his ship and put out to sea. They had favourable winds, and the voyage did not take long. Thorkel brought his ship into Hrutafjord. He rode directly from the ship home to Helgafell, where everyone was glad to see him. Thorkel had greatly increased his prestige by this journey. He had his ship hauled ashore and made secure, and had the timber stored there, where it was safe, for he was too busy with other things to have it brought south that autumn.

Thorkel spent the winter at home. He held a Christmas feast at Helgafell, with a great number of guests, and lived in style and state throughout the winter. Gudrun was by no means averse to this, and said that this was what money was for – to increase one's prestige; and whatever Gudrun needed to entertain in lavish style had to be available.

That winter, Thorkel shared out among his friends many of the valuable treasures he had brought from abroad.

75. A bid for Hjardarholt

AFTER Christmas that winter, Thorkel went north to Hrutafjord to bring his timber home. He rode first to the Dales, and from there to Ljarwoods to his cousin Thorstein Kuggason, where he got men and horses. He then went north to Hrutafjord and stayed there for a while making arrangements for transporting the timber; he collected more horses in that district, for he did not want to have to make more than one journey, if possible. All this took quite a long time, and Thorkel was busy with this far into Lent. Eventually he got the work under way and transported the timber from the north; it took more than twenty horses to do it. He had the timber stacked at Ljaeyr, and was going to take it later by boat over to Helgafell.

Thorstein Kuggason owned a large ferry-boat, which Thorkel intended to use for the homeward journey. Thorkel stayed at Ljarwoods during Lent, for the two kinsmen were very fond of one another.

One day Thorstein mentioned to Thorkel that it would be a

good idea to go over to Hjardarholt: 'I want to make Halldor Olafsson an offer for his land, for he has been very short of stock since paying the Bollasons the compensation for their father's death. That land is exactly what I would most like to own.'

Thorkel told him to have it his own way. They set off in a group of twenty and arrived at Hjardarholt, where Halldor gave them a good welcome and was extremely cheerful. There were few people at home, for Halldor had sent some of his men north to Steingrimsfjord where a whale to which he had a part-claim was stranded.

Beinir the Strong was at home; he was the only man still alive of those who had been there with Halldor's father, Olaf the Peacock.

Halldor had said to Beinir when he saw Thorstein and the others riding up: 'I know quite well what these kinsmen want: they're going to make me an offer for my land, and if I'm right, they will want to call me out for a talk. I presume they will seat themselves one on either side of me, and if they give me any trouble you must set upon Thorstein as soon as I set about Thorkel; you have long been loyal to our family. I've also sent word to the neighbouring farms for more men; I'd like the reinforcements to arrive just when we are finishing our talk.'

As the day passed, Thorstein suggested to Halldor that they should all three go and have a talk – 'For we have some business to discuss with you.'

Halldor said it suited him well. Thorstein told his men they need not come with them, but Beinir accompanied them nevertheless, for things seemed to be turning out very much as Halldor had surmised. They walked a long way out into the homefield. Halldor was wearing a cloak fastened by a long pin-brooch, as was the custom in those days. Halldor sat down on the ground with the two kinsmen on either side of him, so close that they were almost sitting on his cloak; Beinir stood behind them with a large axe in his hand.

Thorstein said, 'My reason for coming here is that I want to buy land from you. I'm making this offer now because my kinsman Thorkel is here with me. I think this would suit both of us

very well, for I'm told you are short of stock although your
land is very valuable. I shall give you a good farm in exchange,
and whatever sum we might agree upon into the bargain.'

Halldor did not seem unenthusiastic at first, and they discussed some of the terms of the sale; and when they thought
Halldor was willing to settle, Thorkel joined in vigorously,
trying to bring the deal to a conclusion. At this point Halldor
began to be evasive, so the others pressed the matter all the
harder, until it came to this – that the harder they pressed, the
further they were from making a deal.

Then Thorkel said, 'Don't you see the way this is going,
Thorstein? Halldor has been delaying the matter for us all day,
and we've been sitting here listening to his trivial and deceitful
talk. If you want to buy the land now, we'll have to come a
little closer.'

Thorstein then said he wanted to know where he stood, and
he asked Halldor to come out into the open about whether or
not he wanted to sell him the land.

Halldor replied, 'I think there's no need to keep you in the
dark about this – you'll be going home tonight without a sale.'

Then Thorstein said, 'I think there's no need, either, to put
off telling you what we've already decided : you're being offered
a choice of two courses, for we believe we have the advantage
over you in numbers. One is that you do this willingly, and
have our friendship in return; the other, and obviously the
worse one, is that we force you to sell me the Hjardarholt lands
now.'

When Thorstein spoke so plainly, Halldor leapt to his feet so
fiercely that the brooch was torn from his cloak, and said,
'Something else will happen before I agree to something against
my will.'

'What will that be?' asked Thorstein.

'An axe will be buried in your head by a slave, thus putting
an end to your insolence and unfairness.'

Thorkel said, 'That is an evil prophecy, and we trust it won't
come true. And now I think you have given ample grounds,
Halldor, for forfeiting your land and getting nothing at all for
it.'

Halldor replied, 'You will be embracing the seaweed in Breidafjord before I'm forced to sell my land against my will.'

With that, Halldor went back to the house; and now the men he had sent for came crowding up to the farm.

Thorstein was furious, and wanted to attack Halldor at once. But Thorkel told him not to – 'For it would be an outrage during this holy season; but when it's over, I won't stand in the way of an encounter with him.'

Halldor said he would be sure never to be unprepared for them. After that they rode away, and talked about the affair at great length. Thorstein said there was no doubt that their journey had been an utter failure: 'But why were you so reluctant, Thorkel, to set upon Halldor and put him to some shame?'

'Didn't you see Beinir standing behind you with his axe raised?' said Thorkel. 'It was a very dangerous situation, for he would have driven the axe into your head as soon as I made a move of any kind.'

They rode back home to Ljarwoods. Lent wore on, and Holy Week came.

76. Thorkel Eyjolfsson's fate

EARLY in the morning of Maundy Thursday, Thorkel made ready to leave. Thorstein tried hard to dissuade him, 'For this weather looks treacherous to me,' he said.

Thorkel said the weather would do all right – 'And don't try to dissuade me, kinsman, for I want to get home before Easter.'

So now Thorkel launched the ferry-boat and started loading it; but Thorstein carried the timber ashore as fast as Thorkel and his companions put it on board.

Then Thorkel said, 'Stop this now, kinsman, and don't try to hinder our departure; for you won't get your way this time.'

Thorstein replied, 'Then the more misguided of us will have his way, for this journey will have grave consequences.'

Thorkel bade him farewell until their next meeting, and Thorstein walked home in great distress. He went into the living-room and asked for a pillow to be placed under his head, and this was done. The maidservant saw tears streaming from his eyes on to the pillow. A little while later a roaring gust of wind struck the house. Then Thorstein said, 'Now we can hear the roar of the killer of my kinsman, Thorkel.'

Meanwhile, to return to Thorkel's journey, he and his men sailed along Breidafjord all day; there were ten of them on board. The wind began to blow very hard, and rose to a full gale before it abated. They sailed fast before the wind, for they were all robust men. Thorkel had the sword 'Skofnung' with him; it was lying in a locker. Thorkel and his men sailed as far as Bjarn Isle – people were watching their progress from both shores – but just then a sudden squall caught the sail and overturned the boat. Thorkel and all the men who were with him were drowned there. The timber drifted far and wide about the islands; the corner-pillars drifted ashore on the island which has been called Staff Isle ever since. 'Skofnung' was jammed in the hull of the boat, and was found on Skofnungs Isle.

On the evening of the day that Thorkel and his men were drowned, Gudrun happened to go to the church at Helgafell after the rest of the household had gone to bed. And as she passed through the lich-gate she saw a ghost standing in front of her. The ghost leaned down towards her and said, 'Grave news, Gudrun !'

Gudrun replied, 'Then be quiet about it, wretch !'

Gudrun went on towards the church, as she had intended, and when she reached the church she thought she saw Thorkel and his men returned home and standing in front of the church. She saw that sea-water was streaming from their clothes. Gudrun did not speak to them, and went into the church and stayed there as long as she thought fit. Then she went back to the house, for she thought that Thorkel and his men would have gone there. But when she came inside there was no one there. And now Gudrun was greatly disturbed by everything that had happened.

On Good Friday, Gudrun sent men to get news of Thorkel's

movements, some in along the coast, and some out to the islands. By then the flotsam had drifted far and wide about the islands and to both shores of the fjord. On the Saturday before Easter, people heard the news and thought it very grave, for Thorkel had been a great chieftain. Thorkel was forty-eight years old when he was drowned, and that was four years before King Olaf the Saint fell.

Gudrun was deeply affected by Thorkel's death, but bore it with great fortitude.

Very little of the church-timber was ever recovered.

Gellir was fourteen years old at this time. He now took charge of the estate with his mother, and took over the chieftaincy. It soon became evident that he was well suited for leadership.

Gudrun became a deeply religious woman, and was the first woman in Iceland to learn the Psalter. She would spend long hours in the church at night saying prayers; and Herdis Bolli's-daughter always accompanied her during these vigils. Gudrun loved Herdis dearly.

It is said that one night young Herdis dreamed that a woman came to her; she was wearing a woven cloak, with her head hooded under a kerchief, and Herdis thought she looked very unpleasant. The woman said, 'Tell your grandmother I'm very displeased with her, for she tosses about on top of me every night, and lets fall on me such searing drops that I'm burning all over. I'm telling this to you because I like you a little better than her, even though there's something a bit uncanny about you, too. But I could still get on with you if I didn't feel there was so much wrong where Gudrun is concerned.'

With that, Herdis woke up and told Gudrun her dream. Gudrun thought it a good omen. Next morning Gudrun had some planks removed from the church-floor where she was in the habit of kneeling on the hassock. She had the ground underneath dug up, and there they found some bones which were blue and evil-looking, and a brooch, and a large witch's wand. People then realized that this must have been a sorceress's grave. The bones were taken far away to a place where people were least likely to pass by.

77. Bolli's return

Four years after the drowning of Thorkel Eyjolfsson, a ship put in at Eyjafjord; it belonged to Bolli Bollason, but most of the crew were Norwegians. Bolli brought with him a great deal of money and many treasures that princes and men of rank had given him. Bolli had such a taste for the ornate when he returned from his travels that he would not wear any clothes that were not made of scarlet cloth or gold-embroidered silk, and all his weapons were inlaid with gold. He was called Bolli the Proud.

He told his crew that he was going west to his own district, and entrusted the ship and its cargo to their care.

Bolli rode from the ship with eleven companions. His companions were all wearing scarlet and rode in gilded saddles; they were all fine-looking men, but Bolli surpassed them all. He was wearing clothes of gold-embroidered silk which the Byzantine Emperor had given him, and over them a scarlet cloak. He was girt with the sword 'Leg-Biter', its pommel now gold-embossed and the hilt bound with gold. He had a gilded helmet on his head and a red shield at his side on which a knight was traced in gold. He carried a lance in his hand, as is the custom in foreign lands. Wherever they took lodgings for the night, the womenfolk paid no heed to anything but to gaze at Bolli and his companions and all their finery. Such was the courtly splendour in which Bolli rode through the western districts until he arrived at Helgafell with his retinue. Gudrun was overjoyed to see her son Bolli.

Bolli did not stay there long before he rode up to Sælingsdale Tongue to see his father-in-law Snorri and his wife Thordis. It was a very happy reunion. Snorri invited Bolli to stay there with as many men as he wished; Bolli accepted, and spent the winter with Snorri along with those who had accompanied him from the north.

Bolli's travels brought him great renown. Snorri took no less pains now to treat him affectionately than he had done when Bolli was staying there before.

78. Saga end

WHEN Bolli had been in Iceland for one year, Snorri the Priest fell ill. His illness did not gain quickly on him, and he lay bedridden for a long time; but when the illness grew worse, Snorri summoned his kinsmen and dependents.

Then he said to Bolli: 'It is my wish that you take over the farm here and my chieftaincy when I die. I desire success and honour for you no less than for my own sons, and my son Halldor, the one who I think will be the foremost of all my sons, is not here in this country now.'[1]

After that, Snorri died; he was then sixty-seven years old. This was one year after the death of King Olaf the Saint, according to Ari the Learned. Snorri was buried at Sælingsdale Tongue.

Bolli and Thordis took over the farm at Tongue, as Snorri had wished, and Snorri's sons accepted this with good grace. Bolli became a man of great eminence, and was well-liked.

Herdis Bolli's-daughter grew up at Helgafell; she was an exceptionally beautiful woman. Orm, the son of Hermund Illugason,[2] asked for her hand, and she was given to him in marriage.[3]

---

1. According to *King Harald's Saga* Halldor Snorrason was for many years a henchman of Harald Hardradi of Norway. Harald fled from Norway to Russia in 1031, the year that Snorri the Priest died, and went to Constantinople *c.* 1035. Halldor Snorrason is said to have taken part in all Harald's campaigns in the Mediterranean for the Byzantine Emperor.

2. Hermund Illugason was the brother of Gunnlaug Serpent-Tongue (cf. Chapter 6, n. 1, p. 54).

3. *Their son was Kodran, who was married to Gudrun Sigmund's-daughter. Kodran's son was Hermund, who was married to Ulfeid, the daughter of Runolf, the son of Bishop Ketil; their sons were Abbot Ketil of Helgafell, and Hrein, and Kodran, and Styrmir.*

Orm and Herdis had a daughter called Thorvor, the wife of Skeggi Brandsson, and from them stems the Skogar kin.

Bolli and Thordis had a son called Ospak.[1]

Gellir Thorkelsson married Valgerd, the daughter of Thorgils Arason of Reykjaness. Gellir went abroad and stayed with King Magnus the Good,[2] and accepted from him a gift of twelve ounces of gold, and many other valuables besides. Gellir's sons were Thorkel and Thorgils.[3]

Gudrun now began to get very old, and lived in such sorrow as has now been described. She became the first nun and anchoress in Iceland. It is commonly said that among women of equal birth, Gudrun was the noblest in the land.

It is said that on one occasion Bolli came to Helgafell; Gudrun was always pleased when he came to see her. Bolli sat with his mother for a long time, and they talked of many things.

Then Bolli said, 'Will you tell me something, mother, that I am very curious to know? Which man did you love the most?'

Gudrun replied, 'Thorkel was the wealthiest and the greatest chieftain, but no one was more accomplished or capable than Bolli. Thord Ingunnarson was the wisest of them and the greatest lawyer; of Thorvald I have nothing at all to say.'

Then Bolli said, 'I understand clearly what you are telling me about the qualities of your husbands; but you have not told me yet which man you loved the most. There's no need to conceal it any longer now.'

'You are pressing me very hard, my son,' said Gudrun. 'But if I must tell someone, then I would rather it were you.'

Bolli begged her to do so.

Then Gudrun said, 'I was worst to the one I loved the most.'

'I think,' said Bolli, 'that the truth has now been told.' And he said she had done right to tell him what he had been so curious to know.

1. *Ospak's daughter was Gudrun, the wife of Thorarin Brandsson; their son was Brand, who established the benefice at Husafell. Brand's son was Sighvat the Priest, who lived there for a long time.*

2. King Magnus the Good was the son of King Olaf the Saint, and ruled over Norway and Denmark from 1035 to 1047.

3. *Thorgils' son was Ari the Learned, whose son was Thorgils, the father of Ari the Strong.*

Gudrun grew to be very old, and people say she became blind. She died at Helgafell, and lies buried there.

Gellir Thorkelsson lived at Helgafell till old age, and many remarkable things are told of him. He plays a part in many other sagas,[1] although very little is said of him here. He had a very distinguished church built at Helgafell, as Arnor Thordarson the Earls'-Poet confirms in the memorial lay he composed about Gellir.[2]

When Gellir was advanced in years he left Iceland and went abroad. He arrived in Norway but did not stay there long; he set off at once on a pilgrimage to Rome, and paid a visit to the Apostle St Peter. He spent a long time in Rome, and then he travelled north and came to Denmark, where he fell ill and lay bedridden for a long time and received the last rites. After that he died, and lies buried at Roskilde. Gellir had taken with him the sword 'Skofnung' but it was never recovered; it had originally been taken from the burial mound of Hrolf Kraki.

When the news of Gellir's death reached Iceland, his son Thorkel took over his father's estate at Helgafell. Gellir's other son, Thorgils, was drowned in Breidafjord when still a young man, and all his crew with him.

Thorkel Gellison was a most worthy man, and was stated to have been a man of great learning.[3]

And there this saga ends.

1. In particular, *Bandamanna Saga*.

2. This memorial lay is now lost. Arnor Thordarson earned his nickname of 'the Earls'-Poet' by being court poet to the Norse earls of Orkney for many years in the 11th century. The main source of his extant poetry is *Orkneyinga Saga*; but he was also court poet to Harald Hardradi of Norway (cf. *King Harald's Saga*). Gellir Thorkelsson died in 1073.

3. Thorkel Gellison was one of the main authorities cited by Ari the Learned in his historical writings. Cf. Introduction, pp. 22–3.

Genealogical Tables

KETIL FLAT-NOSE AND HIS CHILDREN

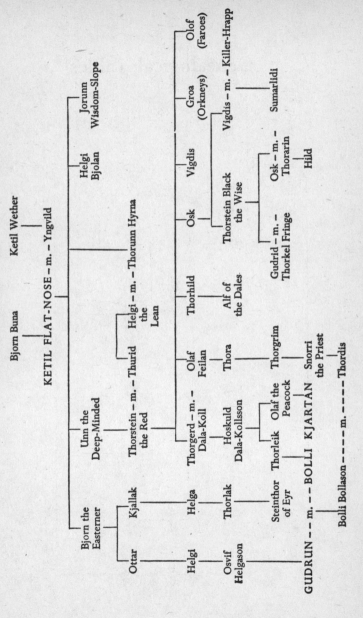

KETIL FLAT-NOSE'S DESCENDANTS INTERMARRY

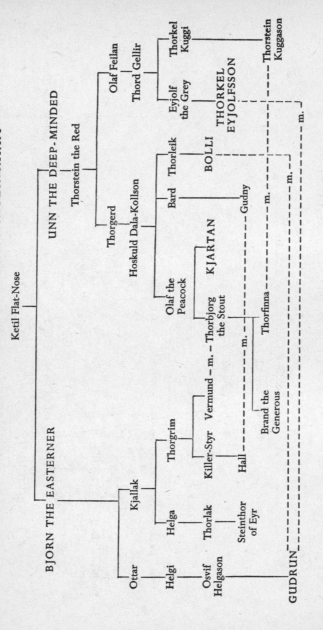

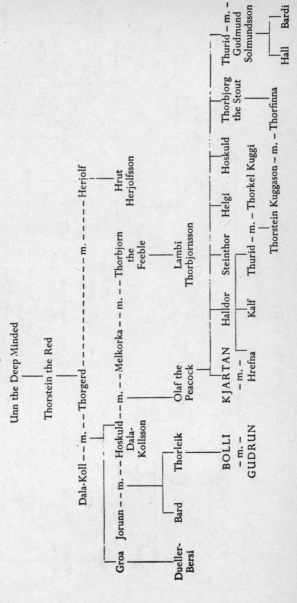

KJARTAN AND BOLLI

Unn the Deep Minded

Thorstein the Red

Groa   Jorunn – – m. – – Hoskuld – – m. – – Melkorka – – m. – – Thorbjorn   Dala-Koll – – m. – – Thorgerd – – – – – – – – – – m. – – – – – Herjolf
Dueller-   Dala-   the
Bersi   Kollsson   Feeble

        Bard   Thorleik   Lambi   Hrut
                                                   Thorbjornsson   Herjolfsson
              BOLLI
              – m. –   Olaf the
              GUDRUN   Peacock

                                         KJARTAN   Halldor   Steinthor   Helgi   Hoskuld   Thorbjorg
                                         – m. –   the Stout
                                         Hrefna   Kalf   Thurid – m. – Thorkel Kuggi   Thurid – m. – Gudmund
                                                                                                           Solmundsson
                                                       Thorstein Kuggason – m. – Thorfinna
                                                                                              Hall   Bardi

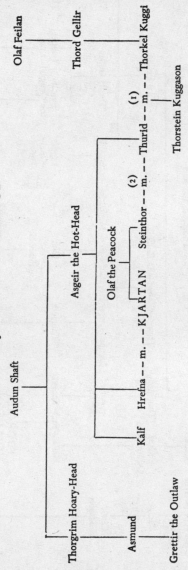

KJARTAN'S MARRIAGE

GUDRUN AND HER SUITORS

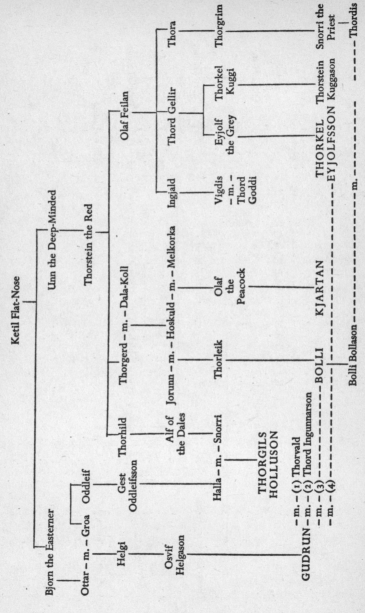

Glossary of Proper Names

THIS Glossary of personal names is not a complete index of all the people who are mentioned in the saga; it is primarily intended as a guide to the parts played by the major characters, to refresh readers' memories about minor characters and relationships, and people of particular historical significance. The numbers refer to chapters, not pages.

Alf of the Dales (*Dala-Alf*), 6 (n. 3, p. 54), married to Halldis Erp's-daughter, 6; grandson of Thorstein the Red, 6; grandfather of Thorgils Holluson, 57; father of Svein and Hunbogi the Strong 62, 63, 64.

Alfdis (*Konal's-daughter*), wife of Olaf Feilan, 7; their children, 7.

An the Black, one of Olaf Hoskuldsson's smiths, 24; rides with Kjartan Olafsson to Saurby, 47; dreams of being disembowelled, 48; ambushed with Kjartan in Svinadale, wounded and healed, nicknamed 'Brushwood-Belly', 49; in the attack on Bolli Thorleiksson, 54; killed 55.

An the White, brother of An the Black, 24; finds the sword stolen from Kjartan Olafsson, 46.

Ari of Reykjaness (*Masson*), ancestor of the Reyknessing kin, 6 (n. 2, p. 55); grandfather-in-law of Gellir Thorkelsson, 78.

Ari Thorgilsson (*Ari the Learned*), cited as a source, 4, 78; grandson of Gellir Thorkelsson, 78.

Armod Thorgrimsson. of Thykkvawood, father of Hrut Herjolfsson's second wife, Thorbjorg, 19; brother-in-law of Gest Oddleifsson, and father of Ornolf and Halldor, 33; host to Gest, 33.

Arnor Thordarson ('the Earls'-Poet'), writes a memorial poem about Gellir Thorkelsson, 78.

Asgaut, a slave belonging to Thord Goddi, 11; accompanies the fugitive Thorolf to Saudafell, 15; rewarded with his freedom, emigrates to Denmark, 16.

Asgeir Audunarson (*Asgeir the Hot-Head*), a farmer in Vididale, 40; father of Kalf and Hrefna, 40; rides to meet his son Kalf and Kjartan Olafsson on their return from Norway, 44; gives Hrefna in marriage to Kjartan, 45; dies, 46.

Asgeir Kjartansson, son of Kjartan Olafsson, 47; fostered by Thorstein Kuggason, 50.

Astrid, of Breidafjord, married to Bard Hoskuldsson, 25.

Tongue, 78; his son Ospak born, 78; asks his mother which man she had loved the most, 78.

Bolli Thorleiksson, Gudrun's third husband: son of Thorleik Hoskuldsson, 25; fostered at Hjardarholt by his uncle, Olaf the Peacock, 27; friendship with his foster-brother, Kjartan Olafsson, 28; given the sword 'Leg-Biter' by his cousin Thurid, 30; Gest's prophecy about him and Kjartan, 33; Olaf's promise to his father, 38; accompanies Kjartan on visits to Gudrun Osvif's-daughter, 39; goes abroad with Kjartan to Norway, 40; baptized, 40; returns to Iceland alone, 41; woos Gudrun Osvif's-daughter, 42; marries Gudrun, 43; reproached by her when Kjartan returns. 44; his gift of horses refused by Kjartan, 45; attends a feast at Hjardarholt when Kjartan's sword is stolen, 46; host to Kjartan at Laugar when Hrefna's head-dress is stolen, 46; beseiged by Kjartan at Laugar for three days, 47; buys Sælingsdale Tongue from Thorarin Thorisson, but the deal is thwarted by Kjartan, 47; ambushes Kjartan in Svinadale and kills him with 'Leg-Biter', 48–9; reconciliation with Olaf the Peacock, 50; moves to Sælingsdale Tongue, 52; his son Thorleik born, 52; enmity from the Olafssons, 53–4; attacked by the Olafssons and killed, 55; his son Bolli born, 56; recalled by Gudrun, 78.

Bork Thorsteinsson (Bork the Stout), grandson of Olaf Feilan and uncle of Snorri the Priest, 7 (n. 3, p. 57); his eminence in Thorsness, 18.

Dala-Alf: see Alf of the Dales.

Dala-Koll: see Koll.

Dueller-Bersi: see Bersi Veleifsson.

Egil Skalla-Grimsson, of Borg: father of Thorgerd, 22; marries his daughter Thorgerd to Olaf the Peacock, 23; grandfather of Kjartan Olafsson, 28.

Einar Rognvaldsson (Turf-Einar), Earl of Orkney; descended from Unn the Deep-Minded, 4 (n. 1, p. 52).

Eldgrim, of Eldgrimsstead; tries to buy horses from Thorleik Hoskuldsson, is refused, 37; tries to steal them, is killed by Hrut Herjolfsson, 37.

Eyjolf Thordarson (Eyjolf the Grey), son of Thord Gellir, 7; father of Thorkel Eyjolfsson, 57.

Eyvind Bjarnarson (Eyvind the Easterner), father of Helgi the Lean, who married Thorunn, daughter of Ketil Flat-Nose, 1; father of Thurid, who married Ketil's grandson, Thorstein the Red, 4; father of Bjorg, from whom stems the Reyknessing kin, 6 (n. 2, p. 55).

Gudmund Solmundsson, of Asbjarnarness, brother-in-law of Kjartan Olafsson; marries Thurid Olaf's-daughter, has a family, 31; welcomes Kjartan Olafsson back to Iceland, 44; invites Kjartan north to his home, 44; attends Kjartan's marriage to Hrefna at Hjardarholt, 45; consulted by his father-in-law, Olaf the Peacock, after Kjartan's death, 50.

Gudrid Thorstein's-daughter, daughter of Thorstein Black the Wise, 10; married to Thorkel Fringe, 10; inherits from her father, 18.

Gudrun Osvif's-daughter, daughter of Osvif Helgason, 32; her four dreams interpreted by Gest Oddleifsson, 33; married at fifteen to her first husband, Thorvald Halldorsson, and divorces him, 34; encourages Thord Ingunnarson to divorce Aud, and marries him, 35; widowed, gives birth to Thord Cat, 36; meets Kjartan Olafsson at the baths at Sælingsdale, 39; dislikes Kjartan's decision to go abroad, refuses to wait three years for him as his betrothed, 40; hears from Bolli Thorleiksson about Kjartan in Norway, 42; wooed by Bolli, marries him, 43; attends feast at Hjardarholt, sees Hrefna's head-dress, 46; attends feast at Laugar where the head-dress is stolen and burned by her, 46; urges Bolli and her brothers to attack Kjartan, 47–8; gloats over Kjartan's death, 49; moves to Sælingsdale Tongue, her son Thorleik born, 52; at the shieling with Bolli when Bolli is attacked, 55; talks to his killers, Helgi Hardbeinsson wipes his spear on her sash, 55; seeks help from Snorri the Priest, 56; her son Bolli born, 56; exchanges farms with Snorri, moves to Helgafell, 56; plans vengeance for Bolli, 59; urges her sons to wreak vengeance on Helgi Hardbeinsson, lures Thorgils Holluson to take part, 60; refuses to marry Thorgils, 65; builds a church at Helgafell, 66; marries her fourth husband, Thorkel Eyjolfsson, 68; shelters Gunnar Thidrandi's-Killer, 69; her son Gellir born, 70; attends Bolli's wedding at Sælingsdale Tongue, 70; fosters her grand-daughter Herdis Bolli's-daughter, 72; interprets Thorkel Eyjolfsson's dream, 74; sees Thorkel's ghost, 76; becomes very religious, 76; becomes Iceland's first nun and anchoress, 78; tells of the loves in her life, 78; dies at Helgafell, 78.

Gunnar Thidrandi's-Killer, sheltered by Gudrun Osvif's-daughter, 69.

Gunnhild, Queen Mother of Norway; bestows her favours on Hrut Herjolfsson, 19; bestows her favours on Hrut's nephew, Olaf Hoskuldsson, 21, 22.

Gunnlaug Serpent-Tongue, son of Illugi the Black, 6 (n. 1, p. 54); uncle-in-law of Herdis Bolli's-daughter, 78 (n. 2, p. 237).

Hakon Haraldsson (Hakon the Good), King of Norway, 9; makes Hoskuld Dala-Kollsson a member of his court, 9; entertains Hos-

pays compensation to the Bollasons, gives Bolli Bollason a sword, 71; refuses to sell Hjardarholt to Thorstein Kuggason, 75.

Hallfred the Troublesome-Poet (Ottarsson), court-poet to King Olaf Tryggvason: refused permission to leave Norway, 40; teams up with Kjartan Olafsson in Norway, 40; converted to Christianity by King Olaf Tryggvason, 40.

Hallgerd Long-Legs, daughter of Hoskuld Dala-Kollsson, 9.

Hallstein the Priest, of Hallsteinsness, a chieftain, 35; befriends the Kotkel family, 35; evicts them under pressure from Gest Oddleifsson, 36.

Harald Fine-Hair, King of Norway: achieves overlordship of Norway, forces Ketil Flat-Nose to emigrate, 2; father of King Hakon the Good, 9 (n. 1, p. 59).

Harald Gunnhildarson (Harald Grey-Cloak), King of Norway: son of Queen Gunnhild and Eirik Blood-Axe, 19; makes Hrut Herjolfsson a member of his court, gives him a ship, 19; entertains Olaf the Peacock and makes him a member of his court, 21; receives Olaf on his return from Ireland, 21; gives Olaf a set of scarlet clothes and a ship, 22; gives Hrut Herjolfsson a gold-inlaid halberd, 37.

Harald Sigurdsson (Harald Hardradi), King of Norway, 50 (n.1, p. 178).

Hardbein Helgason, twelve-year-old son of Helgi Hardbeinsson, 62; in the shieling when his father is killed by the Bollasons, fights by his side, is spared, 64.

Helga Olaf's-daughter, daughter of Olaf Feilan, 7.

Helgi Eyvindarson (Helgi the Lean), one of the first Icelandic settlers: marries Thorunn Hyrna, daughter of Ketil Flat-Nose, 1, 3; emigrates to Iceland with his brothers-in-law, settles at Kristness, 3; brother-in-law of Thorstein the Red, 4 (n. 2, p. 51); ancestor of the Reyknessing kin, 6 (n. 2, p. 55).

Helgi Hardbeinsson, brother-in-law of Thorstein the Black of Hundadale, 54; joins in the attack on Bolli Thorleiksson, 54; kills Bolli with his spear, wipes his spear on Gudrun's sash, prophesies his own death at Bolli Bollason's hands, 55; plans laid to kill him, 59–61; surrounded in his shieling, 62; his attackers described by his shepherd, 63; killed by Bolli Bollason, 64; compensation paid to his sons, 67, 71.

Helgi Ketilsson (Helgi Bjolan), son of Ketil Flat-Nose, 1; emigrates to Iceland, 2; settles at Esjuberg, 3; welcomes his sister Unn the Deep-Minded inhospitably, 5; attends Unn's last feast, 7.

Helgi Olafsson, son of Olaf the Peacock and brother of Kjartan, 28;

identified swimming with his brothers by Gest Oddleifsson, 33; kills the Thorhollusons with his brothers in revenge for Kjartan's death, 49; dissatisfied with settlement over Kjartan's death, hates Bolli Thorleiksson, 51; takes part in the killing of Bolli, 54-5; pays compensation to the Bollasons, 71.

Helgi Osvifsson, son of Osvif Helgason and brother of Gudrun, 31; supports Thord Ingunnarson with his brothers after the divorce from Aud, 35; takes part in the ambush of Kjartan Olafsson, 48-9; outlawed with his brothers, goes to Norway, 51.

Herdis Bolli's-daughter, daughter of Bolli Bollason, 72; fostered by her grandmother, Gudrun Osvif's-daughter, 72; dreams of an old witch buried under the church floor, 76; grows up at Helgafell, marries Orm Hermundsson (the nephew of Gunnlaug Serpent-Tongue), 78.

Herjolf Eyvindarson, a Norwegian landowner: marries Thorgerd Thorstein's-daughter, the widow of Dala-Koll, 7; father of Hrut Herjolfsson, 8; dies, 8.

Hermund Illugason, brother of Gunnlaug Serpent-Tongue, 6 (n. 1, p. 54); father-in-law of Herdis Bolli's-daughter, 78.

Hild Thorarin's-daughter, baby grand-daughter of Thorstein Black the Wise; drowns in the family drowning in Breidafjord, 18.

Hjalti Skeggjason, a chieftain: converted to Christianity by the missionary Thangbrand, 41; blasphemes the heathen gods, is outlawed, 41; goes to Norway, returns to Iceland to convert it to Christianity, 41.

Hord, a man of noble birth: accompanies Unn the Deep-Minded from Scotland to Iceland, 4; settles at Hordadale, ancestor of Gunnlaug Serpent-Tongue and the Gilsbekking kin, 6 (n. 1, p. 54); attends Unn's last feast, 7.

Hoskuld Dala-Kollsson, of Hoskuldstead: son of Dala-Koll and Thorgerd Thorstein's-daughter, 5; inherits Hoskuldstead, 7; welcomes his mother back from Norway, claims her whole estate, 8; marries Jorunn Bjorn's-daughter, their children, 9; protects his followers against Killer-Hrapp, 10; goes to Norway, 11; buys a concubine, Melkorka, 12; fêted by King Hakon the Good, 13; takes Melkorka to Iceland, has a son by her – Olaf the Peacock, 13; gives Melkorka Melkorkustead, 13; gives Olaf to Thord Goddi for fostering in return for his wealth, 16; refuses to give his half-brother Hrut Herjolfsson a share of their mother's estate, is eventually reconciled with him, 19; furious at Melkorka's marriage and Olaf's decision to go abroad, 20-21; supports Olaf's marriage-proposal to Thorgerd Egil's-daughter, 23; blesses Hjardarholt, 24;

tricks his sons into allowing a large inheritance for Olaf the Peacock, 26; dies, 26; his memorial feast, 27.

Hoskuld Olafsson, youngest son of Olaf the Peacock and brother of Kjartan, 28; identified swimming with his brothers by Gest Oddleifsson, 33; kills the Thorhollusons with his brothers in revenge for Kjartan's death, 49; dissatisfied with settlement over Kjartan's death, hates Bolli Thorleiksson, 51; takes part in the killing of Bolli, 54–5; pays compensation to the Bollasons, 71.

Hrapp (Killer-Hrapp), from Breidafjord: joins the attack on Helgi Hardbeinsson, 63; killed by Helgi, 64.

Hrapp Sumarlidason (Killer-Hrapp), of Hrappstead: terrorizes his neighbours in Laxriverdale, 10; dies, is buried under the threshold of Hrappstead, walks after death, is exhumed and removed, 17; causes the drowning of Thorstein Black the Wise's family in the guise of a seal, 18; wrestles with Olaf the Peacock, is disinterred again and cremated, 24.

Hrefna Asgeir's-daughter, daughter of Asgeir the Hot-Head, 40; sister of Kalf Asgeirsson, meets Kjartan Olafsson on their return from Norway, 44; tries on the royal head-dress, 44; marries Kjartan, 45; shows Gudrun the head-dress at a feast at Hjardarholt, 46; the head-dress stolen at a feast at Laugar, 46; teases Kjartan over Gudrun, 47; has a son, Asgeir, 47; goes north and dies of a broken heart after Kjartan's death, 50.

Hrut Herjolfsson, half-brother of Hoskuld Dala-Kollsson: son of Herjolf and Thorgerd Thorstein's-daughter, left behind for fosterage in Norway, 8; goes to Iceland, claims his share of his mother's estate, disputes with Hoskuld, raids his cattle, wins his claim, is reconciled, 19; marries, settles at Hrutstead, has 16 sons, 19; enmity with his nephew, Thorleik Hoskuldsson, 20; settles a freed slave on Hoskuld's land, disputes with Hoskuld and Thorleik Hoskuldsson, 25; kills Eldgrim for trying to steal Thorleik's horses, 37; his son Kari killed by sorcery on Thorleik's instructions, 37; kills the Kotkel family with Olaf the Peacock, 37.

Hunbogi the Strong, son of Alf of the Dales and uncle of Thorgils Holluson: takes part in the attack on Helgi Hardbeinsson, 62; description by Helgi's shepherd, 63; kills one of Helgi's men, 64

Ingibjorg Tryggvi's-daughter, princess of Norway, sister of King Olaf Tryggvason: friendship with Kjartan Olafsson, 41–2; gives Kjartan a head-dress as a wedding-gift for Gudrun, 43.

Ingjald Saudisle-Priest, brother of Hall, 14; tries to capture his brother's killer, Thorolf, but is thwarted by Vigdis, 15.

Ingunn (Thorolf's-daughter), wife of Glum Geirason and mother of

Knut, a farmer, of Hol in Saurby: brother of Aud and brother-in-law of Thord Ingunnarson, 32; fails to prosecute Thord after the divorce from Aud, 35; accompanies Kjartan Olafsson on his last journey, sent home before the battle in Svinadale, 48.

Kolbein, son of Thord Frey's-Priest: held hostage by King Olaf Tryggvason in Norway, 41; released, 43.

Koll (Dala-Koll), a Norwegian chieftain: accompanies Unn the Deep-Minded from Scotland to Iceland, 4; marries Thorgerd Thorstein's-daughter, is given Laxriverdale as a dowry by Unn, father of Hoskuld Dala-Kollsson, 5; attends Unn's last feast, 7; dies, succeeded by Hoskuld, 7, 9.

Kotkel, a Hebridean sorcerer, and his family, 35; protected by Hallstein the Priest, persecutes his neighbours, 35; summonsed by Thord Ingunnarson, drowns him by sorcery, 35; evicted, gets protection from Thorleik Hoskuldsson by bribery, 36; kills Hrut's son Kari by sorcery at Thorleik's request, put to death by Olaf the Peacock, buried under a cairn at Skrattavardi, 37.

Lambi Thorbjornsson, son of Thorbjorn the Feeble and Melkorka, and half-brother of Olaf the Peacock, 22; inherits Melkorkustead, 38; joins in the attack on Bolli Thorleiksson, 54; wounds Bolli, is wounded by him, 55; threatened by Thorgils Holluson, is forced to join the revenge expedition against Helgi Hardbeinsson, 59, 61-62; description by Helgi's shepherd, 63; in the attack on Helgi, 64; returns to Hjardarholt, is rebuked by the Olafssons, 65.

Magnus Olafsson (Magnus the Good), King of Norway: gives valuable gifts to Gellir Thorkelsson, 78.

Melkorka, a concubine, daughter of King Myrkjartan of Ireland: bought as a deaf-mute by Hoskuld Dala-Kollsson, 12; goes to Iceland with Hoskuld, gives birth to Olaf the Peacock, reveals her name and identity, fights with Hoskuld's wife, moves to Melkorkustead, 13; disapproves of Olaf being fostered by Thord Goddi, 16; neglected by Hoskuld, helps Olaf go abroad, marries Thorbjorn the Feeble, 20; gives Olaf a gold ring as token of identity in Ireland, 21; disappointed that Olaf doesn't bring her nurse from Ireland, 22; gives birth to Lambi Thorbjornsson, 22; dies, 38.

Myrkjartan, king of the Irish, father of Melkorka, 13; grandfather of Olaf the Peacock, 20, 21; recognizes Olaf, welcomes him, offers him the throne of Ireland, gives him a gold-inlaid spear and a chased sword, 21.

Odd Thorholluson, son of Thorhalla the Gossip: working on Osvif Helgason's estate, 32; in the ambush on Kjartan, 48; fights

landers hostage, 41; releases the hostages after Iceland accepts Christianity, 43; gives Kjartan a magic sword, 43.

Olof Gudmund's-daughter, grand-daughter of Olaf the Peacock, 31.

Olof Thorstein's-daughter, grand-daughter of Unn the Deep-Minded: marries in the Faroe Islands, 4.

Orm Hermundsson, nephew of Gunnlaug Serpent-Tongue: marries Herdis Bolli's-daughter, 78.

Orn, a Norwegian skipper: takes Olaf the Peacock abroad, 20; accompanies Olaf to Ireland, 21; returns with Olaf, 22.

Ornolf Armodsson, son of Armod of Thykkvawood, and nephew of Gest Oddleifsson, 33; friendly with Thorleik Bollason, 59; foster-brother of Thorgils Holluson, 59; not a witness to Gudrun's promise of marriage to Thorgils, 60; joins the attack on Helgi Hardbeinsson, 62; description by Helgi's shepherd, 63; attacks Helgi, 64; stays at Helgafell on the way home, 65.

Osk Thorstein's-daughter, grand-daughter of Unn the Deep-Minded, 6; mother of Thorstein Black the Wise, 6.

Osk Thorstein's-daughter, daughter of Thorstein Black the Wise, 10; marries Thorarin from Breidafjord, 10; mother of Hild, 18; drowns in Breidafjord, dispute over the inheritance, 18.

Ospak Bollason, son of Bolli Bollason: his descendants, 78.

Ospak Osvifsson, son of Osvif Helgason and brother of Gudrun, 31; supports Thord Ingunnarson with his brothers after the divorce from Aud, 35; speaks ill of Kjartan, 47; takes part in the ambush of Kjartan, 48–9; already outlawed, 50.

Osvif Helgason, of Laugar, father of Gudrun Osvif's-daughter, 32; buys land in Sælingsdale for a shieling, 32; prophecy about him by Gest Oddleifsson, 33; doubts about Gudrun's first marriage, 34; agrees to Gudrun's second marriage, 35; present when Aud wounds Thord Ingunnarson, 35; kinsman of Snorri the Priest, 36; discourages his sons from attacking the Kotkel family, 36; proved right, 39; friend of Olaf the Peacock, 39; urges Gudrun to marry Bolli Thorleiksson, 43; host at a feast at Laugar, 44; attends feast at Hjardarholt when Kjartan's sword is stolen, 46; advises Bolli and Gudrun to buy land at Tongue, 47; worsted by Olaf the Peacock in the lawsuit after Kjartan's death, 50; prophesies disaster for Audun Fetter-Hound, 51; moves to Helgafell with Gudrun, 56; dies, is buried at Helgafell, Gest's prophecy fulfilled, 66.

Ottar Bjarnarson, son of Bjorn the Easterner, 3 (n. 2, p. 50); grandfather of Osvif Helgason, 32 (n. 1, p. 117).

Rognvald of More, Earl of Orkney; descendant of Unn the Deep-Minded, 4 (n. 1, p. 52).

Holluson: takes part in the attack on Helgi Hardbeinsson, 62; description by Helgi's shepherd, 63; battle with Helgi, 64.

Sverting Runolfsson, son of Runolf Ulfsson: held hostage by King Olaf Tryggvason in Norway, 41; released, 43.

Thangbrand, a Norwegian missionary: sent by King Olaf Tryggvason to evangelize Iceland, fails, 41.

Thorarin, from Breidafjord: married to Osk, the daughter of Thorstein Black the Wise, 10; drowns with his family, dispute over the inheritance, 18.

Thorarin, a chieftain, of Langadale: father of Audgisl, 67; deprived of his chieftaincy by Thorgils Holluson, 67.

Thorarin Ragi's-brother, Law-Speaker: married to a daughter of Olaf Feilan, 7 (n. 5, p. 58).

Thorarin Thorisson, a farmer, of Sælingsdale Tongue: sells some land to Osvif Helgason, 32; witnesses An Brushwood-Belly retrieving Kjartan's sword, 46; sells Sælingsdale Tongue to Bolli Thorleiksson, but is forced to sell to Kjartan instead, 47; accompanies Kjartan on his last journey, 47, 49; fights the Thorhollusons when Kjartan is ambushed in Svinadale, 49.

Thorbjorg Armod's-daughter, second wife of Hrut Herjolfsson, 19.

Thorbjorg Olaf's-daughter (Thorbjorg the Stout), daughter of Olaf the Peacock, 28; married to Asgeir Knattarson and, later, to Vermund Thorgrimsson, 31.

Thorbjorn the Feeble, a farmer, of Lambastead in Laxriverdale, 11; marries Melkorka, 20; father of Lambi Thorbjornsson, 22; dies, 38.

Thord Gellir, son of Olaf Feilan, 7; uncle of Vigdis Ingjald's-daughter, 11; disapproves of Vigdis' divorce, 16; reconciliation with Hoskuld Dala-Kollsson, 16; secret contacts with Hrut Herjolfsson alleged, 19; father of Thorkel Kuggi and father-in-law of Thurid Asgeir's-daughter, 40.

Thord Gestsson (Thord the Short), son of Gest Oddleifsson: hears his father prophesy the fate of the Olafssons, 33; takes his father's body to Helgafell, 66.

Thord Goddi, of Goddastead in Laxriverdale: married to Vigdis Ingjald's-daughter, 11; is forced by Vigdis to shelter Thorolf, 14; does a deal with Ingjald Saudisle-Priest, thwarted by Vigdis, 15; divorced by Vigdis, 16; fosters Olaf the Peacock, 16; dies, bequeaths Goddastead to Olaf, 24.

Thord Ingunnarson, of Saurby, Gudrun's second husband: married to Aud, 32; falls in love with Gudrun, 34; divorces Aud and marries Gudrun, 35; assaulted by Aud, 35; prosecutes the Kotkel

claims Gudrun's hand, realizes he has been tricked, 65; killed by Audgisl Thorarinsson, 67.

Thorgrim Thorsteinsson, brother of Bork the Stout, and father of Snorri the Priest, 7 (n. 3, p. 57); his eminence in Thorsness, 18.

Thorhalla the Gossip, a servant on Osvif Helgason's farm, 32; mother of Odd and Stein Thorholluson, 32; meets Kjartan Olafsson, tells Gudrun of Kjartan's movements, 47.

Thorkel the Bald, a farmer, of Thykkvawood: fights the ghost of Hallbjorn Sleekstone-Eye, 38.

Thorkel Eyjolfsson, Gudrun's fourth husband: friend of Snorri the Priest, 57; fights Grim Helguson, 58; persuaded by Snorri to court Gudrun, goes abroad, 58; returns to Iceland, marries Gudrun, 68; tries to arrest Gunnar Thidrandi's-Killer, thwarted by Gudrun, 69; becomes a chieftain, 70; father of Gellir Thorkelsson, 70; sends Thorleik Bollason abroad, 70; marries Bolli Bollason to Thurid Snorri's-daughter, 70; dreams that his beard covers Breidafjord, goes abroad, 74; gets church-timber from King Olaf the Saint, 74; tries to force Halldor Olafsson to sell Hjardarholt to Thorstein Kuggason, 75; drowns on his way home in Breidafjord, 76; recalled by Gudrun, 78.

Thorkel Fringe, a chieftain, of Svignaskard: married to a daughter of Thorstein Black the Wise, 10; gets hold of all the inheritance when Thorstein Black's family drowns in Breidafjord, fakes the ordeal ceremony, 18; sells Hrappstead to Olaf the Peacock, 24.

Thorkel Gellison, son of Gellir Thorkelsson, 78; inherits Helgafell from his father, 78.

Thorkel Kuggi, son of Thord Gellir, 7; married to Thurid Asgeir's-daughter, and father of Thorstein Kuggason, 40; his widow marries Steinthor Olafsson, Kjartan's brother, 52.

Thorkel Whelp, a farmer, of Hol in Saurby: brother of Aud, and brother-in-law of Thord Ingunnarson, 32; fails to prosecute Thord after the divorce, 35; accompanies Kjartan on his last journey, sent home before the battle in Svinadale, 48.

Thorleik Bollason, son of Bolli Thorleiksson and Gudrun, 52; four years old when his father is killed, 56; fostered by Thorgils Holluson, 57; stays at Thykkvawood and at Tongue, 59; wants to avenge his father, 60; joins the expedition against Helgi Hardbeinsson, 62; description by Helgi's shepherd, 63; spots Helgi's ruse, 64; kills Helgi's servant Eyjolf, 64; disapproves of his mother's trick on Thorgils Holluson, 65; attends his mother's marriage to Thorkel Eyjolfsson, 68; goes abroad, becomes a member of King

Thorstein Olafsson (Thorstein the Red), son of Olaf the White and Unn the Deep-Minded, 4; conquers half of Scotland, is killed in Caithness, 4; his daughters and their marriages, 4, 5, 6; family resemblance to his grandson Hrut Herjolfsson, 8.

Thorunn Hyrna, daughter of Ketil Flat-Nose: married to Helgi the Lean, 1, 3; emigrates to Iceland, her descendants, 3.

Thorvald Halldorsson, of Garpsdale, Gudrun's first husband: marries Gudrun, 34; divorced by her, 34; recalled by her, 78.

Thurid Asgeir's-daughter, daughter of Asgeir the Hot-Head and sister of Hrefna: married to Thorkel Kuggi, and mother of Thorstein Kuggason, 40; marries Steinthor Olafsson, 52.

Thurid Eyvind's-daughter, sister of Helgi the Lean: wife of Thorstein the Red, 4.

Thurid Hoskuld's-daughter, daughter of Hoskuld Dala-Kollsson, 9.

Thurid Olaf's-daughter, daughter of Olaf the Peacock, 23; marries Geirmund the Noisy, 29; deserted by him, abandons her baby Groa with him, steals the sword 'Leg-Biter', 30; gives 'Leg-Biter' to her cousin Bolli Thorleiksson, 30; marries Gudmund Solmundsson, 31; meets her brother Kjartan on his return from Norway, 44; invites Kjartan home to Asbjarnarness, 44; urges Kjartan to marry Hrefna, 45.

Torrad Osvifsson, son of Osvif Helgason and brother of Gudrun, 31; supports Thord Ingunnarson with his brothers after the divorce from Aud, 35; takes part in the ambush of Kjartan Olafsson, 48–9; outlawed with his brothers, goes to Norway, 51.

Turf-Einar: *see* Einar Rognvaldsson.

Unn the Deep-Minded, daughter of Ketil Flat-Nose: married to Olaf the White, 1; emigrates to Scotland, 3; flees after her son Thorstein the Red is killed, 4; marries off her grand-daughters in Orkney and the Faroe Islands, 4; first settler of Breidafjord, settles at Hvamm, 5; apportions land to her followers, 6; bequeaths Hvamm to her grandson Olaf Feilan, dies, 7.

Vandrad Osvifsson, son of Osvif Helgason and brother of Gudrun, 31; supports Thord Ingunnarson with his brothers after the divorce from Aud, 35; takes part in the ambush of Kjartan Olafsson, 48–9; outlawed with his brothers, goes to Norway, 51.

Vermund Thorgrimsson, descendant of Bjorn the Easterner, 3 (n. 2, p. 50); marries Thorbjorg the Stout, the daughter of Olaf the Peacock, becomes the father-in-law of Thorstein Kuggason, 31; father of Brand the Generous, 40 (n. 2, p. 143).

Vigdis Hallstein's-daughter, wife of Killer-Hrapp and sister of Thorstein Black the Wise, 10; mother of Sumarlidi, 10; inherits Hrapp-

Chronological Table

As is explained in the Introduction (pp. 24–6), the chronology of *Laxdæla Saga* is inconsistent in many particulars. It is impossible to give a precise chronology for all events of the saga, but this tentative table, based on certain key dates that are more or less verifiable from other sources, gives at least a general framework that readers may find useful.

Settlement of Iceland begins	c. 870
Ketil Flat-Nose emigrates from Norway	c. 890
Unn the Deep-Minded settles in Iceland	c. 915
The Icelandic Althing established	930
Olaf the Peacock born	c. 938
Thorstein the Black drowns	c. 956
Olaf the Peacock goes abroad	c. 956
Olaf the Peacock marries Thorgerd	c. 960
Snorri the Priest born	c. 963
Kjartan Olafsson born	c. 970
Gudrun Osvif's-daughter born	c. 973
Thorkel Eyjolfsson born	979
Gudrun marries Thorvald Halldorsson	c. 989
Gudrun marries Thord Ingunnarsson	?993
Kjartan and Bolli go abroad	998
Iceland converted to Christianity	1000
Gudrun marries Bolli	1000
Kjartan returns to Iceland	1001
Kjartan is killed by Bolli	c. 1003
Olaf the Peacock dies	c. 1006
Bolli is killed	c. 1006
Bolli Bollason born	c. 1007
Gudrun exchanges houses with Snorri, moves to Helgafell	c. 1008
Gudrun marries Thorkel Eyjolfsson	c. 1008
Gellir Thorkelsson born	c. 1009
Thorkel Eyjolfsson drowns	1026
Snorri the Priest dies	1031
Gudrun dies	c. 1060
Ari the Learned born	1068
Gellir Thorkelsson dies	1073

Iceland

The Breidafjord Dales

Laxriverdale

LAXRIVERDALE HEATH

DONUSTEAD ✕

LAX RIVER

LAMBASTEAD ✕

GODDASTEAD ✕

LJARWOODS ✕

LEIDOLFSTEAD ✕

Ija River

HJARDARHOLT ✕

HRAPPSTEAD ✕

HOSKULDSTEAD ✕

SKOGAR ✕

BUDARDALE ✕

ORROSTUDALE

HVAMM ✕

HVAMMSFJORD

KAMBSNESS ✕

HRUTSTEAD ✕

LÆKJARWOODS ✕

Haukadale River Tl.

THYKKVAWOOD ✕

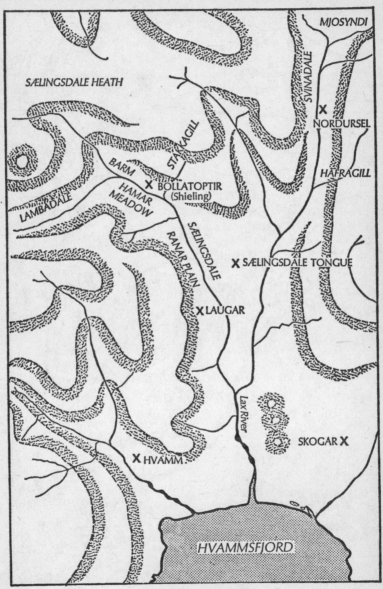

Sælingsdale and Svinadale